HIGH-STAKES RESCUE

USA TODAY Bestselling Author

RITA HERRON

Previously published as *McCullen's Secret Son*
and *The Last McCullen*

HARLEQUIN

 **HARLEQUIN**®

ISBN-13: 978-1-335-42731-1

High-Stakes Rescue

Copyright © 2022 by Harlequin Enterprises ULC

McCullen's Secret Son
First published in 2015. This edition published in 2022.
Copyright © 2015 by Rita B. Herron

The Last McCullen
First published in 2017. This edition published in 2022.
Copyright © 2017 by Rita B. Herron

PLEASE RECYCLE
THIS PRODUCT IS RECYCLABLE

Recycling programs
for this product may
not exist in your area.

For questions and comments about the quality of this book, please contact us at CustomerService@Harlequin.com.

Harlequin Enterprises ULC
22 Adelaide St. West, 41st Floor
Toronto, Ontario M5H 4E3, Canada
www.Harlequin.com

Printed in U.S.A.

CONTENTS

USA TODAY bestselling author **Rita Herron** wrote her first book when she was twelve but didn't think real people grew up to be writers. Now she writes so she doesn't have to get a real job. A former kindergarten teacher and workshop leader, she traded storytelling to kids for writing romance, and now she writes romantic comedies and romantic suspense. Rita lives in Georgia with her family. She loves to hear from readers, so please visit her website, ritaherron.com.

McCULLEN'S SECRET SON

To Aunt Nelda,
for her love of cowboys!
Love, Rita

Chapter One

The last place Brett McCullen wanted to be was back in Pistol Whip, especially on the McCullen ranch.

He pulled down the long drive to his family's ranch, Horseshoe Creek, his leg throbbing from his most recent fall. Damn, he loved rodeo and riding.

But maybe at thirty, he was getting too old to bust his butt on the circuit. And last week when he'd woken up in bed with one of the groupies, some hot, busty blonde named Brandy or Fifi—hell, after a while, they all sounded and looked the same—he'd realized that not a soul in the damn world really cared about him.

Or knew the Brett underneath.

Maybe because he was good at the show. Play the part of the bad boy. The fearless rider. The charmer who smiled at the camera and got laid every night.

Easier than getting *real* and chancing getting hurt.

He cut the lights and stared at the farmhouse for a minute, memories suffusing him. He could see him and his brothers, playing horseshoes, practicing roping on the fence posts, riding horses in the pasture, tagging along with their daddy on a cattle drive.

His oldest brother, Maddox, was always the responsible one—and his father's favorite. Ray, two years younger than Brett, was the hellion, the one who landed in trouble, the one who butted heads with their father.

Brett could never live up to his old man's expectations, so he figured why try? Life should be fun. Women, horseback riding, rodeos—it was the stuff dreams were made of.

So he'd left home ten years ago to pursue those dreams and hadn't questioned his decision since.

But Maddox's phone call had thrown him for a loop. How could he deny his father's last request?

Hell, it wasn't like he hadn't loved his old man. He was probably more like him than Maddox or Ray. He'd always thought his father had a wild streak in him, that maybe he'd regretted settling down.

Brett hadn't wanted to make the same mistake.

He walked up the porch steps and reached for the doorknob, then stepped inside, back into a well of family memories that reminded him of all the holidays he'd missed.

Last year, he'd seen daddies shopping with their kids for Christmas trees, and mothers and kids at the park, and couples strolling in the moonlight, and he'd felt alone.

Mama Mary, his dad's housekeeper and cook and the woman who'd taken care of him and his brothers after their mother passed, waddled in and wrapped him into a hug.

"You're a sight for sore eyes," Mama Mary said with a hearty laugh.

Brett buried his head in her big arms, emotions churning through him. He'd forgotten how much he loved Mama Mary, how she could make anything feel all right with a hug and her homemade cooking.

She leaned back to examine him, and patted his flat belly.

"Boy, you've gotten skinny. My biscuits and gravy will fix that."

He laughed. Mama Mary thought she could fix any problem with a big meal. "I've missed you," he said, his voice gruff.

She blinked away tears and ushered him into the kitchen. The room hadn't changed at all—still the checkered curtains and pine table, the plate of sausage and bacon left from breakfast. And as far back as he could remember, she'd always had a cake or pie waiting.

"Sit down now and eat. Then you can see your daddy." She waved him to a chair, and he sank into it. Dread over the upcoming reunion with his father tightened his stomach. Grateful to have a few minutes before he had to confront him, he accepted the peach cobbler and coffee with a smile.

Without warning, the back door opened and his little brother, Ray, stood in the threshold of the door. Ray, with that sullen scowl and cutting eyes. Ray, who always seemed to be mad about something.

Ray gave a clipped nod to acknowledge him, then Mama Mary swept him into a hug, as well. "Oh, my goodness, I can't tell you how much it warms my heart to have you boys back in my kitchen."

Brett gritted his teeth. It wouldn't be for long, though. As soon as he heard what his father had to say, he was back on the road.

A tense silence stretched between them as Mama Mary pushed Ray into a chair and handed him some pie and coffee. Just like they did when they were little, Brett and Ray both obeyed and ate.

"Maddox is on his way home now," Mama Mary said as she refilled their coffee.

Brett and Ray exchanged a furtive look. While the two of them hadn't always seen eye to eye, Ray and Maddox had clashed *big*-time.

Brett had always felt the sting of his big brother's disapproval. According to Maddox, Brett didn't just leave but *ran* at the least hint of trouble.

Footsteps echoed from the front, and Brett braced himself as Maddox stepped into the kitchen, his big shoulders squared, that take-charge attitude wafting off him.

"Now, boys," Mama Mary said before any of them could start tangling. "Your daddy had a rough night. He's anxious to see you, so you'd best get upstairs."

An awkwardness filled the air, but Brett and Ray both stood. His brothers were here for one reason, and none of them liked it.

"I'll go first." Brett mustered up a smile. Pathetic that he'd rather face his father on his deathbed than his brothers.

Ray and Maddox followed, but they waited in the hall as he entered his father's bedroom.

The moment he spotted his father lying in the bed, pale, the veins in his forehead bulging, an oxygen tube in his nose, he nearly fell to his knees with sorrow and regret. He should have at least checked in every now and then.

Although he had come back once five years ago. And he'd hooked up with Willow James. But that night with her had confused the hell out of him, and then he'd fought with Maddox the next day and left again.

"Brett, God, boy, it's good to see you."

Emotions welled in Brett's chest, but he forced himself to walk over to his father's bed.

"Sit down a spell," his father said. "We need to talk."

Brett claimed the wooden chair by the bed, and braced himself for a good dressing-down.

"I want you to know that I'm proud of you, son."

Proud was the last thing he'd expected his father to say.

"But I should have come back more," he blurted.

His father shook his head, what was left of his hair sticking up in white patches. "No, I should have come to some of your rodeos. I kept up with you, though. You're just as talented as I always thought you'd be."

Brett looked in his father's eyes. Joe McCullen looked weak, like he might fade into death any second. But there was no judgment or anger there.

"I'm glad you followed your dreams," his father said in a hoarse voice. "If you'd stayed here and worked the ranch, you'd have felt smothered and hated me for holding you back."

Brett's lungs squeezed for air. His father actually understood him. That was a surprising revelation.

"But there is something you need to take care of while you're here. You remember Willow?"

Brett went very still. How could he have forgotten her? She was his first love, the only woman he'd *ever* loved. But his father had discouraged him from getting too involved with her when he was younger.

So he'd left Pistol Whip, chasing a more exciting lifestyle.

Willow had wasted no time in moving on...and getting married.

She even had a child.

Her last name was what, now? Howard?

"Brett?"

"Yes, I remember her," he said through clenched teeth. "I heard she's married and has a family." That was the real reason he hadn't returned to Pistol Whip more often.

It hurt too damn much to see her with another man.

"That girl's got troubles."

Brett stiffened. "Why are you telling me this?"

"Because I was wrong to encourage you to break up with her," his father murmured. "I've made my mistakes, son. I don't want you to do the same."

His father reached out a shaky hand, and Brett took it, chilled by his cold skin.

"Promise me you'll check on her and her boy," his father murmured.

"That's the reason you wanted to see me?"

"Yes." His father coughed. "Now send Ray in here. I need to talk to him."

Brett squeezed his father's hand, then headed to the door. If his father wanted him to check on Willow, something bad must have happened to her.

His heart hammered at the thought of seeing her again. But he couldn't refuse his father's wishes.

He'd pay her a visit and make sure she was okay. Then he'd get the hell out of Pistol Whip again.

When his father was gone, there was no reason for him to stick around.

Three days later

BRETT MCCULLEN WAS back in town.

Willow James, Willow Howard technically, although she was no longer using her married name, rubbed her chest as if the gesture could actually soothe the ache in her heart. Brett was the only man she'd ever loved. Ever would love.

But he'd walked away from her years ago and never looked back.

She sat in her car at the edge of the graveyard like a voyeur to the family as they said their final goodbyes to their father, Joe. Part of her wanted to go to Brett and comfort him for his loss.

But a seed of bitterness still niggled at her for the way he'd deserted her. And for the life he'd led since.

He'd always been footloose and fancy-free, a bad-boy charmer who could sweet-talk any girl into doing whatever he wanted.

He'd taken her virginity and her heart with him when he'd left Pistol Whip to chase his dreams of becoming a famous rodeo star.

He'd also chased plenty of other women.

Her heart squeezed with pain again. She'd seen the news footage, the magazine articles and pictures of his awards and conquests.

She'd told herself it didn't matter. She had the best part of him anyway—his son.

Sam.

A little boy Brett knew nothing about.

If Brett saw Sam in town, would he realize the truth? After all, Sam had Brett's deep brown eyes. That cleft in his chin.

The same streak of stubbornness and the love of riding.

A shadow fell across the graveyard, storm clouds gathering, and the crowd began to disperse. She spotted Brett shaking hands with several locals, his brothers doing the same. Then he lifted his head and looked across the graveyard, and for a moment, she thought he was looking straight at her. That he saw her car.

But a second later, Mama Mary loped over and put her arm around him, and Brett turned back to the people gathered at the service.

Chastising herself for being foolish enough to still care for him after the way he'd hurt her, she started the engine and drove toward her house. She didn't have to worry about Brett. He'd bounce back in the saddle in a day or two and be just fine.

But she had problems of her own.

Not just financial worries, but a no-good husband who she was scared to death of.

Dread filled her as she drove through town and ventured down the side street to the tiny house she'd rented. Her biggest mistake in life was marrying Leo Howard, but she'd been pregnant and on the rebound and had wanted a father for her son.

Leo was no father, though.

Well, at first he'd claimed he was. He'd promised her security and love and a home for her and her little boy.

But as time wore on, she realized Leo had secrets and an agenda of his own.

They hadn't lived together in over three years, but last night he'd come back to town.

Hopefully he had the divorce papers with him, so she could get him out of her life once and for all.

Mentally ticking off her to-do list, she delivered three quilts she'd custom made from orders taken at the antiques store, Vintage Treasures, where she displayed some of her work. When she'd had Sam, she'd known she had to do something to make a living, and sewing was the only skill she had. She'd learned to make clothes, window treatments and quilts from her grandmother, and now she'd turned it into a business.

She did some grocery shopping, then dropped off the rent check. Earlier, she'd left Sam at her neighbor's house, hoping to meet with Leo alone.

She pulled in the drive, noting that Leo had parked his beat-up pickup halfway on the lawn, and that he'd run over Sam's bicycle. Poor Sam. He deserved so much better.

Furious at his carelessness, she threw her Jeep into Park, climbed out and let herself in the house, calling Leo's name as she walked through the kitchen/living room combination, then down the hall to the bedrooms.

When Leo didn't answer, dread filled. He was probably passed out drunk.

Fortified by her resolve to tell him to leave the signed divorce papers so she'd be rid of him for good, she strode to the bedroom. The room was dark, the air reeking of the scent of booze.

Just as she'd feared, Leo was in bed, the covers rumpled, a bottle of bourbon on the bedside table.

Anger churned through her, and she crossed the room, disgusted that he'd passed out in her house. She leaned over to shake him and wake him up, but she felt something sticky and wet on her hand.

She jerked the covers off his face, a scream lodging in her throat. Leo's eyes stared up at her, wide and vacant.

And there was blood.

It was everywhere, soaking his shirt and the sheets…

Leo was dead.

Chapter Two

Willow backed away from the bed in horror. The acrid odor of death swirled around her. There was so much blood…all over Leo's chest. His fingers. Streaking his face where he must have wiped his hand across his cheek.

Nausea rose to her throat, but she swallowed it back, her mind racing.

Leo was…really dead. God…he'd said he was in trouble, but he hadn't mentioned that someone was after him…

She had to get help. Call the police.

Sheriff McCullen.

Her head swam as she fumbled for the phone, but her hand was sticky with blood where she'd touched the bedding.

She trembled, ran into the bathroom and turned on the water, desperate to cleanse herself of the ugly smell. She scrubbed her hand with soap, reality returning through the fog of shock.

Where was the killer? Was he still in the house?

She froze, straining as she listened for signs of an intruder, but the house seemed eerily silent.

Sam… Lord help me. Her neighbor would probably drop Sam off any minute. She couldn't let him come home to this.

Panicked, she dried her hands, then ran for the phone again. But a shadow moved across the room, and she suddenly realized she wasn't alone.

Terrified, she dived for the phone, but the figure lunged at her and grabbed her from behind. Willow screamed and tried to run, but he wrapped big beefy hands around her and immobilized her.

His rough beard scraped her jaw as he leaned close to her ear. "You aren't going to call the cops."

Fear shot through her. "No, no police."

He tightened his grip around her, choking the air from her lungs. "If you do, you'll end up like your husband."

Willow shook her head. "Let me go and I promise I'll do whatever you say."

A nasty chuckle rumbled in her ear. "Oh, you'll do what we want, Willow. That is, if you want to see your little boy again."

"What?" Willow gasped.

He twisted her head back painfully, as if he was going to snap her neck. She tried to breathe, but the air was trapped in her lungs. "Please...don't hurt him."

"That's up to you." He shoved her head forward, and she felt the barrel of his gun at the back of her head. "We'll be in touch with instructions."

Then he slammed the butt of the gun against her head. Pain shot through her skull, and the world spun, the room growing dark as she collapsed.

BRETT HAD MUDDLED his way through the funeral and tacked on his polite semicelebrity smile as the neighbors offered condolences and shared the casseroles that had been dropped off.

He didn't know why people ate when they were grieving, but Mama Mary kept forcing food and tea in his hands, and he didn't have the energy to argue. He'd grown accustomed to cameras, to putting on a happy face when his body was screaming in pain from an injury he'd sustained from a bull ride.

He could certainly do it today.

"Thank you for coming," he said as he shook another hand.

Betty Bane's daughter Mandy slipped up beside him and gave him a flirtatious smile. She looked as if she'd just graduated high school. *Jailbait.* "Hey, Brett, I'm so sorry about your daddy."

"Thanks." He started to step away, but she raised her cell phone. "I know it may not be a good time, but can I get a selfie with you? My friends won't believe I actually touched *the* Brett McCullen!"

She giggled and plastered her face so close to his that her cheek brushed his. "Smile, Brett!"

Unbelievable. She wanted him to pose. To pretend he hadn't just buried his old man.

He bit the inside of his cheek to keep from telling her she was shallow and insensitive, then extricated himself as soon as she got the shot. He shoved his plate on the counter, wove through the crowd and stepped outside, then strode toward the stable.

He wanted to be alone. Needed a horse beneath him, the fresh air blowing in his face and the wild rugged land of Horseshoe Creek to make him forget about the man he and his brothers had just put six feet under.

Or…he could take a trip down to The Silver Bullet, the honky-tonk in town, and drown his sorrow in booze and a woman.

But the thought of any female other than the one he'd

left behind in Pistol Whip didn't appeal to him. Besides, if the press got wind he was there, they'd plaster his picture all over the place. And he didn't need that right now. Didn't want them following him to the ranch or intruding on his brothers.

A heaviness weighed in his chest, and he saddled up a black gelding, climbed atop and sent the horse into a sprint. Storm clouds had rolled in earlier, casting a grayness to the sky and adding to the bleakness of the day.

He missed the stars, but a sliver of moonlight wove between the clouds and streaked the land with golden rays, just enough to remind him how beautiful and peaceful the rugged land was.

To the west lay the mountains, and he pictured the wild mustangs running free. He could practically hear the sound of their hoofs beating the ground as the horses galloped over the terrain.

Cattle grazed in the pastures, and the creek gurgled nearby, bringing back memories of working a cattle drive when he was young, of campfires with his father and brothers, of fishing in Horseshoe Creek.

He'd also taken Willow for rides across this land. They'd had a picnic by the creek and skinny-dipped one night and then…made love.

It was the sweetest moment he'd ever had with a woman. Willow had been young and shy and innocent, but so damn beautiful that, even as the voice in his head cautioned him not to take her, he'd stripped her clothes anyway.

They'd made love like wild animals, needy and hungry, as if they might never be touched like that again.

But he and his brothers had been fighting for months. His father had started drinking and carousing the bars, restless, too. He'd met him at the door one night when he'd been in the barn with Willow, and warned Brett that if he ever wanted to follow his dreams, he needed to leave Willow alone.

His father's heart-to-heart, a rarity for the two of them, had lit a fire inside him and he'd had to scratch that wandering itch. Like his father said, if he didn't pursue rodeo, he'd always wonder if he'd missed out.

That was ten years ago—the first time he'd left. He'd only been back once since, five years ago. Then he'd seen Willow again…

He climbed off the horse, tied him to a tree by the creek, then walked down to the bank, sat down, picked up a stone and skipped it across the water. The sound of the creek gurgling mingled sweetly with the sound of Willow's voice calling his name in the moonlight when they'd made love right here under the stars.

He'd made it in the rodeo circuit now. He had fame and belt buckles and more women than any man had a right to have had.

But as he mourned his father, he realized that in leaving, he'd missed something, too.

Willow. A life with her. A real home. A family.

Someone who'd love him no matter what. Whether he lost an event, or got injured and was too sore to ride, or…too old.

He buried his head in his hands, sorrow for his father mingling with the fact that coming back here only made him want to see Willow again.

But she was married and had a kid.

And even if she had troubles like his father said, she could take care of them herself. She and that husband of hers…

He didn't belong in her life anymore.

WILLOW ROUSED FROM unconsciousness, the world tilting as she lifted her head from the floor. For a moment, confusion clouded her brain, and she wondered what had happened.

But the stench of death swirled through the air, and reality surfaced, sending a shot of pure panic through her.

Leo was dead. And a man had been in the house, had attacked her.

Had said Sam was gone…

She choked on a scream, and was so dizzy for a second, she had to hold her head with her hands to keep from passing out. Nausea bubbled in her throat, but she swallowed it back, determined not to get sick.

She had to find her son.

A sliver of moonlight seeped through the curtains, the only light in the room. But it was enough for her to see Leo's body still planted in her bed, his blood soaking his clothes and the sheets like a red river.

Who was the man in the house? Was he still here? And why would he kidnap Sam?

Shaking all over, she clutched the edge of the dresser and pulled herself up to stand. Her breathing rattled in the quiet, but she angled her head to search the room. It appeared to be empty. She staggered to the kitchen and living room.

Both were empty.

Nerves nearly immobilized her, but she held on to the wall and made herself go to Sam's room. Tears blurred her eyes, but she swiped at them, visually scanning the room and praying that the man had lied. That her little four-year-old boy was inside, safe and sound. That this was all some kind of sick, twisted dream.

Except the blood on the bed and Leo's body was very real.

At first glance, her son's room seemed untouched. His soccer ball lay on the floor by the bed, his toy cars and trucks in a pile near the block set. His bed was still made from this morning, his superhero pillow on top, next to the cowboy hat he'd begged for on his birthday.

But this morning his horse figurines had been arranged by the toy barn and stable where he'd set them up last night when he was playing rodeo. She was afraid he had his father's blood in him.

The horses were knocked over now, the toy barn broken. Sam was supposed to be at Gina's...

Her mind racing, she hurried to retrieve her cell phone from her purse and called her neighbor. *Please let Sam still be there.*

The phone rang three times, then Gina finally answered. "Hello."

"Gina, it's Willow. Is Sam there?"

"No, his father picked him up. I hope that was all right."

Willow pressed her hand to her mouth to stifle a sob. So Sam had come home with Leo.

Which meant he'd probably witnessed Leo's murder.

Fear squeezed the air from her lungs. The man who'd attacked her, warned her not to call the police, that she'd hear from him...

But when?

And what was happening to Sam now?

BRETT FELT WRENCHED from the inside out. He'd been living on adrenaline, the high of being a star, of having women throwing themselves at him, and everyone wanting a piece of him for so long, that he didn't know what to do with himself tonight.

He knew one thing, though—he did not want a picture

of himself at his father's graveside all over the papers. He'd told his publicist that, and banned her from making any public announcement about his father's death.

Grieving for his father and returning to his hometown were private, and he wanted to keep it that way.

Night had fallen, the cows mooing and horses roaming the pastures soothing as he rose from the creek embankment, climbed on his horse and headed back to the farmhouse. The ranch hands would have been fed by now, the days' work done, until sunrise when the backbreaking work started all over again.

If he had to stay here a couple of days to wait on the reading of the will, maybe he'd get up with the hands and pitch in. Nothing like working up a sweat hauling hay, rounding cattle or mending fences to take his mind off the fact that he'd never see his daddy again.

It made him think about his mother and how he'd felt at eight when she'd died. He'd run home from the school bus that day, anxious for a hug and to tell her about the school rodeo he'd signed up for, but the minute he'd walked in and seen his daddy crying, he'd known something was terribly wrong.

And that his life would never be the same.

Damn drunk driver had turned his world upside down.

Shaking off the desolate feeling the memory triggered, he reminded himself that he had made a success out of himself. He had friends...well, not friends, really. But he was surrounded by people all the time.

He'd thought that the crowd loving him would somehow fill the empty hole inside him. That having folks cheer for him and yell his name meant they loved him.

But they loved the rodeo star. If he didn't have that, no one would give him a second look.

The breeze invigorated him as he galloped across the pasture. When he reached the ranch, he spotted Maddox outside with a woman. Moonlight played off the front yard, and he yanked on the reins to slow his horse as he realized he was intruding on a private moment. He steered the animal behind a cluster of trees, waiting in the shadows.

Maddox was on his knees, and so was the woman he was with. They were kissing like they couldn't get enough of each other.

The two of them finally pulled back for a breath, and Brett froze as he saw Maddox slide a ring on the woman's finger.

His brother had just proposed.

He should be glad for Maddox. His older brother had taken his mother's death hard, and he and their daddy had been close.

Maddox had obviously found love. Good for him.

He tightened his fingers around the reins, turned the gelding around and rode back to the stables.

Something about seeing Maddox with that woman made him feel even more alone than he had before.

WILLOW COULDN'T STAND to look at Leo's dead body.

She needed to call the police. But what if the killer was watching her and the sheriff came, and he saw her and hurt her son?

She paced to the living room, frantic. She needed help. She couldn't do this alone.

But calling Sheriff McCullen was out of the question.

Brett's face flashed behind her eyes. She hadn't talked to him since he'd left five years ago. When they'd made love that night, she'd thought that Brett might be rethinking his career, that he might have missed her. That he might have contemplated returning to her.

But the next day he'd left town without a word.

Still, he was Sam's father. Even if he didn't know it.

Heaven help her…he'd be furious with her for not telling him. Although years ago, he'd made it plain and clear that he didn't intend to settle down or stay in Pistol Whip. A wife and a child would have cramped his style and kept him from chasing his dreams.

And Willow refused to trap him. He would only have resented her and Sam.

Would he help her now?

She picked up Sam's photo and studied her precious little boy's face, and she decided it didn't matter. It might be a bad time for Brett, but her son was in danger, and she'd do anything to save him.

Her hand trembled as she phoned the McCullen house. Mama Mary answered, and she asked to speak to Brett.

"He's out riding, can I take a message or tell him who called?"

"It's Willow James. And it's important," she said. "Can you give me his cell phone number?"

"Why sure thing, Ms. Willow." Mama Mary repeated it and Willow ended the call abruptly, then called Brett's mobile. Nerves gripped her as she waited on him to answer. What if he didn't pick up? He might not want to talk to her at all.

The phone clicked, then his deep voice echoed back. "Hello."

"Brett, it's Willow."

Dead silence, then his sharp intake of breath. "Yeah?"

"I'm sorry about your father," she said quickly. "But I…need to see you tonight."

"What?" His voice sounded gruff, a note of surprise roughening it.

"Please," Willow cried. "I...can't explain, but it's a matter of life and death."

Chapter Three

Brett clenched his phone in a white-knuckled grip as he paced the barn. He hadn't seen or talked to Willow in years, and she hadn't attended his father's funeral today. Even as he'd told himself he didn't care if she came, he'd looked for her.

But now she wanted to see him?

It's a matter of life and death.

What the hell was going on?

He cleared his throat. Once upon a time, he'd have jumped and run at a moment's notice if Willow had called. But she was a married woman now. "What's wrong, Willow?"

"I can't explain on the phone," she said, her voice strained. "Please, Brett... I don't know what else to do. Who to call."

His gut tightened at the desperation in her voice. "Willow—"

"Please, I'm begging you. I need your help."

"All right, I'll be right there." He didn't bother to ask for her address. He knew where she lived. Mama Mary had managed to drop it in the conversation once when he'd had a weak moment and had called home.

He'd already unsaddled his horse, so he jogged back to the house and climbed in his pickup truck.

Thankfully, Maddox and his lady friend had gone inside, and he had no idea where Ray was, so he didn't have to explain to anyone. Not that he had to tell them where he was going.

He hadn't answered to anyone in a long time.

Well, except for his publicist and fans and the damn press.

He drove from the ranch, winding down the drive to the road leading into town, the quiet of the wilderness a reprieve from the cities he'd traveled to. A few miles, and he drove through the small town, noting that not much had changed.

At this late hour, the park was empty, the general store closed, yet country music blared from The Silver Bullet, and several vehicles were parked in the lot. He wasn't surprised to see Ray's. He was probably drowning his sorrows.

Inside, the booze and music was always flowing, the women footloose and fancy-free. Just his type.

Another night maybe…

He turned down the street toward Willow's, anxiety needling him. He'd never stopped loving her. Wanting her.

But she was taken. And he had a different life now. A life he'd chosen. Another rodeo coming up, another town…

Children's bikes and toys dotted the yards, suggesting the neighborhood catered to young families. The house at the end of her block, a small rustic log cabin, was Willow's and was set way back from the road, offering privacy. A beat-up pickup truck that had obviously run over the child's bike sat crooked, half in the drive, half in the yard.

His father had said Willow had troubles... Did it have to do with the man she'd married? Judging from the sloppy way the truck was parked, and the fact that he'd run over the bike, maybe he'd been drinking...

Not your problem, Brett.

Except that Willow said she needed him.

He scanned the outside to see if her old man was lurking around. Did he know that Brett and his wife had had a romantic relationship years ago?

He braced himself for trouble as he parked and walked up to the front door. Barring a low-burning light in the bedroom, the house looked dark.

The hair on the back of his neck prickled as he rang the doorbell. Something didn't feel right...

He waited several seconds, then knocked and called through the door, "Willow, it's me. Brett."

The sound of footsteps on the other side echoed, then the lock turned, and the door squeaked open. His breath stalled in his chest as Willow appeared, the door cracking just enough to see her face.

"Brett?" Her face looked ashen, and a streak of blood darkened her hair.

"Yeah, it's me."

Panicked at the sight of her disheveled state, he pushed open the door and stepped inside. "What the hell's wrong?"

She slammed the door shut, then locked it and turned to face him, her eyes wide with fear. "Help me," she whispered as she threw herself into his arms.

Brett's stomach churned as he pulled her trembling body against him and wrapped his arms around her.

WILLOW SANK INTO Brett's arms, the terror she'd felt since she'd arrived home pouring out of her as he held her. She tried to battle the tears, but they overflowed, soaking his shirt.

"Shh, it's all right," Brett murmured into her hair. "Whatever's wrong, we can fix it."

She shook her head against him. "That's just it, I don't know if I can."

Brett stroked her hair, and rubbed slow circles along her back. For the first time in years, she felt safe. Cared for.

But he was only being nice. He had his own life, and when she confessed the truth about Sam, there was no telling how he'd react. He might hate her.

Or he might leave town and not get involved in her troubles. A murder case could ruin his reputation.

But really—none of that mattered. Not when Sam was in danger.

"Willow," Brett said softly. "Honey, you've got to tell me what's wrong. What happened?"

Brett slipped a handkerchief into her hands and she wiped her face. Then she looked up into his eyes.

He had the darkest, most gorgeous eyes she'd ever seen. Eyes she'd gotten lost in years ago.

She wanted to soak in his features, but looking at that handsome, strong face only reminded her of her little boy who looked so much like him that it hurt.

He rubbed her arms. "Willow, talk to me."

"I…don't know where to begin." *With the body of her dead husband*? *Or Sam*?

"You said it was a matter of life and death. I know you're married, that you have a little boy." She squeezed her eyes shut, unable to look at him for a moment.

"I noticed the pickup truck outside and the crunched bike. Is that what this is about?"

"I wish it was that simple," she said on a shaky breath.

Brett led her over to the sofa and she sank onto it, her legs giving way. He joined her, but this time he didn't touch her.

"Your husband? Is he here? Did he hurt you?"

Emotions threatened to overcome her again, and she glanced at the phone, willing it to ring. Willing the caller to tell her how to get her little boy back and end this horror.

"Did he?" Brett asked, his voice harsh with anger.

She shook her head. "Not exactly."

Brett shot up from the seat, his jaw twitching. "Come on, Willow, tell me what the hell is going on."

"He's dead," Willow blurted. "Leo is…dead."

Brett went stone still and stared at her. "What do you mean, *dead*?"

"In there," Willow said. "When I got home tonight, I found him."

He glanced around the bedroom, then exhaled noisily. "How did he die?"

"Someone shot him." Her voice cracked. "There's blood…everywhere."

Brett released a curse and strode to the bedroom. Willow jumped up and raced after him, trembling as he flipped on the overhead light. The stark light lit the room, accentuating the grisly scene in her bed. Leo staring at the ceiling with dead eyes. Blood on his clothes and the sheets.

Brett choked back an obscenity. "Who shot him?"

"I don't know," Willow whispered. "I…found him and was going to call the police, but then a man jumped me."

Brett pivoted, his eyes searching her face, mouth pinched with anger as he lifted his hand and touched her forehead. She didn't realize she'd been bleeding, but he drew his hand back and she saw blood streaking his finger. "He hurt you?"

"I'm all right. He grabbed me from behind, and he said… He told me not to call the police, that he…had Sam."

"Sam?"

Willow's lungs strained for air. "My little boy. He has him, Brett. And he said if I called the police, I'd never see him again."

BRETT GRITTED HIS TEETH. "You mean he kidnapped your child?"

"Yes," Willow cried. "I have to get him back."

Brett stared at the man lying dead in Willow's bed.

Her husband.

He'd never met the man but had heard he was a businessman, that he'd done well for himself.

So why had someone wanted him dead? And why kidnap Willow's son?

"I don't know what to do," Willow said "I…can't leave Leo there. But if I call the sheriff, he'll send police and crime workers, and I might never see Sam again."

Cold fury seized Brett's insides. What kind of person threatened a small child?

"How old is Sam?" he asked.

"Four," Willow said. "He's just a little guy, Brett. He has to be terrified." Her voice cracked again, her terror wrenching Brett's heart. "And if he saw Leo murdered, then he may be traumatized."

He also might be able to identify the killer.

But Brett bit back that observation because it would only frighten Willow more.

If her son could identify her husband's shooter, the killer might not let Sam live anyway, no matter what Willow did.

Brett tried to strip the worry from his voice. "What does this man want from you, Willow?"

"I have no idea." She looked up at him with swollen, tear-stained eyes. "He said to wait for a call."

Brett turned away from the sight of the bloody, dead man. "I know you're scared, but think about it—why would this man take Sam? Did your husband have a lot of money?"

Willow shook her head back and forth, sending her hair swaying. It was tangled from where she'd run her hands through it, the long strands even more vibrant with streaks of gold and red than he remembered.

He tried to dismiss memories of running his hands through it, of the way it felt tickling his belly when she'd loved him, but an image teased his mind anyway.

"Are you sure? Maybe he had some investments? Stocks?"

"If he had any money, I didn't know about it," Willow said. "He didn't even have a savings or checking account in town. It's one of the things we argued about."

Brett arched a brow. He didn't have a bank account in town—which meant he was probably hiding one somewhere else? "One of the things?"

Her face paled. "Yes." She closed her eyes, a pained sound escaping her. "You might as well know. We weren't getting along. We hadn't for a while. Leo moved out three years ago."

Brett tried to assimilate that information. "What has he been doing?"

"I don't know," she said in a choked whisper.

"Was he giving you any money to live on? Helping out with the boy?"

Willow worried her bottom lip with her teeth. "No. He...didn't want to be a father to Sam."

An odd note crept into her voice.

"What kind of father doesn't want to be there for his kid?"

Willow didn't respond, making Brett even more curious about her husband and how he'd treated her.

"Willow, talk to me. What happened between you two? Was he abusing you and Sam?"

Willow cut her eyes away. "When we met, he was kind, charming. But the last year he'd been drinking too much, and his temper erupted."

"And he took it out on you and Sam?"

Willow shrugged. "At first it was just verbal. But... he hit me once. Then he started in on Sam, and I told him to leave." A fierce protectiveness strengthened her voice. "I would never let him hurt my son. I asked him for a divorce."

"How did he take that?"

"He was angry, but he left. Frankly... I think he wanted out."

"You don't know what he's been doing since?"

"No, I have no idea."

He was obviously in trouble.

Dammit. Even though he and his brother were hardly talking, Brett's first instinct was to call Maddox.

But that would endanger Willow's son.

Besides, Maddox had always been by the book. He'd

want to call in the authorities, issue an Amber Alert, all the things they should be doing.

But if they did those things, Willow's little boy could end up dead like his father.

He couldn't allow that to happen.

So he made a snap decision. He'd bury Leo's body and protect Willow until they found Sam.

Chapter Four

Willow couldn't drag her eyes away from Leo's dead body. She couldn't believe this was happening.

She'd hated that her marriage had fallen apart, but it hadn't been right from the beginning. She'd never loved Leo and he knew it.

And truthfully, she didn't think he'd ever loved her.

But she'd been hurt with Brett, and lonely and a single pregnant woman with nowhere to turn. Leo had offered her security and comfort.

For a little while. Then everything had changed and the charming man who'd swept in like a hero had disappeared and become…someone she was afraid of.

Someone Sam was afraid of.

That was when she'd known she had to get out.

The blood on her hands mocked her. She hadn't loved Leo but she'd never wished him dead.

And where was her precious little boy? Was he safe? Hurt? Scared?

A tremor rippled through her. Of course he was scared. He'd been taken from his home.

"We'll bury him on the ranch somewhere," Brett said. "It's too dangerous to do it in your neighborhood."

Willow rubbed her hands up and down her arms as

if to warm herself. "But what about Maddox? He's the sheriff and…your brother."

Brett's look darkened. "I know that," Brett said. "I'll talk to him and explain once we get your little boy back."

Willow's heart constricted. "I'm sorry for putting you in this position, Brett. You could get in trouble with the law. But… I didn't know who else to call."

Brett clasped her arms and forced her to look at him. "Don't worry about me, Willow. I can handle whatever happens. But we can't go to Maddox yet. We have to play by this bastard's rules, until we find Sam."

How could she argue with that? She'd give her life for her son's.

And if Brett knew that Sam was his, he'd do the same.

He probably would anyway, just because he was a McCullen. Joe McCullen had taught his boys old-fashioned values, that men were supposed to protect women and children.

Brett moved over by the bed. "I need to get him in the back of my pickup."

"Why? Aren't we going to bury him in the backyard?"

"No," Brett said. "You live in a neighborhood. And if anyone comes asking about Leo and is suspicious, this is the first place they'd look." He glanced down at the floor and indicated the braided rug. "Let's wrap him in the sheet and I can use the rug to slide him outside."

"But what if a neighbor sees us?"

Brett's jaw tightened. "Your house is set far enough back from the road, so unless someone is in the drive, we should be all right. But I'll move my truck up to the garage and we can go through there just to be safe."

Willow agreed, although she knew what they were doing was wrong. *Illegal*. That they could both be charged.

But nothing mattered now except saving Sam.

BRETT HATED THE FEAR in Willow's eyes. If he had hold of the bastard who had hurt her and taken her little boy, he'd pound his head in.

He started to roll Leo in the sheet, but doubts hit him. He'd seen enough crime shows to know that as soon as he touched the man or the bedding, he was contaminating evidence. Evidence that could lead to the killer and the person who had abducted Sam.

Besides, he'd gotten in a sticky situation once. Had been accosted by the jealous lover of a rodeo groupie he'd dated, a man who'd tried to make it look as if he was the guilty party. He'd seen how the police handled the situation. If it hadn't been for a savvy detective who paid attention to detail, Brett might have gone to jail.

Maybe he *should* call Maddox.

But the kidnapper's warning taunted him. Willow's little boy was in danger.

He couldn't take the chance on that child getting hurt. Pain tugged at his chest. He'd once thought he and Willow would have a family together.

But he'd left and she'd met Leo, and their lives had gone down another path.

Still, her little boy shouldn't suffer.

He removed his phone and snapped some pictures of the man, the wounds to his chest, the blood on the sheets, and the room.

"What are you doing?" Willow asked.

"We'll be destroying evidence here," Brett said. "I

should document how we found Leo to show Maddox when we tell him."

Willow's face paled. "I can't believe this is happening, Brett. I…don't know why anyone would want to kill Leo."

Brett clenched his jaw. "We'll talk about that once we take care of him." He studied the scene again, then snapped a picture of the bullet hole in Leo's chest. "Do you have plastic gloves?"

She nodded and hurried to the kitchen. Seconds later, she returned with two pairs of latex gloves and they both pulled them on. "Let's roll him in the sheet onto the floor. Then I'll wrap him in the rug and drag him outside."

Tears glittered in Willow's eyes, but she jumped into motion to help him. The man's shirt was soaked in blood, his eyes wide with shock, his mouth slack, one hand curled into a fist as if he might have been holding something.

If he had, the killer had taken it.

"Did Leo own a gun?"

"What man in Wyoming doesn't?" Willow asked.

"What kind?"

"A pistol and a shotgun," Willow said. "But he took them when he moved out."

"Look around for bullet casings. Maddox will want them to help with the case." Willow walked around, searching the floor and the bathroom, but shook her head. "I don't see any."

"How about you? Do you have a gun?"

Willow shook her head. "No, I didn't want weapons in the house with Sam."

Good point.

"When did you learn about crime scenes?" Willow asked.

Brett shrugged. He didn't intend to share the story about that debacle with the rodeo groupie. "Television."

She frowned as if that surprised her, but he wrapped the sheet around Leo, gritting his teeth as Willow's husband stared up at him in death.

Blood had dried onto the sheet and soaked through to the mattress. Rigor had set in and Leo was a deadweight. Willow gasped as he eased the man to the rug.

"Strip the rest of the bedding," Brett said. "And bag it. We'll keep it to give to Maddox later."

Willow looked ill, but she rushed back to the kitchen and returned a moment later with a big garbage bag.

While he wrapped the top sheet tighter around Leo, she stripped the fitted sheet and comforter and jammed it in the plastic bag. Her ragged breathing rasped between them as she added the pillowcases, then she stood and stared at the bed for a moment as if she'd never be able to sleep in it again.

Brett wanted to comfort her, but he needed to get rid of Leo's corpse before anyone discovered what they'd done.

THE SCENT OF the blood on her sheets and the image of Leo lying dead in her bed made Willow feel ill.

She didn't know how she'd ever sleep in this room again.

"What should I do with these?"

"We'll bury them with Leo."

The thought of digging a hole for her husband sent bile to her throat. But as Brett dragged Leo's body on that rug into the hall, she glanced in Sam's room again, and determination rifled through her.

That empty room nearly brought her to her knees.

Determined to bring her son home no matter what,

she followed Brett with the garbage bag. He pulled Leo through the hallway to the kitchen. She opened the garage door, and he left Leo in the garage, then backed his pickup around to the exterior garage door, which faced the side of the drive.

Anger at Leo mushroomed inside her.

Leo had a temper, was manipulative and secretive and…he had gotten rough with her more than once. But the day he'd put his hand on Sam, she'd ordered him to leave and told him she wanted a divorce.

Nobody would hurt her baby.

Except Sam might be hurt now… All because of the man she'd exchanged vows with. She leaned over Leo and stared at him, a mother's temper boiling over. "What did you do to get my son kidnapped?"

Of course he didn't answer. He simply laid there with his mouth slack and his eyes bulging. If possible, his face looked even paler beneath the kitchen lights.

Brett appeared a second later, wiping sweat from his brow with the back of his sleeve. He planted his hands on his hips and looked down at Leo, then up at her.

"Are you okay, Willow?"

A sob caught in her throat, and she shook her head. "How can I be all right when Sam is missing? When he might be crying for me right now?"

Silence stretched full of tension for a minute. "Then let's get this done."

Brett sounded resigned, and Willow questioned again whether she should have called him. But what else could she do?

Brett knelt and grabbed the end of the rug, and Willow decided she couldn't allow him to do this alone. She set the garbage bag down, flipped off the garage light so they couldn't be seen through the front window, then grabbed the opposite side of the rug and helped Brett drag Leo through the garage.

She was heaving for breath by the time they reached the threshold of the exterior door. Leo's body was so heavy that she didn't know how Brett would lift him.

The garage door was situated on the side of the house and wasn't visible from the street, but in silent agreement they paused to check and make sure there weren't any cars passing or anyone walking by.

"It's clear." Brett stooped down, scooped Leo up—still wrapped in the rug—and threw him over his shoulder. She bit down on her lip to stifle a gasp as Leo's arm swung over Brett's back. The dried blood on his hand and face looked macabre in the moonlight.

Brett struggled for a minute with the weight, then maneuvered Leo's body into the truck bed. He climbed in and threw an old blanket over the body, and she tossed the bag of linens in the back with him.

"I'd tell you to stay here," Brett said, "but it's not safe, Willow. Come with me and I'll bring you back later."

The last thing Willow wanted to do tonight was bury Leo, but she had started this and she had to see it through. At least until she got Sam back.

"Let me get my phone in case the kidnapper calls tonight."

BRETT SAID A SILENT prayer that the kidnapper would call, but as Willow went to retrieve her phone and purse, he had a bad feeling. What did the kidnapper want?

Money? Or something else?

All questions to pursue once they got rid of Leo's body. Damn, he couldn't believe he was doing this. Actively covering up a crime. If his agent and his fans found out, his career would be over.

Hell, if Maddox didn't help him out when he finally explained things, his life as a free man would be over.

But he couldn't let Willow down.

His phone buzzed, and he checked the caller ID. Kitty. Another pesky immature groupie.

Dammit, he'd slept with her twice, then broken it off, but she'd become obsessed with him. He'd warned her that he'd take out a restraining order if she didn't leave him alone.

He'd hoped coming home for a while might give her the time and distance she needed to move on.

Willow locked the house and closed the garage door and he let the call roll to voice mail, then covered Leo's body in the bed of the truck. If he got stopped…no, that was not going to happen.

He removed the latex gloves and Willow did the same. He stuffed both pairs in his pocket, then opened the passenger side for Willow, and she climbed onto the seat, her hand shaking as she gripped the seat edge. The wind kicked up, stirring leaves and rattling the windows as he hurried to the driver's side, jumped in and started the engine.

The moon disappeared behind storm clouds as he eased onto the street. Senses on alert, Brett searched right and left, then in the rearview mirror, looking for someone who might be watching.

For all he knew, the killer/kidnapper might have hung around to see if Willow called the law.

Willow leaned against the doorframe, looking lost and shaken, and so terrified that Brett's heart broke. In spite of the fact that he was digging a hole for himself with the law and his own brother, he pulled her hand in his.

"We'll get Sam back, Willow. I promise."

"But what if—"

"Shh." He brought her hand to his mouth and kissed her fingers. "Everything will be all right. I swear."

Tears trickled down her cheeks, and she broke into another sob. Brett pulled her over beside him and wrapped his arm around her as he drove. She collapsed against him, her head against his chest, her arm slipped around his waist.

The two of them had ridden just this way in high school, hugging and kissing as they'd driven up to Make-Out Point. But tonight, they wouldn't be making out or... making love.

Tonight they were hiding her husband's body, and she was almost despondent over her missing son.

Still checking over his shoulder as he turned onto the highway, a siren wailed from the right, and he tensed. A fire engine, ambulance, police?

Suddenly blue lights swirled against the night sky as a police car careened around the corner and flew toward them.

Brett's chest constricted. He was about to get caught with a dead body in his truck.

SAM CURLED INTO a little ball, hugged his knees to his chest and leaned against the wall. He was shaking so badly, he thought he might pee his pants. He hadn't done that since he was two.

Where was he? And why had that man with the bandana over his face grabbed him and thrown him in the trunk of his car?

Sam hated that trunk. He hated the dark.

Swiping at tears, he clutched the ratty teddy bear the man had tossed into the room with him. He didn't want the old dusty thing. He wanted his dinosaur and his mommy and his room with all his toys.

But he clutched the bear anyway because it made him feel like he wasn't all alone.

Outside the dark room, footsteps pounded and two men's voices sounded. Loud. Mad. They were barking at each other like dogs.

They had been mad at Daddy. Then one of them had pulled that gun and shot him.

Sam closed his eyes, trying to forget the red blood that had flown across the bed like a paintball exploding. Except it wasn't paint.

He couldn't forget it.

Or that choked gurgling sound Daddy had made.

He started shaking and had to hug his legs with his arms to keep his knees from knocking. He had to be quiet. Make them think he was asleep or they'd come back and get him.

Daddy was dead.

And if he didn't do what they told him, he'd be dead, too.

Chapter Five

Willow clenched her clammy hands together as the sirens wailed closer. Dear Lord, had someone seen them leave with Leo's body?

Brett laid a hand over hers. "It'll be all right."

But they both knew it wouldn't be all right. They'd lose precious time explaining themselves to the police, and even then, they would go to jail and the kidnapper might hurt Sam.

Brett slowed and pulled off the road, but they were both shocked when the police car raced on by.

His relieved breath punctuated the air. "Whew, I thought they had us."

"Me, too." She wiped at the perspiration trickling down the side of her face, but she was trembling so badly a pained sound rumbled from her throat.

Brett pulled her to him for a moment and soothed her. "Hang in there, Willow. I'm here."

She nodded, those words giving her more comfort than he could imagine. She didn't think she could hold it together tonight if she was alone.

They sat there for several seconds, but finally Brett pulled away and inched back onto the road. By the time they reached the ranch, her breathing had finally steadied.

She had always loved Horseshoe Creek, but tonight she found no peace in the barren stretch of land where Brett parked.

Brett kept looking in the rearview mirror and across the property as if he thought they might have been followed. The land seemed eerily quiet, the wind whistling off the ridges, whipping twigs and tumbleweed across the dirt as if a windstorm was brewing.

This rocky area was miles away from the big farmhouse where Brett had grown up, the pasture where the McCullen cattle grazed, from the stables housing their working horses and the bungalows where the ranch hands lived.

The truck rumbled to a stop, and Brett cut the engine. He turned to her for a moment, the tension thick between them. "His body should be safe out here until we get your son back."

Willow bit down on her lip as the full implications of what they were doing hit her. Not only was she compromising evidence and disposing of a body, but when the truth was revealed, she would look like a bitter ex-wife—one who might have killed Leo and then called an old boyfriend to help her dispose of his body.

She could go to jail and so could Brett.

It would also drive a bigger wedge between him and his brother Maddox.

But what other choice did she have?

She touched the knot on the back of her head where the intruder had hit her, then looked down at her cell phone, willing it to ring.

Poor little Sam must be terrified. Wondering where she was. Wanting to be home in his own bed.

Resigned, she reached for the door handle. "Let's get

this done and pray the kidnapper calls tonight, then we can explain everything to Maddox."

Brett's eyes flashed with turmoil at the mention of his brother, compounding her guilt. The men had just buried their beloved father and now she was asking *this* of him.

She hated herself for that.

But Sam's face flashed in her mind, and she couldn't turn back.

"WAIT IN THE TRUCK," Brett told Willow.

Brett jumped out of the pickup, walked to the truck bed and retrieved a shovel. Yanking on work gloves, he strode to a flat stretch between two boulders, a piece of land hidden from view and safe from animals scavenging for food.

A coyote howled in the distance and more night sounds broke the quiet. His breath puffed out as he jammed the shovel in the hard dirt and began to dig. Pebbles and dry dirt crunched, and he looked up to see Willow approaching with a second shovel.

"I told you to stay in the truck."

"This is my mess," Willow said. "I...have to help."

Brett wanted to spare her whatever pain he could. "Let me do it for you, Willow, *please.*"

Her gaze met his in the dim light of the moon, and she shook her head, then joined him and together they dug the grave.

It took them over an hour to make a hole deep enough to cover Leo so the animals wouldn't scavenge for him. Willow leaned back against a boulder, her breath ragged. She looked exhausted, dirty and sweaty from exertion, and shell-shocked from the events of the night.

He returned to the truck, dragged Leo's body inside

the rug from the bed, then hauled him over his shoulder and carried him to the grave. Before he dumped him inside, he retrieved a large piece of plastic from his trunk and placed it in the hole to protect the body even more.

Willow watched in silence as he tossed Leo into the grave, then he shoveled the loose dirt back on top of him, covering him with the mound until he was hidden from sight.

But he had a bad feeling that even though Leo was covered, Willow would still continue seeing his face in her mind.

He smoothed down the dirt, then stroked her arm. "It's done. Now we wait on the ransom call."

She nodded, obviously too numb and wrung out to talk, and he led her back to the truck. He tossed the shovels in the truck bed, grabbed a rag and handed it to Willow to wipe her hands.

She looked so shaken that he decided not to take her back to that house. There were a couple of small cabins on the north side of the ranch that weren't in use because they'd reserved that quadrant to build more stables. Even though he was a bull rider, he also did trick riding, so his father had wanted Brett to handle the horse side of the business. But when Brett left town, Maddox and his father had put the idea on hold. "I'm going to take you to one of the cabins to get some rest."

Willow didn't argue. Her hand trembled as she fastened her seat belt, then she leaned her head back and closed her eyes. He drove across the property to the north, where he hoped to find an empty cabin.

Five minutes later, he found the one he was looking for just a few feet from the creek. He parked and walked around to help Willow out. The door to the place was un-locked—so like the McCullens. Trustworthy to a fault.

The electricity was on, thank goodness, and the place was furnished, although it was nothing fancy, but the den held a comfortable-looking sofa and chair and a double bed sat in the bedroom, complete with linens. He and Willow had sneaked out to this cabin years ago to make love in the afternoon.

Her eyes flickered with recognition for a moment be-fore despair returned.

"Thank you for coming tonight," Willow said in a raw whisper.

He gestured toward the bedroom. "Get some rest. I'll hang around for a while."

She looked down at her hands, still muddy from the dirt and blood. "I have to wash up first."

He ducked into the bathroom and found towels and soap. The place was also fairly clean as if someone had used it recently. His father was always taking someone in to help them out so he wasn't surprised.He still felt like he'd walk into the main house and find him sitting in his chair. But he was gone.

Willow flipped on the shower, then reached for the button on her shirt to undress.

It was too tempting to be this close to her and not touch her, so he stepped into the hall and shut the door to give her some privacy. Self-doubts over his actions tonight assailed him, and he went to his truck, grabbed a bottle of whiskey and brought it inside.

As much as he wanted to comfort Willow and hold her tonight, he couldn't touch her. She'd only called him to help her find her son.

And he would do that.

But tonight the stench of her husband's dead body permeated his skin, and the lies he would have to tell his brother haunted him.

IMAGES OF DIGGING her husband's grave tormented Willow as she showered. No matter how hard she scrubbed, she couldn't erase them.

Leo was dead. Shot. Murdered.

And Sam was missing.

Her little boy's face materialized, and her chest tightened. Sam liked soccer and climbing trees and chocolate chip cookies. And he had just learned to pedal on his bike with training wheels. Only Leo had run over his bike.

Where was Sam now? Was he cold or hungry?

She rinsed, dried off and looked at the clock. It was after four. Was Sam asleep somewhere, or was he too terrified to sleep? His favorite stuffed dinosaur was still in his room…

She found a robe in the closet and tugged it on, then checked her phone in case she'd missed the kidnapper. But no one had called.

Tears burned the backs of her eyelids. Why hadn't they phoned?

Nerves on edge, she walked into the kitchen and spotted a bottle of whiskey on the counter. Brett had always liked brown whiskey. In fact, in high school, he'd sneaked some of his father's to this very cabin and they'd imbibed before they'd made love.

She couldn't allow herself to think about falling in bed with Brett again.

This was an expensive brand of whiskey, though, much more so than the brand Joe McCullen drank. Of course, Brett had done well on the rodeo circuit.

Both financially and with the women.

An empty glass sat beside the bottle, and she poured herself a finger full, then found Brett sitting in the porch swing with a tumbler of his own.

He looked up at her when she stepped onto the porch, his handsome face strained with the night's events.

"I should go home," Willow said from the doorway.

Brett shook his head. "Not tonight. We'll pick up some of your things tomorrow, but you aren't staying in that house until this is over and Leo's killer is dead or in jail."

"But—"

"No buts, Willow." He sipped his whiskey. "It's not safe. Besides, we shouldn't disturb anything in the house, so when we do call Maddox in, he can process the place for evidence."

He was right. "I realize this is putting you in a difficult position with Maddox."

Brett shrugged. "That's nothing new."

Willow sank onto the swing beside him. She'd never had siblings although she'd always wanted a sister or a brother, especially when she was growing up. Her mother had died when she was five, and she'd been left with her father who'd turned to drinking to drown his problems. That alcohol had finally killed him two weeks before she'd graduated from high school.

Another reason she'd gravitated toward Brett and it had hurt so much when he'd left town. She had literally been alone.

"I know you've had issues, Brett, but your father just died, and you and your brothers should be patching things up." She took a swallow of her own liquor, grateful for the warmth of the alcohol as it eased her nerves. "Family means everything, Brett. When you don't have one anymore, you realize how important it is."

Brett's gaze latched with hers, but the flirtatious gleam she'd seen years ago and in the tabloids was gone. Instead, a dark intensity made his eyes look almost black.

"I'm sorry you lost yours. I know that last year with your dad was rough."

It was Willow's turn to shrug, although it was Brett leaving a second time that had sent her into Leo's arms. Made her vulnerable to his false charm.

"My family is Sam now. I can't go on if something happens to him."

Brett reached out and covered her hand with his. "We will find him, I promise. And I'll make sure whoever abducted him pays."

She desperately wanted to believe him.

"There's something I have to ask you, Willow."

A knot seized her stomach at his tone. "What?"

"Where were you earlier today?"

Willow tensed. "Why? You don't think *I* shot Leo, do you?"

He hesitated, long enough to make her think that he had considered the possibility. That hurt.

"No," he finally said. "But I have to ask, because the police will."

Willow sucked in a sharp breath. "I did errands, had to drop off some of my orders. Sam was staying with my neighbor Gina, but apparently Leo picked him up." That sick feeling hit her again.

"This other woman can corroborate your story?"

Willow pinched her lips together, angry. "Yes, Brett."

Would she need a more solid alibi to prove that she hadn't killed her husband?

THE PAIN IN Willow's eyes made Brett strengthen his resolve to help her. "Do you have any idea who abducted Sam?"

She shook her head, her hair falling like a curtain around her face. "I didn't recognize the man's voice. And he wore a ski mask."

"You said that Leo didn't have a bank account? Where did he keep his money?"

Willow traced her finger along the rim of her glass. "He kept cash in a safe when he lived with me. But he cleaned that out when he left."

"It seems odd that a businessman wouldn't have had bank accounts, maybe even a financial advisor."

"I thought so, too, but he just got defensive every time I mentioned it."

Brett rocked the swing back and forth with his feet. "Where did he go when he moved out?"

"I don't know."

"He didn't send child support?"

"No. And I was okay with that. When he left, I was so glad to have him out of my life, out of Sam's life, that I didn't want anything from him."

Brett willed his temper in check. The McCullen men had been raised to protect women, and to honor them. No man ever laid a hand on a woman or child.

"How bad was it?" he asked gruffly.

Willow sighed wearily. "At first it was just arguments. He wanted to control everything, from the money I spent, to how I took care of the house. I stood my ground, and he didn't like it."

"Good for you."

A small smile tilted her mouth. "He was nice in the beginning, Brett, but he changed once we married. Nothing I did was right. And he was always traveling and refused to tell me where he was going."

"You think he was having an affair?"

Willow shrugged. "It wouldn't have surprised me."

Brett contemplated that idea. What if Leo had been seeing another woman and she had killed him?

Still, why would that woman abduct Sam?

Unless she thought Willow had Leo's money.

"Tell me about his business," Brett said. "What did Leo do for a living?"

"When we first met, he said he'd made it big with some investment, something about mining uranium."

Made sense. Wyoming was rich in rare earth elements and mining.

"Did he say how much money he made? Thousands? A million?"

Willow bit down on her lip. "No. He just said he'd— we'd—be taken care of for life."

Brett considered the small house where Willow lived. "If he had so much money, why were you living in that little place?"

Willow frowned. "I moved there after Leo left. I wanted a fresh start."

"Where was your other house?"

"Cheyenne," Willow said. "But it was a rental, too. He said he was holding out to buy a big spread and build his dream house. But he never started anything."

"Did he have a business card? Or was there a business associate he mentioned?"

"No." Willow's voice cracked. "I'm sorry. I'm not being much help."

She obviously hadn't known much about her husband, which seemed odd to him. Willow had always been honest, trusting, and she valued family but she was also cautious because her father had had problems.

So why had she been charmed by Leo? Had his money appealed to her?

That also didn't fit with the Willow he'd known.

"Did Leo have any family? A sister? Brother? Parents?"

"No," Willow said. "He lost both his parents." Willow leaned against the back of the porch swing, her face ashen. "Looking back, Brett, I feel like I didn't know Leo at all."

Brett tossed back the rest of his whiskey. "You're exhausted now, but maybe tomorrow you'll remember more."

If he was lucky, he'd find something in the house to add insight into Willow's dead husband.

Knowing more about him might clue them in to the reason for his death.

He patted Willow's hand. "Go inside and try to get some sleep."

"How can I sleep when I don't know where Sam is? He must be scared…and what if he's hurt? What if that man did something to him?"

Brett cupped her face with his hands. "Listen to me, Willow. If this man wanted something from Leo, and he didn't get it, he's going to use Sam as leverage. So if we figure out what kind of trouble Leo was in, we can figure out how to save your son."

He coaxed her to stand. "Try to rest until he calls with his demands."

Willow glanced down at his hand. "Are you staying here?"

He wanted to. But that would be too tempting.

"No. I'll run back to the farmhouse to shower. I'll bring you some breakfast in a little while, then we can stop by your house for some of your things."

He opened the door and ushered her inside. "Now lock up. You'll be safe here. And when the kidnapper calls, phone me and I'll come right over."

Her golden eyes flickered with fear, but she nodded and slipped inside. He waited until he heard the door lock, then hurried to his truck before he went inside and crawled in bed with her.

Tension thrummed through him as he drove back to the farmhouse and parked.

Just as he let himself inside the house, Maddox was jogging down the steps. His gaze roved over Brett's dirt-stained clothes, a disapproving scowl stretching his mouth into a thin line.

"We just buried our father, and you went out partying, huh?" Maddox muttered. "Some things never change, do they?"

Brett bit his tongue to keep from a retort.

Unable to tell him the truth, he let his brother believe the lesser of the evils, pasted on a cocky grin like he would after an all-night drunk and climbed the steps to his old room.

If his brother knew that he'd buried a murdered man on McCullen land, he'd lock him up and never talk to him again.

Chapter Six

Too on edge to sleep, Brett showered, anxious to wash the stench of Leo's dead body off him.

But all the soap in the world couldn't erase the memory of what he'd done.

He envisioned the headlines—Rodeo Star Brett McCullen Arrested for Covering Up a Murder, for Tampering with Evidence in a Homicide...

The list could go on and on.

If—no, *when*—it was revealed that he and Willow shared a past, people might think that the two of them had plotted to kill her husband so they could be together.

Perspiration beaded on his neck as he buttoned his shirt.

The only way to make sure the two of them weren't charged was to find out who had killed Leo. Then they could recover Willow's little boy and turn the situation over to Maddox.

He dressed in jeans, fastened his belt and yanked on his cowboy boots. Then he packed a duffel bag of clothes in case he needed to stay with Willow and stowed them in his Range Rover.

His eyes felt bleary from lack of sleep, but he couldn't rest right now. He had to find some answers.

Willow and her little boy were depending on him.

The first place he would start was Leo's truck. It had been left in Willow's drive. Maybe there was something inside it that would give him a lead.

The scent of strong coffee and bacon wafted through the air as he entered the dining room. Mama Mary was humming a gospel song in the kitchen, but she had set out coffee and juice along with hot biscuits, bacon and eggs on the sideboard.

He poured himself a mug of coffee, then made a breakfast sandwich and wolfed it down. She ambled in just as he was finishing, her eyes probing his.

"How you doing this morning, Mr. Brett?"

He and his brothers always said Mama Mary had eyes in the back of her head, and a sixth sense that told her when one of them had been bad. She was giving him that look this morning.

He shrugged. "Okay."

"Hmm-hmm."

If guilt wasn't pressing against his chest so badly he would have chuckled. "It's hard being back here without Dad," he said, hoping she'd think his grief was all that was eating at him.

"I know. We're all gonna miss your daddy." She patted his shoulder and poured him another cup of coffee. "Best remember that and take care to make up with the ones still on this side of the ground."

He understood her not-so-subtle message.

Unfortunately his actions the night before would only create a bigger chasm and garner more disapproval from his older brother. He never could measure up to Maddox.

She cleared his plate. "Maddox wanted to check the

fence on the west side before he went to the sheriff's office."

How Maddox handled being in the office and the ranch was beyond Brett. But then again, Maddox was the one who *could* do it all and make it look easy at the same time.

Hadn't his father told him that a million times?

"You know Maddox got engaged to this pretty lady named Rose?" Mama Mary said with a sparkle in her eye.

Brett nodded. "Is that her name?"

"Yeah, she's a sweetheart. Owns the antique store in town where Willow sells her quilts. Poor Rose had some trouble a while back, but Maddox handled it for her."

"I'm sure he did." He didn't mean to sound surly, but his tone bordered on sarcastic.

Mama Mary gave him a chiding look, and he grabbed one of the to-go mugs on the sideboard, filled it with coffee, wrapped an extra biscuit and bacon in a napkin for Willow and gave Mama Mary a peck on the cheek.

"Thanks for breakfast. I haven't had biscuits like that since I left here."

She grinned with pride, and he hurried away before she asked him where he was going. He could lie to Maddox, but it was harder to lie to Mama Mary because she could see right through him.

Wind stirred dust around his boots, and the temperature had dropped twenty degrees overnight. As he drove across the ranch, the beauty of the land struck him along with memories of riding with his brothers as a kid. The campouts and cattle drives. The horseshoe contests and trick riding.

When he'd left Pistol Whip, he'd been young and

eager for travels, to see new places, to escape the routine of ranch life, and he'd enjoyed the different towns and women.

This morning, though, the land looked peaceful. The women's faces a blur.

There was only one woman he'd ever really cared about, and that was Willow.

By the time he reached her place, worry for her son dominated his mind.

Knowing Willow must be frantic, he scanned the outside of her rental house and the property when he arrived. Everything appeared as he'd left it the night before.

Leo's truck was still parked on the lawn, the little boy's bike mangled.

He yanked on a pair of work gloves to keep from leaving fingerprints, then climbed out and walked over to the truck. For a man who supposedly had landed a windfall, the truck was old and shabby looking. Barring a few tools, the truck bed was empty.

The door to the cab was unlocked, as if the man had gotten out in a hurry. Brett slipped inside and checked the seat. Nothing.

No papers, computer or cell phone. No gun.

He opened the glove compartment and found a wallet with a driver's license and a hundred dollars in cash.

He didn't find an insurance card, but found a tiny slip of paper with a name and phone number.

It was a woman's name. Doris Benedict.

Brett's instincts kicked in. If Leo had another woman on the side, maybe she'd killed him.

He jammed the paper in his pocket. It was a place to start.

Willow dozed to sleep but dreamed of her little boy and Brett, and woke up in a sweat.

In the dream, Sam looked so much like his father sitting on that horse that it nearly took her breath away and resurrected memories of watching Brett at the rodeo when he was eighteen.

She'd fallen in love with him that day. He'd looked so handsome with his thick hair glinting in the sunlight. When he'd turned his flirtatious smile on her, she hadn't been able to resist.

She had been alone so long. Dubbed poor white trash because her father had been a mean drunk and she was motherless. The very reason she'd been determined to be a good mother to Sam.

But now he was missing because she'd been fooled by Leo's promises and wound up marrying a mean drunk herself.

But that day Brett had made her feel so special…not like poor trash. All the other girls at the rodeo wanted Brett McCullen, the up-and-coming rodeo star.

But after he'd received his buckle for winning, he'd walked over to her and kissed her right in front of the crowd.

How could she *not* have fallen in love with him?

It didn't matter.

Brett hadn't wanted her the past few years. He had plenty of women. And he certainly didn't intend to stay in Pistol Whip and settle down.

She had done the right thing. If she'd told Brett she was pregnant five years ago, he might have stuck around, but he would have resented her. And that would have destroyed their love.

She found some coffee in the kitchen and brewed a

pot, then carried a mug and her phone to the front porch and sat down, praying it would ring with news about how to get Sam back.

BRETT DROVE BACK to the cabin, anxious to check on Willow. Hopefully the kidnapper would phone today with his demands.

But if Willow didn't have the money, what did they want?

Willow was sitting on the porch, sipping coffee and looking so damn lost and pained that his lungs squeezed for air. He'd do anything to make her happy again.

But the only way to do that was to put her son back in her arms.

He parked, then carried the biscuit in one hand as he walked up to the porch.

He handed her the food. "Any word?"

She unwrapped the biscuit, although she rewrapped it as if she couldn't eat. That, and the desolate look in her eyes, told him all he needed to know.

"I searched Leo's truck and found a woman's name scribbled on a slip of paper, Doris Benedict. Do you know her?"

"No. Who is she?" Willow ran a hand through her hair, the wavy strands tangling as the wind picked them up and whipped them around her face. Winter was blowing in to Pistol Whip with its cold and gusty windstorms.

"I don't know," Brett said. "But maybe she knows something about Leo that can help us."

Willow rose from the porch swing, her face even more pale in the early morning light. "I'll go with you."

"Are you sure? We don't know what we'll find—what her relationship with Leo was."

"I don't care if they were lovers," Willow said staunchly. "I was done with Leo a long time ago. But if she can help us find Sam, I have to talk to her."

Brett gave a clipped nod. She'd been done with Leo a long time ago—had she *loved* him, though?

At one time he'd thought she loved *him*. But when he'd left town, she'd completely cut him out of her life.

She disappeared inside the cabin and returned a moment later with her purse over her shoulder. But she kept her phone clutched in one hand. Her fingers were wrapped so tightly around it that they looked white.

She didn't look at him as she started down the steps. "Let's go."

Brett followed her, climbed in the truck and started the engine, the tension between them thick with unanswered questions as he drove toward the woman's address.

Doris Benedict lived in Laramie, in a stone duplex on the outskirts of town. Dry scrub brush and weeds choked the tiny yard. No children's toys outside, so she must not have kids. Although the duplex didn't look fancy or expensive, a fairly new dark green sedan sat in the drive.

Brett and Willow walked together to the front door. Willow folded her arms while he buzzed the doorbell. A car engine rumbled from next door while voices from another neighbor herding her kids out to the bus stop echoed in the wind.

He punched the doorbell again, and a woman's voice shouted from inside that she was coming. A second later, the door opened, and a young woman with a bad dye job and sparkling earrings that dangled to her shoulders stood on the other side.

He guessed her age to be about thirty-four, although

she had the ruddy skin of a heavy smoker, so she could have been younger.

Her flirtatious smile flitted over him. "You're that rodeo star?"

He nodded. "Yes, ma'am. Brett McCullen."

When her gaze roved from him to Willow, her ruby-red lips formed a frown. "What do you want?"

Brett narrowed his eyes at the contempt in her voice.

"My name is Willow James, um Willow Howard—"

"I know who you are." Doris reached for the door as if to slam it in their faces, but Brett caught it with one hand.

Willow looked stunned. "How do you know me?"

Doris removed a cigarette from the pack in the pocket of her too-tight jeans. "Leo married you."

Brett frowned. "How do you know Leo, Ms. Benedict?"

The woman angled her face toward him, her eyes menacing. "He and I dated a while back."

"How far back?" Brett asked.

She lit her cigarette, tilted her head back and inhaled a drag, then glared at Willow. "About five years. I thought we were going to get hitched, but then he married you."

"You dated Leo?" Willow asked.

The woman pushed her face toward Willow. "What's that supposed to mean? You don't think he'd go out with a woman like me?"

"It's not that," Willow said quickly. "It's just that Leo never mentioned his prior relationships."

Doris chuckled. "Honey, there's a lot of things Leo didn't tell you."

Willow's breath rasped out. "Like what?"

Doris blew smoke into the air. "Why don't you ask him?"

Willow glanced at him and he gave a short shake of his head, silently willing her not to divulge that Leo was dead. Not yet.

"When was the last time you saw him?" Brett asked.

Doris shrugged. "About a month ago."

"You were seeing him while he was married to Willow?" Brett asked.

Doris poked him in the chest. "Don't judge me, Brett McCullen. Leo loved me."

"Then why did he marry me?" Willow asked.

Doris laughed again. "Because you were respectable. And Leo needed a respectable wife so nobody in town would ask too many questions."

"Why didn't he want them asking questions?" Brett asked.

Doris tapped ashes on the porch floor at Willow's feet. "Again—why don't you ask him?"

"Because I'm asking you," Willow said, her voice stronger. "You obviously don't like me and wanted Leo for yourself. So when I filed for divorce, did he come to you?"

Doris's eyes widened in shock. "You were divorcing Leo?"

Brett scrutinized her body language. She sounded sincerely surprised. But if she'd discovered he and Willow weren't together, and he still didn't want her, she might have killed him out of anger.

Although she didn't appear to be the motherly type. So if she had killed Leo, why kidnap Sam?

SAM HUGGED THE RAGGEDY stuffed animal under his arm and rubbed his eyes. He wanted his mommy.

But he remembered what had happened the night before and tears filled his eyes. Those bad men…two of them. One with the scarf over his mouth and the other with that black ski mask.

All he could see was their eyes. Mean eyes.

And the tattoo. Both of them had tattoos on their necks. One had a long rattlesnake that wound around his throat. The other had crossbones like he'd seen on some of the T-shirts at Halloween.

Those crossbones meant poison or the devil or something else evil.

Just like the bad men.

Red flashed behind his eyes, and he heard the gunshots blasting like fireworks. He covered his ears to snuff them out just like he'd done at his house.

But he'd peeked from the closet and seen his daddy and all that blood ran down his shirt. Then Daddy's eyes had gone wide, like they did on TV when someone was dead.

He didn't much care if he was dead, and he felt real bad about that. Kids were supposed to love their fathers. But he couldn't help it—his daddy had been mean to his mommy.

He didn't want to be dead, too, though.

He sat up on the cot and pushed the curtain to the side and looked through the dirty window. A spider was crawling across the windowsill, and a tree branch was beating against the glass.

He tried to see where he was, but all he saw was woods.

Big trees stuck together, so close that he couldn't see past them or even between them for a path.

He pushed at the window to open it and climb out. He was scared of the woods and the dark, but he'd rather run in there than be stuck here with these bad men with the tattoos and guns.

But the window wouldn't move. He pushed and shoved. Then he saw nails. They were hammered in the edge to keep it closed.

His chin quivered. They had locked him in here, and he was never going to get out.

Footsteps pounded outside the door, and he dropped back onto the bed, rolled to his side, grabbed the blanket and pulled it over him, then pretended to be asleep.

The door screeched open, then the snake-man's voice said, "What are we gonna do with the kid?"

"Dump him when we get what we want."

Sam pressed his hand over his mouth to keep from crying out loud.

Their boots pounded harder. They were coming toward him.

He squeezed his eyes shut, swallowing hard not to let the tears fall. Then one of them jerked the blanket off his head.

"Say *hi* to your mother, kid," Snake man said.

Sam couldn't help it. A tear slid down his cheek. Then the big man snapped a picture of him with his phone.

A second later, he tossed the blanket back to him, then stalked across the room. The big man's words echoed in his head.

They were calling his mommy. Maybe she'd come and get him.

But they said something else. They were going to dump him when they got what they wanted. Would he ever see his mommy again?

Chapter Seven

Willow couldn't take her eyes off Doris.

Leo had been involved with *this* woman?

Doris was the complete opposite of her. Everything from her low-cut top to those red high-heel boots screamed that she liked the wilder side of life.

She'd considered the fact that during their marriage Leo had cheated on her. He was a womanizer and liked to flirt. And he'd lost interest in her early on, almost as soon as they'd exchanged vows.

But now she realized he and Doris had rolled in the hay while Willow had wondered what was wrong with her, if she didn't possess enough sex appeal to please him.

She certainly hadn't had enough to keep Brett in town. He'd wanted other women, too.

But Doris said Willow had been a tool to make Leo look good. For what reason?

Who had he wanted to impress?

And if Doris had killed Leo, why had she admitted that she knew *her*?

"Can we come inside for a minute?" Willow asked. "I need to use your restroom." What she really needed was to know if Sam was inside the house.

Doris glared at her, but waved them inside the foyer. "First door on the left."

Willow hurried down the hall, but she did a quick visual as she passed the small living room. Basic furniture, hair and makeup magazines on the oak coffee table, but no toys or children's books.

She ducked in the bathroom and closed the door, then checked the closet and cabinet. Sam wasn't hidden inside, and there were no kids' toothpaste or toys. She flushed the toilet, so as not to draw suspicion, then ran some water in the sink. When she finished, she slipped out and peered into the kitchen. Doris was handing Brett a cup of coffee.

She tiptoed down the hall to the bedrooms. One on the left that looked ostentatious with a hot-pink satin comforter, a silk robe tossed across a chaise and a door that probably led to a master bath. She veered into the second bedroom, which was filled with junk. Boxes of items Doris had obviously ordered online. She didn't see any signs of Sam or a child anywhere, though. She checked the closet and found more boxes stacked, many of them unopened. Many from expensive department stores.

How does the woman support her shopping habit?

Brett's voice echoed as she made her way back to him.

"Where were you yesterday, Doris?" Brett asked.

Doris tapped cigarette ashes into a coffee cup she held in her hand. "I was out. Why you want to know?"

"Out where?" Brett asked.

"Honey, you sound like a cop, not a cowboy"

Doris batted her lashes at Brett and traced a finger along his collar. Willow bit her lip. Surely Brett wouldn't be attracted to Doris like Leo had…

Brett winked at her, irking Willow even more. "Just

indulge me, Doris," Brett said smoothly. "Were you with Leo?"

Anger flickered in the woman's eyes for a brief second. "No. I had to pull a double shift at Hoochies."

Willow inhaled to stem a reaction. Hoochies was a well-known bar where the waitresses offered dessert on the side.

"I suppose someone at Hoochies can verify that," Brett said.

Doris jerked her hand back. "You said that like I need a damn alibi."

Willow couldn't resist. She didn't like the fact that Leo cheated on her with this woman or that she'd touched Brett, and that Brett didn't seem to mind. "Maybe you do."

Panic tinged Doris's voice. "Did something happen to Leo?"

Willow shrugged. "Do you know anyone who'd want to hurt him?"

Doris took a step toward Willow. "Where is he? What happened? Is he hurt?"

For a millisecond, Willow almost felt sorry for the woman. Doris actually loved that lying bastard. "It's possible."

Doris grabbed Willow's arm. "What's that supposed to mean?"

Willow extracted herself from the woman's claws. "Just answer the question. Do you know anyone who'd want to hurt him?"

Doris glanced at Brett as if she wanted assurance that Leo was okay, but Brett maintained a straight face.

"Did he owe someone money?" Brett asked.

"Maybe." Doris's voice cracked. "I know he got in some trouble a while back."

"What kind of trouble?" Brett asked.

"Something with the law," Doris said in a low voice. "He never told me exactly what."

Willow grimaced. He'd certainly never shared that information with her either.

"And then there was his old man. The two of them didn't get along."

"His father?" Willow asked, her breath catching.

"Yeah," Doris said as she snatched another cigarette and lit up. "I don't know what happened between them, but there was some bad blood."

Willow forced herself not to react. Leo had claimed both his parents were dead.

Was everything he'd told her a lie?

BRETT SCHOOLED HIS FACE into a neutral expression, although it was all he could do not to punch his fist through a wall.

How had a man like Leo won Willow's sweet heart?

And why would a man cheat on Willow with Doris, when Willow was the most beautiful, tenderhearted, desirable woman in the whole damn world?

"What was his father's name?" he asked.

Doris shrugged. "Hell, I don't know. Every time I tried to ask him, he got mad. Told me it was none of my business."

Brett shifted. He wished she'd give him something concrete. Although this could be a lead. If Leo had been in trouble before, especially with the law, he probably had an arrest record.

Another thought occurred to him. One of his buddies

had won thousands in the rodeo circuit, but he'd lost it all in Vegas.

"Was Leo into gambling?"

Doris inhaled and blew smoke into the air, her gaze fixed on him. "You're really scaring me now."

"Listen," Willow said. "Leo disappeared with my savings and I need it for medical expenses for my son."

Brett admired the way Willow told the lie without giving herself away. He watched Doris for a reaction, anything that might tip them off that she knew where Sam was being held.

"I have no idea where Leo is," Doris said instead. "But if I talk to him, I'll tell him about the kid." Her voice grew low, almost sincere. "I hope it's not too serious."

Willow gave a little shake of her head, but real tears glittered on her eyelashes.

"Was he into gambling?" Brett asked. "It could explain the reason he stole from Willow."

"He gambled some, but I don't think he was in big debt for it, if that's what you mean."

"Did he leave any money with you?"

Doris muttered a sarcastic sound. "If he left me money, do you think I'd be living in this dump or working doubles at Hoochies?"

Good point.

Brett crossed his arms. "Did Leo have any friends he might have been staying with?"

"You mean female friends?" She gave Willow a condescending look. "If he had other women, I didn't know about it. Then again, I never thought he'd marry *you*."

Brett cleared his throat. "How about male friends?"

"You mean friends who'd let him hide out with them?" Doris asked with a sarcastic grunt.

Brett nodded.

She stared at the burning tip of her cigarette for a long minute as if in thought. "He mentioned this guy named Gus a while back. But I don't know where he is. I think he might have been in jail."

Brett's instincts kicked in. If Leo and this guy were friends, they might have been in cahoots over something illegal.

He wasn't a cop, but his brother was. He wanted to ask Maddox for his help more than he'd ever wanted to ask him anything in his life.

But the tears Willow had just wiped away haunted him. He couldn't turn to his brother now, not as the sheriff.

Although, if he could use Maddox's computer, he could research Leo's past. His father, his arrest record, this man, Gus…

That information might lead him to whatever Leo was involved in that had gotten him killed.

And then to Willow's son.

"Thank you, Doris." Brett handed her a card with his number on it. "If you think of anything else that might help us find Leo, let me know."

Doris caught his arm before he could leave, but she looked at Willow as she spoke. "If you hear from him, tell him I'm still here."

He expected Willow to show a spark of jealousy, but she gave Doris a pitying look and walked back to the car.

Brett followed, his mind ticking away. First they'd stop by Willow's house for her to pack a bag, then they'd go back to Horseshoe Creek.

Maybe he could sneak onto Maddox's home computer and access his police databases while Maddox was out.

WILLOW CHECKED HER PHONE as Brett drove away from Doris's. "Why haven't they called?"

Brett made the turn onto the highway leading back toward her rental house. "They're probably putting together a list of their demands."

She prayed they were. Although she had no idea what they would want from her. She had a couple of thousand in the bank, but that was all.

"Do you think Doris was telling the truth?" Brett asked.

Willow sighed. "She didn't seem to know Leo was dead. If she had, why wouldn't she have hidden the fact that she knew me?"

"She was pretty up-front about that," Brett agreed. "Did you see anything in the house to indicate Sam was there or had been there?"

Willow shook her head no. "If Doris didn't murder Leo, who did?"

"That's what we're going to find out. I think the key is somewhere in Leo's past."

Willow heaved a breath. "I feel like such a fool, Brett. I thought I knew Leo when I first met him, but I didn't know him at all."

"He showed you what he wanted you to see," Brett said.

Humiliation washed over Willow. She'd made such a mess out of her life, while Brett had risen to success. "It's my fault Sam is missing," she said, her chest aching with guilt. "If anything happens to him…"

Brett squeezed her hand. "Nothing is going to happen to him. If he's anything like his mom, he's a tough little guy."

He was nothing like her and everything like Brett.

But she bit back that comment for now. When they found Sam, she'd have to tell Brett the truth.

For now…she needed him focused and helping her. Because if he knew Sam was his, he'd blame her, too. And she couldn't bear any more guilt.

They lapsed into silence until they reached her house, and Brett parked. Leo's truck was still sitting in the drive, Sam's mangled bike beneath it. She gritted her teeth as they walked up to the front door. "Just pack a bag with some clothes. You can stay at the cabin until this is over."

The scent of blood and death permeated the air as Willow entered the house, then her bedroom. The bloodstain that had seeped through the sheets to the mattress looked even more stark in the daylight.

She rushed to the closet, grabbed an overnight bag, then threw a couple of pairs of jeans, a loose skirt, some blouses and underwear inside. In the bathroom she gathered her toiletries and makeup, then carried the bag back to the hall. Brett was kneeling in front of Sam's room with a dark look on his face.

"What is it?" Willow asked.

He gestured toward the floor. "A bloodstain. It looks like Leo might have initially been shot here, then moved to the bed."

"Why move him to the bed?"

"Perhaps to frame you."

Perspiration beaded on Willow's hand. "And when the police learn that Leo had another woman, they'll assume I killed him out of jealousy."

"It's possible. All the more reason we uncover the truth first."

Willow glanced up from the stain and into Sam's room. Horror washed over her as she realized that Sam could have easily seen Leo being gunned down from his room.

Poor Sam. What would witnessing a cold-blooded murder do to a four-year-old?

And if the killer knew that Sam could identify him, he might not let her have him back even if she did pay the ransom...

Chapter Eight

"Willow?" Brett gently touched her arm. "Are you all right?"

She blinked back tears. "How can I be all right when my little boy is in the hands of a murderer? What if they've hurt him, Brett?"

Brett made a low sound in his throat. "Don't think like that, Willow. We'll find him, I promise."

She nodded, although the fear was almost paralyzing. Finally, though, she stood and went into Sam's room. For a moment, she was frozen in place at the sight of his stuffed dinosaur and the soccer ball and the blocks on the floor. The top to his toy chest stood open, a few of his trucks and cars still inside although several of the toys had been pulled out and lay across the floor.

She ran her finger over the quilt she'd made for Sam. He'd picked out the dark green fabric because it was the color of grass, and he'd asked for horses on the squares. She'd appliquéd them on the squares, then sewed them together for him just a few months ago.

Would he ever get to sleep under that quilt again?

"We should go," Brett said in a deep voice. "I want to use Maddox's computer while he's at his office and see what I can learn about Leo and that man, Gus."

Willow grabbed Sam's dinosaur and the throw he liked, a plush brown one with more horses on it, and clutched them to her. Brett carried her overnight bag, and she followed him outside to his truck.

Sam's sweet little-boy scent enveloped her as she pressed the dinosaur to her cheek, and emotions welled inside her. Last week they'd talked about Christmas and finding a tree to cut down on their own this year. They'd planned to decorate using a Western-themed tree with horse and farm-animal ornaments, since Sam was infatuated by the ranches nearby.

If only he knew his father lived on a spread like Horseshoe Creek, and that he was a rodeo star...

One day, maybe. Although, Sam might hate her for lying to him about his father.

BRETT PARKED AT the ranch house, grateful Maddox's SUV was gone and Mama Mary's Jeep wasn't in the drive. She usually liked to grocery shop or visit friends from the church in the morning or early afternoon, but came home in plenty of time to make supper.

Maddox had another cook who prepared food for the ranch hands, and a separate dining hall for them to eat, as well.

He had no idea where Ray was. He'd made himself scarce since the funeral, probably biding his time until the reading of the will, after which he could head out of town.

"I'm sorry for taking you away from your family," Willow said. "I know this is a difficult time for you and your brothers, and you need to be spending time with them."

He hated to admit it, but he hadn't thought much about

them since Willow's panicked phone call. "Don't worry about us. Our problems have nothing to do with you." Except of course, Maddox would disagree when he discovered Brett was covering up a murder, and he'd buried Willow's husband on McCullen land. Land as sacred to Maddox as it had been to Joe McCullen.

His conversation with his father about Willow having trouble echoed in his head, and he wondered if his dad had known more about Leo than he'd revealed.

The sound of cattle and horses in the distance took some of the edge off Brett's emotions as he and Willow walked up to the house. "You didn't eat your breakfast," Brett said. "I'm sure Mama Mary left something for lunch."

Willow paused to watch a quarter horse galloping in the pasture. "I'm not really hungry, Brett."

"I know, but you have to keep up your strength. I'll get us something if you want to relax in the office."

She mumbled okay, then he ushered her to the corner table in the gigantic office their father shared with Maddox, while Brett hurried to the kitchen and found meat loaf sandwiches already prepared, as if Mama Mary remembered their high school days when the boys had worked the ranch and come in starved.

He poured two glasses of tea and carried them and the sandwiches to the office. Willow nibbled on hers, while he consumed his in three bites. Their father's computer was ancient, but Maddox had installed a new one for the ranch business, one he also used for work when he was out of the office.

He attempted to access police databases, but doing so required a password. He tried Maddox's birthday, then the name of Maddox's first pony and their first dog. None fit.

He stewed over it for a minute, then plugged in their father's birthday. Bingo.

Determined to find answers for Willow, he punched Leo's name into the system. DMV records showed he had a current driver's license, then Brett ran a background check.

"Willow, listen to this. Leo Howard was born to Janie and Hicks Howard thirty-two years ago, although Janie died when Leo was five. His father, Hicks, worked in a factory that made farm equipment, but he suffered debilitating injuries from a freak tractor accident on his own farm six years ago."

Willow nearly choked on the sandwich, and sipped her tea. "I still don't understand why he wouldn't tell me his father was alive."

"It's worth paying his father a visit to find out."

She wiped her mouth on a napkin and peered at the screen over his shoulder.

He ran a search for police records and watched as a photo of a man named Leo Stromberg, then Leo Hammerstein, popped up, both bearing Leo Howard's photo—both aliases.

Willow gasped. "Oh, my goodness. Leo had a police record."

"For stealing from his boss, a rancher named Boyle Gates, but apparently Gates dropped the charges." He scrolled farther. "But it says here he was implicated in a cattle-rustling operation. One of the men, Dale Franklin, was killed during the arrest. The other, Gus Garcia, is in prison serving time for the crime."

"How did Leo escape prison time?"

"Apparently Garcia copped to the crime. Although the police suspected a large cattle rustling operation, Garcia insisted that no one else except Franklin was involved. Franklin died in the arrest. Garcia is still in prison."

"You think he has something to do with Leo and Sam's disappearance?"

"That's what we're going to find out." Brett jotted down Garcia's full name, then the address for Leo's father. "First we'll pay a visit to Hicks Howard, then we'll go see Garcia."

An engine rumbled outside, then quieted, and Brett heard the front door open and slam. He flipped off the computer, ushered Willow over to the table and picked up his tea.

The door to the office screeched open, and Maddox filled the doorway, his broad shoulders squared, that air of superiority and disapproval radiating from him.

"What's going on here?"

Brett shrugged. "Willow stopped by to pay her condolences about Dad."

Maddox tipped his Stetson toward Willow in a polite greeting. "Hey, Willow. Nice to see you. How's your boy?"

Willow's eyes darkened with pain, but she quickly covered her emotions. "He's growing up fast."

Maddox smiled at her, but looked back at Brett. "You're having lunch in Dad's office?"

Brett shrugged and said the first thing that entered his head. "Thought I'd feel closer to Dad this way."

Maddox's brows quirked as if he didn't believe him, but Brett had spoken a half-truth. He did feel closer to his father in this room. He envisioned Joe resting in his big recliner with his nightly shot of bourbon, a book in his hand, his head lolling to the side as he nodded off.

Maddox gave him an odd look, then at least pretended to buy the lie. Brett was grateful for that.

But he picked up his and Willow's plates and tea glasses and carried them to the kitchen, anxious to leave.

The day was passing quickly, and he didn't want Willow to spend another night without her son.

EARLY AFTERNOON SUNLIGHT faded beneath the gray clouds as Brett maneuvered the long drive to Hicks Howard's farm. The place was miles from nowhere and looked as if it hadn't been operational in years. Run-down outbuildings, overgrown pastures and a muddy pond added to the neglected feel.

If Leo had come here, it had probably been to hide out. But if he was in trouble, whoever he'd crossed had found him anyway.

Willow checked her phone again, willing it to ring with some word on Sam. Why hadn't the kidnapper called yet?

Terrifying scenarios raced through her head, but she forced herself to tune them out. She had to think positive, had to believe that she would bring Sam home.

Willow tensed, her chest hurting. Maybe she should tell Brett that Sam wasn't Leo's now. But…she wasn't ready for his reaction, for the anger, to explain why she'd kept her secret for so long.

Granted, she'd had her reasons. Brett had left her to sow his oats. He hadn't wanted to settle down. If he'd stayed around, he would have known about Sam.

Brett rolled to a stop beside a tractor overgrown by weeds. It looked as if it hadn't been used in a decade. A rusted pickup covered in mud sat under an aluminum shed.

As he approached, a mangy-looking gray cat darted

beneath the porch of the wooden house. Boards were rotting on the floor, and the shutters were weathered, paint peeling.

Brett knocked on the door, and a noise sounded inside. Something banging, maybe a hammer. He knocked louder this time, and a minute later, the hammering stopped and a man yelled to hang on.

The door opened and a craggy, thin, balding man leaning on a walker stared up at them over wire-rimmed glasses. "If you're selling something, I don't want it."

"We're not selling anything. We just want to talk." Brett gestured to Willow, and she introduced herself. "Mr. Howard, I was married to your son, Leo."

"What?" The man grunted as he shifted his weight. "I hate to say it, honey, but you don't look like Leo's type." He raked his gaze up and down her body. "My son usually goes for the more showy girls."

Remembering Doris, she understood his point. "Did Leo tell you he was married?"

The older man scratched at the beard stubble on his chin. "No, but he didn't come around much."

"Why was that?" Brett asked.

Mr. Howard wrinkled his nose. "Why you folks asking about my son? Is he in some kind of trouble?"

"Would it surprise you if I said he was?" Brett asked.

"No. Leo was always messing up, skirting the law. From the time he was a teenager, he hated this farm. I was never good enough for him, never made enough money." He gestured at the walker and his bum leg. "When he left here, he said he was going to show me that he wasn't stupid like me. That he'd be rich one day."

"Was he?" Willow asked.

Howard shrugged. "About five years ago he came

back with a duffel bag of money, all puffed up with himself. But when I asked him how he got it, he hem-hawed around."

"You thought he'd gotten it illegally?" Willow asked.

His head bobbed up and down. "I confronted him, and that's when he came at me." He gestured toward his leg. "That's how come I had my accident."

Willow's pulse hammered. Leo had caused his father's accident? No wonder he hadn't told her about him…

THE MORE BRETT learned about Leo Howard, the less he liked him. "Did he give you an indication as to how he got the money?"

"At first I thought he probably won it at the races, but when I was in the hospital after my leg got all torn up, the sheriff over in Rawlins stopped by and asked me if Leo stole some money from his boss. Some big hotshot rancher."

"Boyle Gates?"

"Yeah, I believe that was his name."

"Gates dropped the charges?" Brett asked.

Howard coughed. "Yeah. Don't ask me why, though."

Brett studied the old man. "You must have been angry at your son for the way he treated you."

"Like I said, he was trouble. I did all I could to help him, but it wasn't ever enough."

"Leo and I were separated for the past three years," Willow interjected. "Have you talked to him during that time?"

Howard shook his head no.

"Do you know any of his friends or men he worked with?"

"No, I think he was too ashamed of me to bring any of them around."

Or maybe he'd been too ashamed of his own friends, since they were probably crooks.

KNOWING THAT LEO had hurt his father made Willow feel ill. How had she not seen beneath his facade?

Family meant everything to her. Not money. But obviously Leo had wanted wealth and would use anyone in his path to obtain it.

Brett left his phone number in case the man thought of someone Leo might have contacted the past year.

"You didn't tell him that he has a grandson," Brett said as they settled back inside his truck.

Willow's heart pounded. She hated to keep lying to Brett, especially when he was helping her. But she needed to find the right moment to tell him the truth.

Suddenly her phone buzzed, and she quickly checked the number. *Unknown*. Fear and hope mingled as she punched Connect.

"Hello," Willow said in a choked whisper.

"You want to see your son again?"

"Yes. Please don't hurt him."

Brett covered her hand with his, so they were both holding the phone and he could hear. "We need proof that Sam is all right."

"I told you not to call the cops," the man shouted.

"He's not a cop," Willow said, panicked. "He's just a friend."

"You want to see your son alive, do what we say."

"I will, I promise. Just tell me what you want."

"The half million Leo stashed. We'll contact you with the drop."

Willow's stomach contracted. Leo had a half million dollars stashed somewhere?

"Let me speak to Sam," she whispered.

But the line clicked to silent. A second later, the phone dinged with a text.

Willow started to tremble as she looked at the image. It was a picture of Sam on a cot, clutching a raggedy blanket, tears streaming down his face.

Emotions overcame her and a sob wrenched from her throat. *Sam was alive.*

But he looked terrified, and she had no idea what money the man was talking about, or how to find it.

Chapter Nine

Willow pressed her hand to her mouth to keep from screaming.

Brett dragged her into his arms, and she collapsed against his chest, her body shaking with the horror of that photograph.

"*Shh*, it's going to be all right," Brett said in a low, gruff voice. "We'll find him, I swear."

Willow gulped as she dug her nails into his chest. "What kind of horrible person scares a child like that?"

Brett stroked her hair, his head against hers, as if he wanted to absorb her pain. He'd always acted tough, but he was tenderhearted and had confessed how much he'd hurt when he'd lost his mother. And now he'd lost his dad, and she was dumping on him.

If he knew Sam was his, he'd probably be hurting even more...

Maybe it was best she not tell him yet. They needed to work together and if he was mad at her, that might be impossible.

Besides, when she brought Sam home and he grew attached to Brett, it would be even more difficult when Brett left town.

And he would return to the rodeo. Roaming and riding was in his blood.

He rocked her in his arms, and it had been so long since she'd been held and loved that she savored being close to him again. She had always loved Brett and had missed him so much.

Yet when this was over, Brett would go back to all those other women. If she let herself love him again, she might fall apart when he walked away. And she couldn't do that. She had to be strong for Sam.

Her heart in her throat, she forced herself to release him, then inhaled to gather her composure. She could still feel the tenderness in his arms and the worry in his voice.

He'd promised her he'd find Sam, but they both knew he might not be able to keep that promise. That the men who'd abducted Sam were very bad.

"Willow, did you know anything about Leo having a half million dollars?"

A sarcastic laugh bubbled in her throat. "Of course not. Like I said earlier, he claimed he'd made good money before we married, but I never saw it. He said he'd invested it and when the investment paid off, he was going to buy a big spread for us. But things fell apart shortly after the wedding." And now she realized he'd agreed only because he'd married her as a cover for himself.

Brett veered onto the road and drove away from the Howards' property. "What happened?"

Willow shrugged. She really didn't want to talk about Leo. Leo was the biggest mistake of her life.

"Willow, we were friends once. It might help if you told me."

Friends? He'd been the love of her life.

But right now she needed whatever he could give her.

"Leo acted stressed all the time. *Secretive*. He left for days, sometimes weeks, at a time. And when I asked about his trips, he got angry and said he was trying to make it big. I…told him I didn't care about money, but he was obsessed."

"Just like his father said."

Willow nodded. She didn't care why Leo had stolen money or that he'd lied about his father.

All she cared about was who he'd angered enough to take her son.

BRETT STEERED THE TRUCK toward Rawlins, where the state prison was, hoping Gus Garcia had some answers.

He'd do anything to alleviate Willow's pain. Granted he didn't have a kid, but if he did, he'd be blind with fear right now.

And he'd kill anyone who tried to hurt his child.

Hell, he'd kill anyone who hurt Willow's child.

His phone buzzed, and he glanced at the caller ID display. His publicist and agent, Ginger Redman. Knowing she'd badger him to get back to work, he let it roll to voice mail.

"Aren't you going to answer that?" Willow asked.

"It's not important," Brett said and realized that for the first time in years, his career wasn't his top priority. He'd chased his dreams and become popular and had his picture taken a thousand times.

But he'd missed years with his father, he and his brothers were barely speaking, and he'd lost Willow to another man. They should have had a family together.

But…he'd had a wild streak and had to see what was out in the world.

He glanced at Willow and chewed the inside of his

cheek. He had to admit he'd had a lot of women since he'd left Horseshoe Creek. Not as many as the tabloids reported, but enough so that he couldn't remember all their names or faces.

But the only one he'd ever cared about was the woman sitting in the seat next to him.

"Maybe Leo hid that money in his truck," Willow said, her lost expression tearing at him.

"I searched the truck and didn't find any money." Brett gave her a look of regret. "Can you think of anywhere else he'd hide it? Did he have a safety deposit box?"

Willow rubbed the space between her eyes as if she was thinking hard. "Not that I know of."

"How about a gym locker somewhere? Or an office where he could have had a safe?"

"No. But apparently, I was totally in the dark about what he was doing."

Brett hated the self-derision in her voice. "Willow, it sounds like he was a professional liar. You saw what he wanted you to see."

"So that makes me a big fool." Willow rubbed her forehead again. "What's worse is that I allowed him in Sam's life. I trusted him with my little boy, and now Sam's in danger because of my stupidity."

"It's not your fault," Brett said, as he made the turn onto the road leading to the prison.

"Yes it is. I'm his mother. It's my job to protect him and I failed."

"It was his father's job, as well, Willow. He's the one to blame."

Willow looked down at her hands, the wilderness stretching between them as desolate as the silence. Wind whistled through the car windows, signs of winter evident in the dry brush and brittle grass. Trees swayed in the gusty breeze, the wind tossing tumbleweed and debris across the road.

"Sam is afraid of storms," Willow said, her voice cracking.

"Just hang on," Brett said. "We'll find that money. And if we don't, I'll tap into my own resources."

Willow's eyes widened. "I know you've done well, Brett, but you don't have that kind of money, do you?"

Brett gulped. "Not half a million," he said. "But I can put together a hundred thousand. And if push comes to shove, I could sell Maddox my share of the ranch."

Willow's lip quivered, and he wanted to drag her into his arms. But he'd reached the drive to the prison and the security gate, so he squared his shoulders and pulled up to the guard's station, then reached for his ID.

EMOTIONS NEARLY OVERWHELMED WILLOW. Brett had offered to give her the money to save Sam, when he had no idea he was his own son.

Guilt choked her.

She should have told him about Sam. She should tell him now.

But…there was so much to discuss. And at the moment, they had to focus on finding Sam. Then she'd tell Brett everything.

And pray that he'd forgive her.

But would he want to stay around and be part of Sam's life? Or would he head back to his rodeo life with the groupies, late-night parties and the fame?

The guard requested their ID and asked who they'd come to visit, then recognized Brett and practically dove from his booth to shake his hand.

Willow tamped down her insecurities. Brett was a celebrity. She was a small-town mom who sold quilts for a living. They lived different lives now, lives that were too far apart for them to even consider a relationship.

The guard waved Brett through and must have radioed ahead, because when they reached the prison entrance, another guard greeted them with enthusiasm and the warden rushed to shake his hand. It took a few seconds to clear security, then the warden escorted them to his office.

"You want to see Gus Garcia?" The warden's tone was questioning. "May I ask why?"

She and Brett hadn't strategized, so she used the most logical story that came to mind. "I think he might have information about my husband," Willow said. "He left me and my son, and I'm trying to get child support."

"*Ahh*, I see." He motioned for the guard to take them to a visitor's room, and Willow and Brett followed the guard down the hall.

Barring a bare table and two straight chairs, the room was empty. A guard escorted Garcia inside, the inmate's handcuffs and shackles clanging as he walked. Willow's stomach quivered with nerves at the beady set to his eyes.

He was short and robust with a shaved head, a tattoo of a cobra on one arm, and scars on his arms and face. "Keep your hands where I can see them and no touching," the guard ordered.

The beefy man shoved Garcia into a chair, and Brett gestured for Willow to sit while he remained standing, his arms crossed, feet spread. His stance defied Garcia to start something.

"What do you want with me?" Garcia asked.

"My husband was Leo Howard," Willow began.

Garcia looked genuinely shocked. "Howard got married?"

"Yes," Willow said. "Five years ago."

Garcia chuckled. "That's a surprise."

Brett cleared his throat. "We need to know what happened between you and Howard and those other men the police suspected were working with you on that cattle-rustling ring." Brett hesitated, obviously studying Garcia's reaction. "You took the fall for them. Why?"

"Who the hell told you to come and talk to me?" Garcia's eyes darted sideways as if he thought he was being lured into a trap.

"Look, we don't care what you did," Brett said. "But we suspect that you were working with a group, and that Howard was involved. We also believe that Howard took the money you all made, and tried to cut your partners out of their share.

Anger slashed on Garcia's face, and he stood. "I don't know what you're talking about. Now, leave."

"Please," Willow said.

"I don't know where any money is." Garcia waved his handcuffs in the air. "How could I? I've been locked up in this hellhole."

"But Leo worked with you, didn't he?" Willow cried. "Did he promise you he'd keep your share if you took the fall?"

Garcia turned to leave, but Willow caught his arm. He froze, his body teeming with anger. The guard stepped forward, but Willow gave him a pleading look and the guard stepped back.

Willow lowered her voice. "Please, Mr. Garcia. I think Leo swindled or betrayed your partners. Now they've kidnapped my son. If I don't give them that money, there's no telling what they'll do to him."

Garcia's eyes glittered with a warning that made Willow shiver and sink back into the chair. If he didn't have the answers they needed or refused to help her, how could she save Sam?

BRETT TRIED TO get into Gus Garcia's head, but he didn't know what made the man tick. The only reason he could fathom that the man had confessed and covered for his partners was money.

But if he thought his partners had betrayed him, why wouldn't he want to help them now?

"Listen, Mr. Garcia, I don't understand why you'd cover for Howard or anyone else, but if you tell us where Leo hid the money or who's holding it, I'll write you a check myself. How does a hundred thousand sound?"

Garcia heaved a breath, sat down, looked down at his scarred hands and studied them as if he was wrestling with the decision.

When he lifted his head, his eyes were flat. "I told you I don't know where any money is. Maybe he hid it in that house he lived in at the time."

"What house?"

Garcia shrugged. "Some place in Cheyenne."

Anger shot through Brett. He would find this house, but he wanted more. "Listen to me, a little boy's life may depend on us finding that cash."

A gambit of dark emotions splintered Garcia's face. "Leo was a liar and a thief. I ain't heard from him since I was incarcerated."

Brett stood with a curse, then tossed his card at the man. "If you think of anything that can help us, call me."

Willow looked pale as the guard led Garcia out.

"What do we do now?" she asked.

"Find that damned house where Leo lived. Maybe he did hide it somewhere inside."

Frustration knotted Brett's insides, though. Finding the money there was a long shot. And they were running out of leads.

If they didn't turn up something soon, he'd contact his financial advisor to liquidate some funds. It wouldn't be the full ransom, but it might be enough to fool the men into releasing Sam.

GUS'S GUT CHURNED as the guard led him down the hall and shoved him back into his cell.

He wanted to punch something, but that guard was watching him with eagle eyes, and if he misbehaved they'd throw him in the hole. Worse, it would go on his record, and so far he'd managed to stay clean this past year.

If he messed up, he wouldn't make parole. And making parole meant everything to him.

But dammit, nothing was right.

Leo and those other two sons of bitches that he took the fall for were supposed to lay low and give him his cut when he was released.

But it sounded as if Leo had betrayed them and run off with the money.

He gritted his teeth as the cell door slammed shut. He hated that sound.

Why had he let them coerce him into lying for them?

His wife's and little girl's faces flashed in his mind and his heart felt heavy. He knew why. He'd had no choice.

They'd threatened Valeria and his kid. That was the only reason he'd helped them with the rustling operation in the first damn place.

And the woman claimed they might hurt her little boy if they didn't get what they wanted.

Indecision tormented him. McCullen had offered him enough money that he could take his family far away and live the good life, if he talked.

But if he talked, they would go after *his* family.

All he had to do was wait out one more year of his sentence, and he'd be a free man, then he'd be released and he'd protect them.

They were the only thing in the world that he had to live for.

Chapter Ten

Willow fought a sense of despair as they drove away from the prison. "Do you think Mr. Garcia is lying? Holding out for his share of that half million?"

Brett started the engine and drove through security. "I don't know. I think there's more to the story. If he thinks his partners, or Leo, are trying to cut him out, he probably would have taken the hundred thousand I offered him. That's a lot of money for an ex-con."

He was right. Which worried her even more. If Garcia didn't know where the money was, how could *they* find it?

"Do you know the address of the house where Leo lived after you separated?" Brett asked.

Willow racked her brain. "I think I can find it. A few bills came after Leo left and I forwarded them to him." She searched her phone, but she hadn't entered it in the contact information.

Frantic, she accessed her notes section and scrolled through them. "Here it is. 389 Indian Trail Drive. It's outside Cheyenne."

"It'll take us a while to get there," Brett said. "I know you didn't sleep last night, Willow. Close your eyes and rest while I drive."

Willow looked out at the desolate countryside with the mountain ridges in the distance and the rocky barren land, and fresh tears threatened.

Where was her little boy? Was he cold or hungry? Were the men holding him taking care of him?

The storm clouds were thickening, growing darker. Sam would be getting anxious about the weather, about not coming home. He needed her.

BRETT WAITED UNTIL Willow's breathing grew steady, and she'd fallen into a sound sleep. His phone buzzed again. *Kitty. Dammit*, she was persistent.

He ignored it and phoned his financial planner and manager, Frank Cotton.

"What's up, Brett? Do you have some new investments you need handling?"

"Not exactly. I want you to see how much cash I can liquidate and how quickly."

A tense silent moment passed. "You want *cash*? May I ask the reason? Are you planning a big trip somewhere? Are you purchasing property?"

No, but he might need to sell to Maddox. Only if he asked Maddox, his brother would want an explanation. He could approach Ray, but he doubted Ray had the money to buy him out.

"I'm not ready to discuss my plans yet," Brett said. "But it's important. And Frank, keep this matter confidential."

"Brett, don't tell me you knocked up some young girl."

Brett ground his molars. Was that what Frank thought of him? What others thought about him? "Thanks for the vote of confidence, Frank, but it's nothing like that.

Just do what I ask and keep your mouth shut." Furious, he hung up.

Snippets of his past flashed back. The rodeo groupies clamoring after him after his rides. Throwing themselves at him in hotels and bars. All wanting a piece of the celebrity.

Girls with no real clear dreams of their own, except to bag a man and live off his money.

Unlike Willow, who'd built her own life and was devoted to her little boy. Shy Willow who'd stolen his heart, but hadn't made demands on him when the itch to leave Pistol Whip had called his name.

No wonder Frank thought he might have knocked up some young thing. He had left a trail of women across the states. But he didn't remember their names or faces.

Only they'd filled that empty void in his bed, when he'd craved loving from a woman, and Willow wasn't there.

His father's praise for following his dreams echoed in his ears. He'd always thought he and his daddy were alike, that his father had regretted marrying and settling down so young. Had regretted being saddled with three boys to raise.

Brett had been determined not to make the same mistake.

But now he'd achieved success and fame, and plenty of money, but this past year he'd been restless as hell.

Lonely.

How could he have been lonely, when all he had to do was walk into a bar and he'd have a pretty woman in his bed for the night?

He glanced over at Willow, and the answer hit him

swift and hard. He was lonely because none of those women were Willow.

His phone buzzed. *Maddox*.

He took a deep breath and connected the call. "Yeah?"

"What the *hell* were you looking for on my computer?"

Brett gripped the steering wheel as he veered onto the highway toward Cheyenne. "I just needed to do some research. What's the big deal?"

"The big deal is that you used my password to access police files. Why were you looking at arrest records?"

Brett's temper flared. "You checked up on me?"

"I knew you were lying earlier, so I checked the browser history." Maddox released an angry sigh. "Now tell me what you were doing? Are you in some kind of trouble?"

First Frank, now his brother. And here, he'd considered confiding in Maddox.

"Can't you just trust me for once?" Brett snapped.

A heartbeat passed. Brett didn't know if Maddox planned to answer.

"Listen, Brett, if you are in trouble, tell me. I know we don't always see eye to eye, but I'll see what I can do to help."

Emotions twisted Brett's chest. Would Maddox put himself on the line to help him?

Maybe, but he couldn't take the chance. Not with Sam's life.

"Actually I might need you to buy me out of the ranch."

A longer silence this time, one that reeked of disappointment. "So that's it? You made a fortune out there on the circuit, but you've blown it all. What are you into, Brett? Gambling? Women?"

His words cut Brett to the bone. "I'm not into anything."

Maddox didn't seem to hear him, though. "I knew you didn't care about Dad or me or Ray, but I thought you might have some allegiance to Horseshoe Creek."

His brother's disgusted voice tore at Brett. He *did* care about all of them. And he wanted part of that land more than he'd realized. Horseshoe Creek was his home. His roots.

Where he'd always thought he'd return once his wild days ended. Of course, like a fool, he'd thought Willow would be waiting...

Maddox heaved a breath. "How soon would you need to be bought out?"

Brett's gut churned. "As soon as possible."

Maddox cursed. "All right. I'll see what I can do. If I see Ray, I'll mention it to him, in case he wants part of your share."

Brett hated the thought of selling out to his brothers. Even more, he hated that Maddox thought he didn't give a damn about Horseshoe Creek.

But if they didn't locate the money Leo had stolen, he would sell his share in a heartbeat to save Willow's son.

WILLOW STIRRED FROM a restless sleep as Brett rolled to a stop in front of a small brick ranch house set off the road with a garage to the left and a barn out back. The house looked fairly well kept, although the barn was rotting and obviously wasn't being used for farming.

"Was Leo living here with someone else?" Brett asked.

"I don't know. It's possible."

Brett turned to her. "Were you the one who asked to get out of the marriage, Willow?"

"Yes." She reached for the doorknob. "But he didn't argue. He wanted out. That much was obvious." Doris's words echoed in her head. Leo needed a respectable wife so nobody in town would ask questions.

But respectable to *whom*? He hadn't told his father about her or Sam.

"He was the fool for not wanting to be with you," Brett murmured.

Willow swallowed hard. "You left me, too, Brett." She regretted the words the moment she said them.

Brett's eyes flickered with pain and truth of her statement.

"It doesn't matter now," Willow said. "All that matters is getting Sam back."

Brett's gaze latched with hers, and he started to say something, but she opened the door and hurried up the sidewalk. This was not the time for a personal discussion of the past.

That would come. But first she had to bring Sam home.

Brett caught up to her just as she punched the doorbell. He surveyed the property as if looking for signs of trouble. The door squeaked open, and a middle-aged woman in a nurse's uniform appeared at the door. Behind her, Willow noticed a white-haired woman in a wheelchair.

"Can I help you?" the woman asked.

"My name is Willow James, and this is Brett McCullen." Brett tipped his Stetson in greeting, and Willow forged ahead. "We'd like to talk to you, Miss…?"

"Eleanor Patterson," the woman said. "What's this about?"

Willow offered her a tentative smile. "I was married

to a man named Leo Howard who lived in this house. How long have you lived here?"

"Just a few months. We needed a one-story, so we found this place."

"Did you know Mr. Howard?" Brett asked.

Eleanor angled her head toward Brett, her eyes narrowed, then lighting up in recognition. "You look familiar."

Brett's handsome face slid into one of his charming smiles. "You might recognize me from the rodeo circuit, ma'am."

She snapped her fingers. "That's where it was. My goodness, you're more handsome in person than you are in the magazines."

Irritation nagged at Willow.

"Thanks," Brett said with a smile. "Ma'am, we don't mean to bother you, but did you know Leo Howard?"

"No, the house was vacant when the Realtor showed it to me."

"Did the previous tenant leave anything here when he left?" Willow asked. "Maybe some boxes or papers."

"I really don't know." Eleanor gestured toward the older woman in the chair. "Now if you'll excuse me, it's time for her medication."

"Please think hard," Willow said. "I'm looking for some important documents that I think he put somewhere."

Eleanor looked back and forth between them, then sighed. "The house was basically empty, but now that I think about it, there were a few old boxes in the attic."

"Would you mind if we take a look?" Brett gave her another flirtatious smile, and she waved him toward the hallway where a door led to an attic. Willow followed him, uneasy at the way the woman in the wheelchair watched them, as if she thought they intended to rob her.

Dust motes drifted downward and fluttered through the attic as they climbed the steps and looked across the dark interior. Three plain brown boxes were stacked against the far wall, a ratty blanket on top.

They crossed the space to them, and Brett set the first box on the floor. Willow opened it and began to dig through it while Brett worked on the second box. Flannel shirts, jeans and a dusty pair of work boots were stuffed in the box Willow examined, along with an old pocket watch that no longer worked, and a box of cigars.

Odd. Leo hadn't smoked.

"There's a couple of fake IDs in here," Brett said. "A few letters, it looks like from Doris, but Leo never opened them."

Willow spotted another envelope in the box and removed it. Inside, she found several photographs. "Look at these." She spread them out—a picture of Leo's father, then Doris, then Gus Garcia and two other men. Were those Leo's partners?

He slid another box over between them and lifted the top. Inside lay a .38 caliber gun and some ammunition. Beside it, he found another driver's license under the name of Lamar Ranger, yet it bore Leo's photo.

Oddly another pair of boots sat inside. Curious, Brett searched inside the boot but found nothing. Still wondering why the boots were stowed with the gun instead of the other box of clothes, he flipped the boots over and noticed one of the soles was loose.

"What is it?" Willow asked.

Brett removed his pocketknife and ripped the sole of

the shoe off and found a folded piece of paper inside. He opened it and spread it on the floor, his heart thundering.

"A map."

Willow leaned closer to examine it. "You think this map will lead us to the place where Leo stashed the money?"

"That's exactly what I'm thinking." He folded it and put it in his pocket, then set the gun and fake ID in one box to take with them. They might need them for evidence.

Willow brushed dust from her jeans as they descended the steps and shut the attic.

Eleanor appeared in the hallway, her brows furrowed. "Did you find what you were looking for?"

"Not really," Brett said. "But we're taking this one with us. The boots are special to Willow."

Willow thanked her, then she and Brett hurried outside to his truck. She hoped Brett was right. If that map led them to the money, she could trade it for Sam and bring him back home where he belonged.

BRETT'S PULSE HAMMERED as he drove away from Eleanor's. He waited until they'd reached the dirt road he'd seen on the map, then pulled over, unfolded it and studied it.

"Where is it?" Willow asked.

Brett pointed to the crude notations on the map. Symbols of trees and rocks in various formations that must be significant, signs that would lead the way to his hiding spot.

"If it's there, and we find it," Willow said, "maybe we can end this tonight."

Brett gave a quick nod, although he was still worried that the kidnapper would hurt Sam.

He fired up the engine again, and turned onto the dirt road while Willow pointed out the landmarks.

"There's the rock in the shape of a turtle." A hundred feet down the road. "Those bushes, they form a ring." Another mile. "There's the creek."

He made each turn, the distance growing closer until he spotted the ridge with water dripping over it creating a small waterfall. Willow tapped the map. "Hopefully it's in this spot, hidden under the falls."

Brett pulled over and parked, then got out. The shovels they'd used to bury Leo were still in the back, so he retrieved them and carried them along the trail to the ridge overhang.

Willow knelt and they both examined the wall of rock. She pointed to an etching of a star. "I think the money may be buried here."

Brett propped one shovel by the rock and began to dig. Willow yanked her hair back into a ponytail, and jammed the second shovel into the dirt.

For several minutes they worked, digging deeper, but suddenly a gunshot sounded and pinged off the rock beside him.

Brett threw an arm around Willow and pushed her down, just as a second bullet whizzed by their heads.

Chapter Eleven

"Who's shooting at us?" Willow cried.

"I don't know, but the shot is coming from behind that boulder." Brett gestured toward the bushes beside the falls. "Run behind those bushes."

Willow remained hunkered down, but crept toward the left by the brush. Another shot pinged off the rocks at their feet, and he grabbed her hand and dragged her from the ledge behind some rocks.

"Stay down, Willow."

"What are you going to do?"

"Find out who the hell is firing at us."

Willow grabbed his arm to hold him back. "Please don't go, Brett. I don't want you to get hurt."

"I'm not going to wait here like a sitting duck." Brett ushered her down to the ground, then grabbed his shovel and circled back behind more bushes and trees so he could sneak up on the shooter.

Rocks skittered and a man scrambled down a path. Brett chased after him, but the man veered to the right and cut through a patch of brush to a black sedan parked behind a boulder.

Brett looked back and motioned for Willow to meet him at the car. She took off running, and he jogged down the path, trying to catch up with the shooter. By the time they reached the truck, the sedan roared away.

Brett tossed the shovel into the back of the truck, grabbed his rifle and started the engine. Willow jumped inside, looking shaken. He hit the accelerator and sped behind the sedan, determined to catch him.

"Can you see the tag number?"

Willow leaned forward and squinted as the driver spun onto a side dirt road. "SJ3... I can't see the rest."

The truck bounced over ruts in the road, spitting dust and gravel as he closed the distance. Tires squealed and the driver sped up, trees and brush flying past as he maneuvered a turn. A tire blew and the car swerved. The driver tried to regain control, but he overcompensated and the car spun in a circle, then careened toward a thicket of trees.

The passenger side slammed into the massive trunk, glass shattering and spraying the air and ground.

Brett grabbed his rifle as he slowed to a stop, and motioned for Willow to stay inside the truck.

"Be careful, Brett. He tried to kill us."

He certainly had, and Brett aimed to find out the reason. And if the bastard had Sam, he'd shove this rifle down his throat.

He raised the gun in front of him, scrutinizing the car as he inched forward. The passenger side was crunched, but the driver's side was intact. Still, the front windshield had shattered, and he didn't see movement inside.

Instincts as alert as they were when he climbed on a bull, he crept closer, his eyes trained on the driver. Daylight was waning, the sun sinking behind clouds that threatened rain, the temperature dropping.

He kept the gun aimed as he carefully opened the car

door. It screeched, but opened enough for him to see that the driver was alive. Blood dotted his forehead where he'd hit his head.

Brett jammed the gun to the man's temple, then snagged him by the shirt collar so he could see his face. White, about forty years old, scruffy face, scar above his right eye.

"Who the hell are you?" Brett asked.

The man groaned and tried to open his eyes. He wiped at the blood with the back of his hand. Brett jammed the tip of the rifle harder against his skull, and the man stiffened.

"Don't shoot, buddy. Please don't kill me."

"You tried to kill me and the woman I was with." Anger hardened his tone. "I want to know the reason."

"I wasn't going to kill you," the man said, his voice cracking. "I just wanted to scare you off."

Brett clenched his jaw but kept the gun at the man's head. "Why?"

"Because Eleanor called and said she thought you knew where the money was."

So Eleanor had lied. "Was she working with Leo or *sleeping* with him?" Brett asked.

"Neither, I'm Eleanor's husband, Ralph," the man said. "She takes care of Leo's grandmother. Leo stayed with her for a while, then moved out."

"Where did he move?"

"I don't know. He told Eleanor he'd pay her to be the old lady's nurse, but then he left her high and dry, and me and Eleanor have been trying to pay the bills."

"I thought she said she didn't know Leo."

"She didn't. They set it up over the phone."

Unfortunately he believed the man. Leo had been scum through and through.

The man fidgeted. "Did you find the money?"

"You know about the money?" Brett asked.

"Leo's grandmother told us he had a big bagful. She wanted it to help us. And Leo owes us—"

"We haven't found any cash," Brett said. "And before you ask, I was not working with Leo. He's a dirt bag who *stole* that money. He married the woman you were shooting at and lied to her, then he turned up dead. The people he betrayed kidnapped her son."

The man's eyes widened in shock. "Leo's dead."

"Yeah and if I don't find that money, that little boy may be, too." Brett gripped him tighter. "Do you know where he is?"

The man shook his head back and forth, his eyes panicked. "No, I like kids. I'd never do anything to hurt one."

"What about the men Leo was in cahoots with? Did you know them?"

"No, I swear. When Leo called Eleanor to hire her, she said he seemed nervous. But she likes geriatric patients and wanted to help the old woman."

"She didn't mention a name, or maybe a place Leo said he was going when he left that house? Maybe another address?"

He shook his head again. "If he had, I would have paid him a visit myself. When you showed up, we thought you might lead us back to him."

Brett released the man with a silent curse.

He turned and walked back toward Willow, hating that he had no answers yet.

WILLOW COULDN'T BELIEVE her eyes. Brett was letting the man who'd tried to kill them go.

"Who was he?" Willow asked as soon as he returned to the truck. "Why was he shooting at us?"

"Eleanor's husband. The woman in the wheelchair was Leo's grandmother. He hired Eleanor as a caretaker, but ran off without paying her."

"He really was awful," Willow said, her heart going out to the elderly woman.

"Apparently Eleanor and her husband were desperate financially. They thought you and I knew where Leo was, or at least where his money was, so he followed us. He wasn't trying to kill us, just scare us off so he could take the cash."

"So Leo wrecked that couple's lives, just like he did mine." Willow grimaced. Of course it was her fault for trusting him, for allowing him to be around Sam.

Brett started the truck and drove back toward the falls. When he parked this time, he managed to get closer to the area where they were digging. He carefully scanned for anyone else who might have followed.

"You can stay in the truck, Willow. I have to see if the money is there."

"No, I'm going with you."

Again, they grabbed the shovels and strode to the ridge, then ducked below the falls. The hole they'd started was still there, so he jammed the shovel in and continued to dig for the money.

Minutes ticked by, the wind picking up as rain began to fall, slashing them with the cold moisture. By the time he'd dug a few feet, the shovel hit rock. "It's not here."

"It has to be," Willow said, desperate.

Brett wiped his forehead with the back of his sleeve. "Let me try a different spot."

They spent the next hour digging around the original location, but again and again, hit stone.

Finally Willow leaned against a boulder. "If he put it here, someone must have already found it."

"Or he moved it," Brett said.

Willow shivered from the cold and the ugly truth. Another night was setting in.

Another night she'd have to wonder where her little boy was and if she'd ever see him again.

THEY MADE THE DRIVE back to Horseshoe Creek in silence. Brett hated the strain on Willow's face, but he understood her fear because he felt it in his bones.

He'd been certain that map would lead them to the money.

But Leo could have already retrieved the cash and moved it. Only where had he put it?

Maddox's truck was parked at the main house, so Brett bypassed it and drove straight to the cabin. "Was there any place that was significant to Leo? A place he liked to go riding?"

Willow rubbed her forehead. "Not that I know of."

"How about a place he took you and Sam?"

She looked out the window, as if she was lost in thought. "Honestly, Brett, Leo never spent much time with Sam."

He gritted his teeth. The poor kid. He needed a father. And it sounded like Leo hadn't been one at all.

Brett thought about his own father and how much he missed him now. They'd clashed over the years, but even when Joe McCullen was hard on him, Brett had known it was because his old man cared about him. That he was trying to raise him to be a decent man.

They walked up to the cabin together, and he unlocked the door. He ached for his father, for Willow and for her son, who was probably scared right now and wanted his mother.

"I'm sorry he let you down, Willow." He turned to her, his heart in his throat. "I'm sorry I let you down, too."

Willow's face crumpled, and tears trickled down her eyes. "Brett, what if—"

"Shh." He pulled her into his arms and stroked her hair. "Don't think like that. These guys want that money. If we don't find the cash Leo stole, I'll pay. I already called my financial manager and he's working on liquidating some funds."

Willow looked up at him with such fear and tenderness that he knew he'd do anything in the world to make it right for her. Then she lifted her hand to his cheek, and he couldn't resist.

He dipped his head and closed his mouth over hers.

Overwhelmed with affection for her, he cradled her gently, and deepened the kiss, telling her with his mouth how much he cared for her. How much he'd missed her.

How much he wanted to alleviate her pain.

Willow leaned into him and ran her hands up his back, clinging to him just as she once had when they were friends and lovers. Regret for the years he'd missed with her swelled inside him.

He stroked her hair, then dropped kisses into it, then down her ear and neck and throat. She rubbed his calf with her foot, stoking his desire, and he cupped her hips and pressed her closer to him.

Need and hunger ignited between them, and their

kisses turned frenzied and more passionate. He inched her backward toward the sofa.

But his phone buzzed, and they pulled apart. Their ragged breathing punctuated the air as he checked the caller ID. *Unknown.*

He punched Connect. "Brett McCullen."

A second passed.

"Hello?"

"Mr. McCullen, you talked to my husband, Gus, today at the prison."

Brett straightened. "Yes. I was hoping he could help me. Did he give you my number?"

"Yes, although he didn't want me to call. But he explained to me about the little boy. I'm...sorry."

Brett frowned.

"I...think I might be able to help."

"You can help? *How?*"

"I can't discuss this over the phone. Can you meet me?"

"Of course. Just tell me the place."

"The Wagon Wheel. An hour."

The Wagon Wheel was a restaurant/bar near Laramie. "I'll be there."

Chapter Twelve

"Who was that?" Willow asked when Brett pocketed his phone and reached for his hat.

"Gus Garcia's wife. She wants to meet me tonight."

Willow's heart jumped to her throat. "She knows where Sam is."

Brett grabbed his keys. "She didn't say. But if she has any information that might lead to that money, I need to go."

Willow reached for her jacket, but Brett placed his hand on her arm.

"I can handle this if you want to stay here and rest."

Willow shook her head. "No way. Besides, if this woman holds back, maybe I can appeal to her on a woman-to-woman basis."

Brett's mouth twitched slightly. "I can't argue with that."

The wind splattered them with light raindrops as they ran to his truck. As Brett drove toward The Wagon Wheel, silence fell between them, thick with fear for Sam. Still, Willow couldn't help but remember the kiss they'd shared. A hot, passionate, hungry kiss that only made her crave another.

And reminded her how much she'd loved Brett.

And how painful it had been when he'd left her years ago.

She couldn't allow herself to hope that they could rekindle that love. And when Brett discovered Sam was his…

She'd face that when they got her little boy back.

It took half an hour to reach The Wagon Wheel, a bar/restaurant that specialized in barbecue and beer. Pickups, SUVs and a couple of motorcycles filled the parking lot, the wooden wheel lit up against the darkness.

Willow pulled her scarf over her head as they hurried to the door. Country music blared from the inside as they entered. The place was rustic with deer and elk heads, saddles, saddle blankets and other ranch tools on the walls. Wood floors, pine benches and tables, and checkered tablecloths gave it a cozy country feel.

Willow dug her hands in her jacket pockets. "How do we recognize her?"

Brett shrugged, but his phone buzzed with a text. When he looked down, the message said, Back booth on the right.

"That way." Brett led Willow to the rear of the restaurant where a small Hispanic woman with big dark eyes sat with her hands knotted on the table.

"Mrs. Garcia?"

She nodded, her gaze darting over Willow, then she looked back down at her hands as if wrestling with whether or not to flee.

Willow covered the woman's hand with her own and they slid into the booth. "I appreciate you meeting us. My name is Willow. Tell me your name."

"Valeria," the woman said in a low voice. "I…my husband will be upset that I come."

Willow squeezed her hand. "I don't want to cause you trouble, but my son is missing, Valeria, and I need help."

Valeria gave them both a wary look. "You don't understand. My husband…he not talk because he scared for me and little Ana Sofia."

Willow's heart pounded. "Ana Sofia?"

"Our little girl. She's eight." Valeria pulled a photo from her handwoven purse and showed it to them. "She… is so sweet and so tiny. And Gus went to prison so those bad men wouldn't kill us."

Willow tensed. "Someone threatened your little girl?"

Valeria nodded and curled her fingers into Willow's. But she looked directly at Brett, her eyes pleading, "If I talk to you, you take us some place where they can't hurt us?"

Brett spoke through clenched teeth. "Yes, ma'am. I promise. I'll pay for protection for you myself."

BRETT HAD NO patience for any man who would hurt a woman. "Who threatened you and your daughter, Valeria?"

"If I tell you, they may hurt my Gus."

"He's in prison," Willow said.

Brett understood Mrs. Garcia's fear, though. If someone wanted to get to Gus, they could.

"No one will know about this conversation," Brett assured her.

"Just tell us what happened," Willow said softly.

Valeria pulled her hand from Willow's and twisted them together in her lap. "*Sí.* I do this for the little boy, miss. I cannot stand for anyone to hurt children."

"Neither can I," Willow said, a look of motherly understanding passing between the two women.

"You see, Gus, he work for this rancher named Boyle Gates. Mr. Gates have big spread, but some say he cheat and steal so he be biggest, wealthiest rancher in Wyoming."

"What exactly did Gus do for Gates?" Brett asked.

"He was ranch hand," Valeria said. "Gus proud man. He work hard. But one day Mr. Gates accuse him of stealing money from his safe in house. My Gus not do it, but man named Dale Franklin say he saw Gus take it."

"Dale Franklin? He died, didn't he?"

"Yes." Her voice quivered. "Gus think they kill him. He was working with a rustling cattle ring. They tell Gus they do same to him and us if he not help them."

"What exactly did they want him to do?" Brett asked.

She dabbed at her eyes with a colorful handkerchief. "Steal cattle." Her lip quivered. "Gus not want to, but they say they fix things with Mr. Gates so he keep job and they pay him, too. He still say no, but then they talk about hurting me and our Ana Sofia, he go along."

"And when the men were caught, Gus took the fall to protect you."

She nodded, her eyes blurring with tears. "Gus try to be good in prison so he get out one day. That reason he not talk to you."

"You said *they*, but you only mentioned a man named Dale Franklin. Who else was involved?" Willow asked.

Valeria looked nervous again, but Brett assured her once more that he would protect her and her child. "I'll also do whatever I can to help Gus get paroled. Just give me the men's names."

Valerie heaved a big breath. "Jasper Day and Wally Norman."

"Do they still work for Mr. Gates?" Brett asked.

She shrugged. "I think Mr. Norman, he wind up in prison, too. Not sure he still there."

"Valeria, whoever is holding Sam believes Leo Howard had that money and stashed it somewhere. Do you or Gus know where he would have hidden it?"

She shook her head no. "Mr. Howard was leader. Gus said he was brains."

Brains without a conscience.

Brett wished the bastard was still alive so he could beat the hell out of him. Because of him, Willow's little boy was in danger.

"Valeria, where is your little girl now?"

"At Miss Vera's. I clean her house."

"Let us follow you and pick up Ana Sofia. There's an extra cabin on my family's ranch where the two of you can stay. You'll be safe there."

Willow took Valeria's hands in hers. "I promise, no one will look for you at Horseshoe Creek."

Brett's gut tightened. He should discuss this with Maddox first, but Horseshoe Creek was as much his land as it was his brother's.

That is, until he sold his share to Maddox. Then he would have no stake in the land. No ties to it himself.

Was that what he wanted?

No, but he'd do it for Sam.

Willow followed Valeria inside the small shack where Valeria lived. Ever since her husband had been incarcerated, the poor woman had been cleaning Ms. Vera's house, as well as rooms at a motel to put food on the table.

Willow didn't condone Mr. Garcia's illegal activities, but if he'd been coerced to help the other men out of fear, she could understand. Just look at the lengths she had gone to in the past couple of days for her own son.

Little Ana Sofia was a tiny dark-haired girl with waist-length black braids and the biggest brown eyes Willow had ever seen. She clung to her mother's skirt as Valeria explained that they were taking a trip for a few days.

The child's questioning look only compounded the turmoil raging inside Willow.

How could she ever have married a man who would threaten a family like Leo had?

Had she been that desperate for a father for her baby?

No...she'd been desperate to forget Brett. She'd seen the tabloids of the women throwing themselves at him and had needed comfort. And Leo had stroked her ego—at first.

All part of his ruse to cover up the fact that he was a criminal.

"This is Miss Willow," Valeria said. "She and Mr. Brett are going to let us stay on their ranch."

Not *her* ranch. Brett's and his brothers'. But Willow didn't comment. At one time she'd fantasized about marrying Brett and the two of them carving out a home on a piece of the McCullen land.

But that dream had died years ago.

"Hi, Ana, you have beautiful hair." Willow stroked one of her braids. "And beautiful big eyes."

"They're like my daddy's." Ana's lower lip quivered. "But I don't get to see him anymore."

Valeria looked stricken, but Willow patted the little girl's back. "Well, maybe one day soon, you will. And you can tell him all about the horses and cows you see on Mr. Brett's ranch. Would you like that?"

"I like horses," the little girl said.

Valeria hugged Willow. "Thank you, Miss Willow."

Willow's throat closed. "No, Valeria, thank you."

Because of Valeria's courage, they might have a lead on how to find the money Willow needed.

WILLOW HELPED VALERIA and her daughter settle into a cabin near the one where Brett and Willow were staying. The sound of an engine made him step outside the cabin, and he cursed.

Maddox in his police SUV. What was he doing here?

Wind battered the trees and sent a few twigs and limbs down, a light rain adding to the cold dreariness as evening set in.

Brett jammed his hands in his pockets and waited, contemplating an explanation as Maddox parked and strode up to the porch. Rain dripped from his cowboy hat and jacket as he ducked under the roof.

"What's going on, Brett?"

Brett tensed at his brother's gruff tone. Maddox had a way of saying things that reeked of disapproval even without using specific words.

"I decided to stay in that cabin over there. And a friend of mine needed a place, so she's staying here."

Maddox arched a brow. "A woman? She's not staying with *you*?"

Brett swallowed back a biting retort. He'd be damned if he'd admit that Willow was staying with him. "No, she just needs a safe place for her and her little girl for a few days."

Maddox crossed his arms. "Brett, is this woman one of your conquests?" He lowered his voice. "Is the kid *yours*?"

Anger slashed through Brett. "You *would* think the worst of me, wouldn't you?" He squared his shoulders, making him eye to eye with Maddox. "I wouldn't do that to a woman. And if the child *was* mine, I'd take responsibility."

Animosity bubbled between them, born of years apart—and the years they'd fought as kids.

"I'm sorry," Maddox said quietly. "I guess I jumped to conclusions."

Brett released a tense breath. Maddox didn't apologize often.

"She's in trouble," Brett said in a low voice. "Can't you just trust me for once, Maddox, and let her stay here without asking questions?"

Maddox studied him for another full minute, then gave a clipped nod. "Okay, little brother. Do you want me to have my deputy or one of the ranch hands drive by and check on them tonight?"

Brett shrugged. "Maybe one of the ranch hands. I don't think the deputy needs to come." Sweat beaded on his brow. What if the deputy drove around and found Leo's grave?

"Okay, I'll tell Ron to swing by."

"Thanks, Maddox."

Maddox made a clicking sound with his teeth. "I guess it's time we both start trusting each other, right?"

"Right." Brett's gut knotted with guilt as Maddox strode back to his SUV. Maddox would kick his butt when he learned what Brett had done.

It would also destroy any chance of a reconciliation between him and his brother.

WILLOW BATTLED TEARS as she listened to Brett's conversation with Maddox. Brett wouldn't have abandoned a child.

She should tell him about Sam.

After all, he was putting his relationship with his brother on the line for her. She owed him the truth. But he cut her off before she could speak.

"I'm going to see that rancher tonight. Stay here with Valeria."

Willow glanced down at her phone, willing it to ring. But the picture of little Sam that the kidnapper had sent stared back.

She wrapped her coat around her. "No, I'm going with you. I want to see his reaction to the picture of my son."

SAM PUSHED ASIDE the grilled cheese the man set in front of him. "I want my mommy."

"Well, your mommy's not here, kid. Now eat the sandwich."

Sam picked at the burnt edge, then set the plate on the floor "It's black. And it gots the crust on it and Mommy cuts the crust off."

The man's pudgy face puffed up like a big fat pig's. Then he picked up the sandwich and shoved it toward Sam's mouth.

Sam's stomach growled, but he hated the man, and he wasn't going to eat the nasty thing so he turned his head away.

The mean man probably put roaches in the sandwiches or spiders or maybe he even spit tobacco in it. He'd seen him spitting that brown stuff in that can.

"Fine, you little brat. Starve." He hurled the sandwich at the wall. It hit, then fell to the floor, a mangled mess.

Sam fought tears. "When are you gonna take me back?"

The man glared at him, then slammed the door. Sam

heard the key turning and threw himself at the door, beating on it. "I wanna go home! Let me go!"

He beat and beat until his fists hurt, and snot bubbled in his nose.

Don't be a baby, he told himself. *Cowboys don't cry.*

He wiped his nose on his sleeve and looked around the dingy room. He needed to find a way out, but those windows were nailed shut.

He hunted for something sharp to use to stab the man with if he came back. A knife or a nail or a pair of scissors. But he couldn't find anything but a broken plastic comb.

The rope they'd first tied his hands with was on the floor. It wasn't long enough to make a lasso like the cowboys used.

He wound the rope around his fingers and tried to remember the knots he'd seen in that book he sneaked from the library. It had pictures of roping calves and horseback riding and trick riding.

His mama had another book in the table by her bed, too. She pretended she didn't like rodeos, but he'd seen her looking at pictures of that famous rodeo star. Only those pictures made her cry.

He laid the rope in his lap and twisted and turned it, then tried again and again. If he could trip that mean man, and tie him up like a calf, he could run and run till he found his mommy again.

Chapter Thirteen

Brett waited until the rancher showed up to guard Valeria and her daughter.

"Is she running from a husband?" Ron asked.

Brett shrugged, not wanting to explain. "Something like that."

"I'll make sure no one bothers her tonight."

"Thanks." Brett shook the man's hand. One thing he could always count on was that Maddox hired good men.

He met Willow at the truck. His phone buzzed again as he drove toward Gates's ranch. *Kitty.* He ignored the call.

Why couldn't she take the hint? A second later, his phone rang again.

"Aren't you going to answer that, Brett?"

"No, it's no one important."

Willow's brows lifted. "It's your girlfriend, isn't it?"

Brett's pulse clamored. He didn't want to discuss the women in his past with Willow. "I don't have a girlfriend."

Willow released a sardonic laugh. "Oh, that's right. You have a different woman in every city."

He hated that she was right. "Where did you get that idea?"

"Pictures of you and your lovers are plastered all over

the rodeo magazines. How could I *not* know? Let's see. There was Bethany in Laredo, Aurora in Austin, then Carly in Houston, Pauline in El Paso—"

Brett held up a hand. "Okay, so I've dated a few women. *You* got married." And had a child with another man. And within a year after his last visit home. A visit that had made him think they might have a future.

But she'd squashed that with her wedding.

"You're right. I guess we both moved on."

Had they? Or had he just been biding time, hoping one day to reconcile with Willow?

The rain fell harder, slashing the windshield and roof, forcing him to drive slower through the rocky terrain.

"By the way, congratulations on all your success, Brett." Willow looked out the window as she spoke. "You followed your dreams and became exactly what you always wanted to be."

Brett gripped the steering wheel as he sped around a curve and headed down the long road toward Gates's spread, the Circle T. Willow's words taunted him.

He had achieved success on the circuit. And he didn't have to go without a woman. There were plenty of groupies out there. But they wanted the same thing—the fame, the money, the cameras…

All carbon copies. *Shallow.*

None of them wanted the real Brett or cared to know about his family. Or that sometimes he regretted leaving Pistol Whip and the chasm between him and his brothers. That when his mother died, he'd fallen apart and missed her so much that he'd cried himself to sleep every night.

That he wanted to be as perfect as Maddox, but he hadn't been, so he'd joked his way through life. That the only thing he'd been good at was riding.

He'd certainly screwed up with Willow.

Willow gestured toward the turnoff for the ranch. "There's the sign for the Circle T."

He'd read about Gates's operation. He owned thousands of acres, raised crops and had made a name for himself in the cattle business.

At one time, Brett's father had wanted to make Horseshoe Creek just as big. He'd wanted him and Ray to help Maddox—with the three of them working together, it might have been possible.

But Brett had needed to stretch his wings. And Ray… he'd had too much anger in him. He couldn't get along with Joe or Maddox.

Willow grew more tense as they approached the house, and kept running her finger over the photo of Sam that the kidnapper had texted.

Brett put thoughts of Horseshoe Creek and his own problems behind. He could live with Maddox hating him when this was over.

As long as he put Sam back in Willow's arms.

EVEN THOUGH IT was dark and raining, Willow could see that the Circle T spanned for miles and miles. She'd heard about the big operation and that Gates was a formidable man.

Had he earned his money and success by being involved with crooks like Leo?

She tugged her jacket hood over her head, ducking against the wind and rain as she and Brett made their way to the front door. A chunky woman in a maid's uniform answered the door and escorted them to a huge paneled office with a large cherry desk, and corner bar. Dozens of awards for Gates's quality beef cattle adorned the wall.

The maid offered them coffee, but she and Brett both declined. Her stomach was too tied in knots to think about drinking or eating anything.

A big man, she guessed around six-one, two hundred and eighty pounds, sauntered in wearing a dress Western shirt and jeans that looked as if they'd been pressed. An expensive diamond-crusted ring glittered from one hand, while a gold rope chain circled his thick neck.

Brett introduced them and shook the man's hand. Gates removed his hat and set it on his desk in a polite gesture as he greeted Willow.

Gates pulled a hand down his chin. "McCullen, you're one of Joe's boys, the one that's the big rodeo star, aren't you?"

"Yes, sir."

"I was sorry to hear about your daddy," Gates said. "He was a good man."

"Yes, he was." Brett's expression looked pained. He obviously hadn't expected condolences from the man.

"Care for a drink?" Gates gestured toward the bar, but Brett and Willow declined.

"So what do I owe the honor? You here to find out my trade secrets?" Gates emitted a blustery laugh.

Brett laughed, too, but it sounded forced. "No, sir, although if you want to share, I'm sure my brother Maddox would love to talk."

Gates harrumphed. "I guess he would."

Willow squared her shoulders. "Mr. Gates, did you know my husband, Leo Howard?"

Gates's mustache twitched with a frown as he claimed a seat behind his desk. "Name don't ring a bell."

"How about Gus Garcia?" Brett asked.

Gates's chair creaked as he leaned back in it. "That

bastard tried to steal from under me. Why are you asking about him?"

"We believe that the men Garcia partnered with were in cahoots with Leo Howard."

Willow watched for a reaction, but the man didn't show one. "I don't understand. Garcia confessed and is in prison. I don't know about any partners. But since they locked Garcia up, I haven't had any more trouble."

"You knew a man named Dale Franklin was killed during the arrest? Two other men, Jasper Day and Wally Norman were also involved."

Gates planted both hands on the desk. "All I know is that after they put Garcia away, I cleaned house around here, brought in a whole new crew of hands."

He'd cleaned house to protect his business from corruption? Or to eliminate suspicion from himself for illegal activities?

Brett leaned forward, hands folded. "Do you know where we could find Day or Norman?"

"No, and I don't want to know."

Willow stood and approached his desk. "Mr. Gates, I think my ex-husband and those men rustled cattle and made a lot of money doing it, that they stashed the money somewhere, and I need to know where it is."

Gates shot up from his seat, his jowls puffing out with rage. "What the *hell*? You think I had something to do with them? Listen here, woman, they stole *from* me, not *for* me."

"Mr. Gates," Brett said, holding out a calming hand. "We aren't accusing you of anything. We just want to know if you have any idea where either of those men are."

"No." Gates started around his desk. "Now you two have worn out your welcome."

Willow flipped her phone around and jammed it in the man's face. "Look, Mr. Gates, someone kidnapped my little boy. His name is Sam. I think Day and Norman are responsible. They're demanding the money Leo made off the cattle rustling in exchange for my son. If I don't find it, I might not see my son again."

BRETT STUDIED GATES for telltale signs that he was behind the kidnapping. Gates was a formidable man. If Leo had stolen from him, he had motive for murder.

But Gates paled as he studied the photograph. "You think those men sent that to you?"

"The man didn't identify himself," Willow said. "But he said he wanted the money Leo stole. And if I don't find it, they'll hurt my little boy."

Gates pinched the bridge of his nose. "I'm sorry about your child, miss, but I don't know anything about a kidnapping or any money. And that's the gospel."

"Are you sure?" Brett asked. "You've built an empire awfully quickly. Maybe we should have your herd checked to make sure some of your cattle weren't stolen?"

Gates whirled on Brett in a rage. "How dare you come to my house and suggest such a thing. Now, get out."

"Mr. Gates," Willow cried. "If you have any idea how to find my son, please help me."

Gates's tone rumbled out, barely controlled. "I told you, I don't know anything."

Brett crossed his arms. "Think about it, Gates. Kidnapping is a capital offense. If you help—"

Gates stepped forward and jerked Brett by the arm. "I said get out."

WILLOW WAS TREMBLING as she and Brett left the Circle T.

"Do you think he was lying about knowing Leo?"

Brett's brows were furrowed as he drove away. "I think he's a ruthless man who's made a lot of money fast."

"What are we going to do now?" Willow asked. Her hopes were quickly deflating.

"I've been trying to think of another place where Leo might hide the money. You said his mother died. Where is she buried?"

Willow wrung her hands together. "I don't know. He didn't like to talk about her."

The windshield wipers swished back and forth as the rain fell, the night growing longer as she imagined little Sam locked in some scary place alone.

Brett punched in a number on his phone. "Mr. Howard, this is Brett McCullen again. Can you tell me where your wife was buried?" A pause. "Thank you."

He ended the call and spun around in the opposite direction. "She's in a memorial garden not far from Laramie."

Willow closed her eyes as he drove, but rest didn't come. Images of Sam flashed through her mind like a movie trailer. Sam being born, that little cleft chin and dimple so similar to Brett's that it had robbed her breath.

Sam, the day he'd taken his first step—they had been outside in the grass and he'd seen a butterfly and wanted to chase it. A smile curved her mouth as she remembered his squeal of delight when he'd tumbled down the hill and the butterfly had landed on his nose.

Then Christmas when he'd wanted a horseshoe set. And his third birthday when she'd taken him to the county fair, and he'd had his first pony ride. Dressed in a cowboy shirt, jeans and hat, he'd looked like a pro sitting astride the pony.

He would have loved to watch Brett at the rodeo.

But she'd known watching Brett compete would be difficult.

Every time she'd seen a tabloid with his photograph or a picture of a woman on his arm or kissing him, she'd cried. So she'd finally avoided the rodeo magazines.

Although how could she escape Brett when each time she looked at Sam, she saw his father's face?

Exhausted, she must have dozed off because when she stirred, they'd reached the graveyard. Rain and the cold made the rows of granite markers and tombstones look even more desolate.

Brett parked and reached for the door handle, but she caught his arm. "You aren't going to disturb that poor woman's grave, are you?"

A dark look crossed Brett's face. "We put Leo in the ground, Willow. I'll do whatever I have to in order to save Sam."

Tears blurred her eyes. She thought she'd loved Brett before, but even if he walked away when she got Sam back, she would always love him for what he'd done to help her.

"WHAT THE *HELL* have you done?"

He clenched the phone, his knuckles white. "I did what I had to do."

"You kidnapped a kid? What were you thinking?"

"I was thinking about getting that damn money. Howard refused to tell me where he hid it."

"So you killed him?"

"He came at me and tried to grab the gun from me. It just went off."

"This is some screwed-up mess. I don't want to go to prison for kidnapping."

"What about me? I could be charged with murder." His breath quickened. "That's the reason I took the kid. I need that money to skip the country. And I figured Howard must have told his wife where it was."

"But she claims she doesn't know. She's hooked up with one of those McCullen boys and they're asking questions all over the place."

"The woman has to be lying. Let her sweat a little over the kid and she'll give it up."

Chapter Fourteen

Brett felt as if the walls were closing in. Like the fear that chewed at his gut before he rode a bull these days. The fear that he might not come out whole… Or even alive.

But he didn't care if he died, if Willow got her son back.

Still, he was playing a dangerous game. Burying dead bodies, hiding the truth from the law, desecrating a grave when he'd been taught all his life to respect the dead.

Surely Leo wouldn't have dug deep enough to disturb his mother's coffin, and he would have needed equipment if he actually stored the cash inside the casket. So it made sense that he would have dug a shallow hole.

The rain splattering the grave marker reminded him of Willow's tears and the fact that they'd just buried his father, and his tombstone hadn't been ready at the funeral. Maddox had ordered it.

He wondered what Maddox had written on the headstone.

Pushing his own grief aside, he examined the dirt on Mrs. Howard's grave, looking for signs that it had been disturbed lately. Of course, Leo could have buried the money here when he'd first married Willow.

Then he'd sat back biding his time until interest in

the cattle rustling case died down and no one was looking for him.

Rain dripped off his Stetson and down into his shirt collar as he dug deeper, raking the dirt aside. Another shovelful of dirt, and he moved slightly to the right to check that area. The wet dirt was packed, but he dumped it aside, only to find more dirt.

Questions about Leo pummeled him as he continued to explore one spot then the next. Could Leo have hidden the money in Willow's house? No…she said she'd rented that place after they'd separated…

But he had gone back to see her the day he'd died…

Irritated that he had no answers, he kept digging, but forty-five minutes later, he realized his efforts were futile.

Leo had not buried the money in his mother's grave. Maybe he had some kind of moral compass after all.

Whispering an apology to the woman in the ground, he covered the grave with the dirt again, making quick work of the mess he'd made, then smoothing it out to show some respect.

Finally satisfied that he hadn't totally desecrated the memory of the woman in the ground, he wiped rain from his face and strode back to the truck. Willow sat looking out the window over the graveyard, her eyes a mixture of hope and grief.

He wanted to make her smile again. Fill her mind with dreams and promises of a happy future, the way they'd once done when they sneaked out to the barn and made love.

"It wasn't there, was it?" she said, her voice low. Pained. Defeated.

"I'm sorry." He climbed in and reached for her, but she turned toward the window, arms wrapped around her waist, shutting down.

That frightened him more than anything. If they didn't find Sam tonight, it would be the second night she'd been without her son. The second terrifying night of wondering if he was dead or alive.

WILLOW WAITED IN the truck as Brett stopped by the cabin to check on Valeria and Ana Sofia.

When he returned to the truck, he waved to the rancher Maddox had asked to watch the woman and her child. Ron had parked himself outside the cabin and seemed to be taking his role of bodyguard seriously.

"I'm glad she's safe. She was a brave lady to help me," Willow said, her heart in her throat.

Brett drove to the cabin where they were staying. "Don't give up, Willow. I'm still working on liquidating some funds. At least enough to make a trade and satisfy these men."

She murmured her appreciation, although hope waned with every passing hour.

Brett tossed her an umbrella and she ran through the sludge up to the cabin door. As soon as they entered, she ducked into the bathroom and closed the door. Tears overflowed, her sobs so painful, she couldn't breathe.

She flipped on the shower water, undressed, climbed in and let the hot water sluice over her, mingling with her tears. When the water finally cooled, she forced herself to regain control, dried off and dragged on a big terry-cloth robe. She towel dried her hair, letting the long strands dangle around her face, took a deep breath and stepped into the den.

Brett was standing with a drink in his hand, his eyes worried as he offered her the tumbler. "Drink this. I need to clean up."

She hadn't noticed how muddy and soaked he was, but he'd been out in the freezing rain digging for that money for over an hour. He had to be cold and exhausted.

But he still looked as handsome as sin.

She accepted the shot of whiskey and carried it to the sofa where he'd lit a fire. Tired and terrified, she sank onto the couch and sipped the amber liquid, grateful for the warmth of the fire and the alcohol that burned from the inside out.

The flames flickered and glowed a hot orange red, the wood crackling as the rain continued to beat like a drum against the roof. The shower kicked on, and she imagined Brett standing beneath the water, naked and more virile than any man had a right to be.

It would have been romantic, if she wasn't so worried about Sam.

The door opened and Brett walked in, his jeans slung low on his lean hips, his chest bare, water still dotting the thick, dark chest hair. Her breath caught, her body ached, the need to be with him so strong that she felt limp from want and fear.

If she allowed herself to lean on him, she would fall apart when he left.

"Let me grab a shirt." He ducked into the bedroom, saving her from herself. But a light knock sounded on the door.

Assuming it was Maddox, or perhaps Ron, bringing Valeria and her daughter over, she walked over and opened the door.

A blond-haired woman in a short red dress and cowboy boots stood on the other side aiming a pistol at Willow's heart.

BRETT JAMMED HIS ARMS in his shirtsleeves, determined to dress before he wrapped Willow in his arms and dragged her to bed. She looked so sad and frightened and desolate on that couch. And her tear-swollen eyes when she'd emerged from the bathroom had torn him inside out.

He was buttoning the first button when he stepped back into the hallway and saw Kitty at the door. His heart began to pound. What was *she* doing here? How had she found him?

"Who…are you?" Willow whispered. "What do you want?"

Brett inched closer, shock hitting him at the sight of her fingers wrapped around that pistol. "Kitty? What the *hell* are you doing?"

Kitty waved the gun in Willow's face. "You *bitch*. You can't have Brett. He's mine."

Willow lifted her hands in surrender. "You… I saw your picture with Brett."

Brett gritted his teeth. The gossipmongers made it look as if he and Kitty were a hot item. That he was constantly entertaining women in hotels and his RV, even in the stables between rides. That he even indulged in orgies with women he met online and at the honky-tonks.

"You can't have him," Kitty screeched. "I love Brett and he loves me, don't you, sugar?"

Brett recognized the psycho look in Kitty's eyes. It was the same look she'd had the night she broke into his hotel room and he found her waiting in his bed, naked and oiled, crying and threatening suicide if he didn't marry her that night.

He inched closer, watching her for signs that she intended to fire that gun. "Kitty, it's all right. Just put down the pistol. This is not what you think."

She glared at him, then at Willow. "Not what it looks like? You're both half-naked and alone in this cabin." She waved the gun at Willow. "But you can't have him. Brett and I are meant to be together."

Willow lifted her chin. "Brett is just an old friend. Nothing is happening here. I swear."

Just an old friend? Was that how she saw him?

Kitty's hand trembled, and she fluffed her long blond curls with her free hand. "Is that true, Brett? She means nothing to you?"

Brett swallowed hard, and gave Willow a look that he hoped she understood. One that silently encouraged her to play along. "That's right. Willow and I knew each other in high school. I'm just helping her out with a problem."

Kitty moved forward, hips swaying as she curved one arm around Brett's neck. "Then you've told her about us?"

Brett kept his eyes on the gun.

"I saw the pictures of you two together, Kitty," Willow cut in. "You're a lucky girl to have Brett."

"No, I'm the lucky one." Brett lifted a hand to stroke Kitty's hair and pasted on his photo-ready smile. Even the times he'd been sick or bruised and half-dead from being thrown, he'd used that smile. "Come on, honey. Let's go outside and take a walk. I'll show you my ranch."

Kitty gave Willow a wry look as if to say she'd just won a victory, and Brett ushered Kitty toward the door. "You'll love Horseshoe Creek."

Kitty batted her lashes at him, her eyes full of stars. Or maybe she was high on drugs.

She leaned into him, and he stepped onto the porch with her, then escorted her down the steps. When they'd reached the landing, he made his move. He grabbed the gun from her, then twisted her arm behind her back, and pulled her against him so she couldn't move. "This is it, Kitty. You've gone too far."

She struggled to get away, but he kept a strong hold on her arm and yelled for Willow. The door screeched open, and Willow poked her head out.

"Brett?"

"Call Maddox," he said between gritted teeth. "She's going to jail."

WILLOW WAS STILL trembling when Maddox arrived. She tightened the belt on her robe and waited inside while Brett explained the situation to his brother.

The rain had died down enough for her to hear Brett's explanation through the window. "She's been stalking me for months, Maddox. But tonight she went too far. She pulled a gun on Willow."

Kitty jerked against the handcuffs, her sobs growing louder. "How can you do this to me, to *us*, Brett. I love you! I thought we were going to get married!"

"We had two dates, that was it," Brett said to his brother. "I swear. I didn't lead her on, Maddox. There was never anything between us."

Maddox raised a brow. "Willow's here?"

Willow ducked behind the curtain. She didn't care if Maddox knew she was visiting Brett, but she didn't want to face him. He probably thought she was cheating on her husband with Brett.

Worse, if he asked questions about Leo, she didn't want to lie.

"Yes," Brett said. "But that's not what this is about. I need you to take Kitty into custody. Contact her family and tell them she needs psychiatric help."

Maddox hauled Kitty into the back of his police SUV. Tears streaked her face, and she was still screaming Brett's name as Maddox drove away.

Willow braced herself as Brett strode in. His hair was damp, his jaw rigid, that spark of flirtatiousness in his eyes gone. He looked angry and worried and…so damn masculine and sexy that her heart tripped.

"You've been breaking hearts everywhere you go, haven't you, Brett?" She regretted the words the moment she said them. The bitter jealousy in her tone gave her feelings away.

THERE WAS NO way Brett was going to let Willow believe that he'd been in love with that deranged woman.

"Willow," he said, his teeth clenched. "I swear, we went out twice, then I realized she was unstable. After that, she started stalking me."

"I saw the pictures, Brett." Her voice cracked. "*Everyone* saw them."

He strode toward her, water dripping from his hair, his eyes luminous with emotions. "You can't believe everything you see in the tabloids. They're trying to sell copies."

"But you slept with her."

"Twice and I was half-drunk at the time. A week later, she broke into my hotel room and was waiting in my bed naked. When I told her to leave and pushed her out the hotel door, the press snapped a picture and turned it into something lurid."

Her eyes glittered with anger and something else… *jealousy?* Was it possible that Willow still cared for him?

"So all the pictures of you and the women were fake?"

His heart hammered as he closed the distance between

them. He knew she was scared for her son and frustrated, and so was he. But he couldn't allow her to think that he didn't care. That he hadn't wanted her every damn day he was gone.

So he tilted her chin up and forced her to look into his eyes. "I wasn't a saint, Willow. But know this, I never kissed a woman without wishing she was you."

Then he did what he'd wanted to do ever since he'd ridden back into town.

He dragged her into his arms and kissed her with all the hunger he'd kept at bay for the past few years. Except this time he wouldn't stop at kissing as he had before. This time he wanted all of Willow.

Chapter Fifteen

Willow clung to Brett's words. None of those women had meant anything to him. When he'd closed his eyes, he'd seen her face.

Just as she had imagined Brett holding her when she was in Leo's arms.

Leo had known that she hadn't loved him. He'd felt it. Not that she had anything to feel guilty about. Apparently he'd never loved her either.

Of course he'd acted like he had. He'd showered her with attention and gifts and affection at a time when she'd been most vulnerable.

But it had all been a lie.

Brett's lips fused with hers, and she welcomed the sensations flooding her. Anything to soothe the pain and fear clawing at her heart.

Brett stroked her hair, then ran his hands down her back, pulling her closer to him so she felt the hard planes of his body against her curves. Her pulse raced, need and desire mingling with the desperateness that she'd felt since he'd walked back into her life.

He'd come the minute she'd called. Would he have come sooner if she'd had the courage to ask?

He made a low sound in his throat, and her hunger

spiraled. "Willow, I want you," he said in a gruff whisper against her neck.

She tilted her head back, shivering at his breath on her skin. "I want you, too."

Brett swung her up into his arms and carried her to the bedroom. She kissed him frantically, urging him to do more, and he set her on her feet, then looked into her eyes.

"I've wanted you every day since I left Pistol Whip."

"I've wanted you, too, Brett." It had always been him. No one else. There never would be.

But her voice was lost as he nibbled at her lips again and drove his mouth against hers. They kissed, the passion growing hotter as he probed her mouth apart with his tongue. Lips and tongues mated and danced, his fingers trailing over her back, down to her waist, then one hand slid up to cup her breast.

Her breath caught and her nipple stiffened as he stroked her through her robe. She wanted him naked, touching and loving her everywhere.

Her whispered sigh was all the encouragement he needed. He cupped her face and looked into her eyes again, and for a second, the young boy she'd fallen in love with stood in his place.

All their dreams and fantasies, whispered loving words, kisses and secret rendezvous… She was back in the barn with Brett, hiding out with the boy she loved.

Then there was the night he'd come back to Pistol Whip. He'd shown up on her doorstep and she'd taken one look at him standing in the rain and invited him into her bed.

They'd made love as if they'd never been apart. They'd also made Sam that night.

Her robe fell to the floor, cool night air brushing

her skin. His breath rasped out with appreciation as he cupped both breasts in his hands.

"You're so beautiful," he murmured.

She blushed at his blatant perusal, but shyness fled as he lowered his mouth and drew one stiff nipple into his mouth. Willow moaned as erotic sensations splintered through her, and she threaded her fingers in his hair, holding him close as he laved one breast, then the other.

Aching to touch him, she popped the first button on his shirt, then the second. He pulled away from her long enough to toss his shirt to the floor. His bare chest was broader than she remembered, dusted with dark hair, his skin bronzed from the sun, although a few scars lined his torso. She wondered how he'd gotten each one of them, but didn't ask. She didn't want to talk.

She wanted to be in his arms, loving him the way she once had when life had been simple and she'd had dreams of a future.

She unbuttoned his jeans, the sound rasping in the silence, and he kicked them off. Her body tingled as his hands skated over her hips. His eyes grew dark and needy, and he pulled her against him.

Her breasts felt heavy, achy, the tingling in her thighs and womb intensifying as he kissed her again and she shoved his boxers down his legs. Finally he stood naked in front of her. Powerful muscles flexed in his chest, arms and thighs, and his sex was thick and long, pulsing with excitement.

She trailed her fingers over his bare chest, and he moaned, then cradled her against him and walked them to the bed. Her head hit the pillow, her hair fanning out, as he nibbled at her neck again, then raked kisses along her neck and throat, moving down to her breasts where he loved her again until she begged for more.

NEED PULSED THROUGH Brett as he coaxed Willow onto the bed. His body ached for her, but the need to assuage her pain was just as strong.

He closed his mouth around one turgid nipple and suckled her, his sex hardening as she moaned his name. She stroked his calf with her foot, raking it up and down as she dug her hands into his hair.

Her hunger spiked his own, and he trailed sweet hungry kisses down her belly to her inner thighs.

"Brett…"

"*Shh*, just enjoy, baby." He flicked his tongue along her thigh, finding his way to the tender spot that made her go crazy. She tasted sweet and erotic, just as he remembered, and he teased her with his tongue until she clawed at his arms, begging him to come to her.

"I need you, Brett," Willow whispered.

He flicked his tongue over and over her tender nub until her body began to quiver and she cried out in release.

"Please, Brett."

Brett's heart pounded with the need to be inside her as he lifted himself and covered her with his body. For a moment, he lay on top of her savoring her tender curves against the hard planes of his chest and thighs. But she rubbed her hands down his back, then splayed them on his hips and butt, and his sex surged, needing more.

He tilted his head and looked into her passion-glazed eyes, then braced his body on his hands, and grabbed a condom from his jeans' pocket. She helped him roll it on, her fingers driving him insane as she touched his bare skin. When he had the protection in place, he kissed her again, deeply, hungrily, then rose above her and stroked her center with his erection. She groaned again, then slid her hand down and guided him home.

The moment he entered her, he closed his eyes and hesitated, forcing himself to slow down or he was going to explode. She lifted her hips and undulated them, inviting him to move inside her, and he did.

In and out, he thrust himself, filling her, stroking her with his length, pumping harder and faster as they built a natural rhythm. Sweat beaded on his forehead as he intensified their lovemaking, his release teetering on the edge.

Willow clutched at him, rubbing his back as she moved beneath him, then groaned his name as another orgasm claimed her. He kissed her again, then lifted her hips so he could move deeper inside her, so deep that he felt her core. She breathed his name against his neck.

It was the sweetest sound he'd ever heard, a sound he'd missed so much that it tipped him over the edge and his release splintered through him.

WILLOW CLOSED HER EYES and savored the feel of being in Brett's arms. Erotic sensations rocked through her with such intensity that she clung to him, emotions overwhelming her.

Tears burned the backs of her eyelids. She had told herself not to fall in love with Brett again, but that had been futile.

Because she'd never stopped loving him.

Fear made her chest tighten again. She'd barely survived the first time he'd left her. How would she survive this time?

A deep sigh escaped her as he rolled them sideways and tucked her up against him. Brett kissed the top of her head, then disappeared into the bathroom for a moment. She thought he was going to dress and leave her alone, and she already missed him.

But he crawled back in bed with her, pulled her into his embrace and rubbed her arm. His body felt hot against hers as his breathing rasped out. She wanted to stay in his arms forever.

"Willow?"

She tensed, knowing she should confess the truth about Sam.

"I've been thinking. Wondering why Leo came to your house the day he died."

Willow went still. "I hoped he was going to drop the signed divorce papers by."

Brett took a strand of her hair between his fingers and stroked it the same way he had when they were young and in love. "But why that *particular* day? What if he really came back for the money? Maybe he retrieved it from the original place he'd buried it."

Willow turned to look into his eyes. "You think he had it with him that day?"

Brett shrugged. "Maybe he knew his partners were onto him, so he decided to hide it at your house. It wasn't in his truck. And we didn't find it where that map led us or at his mother's grave."

Willow's pulse kicked up, and she shoved the covers back. "Then we need to search my house."

Brett nodded, although before she slid from bed, he pulled her back and kissed her again. Her heart fluttered with love and hope.

When they found the money and Sam was home,

would Brett forgive her for keeping her secret? Was it possible that they might be a family someday?

Her cell phone buzzed, and she startled. Sam?

Brett handed her the phone from the nightstand and she punched Connect. "Hello."

"Do you have the money?"

Panic shot through Willow. "No, but I think I know where it is."

"Where?"

She swallowed, struggling for courage. "Meet me at my house in an hour. Bring my son to me, and you can have it."

BRETT YANKED ON his jeans and shirt while Willow vaulted from bed and threw on her clothes. He hoped to hell he was right, that the money was hidden somewhere at Willow's.

But just to be on the safe side, he grabbed the duffel bag he'd used to bring his clothes in, then packed some newspaper in the bottom.

"What are you doing?"

"If we don't find the money, I'll use this as a decoy until we rescue Sam." He retrieved his rifle from the corner in the den, wishing he had that money from his accounts to cover the newspaper, but hopefully they'd find Leo's money, and he wouldn't need this bag. And if they checked it…well, he had his rifle. He'd do whatever he had to do to get the boy.

He snatched his coat and handed Willow her jacket.

"Let's hurry. I want to look for the money before this bastard arrives." His phone buzzed, though, and he tensed. Maddox.

What if he'd somehow discovered Leo's body on the ranch?

Exhaling slowly, he punched Connect while Willow tugged on her jacket and boots. "Hey."

"Brett, what kind of trouble are you involved in?"

"I told you that woman was stalking me. End of story."

"I'm not talking about her," Maddox said sharply. "I want the truth about what you're doing. You're looking into Willow's husband, aren't you?"

Brett gritted his teeth. Did he know Leo was dead? "Why would you ask that?"

"I've been investigating a cattle-rustling ring that a man named Garcia is serving time for. It's his wife and kid you brought to the ranch, isn't it?"

He should have realized that would arouse Maddox's suspicions. "Maddox—"

"Just shut up and listen. I know you've always had a thing for Willow, and she's at that cabin with you. But her husband is dangerous."

"What do you know about him? Did he hurt her?"

"That's my guess. Dad talked to me one day and said he was worried, that something was off there."

If he'd been around, he would have known himself. And Willow never would have suffered.

Maddox cleared his throat. "He was in with some bad people. That's the reason you were looking up prison records, wasn't it?"

Brett glanced at his watch, impatient. "Yes, Maddox, but I have to go."

"Brett, let me handle the situation. I think Howard was involved with those cattle rustlers. I don't have proof but I'll get it. In fact, I'm trying to locate him to question him now. Does Willow know where he is, Brett? Because if she's covering for him, she could go to jail, too."

Willow looked panicked and tugged him toward the door. "I'll tell her if she hears from him to call you."

He didn't wait on a response. He hung up with a curse. Maddox was smart; it wouldn't take him long to figure out what was going on.

Willow followed him outside where the rain was still beating on the roof as they hurried to his truck.

Wind and rain battered the windshield as he drove, blurring his vision of the road. He flipped the wipers to High, his nerves on edge as he turned onto Willow's road.

The truck bounced over the ruts, mud spewing. He looked over his shoulder to make sure no one was following.

Hell, for all he knew, Maddox might be on his tail.

Willow twisted in the seat, obviously agitated. "They *will* bring Sam, won't they?"

Brett's gut contorted. He'd wondered the same thing.

If Sam could identify them, they might have already ditched him, then planned to take the money and run.

His fingers curled around the rifle on the seat beside him. If they had hurt Willow's little boy, he'd kill the bastards.

WILLOW SCANNED THE OUTSIDE of her house in case the kidnappers had arrived early. Her throat ached from holding back tears.

She was going to see Sam again. She had to see him.

But what if she and Brent were walking into a trap? What if they'd never intended to give her back her son?

Fear almost paralyzed her. Determined not to give

up, though, she forced the terror at bay. She had to stay strong.

Brett parked and got out, carrying his rifle and the duffel bag with him. Memories of finding Leo dead in her bedroom flashed behind her eyes, and nausea climbed her throat. But she forged on, determined to hold it together.

They slogged through the rain and she unlocked the door, her shoulders knotted with anxiety. The den looked just as she'd left it, and so did the kitchen.

Although it felt as if it had been years since she'd been home. She didn't know if she could ever live here again.

"I don't know where he would have hidden it," Willow said.

"I'll search the closets. You search the kitchen. He could have taped an envelope with a key to a safety deposit box under a drawer or table."

Brett strode to the hall closet and began to dig through it. She checked the cabinet and drawers in the kitchen and the desk, under the drawers and table, and on top of the cabinets. The laundry room came next. Her movements were harried as she ripped through plastic storage containers and checked beneath and behind the washer and dryer.

She searched the pantry, but yielded nothing, so she hurried to the bedrooms. Brett was in her room. The sight of the bloodstains was still so stark that it made her stomach turn.

Sucking in a sharp breath, she darted into Sam's room. Sam's toys and clothes were still scattered about as they'd left them. Knowing time was of the essence, she dropped to her knees and searched beneath the bed. Her hand connected with a toy superhero and she pulled it out, along with several odd socks, a ball and a candy wrapper.

Her thoughts raced as she pulled down his covers and checked below his mattress, the bottom of the box spring and the back of the headboard.

Panic was starting to tear at her, and she threw the closet door open and searched the floor. Shoes, toys and a cereal box. On the top shelf she found the extra blankets and sheets she'd folded along with a flashlight, Sam's Halloween costume and boxes of rocks they'd collected at the creek.

She dug through the corner of the closet and found a stack of magazines—rodeo magazines. Her throat closed as she spotted a picture of Brett on the front of one of them. He must have found this in her nightstand drawer.

"Any luck, Willow?" Brett's voice jerked her from her thoughts and she stuffed the magazines back inside.

"No, nothing. You?"

Brett scowled. "No, but I'm going to look around outside."

"I'll check the attic."

He nodded and she rushed to the hall and climbed in the attic while he stepped outside. The rain had slackened, although droplets pinged off the window where the wind shook it from the trees.

Several boxes of old clothing and quilt scraps were stored on one wall. She went to the antique wardrobe and opened it. It would be a perfect hiding place. In fact, Sam had hidden inside it once when they were playing hide-and-seek. After that, she'd made sure that it couldn't be locked so he wouldn't get trapped.

She swung the door open and found fabric scraps from her projects along with boxes of photographs of her and Brett in high school.

But there was no money anywhere.

Outside an engine rumbled in the distance, and she looked out the attic window and saw lights flickering. Was it them?

Did they have Sam?

BRETT FOUND NOTHING in the garage, so he scanned the side of the house for a crawl space or a hiding place but didn't see one.

The sound of the car engine made his nerves spike. He hurried inside and grabbed the rifle along with the duffel bag. Willow raced down the steps from the attic and clutched his arm. "Brett, what are we going to do?"

"Play along with me."

She nodded, although terror filled her eyes. Brett stepped onto the porch, deciding to use the darkness to camouflage the bag. A black sedan pulled up, lights turned off.

He held the rifle beside him, hand ready to draw, the duffel bag in his other hand. Willow's nervous breathing rattled in the quiet.

The sedan door opened and a man wearing a ski mask stepped from the backseat. The driver remained behind the wheel, hidden in the shadows.

The silver glint of metal flickered against the night. "The woman needs to bring the money over here."

"First, we see the boy," Brett said in a tone that brooked no argument.

A hesitation. The wind hurled rain onto the porch and caused a twig to snap and fall in front of the man. He didn't react, except to reach inside the car and snatch something.

Brett feared it was another weapon, but a little boy wearing a jacket appeared, his body shaking. He couldn't see his face well for the shadows, but he cried out for Willow.

"Mommy!"

Willow stepped onto the porch. *"Sam!* Honey, I'm here. Are you all right?"

"I wanna come home!" Sam yelled.

Brett caught Willow, before she barreled forward.

"Send the boy over, then I'll throw you the money," Brett ordered.

A nasty chuckle echoed from the man. "No way. The woman brings the money. When I see it, I release the kid."

Brett's fingers tightened around the rifle. He was a damn good shot. But this was a dangerous game.

Willow's and her son's lives depended on him.

"Fine." Willow grabbed the duffel bag.

"Willow?" Brett reached for her but she shook off his hand.

"I have to do this," Willow said. "I'll do anything for Sam."

Brett's gut churned as she slowly walked down the steps.

"Send the boy," Brett said.

The man took Sam by the collar and half dragged him across the yard. Brett inched down a step, but the man aimed the gun at Willow. "Stay put, McCullen, or they're both dead."

Chapter Sixteen

Willow soaked up the sight of her little boy's features.

His dark eyes were big and terrified, but he was alive. And she didn't see any visible injuries or bruises.

"Are you okay, honey?" she asked softly as she approached Sam.

He gave a little nod of his head, but his chin quivered. "I wanna come home."

"You *are* coming home," Willow assured him. There was no way this man would leave with her son. She'd die first.

The man's gun glinted as she neared him, but that ski mask disguised his face.

Willow clutched the duffel bag to her side. "I have what you came for. Now let my son go."

The man glanced down at the bag. "Closer."

Willow inched forward, but kept the bag slightly behind her, determined to lure Sam away before the man realized the bag was empty.

She hesitated a few inches from him, then stood ramrod straight, her chin lifted. "Let him go."

The man met her gaze, then shoved Sam. "Go on, kid." At the same time, he reached for the bag.

"Mommy!" Sam ran toward her, and she hugged him

to her and threw the bag at the man's feet a few inches from him.

She gripped Sam by the arm just as he ripped open the bag to check the contents. "Run back to the house, Sam!"

He was crying and clinging to her, and she turned to run with him, but the man lunged at her and snatched her arm. "You lying bitch."

"Run, Sam, *run*!" Her head snapped back as the man caught her.

Brett was coming down the steps, his rifle aimed. "Let her go!"

Sam stumbled and fell, crying out for her. "Mommy!"

"Save him," Willow shouted to Brett.

The second man in the car fired his gun, and Brett jumped back slightly, then pressed his hand on his left shoulder. Blood began to ooze out and soak his shirt.

He'd been shot.

"Please let me go," Willow cried. "I don't have your money, and my son needs me."

"Shut up." The man jammed the gun to her head, but Brett started forward again so the man spoke to Brett. "Move another inch and I'll shoot her."

Brett kept his rifle aimed, but froze a few feet from Sam. "Listen, man, she tried to find the money. But she doesn't know where it is."

A litany of curse words filled the air. Sam pushed up from the ground and shook his little fists at the man. "Let my mommy go!"

Sam started to run back toward her, but Brett snatched him by the neck of his jacket. "Stay still, son. I'll handle this."

The man kept the gun to her head and dragged her back toward the sedan. She wanted to fight, but the cold barrel against her temple warned her not to mess with him. She didn't want to die and leave Sam motherless.

Sam was sobbing, so Brett picked him up. Willow saw the moment he looked into Sam's face and realized he was his.

His gaze flew to hers, questions mingling with shock.

The driver of the sedan fired at Brett's feet, though, and he dodged the bullet, protecting Sam with his body.

The kidnapper opened the sedan door. Willow shoved at him, but he grabbed her around the throat, then pressed the barrel of the gun to her head again.

"Don't hurt her. I'll get you some money!" Brett shouted. "I have a hundred thousand of my own I'll give you in exchange for her."

"Get it and we'll talk." The man shoved Willow inside the car.

Willow tried to crawl across the seat to escape out the opposite door, but he slammed the gun against the back of her head, and the world went black.

BRETT'S HEART WAS pounding so loudly, he could hear the blood roaring in his ears. The driver of the sedan spun the vehicle around. The other man fired at Brett again to keep him from chasing them, and Brett clutched Sam and darted behind a tree to protect him.

"Mommy!" Sam screamed as the sedan accelerated. *"Mommy!"*

A cold knot of fear enveloped Brett as the sedan disappeared with Willow inside.

Sam wrapped his arms around Brett's neck and clung to him, his little body trembling with fear.

Sam. *His son.*

The words echoed over and over in his head. Sam was his little boy.

All this time, these years, the past few days—Willow hadn't told him. Had kept the truth from him.

Why? Because she thought he wouldn't have been a good father…

"I want my mommy!" Sam sobbed.

Brett patted the little boy's back, his heart aching for the ordeal Sam had suffered. For the fear and trauma, for the murder he'd witnessed.

And now his mother was gone, snatched at gunpoint in front of his eyes.

He pressed Sam's head to his shoulder and rocked him in his arms. "*Shh*, son, it'll be all right."

"My…mommy…"

Sam's sniffles punctuated the air, wrenching Brett's heart. "I know you're scared, son, and you've been through a lot." Brett's shoulder was starting to throb, and blood soaked his shirt. "But I'm here now. I'm here and I'll make things right."

I'm your father, he started to say. But he didn't want to confuse Sam now. Besides, what had Willow told him?

Sam thought that bastard Leo was his dad…

Rage heated Brett's blood. He would rectify *that* as soon as possible. As soon as he brought Willow home.

Then they would sit down and have a damn long talk.

Sam's cries softened, but his fingers dug into Brett's neck as Brett walked toward his pickup. He needed to take care of the bullet in his shoulder before he passed out. If he did, he wouldn't be any good to Sam or Willow.

They were his priority now.

But how was he going to remove this bullet without seeing a doctor or drawing suspicion from the law?

He carried Sam around to the passenger side of the truck, his lungs squeezing for air when Sam looked up at him with those big eyes. Eyes that looked exactly like his. The cleft in his chin, the dimple…he was a McCullen through and through.

How had he not seen it before?

Because you didn't look.

In the photo he'd seen of Sam, the boy was wearing a cowboy hat. It had hurt too much for him to think about Willow having another man's son, so he hadn't paid attention to the child's features.

But this boy was *his*.

He fastened Sam's seat belt, soaking up his face for a moment, and thinking about what he'd missed. All those baby years. The first time he'd walked. Christmases and birthdays…

Sam wiped at his nose and looked up at Brett. The fear there nearly stalled Brett's heart. "You helping those mean men?" Sam whispered.

Brett nearly choked on a sharp denial. But he didn't want to scare Sam any more than he already was. "No, son." He gently raked a hand over the child's hair, emotions nearly overwhelming him. "I'm a friend of your mommy's. I've been helping her try to get you back from those men."

Sam's eyes narrowed as he looked at Brett's shoulder. "They shot you like they shot Daddy."

Leo was not his father. But Sam *had* witnessed the murder. "Yes, but I'm not going to die, Sam. And I'm not going to leave you." Not ever again. "I'm going to get your mother back. I promise."

Sam's chin quivered, but he gave Brett a brave nod.

Knowing time was working against him, he walked

around to the driver's side and climbed in. He reached inside his pocket and removed a handkerchief, then jammed it inside his shirt over the wound to help stem the blood flow.

Then he cranked the truck and drove back toward Horseshoe Creek.

He was starting to feel weak, and he needed help. Someone to remove this damn bullet and someone to watch Sam, so he could get hold of that cash and trade it for Willow's life.

He didn't know where to go. Who to turn to.

Maddox would be furious when he found out what Brett had done.

But he was the only one who could help him now.

He'd probably lock Brett up when all was said and done.

He glanced over at Sam who was watching him with those big sad eyes.

But Sam was his son, and if there was anything that Maddox cared about, it was family.

Brett would pay the consequences when this was over and go to jail if it came to that.

But he'd save Willow first.

WILLOW STIRRED FROM UNCONSCIOUSNESS, but her head was spinning and nausea rose to her throat. She lifted her hand to the back of her head and felt blood. The car bounced over the rocky road, jarring her and making her feel ill.

She struggled to sit up, but the car veered to the right, throwing her against the side.

"Be still, bitch, or you're going to get it again."

A sob welled inside her, but she sucked it down. "Please let me go. My little boy needs me."

He barked a sinister laugh. "You're the one who screwed up. You should have given me the money instead of getting greedy."

Willow pushed herself to a sitting position. "I'm not *greedy*. I told you I didn't know where the money was and I *don't*."

He grabbed her arm, clenching it so tightly that pain shot through her arm and shoulder. "We know Leo came to see you, that he took the money from where he'd first hidden it. He was supposed to meet us that day with it, but he stopped off at your house first."

"Leo and I have been separated for years," Willow cried. "He came by to drop off divorce papers, not give me money."

"Because you were already keeping it for him," the man snarled.

Willow shook her head back and forth. How could she convince them that she was telling the truth?

And what if she did and they killed her because she was of no use to them anymore?

Then she'd never see Sam again, and he would grow up without a mother...

She closed her eyes and said a prayer. Even if she didn't make it, Brett had recognized that he had a son. He would raise Sam as a McCullen.

Sam will be all right.

Except she wanted to be there to see him grow up, to learn to ride a horse, to play ball and graduate from school and get married one day...

BRETT IGNORED THE PAIN in his shoulder and focused on driving back to the ranch. He had to get Sam to Horseshoe Creek where he'd be safe.

Dark clouds hovered above, threatening more rain, and he took a curve too quickly and nearly lost control. Sam's little face looked pale in the dark, and Brett reached out and squeezed his shoulder.

"I know you've been through it, little man, and you miss your mother, but hang in there a little longer."

"You said you knew her?" Sam said in a small voice.

"Yes," Brett said. "We were friends back in high school." *Friends and lovers. And I'm your father.*

Although Sam obviously had no idea.

Sam suddenly tilted his head to the side. "You're that rodeo star aren't you? I saw your picture in that magazine Mommy had."

Willow had a magazine with his picture in it.

Of course she had. She'd seen pictures of him and Kitty. She thought he was sleeping with a different woman every night.

And he had, he admitted silently.

But would he have if he'd known he had a child? That Willow had delivered his baby?

Regret and heartache ballooned inside him as he turned onto the road leading back to Horseshoe Creek.

Sam sat up straighter, his little face turned toward the window. "Where are you taking me?"

The poor kid had been kidnapped. He probably was wondering what Brett was going to do to him. "We're going to my ranch," Brett said. "Your mommy likes it there. And I have two brothers and a nice lady named Mama Mary who took care of me when I was little. She'll take care of you till your mommy is home."

As soon as he said the words, he felt better. Maddox would be angry, but Mama Mary would love Sam unconditionally with no questions asked.

"You gots horses?"

Brett's mouth twitched. "Yes, buddy. Do you know how to ride?"

"Not really." Sam's voice dropped to a low whisper. "Mommy said I was too little."

Brett rubbed his hand over Sam's head again. "Well, you look pretty big to me. And I know you're tough. So I'll teach you to ride soon. Sound good?"

Sam nodded, and for a moment, Brett saw himself when he was little. Anytime he was upset or mad, he'd ridden across the ranch and the world had seemed better. He could pass that on to his son.

The farmhouse slid into view, and for once, he was relieved to see Maddox's SUV in front of the house. He parked, pressing his hand to his bloody shoulder as he hurried around to help Sam.

The little boy took his hand and jumped to the ground, and Brett held on to him as they walked up the porch steps. When he opened the door, Maddox was standing in the hall, his expression dark.

"Brett, I need to talk to you. This evening I found something—"

Brett cut him off. He had to get the words out fast. "I have to talk to you, too." Brett swayed slightly, his head light from blood loss.

Maddox's gaze took in Sam, then he noticed Brett's bloody shoulder. "Good grief, you've been shot."

Brett nodded and stumbled forward, and Maddox caught him. "It's worse, Maddox. I need your help. Two men...they kidnapped Willow."

Chapter Seventeen

Willow struggled against the bindings around her wrists and feet as the man tossed her into a dark room. A sliver of light managed to peek through the curtains, and she dragged herself on her belly to the bed and slowly clawed her way on top of it.

She pushed the curtain aside, and hoped to escape through the window, but it was nailed shut.

A sob welled in her throat, and she slumped back down on the bed. Was this the room where they'd kept Sam?

She mentally searched for strength. If her little boy had held it together long enough for her to save him, she could do it long enough for Brett to find her.

The most important thing was that Sam was safe.

Safe with his father who probably hated her now for keeping his son from him all these years.

That didn't matter either, not now. Sam was okay and if she died tonight, Brett would take care of Sam. He'd teach him how to play baseball and skip stones in the creek behind the ranch, and how to saddle a horse and trick ride.

Although one day he might teach him to ride a bull and she wasn't so sure about that.

She would miss it all if she was dead, but Sam would be happy with his father. He would raise him to be an honorable, brave McCullen man.

She rolled to her side on the bed and looked across the room. A ratty stuffed animal lay on the floor, along with a piece of rope.

Sam had been here. He'd twisted the rope into the letter *S*. Her heart warmed as she remembered him pretending to rope cattle like the cowboys on TV.

Brett would teach him how to rope calves one day, too.

She wanted to be there for him and see all those things.

She blinked, and struggled to untie her hands, but the ropes cut into her wrists. Frustrated, she drew her knees up and tried to reach her ankles with her hands to untie her feet, but the knot was so tight, she couldn't budge it.

Outside, footsteps pounded and voices echoed through the wall. She forced herself to be very still so she could hear, although it was difficult over the sound of her own roaring heart.

"You took the woman now? What the hell are you doing?"

Willow tensed. That was a woman's voice. It sounded familiar, but it was too muffled for her to place.

"I thought she was lying about the money."

"But what if she doesn't know where it is?"

"That cowboy said he'll pay us. It won't be half a million, but it'll be enough to get out of the country so we can lie low for a while."

"All right. But give the man a deadline. The longer you wait, the more likely we are going to get caught."

"Twenty-four hours. That's the deadline. If he doesn't produce the money by then, kill her."

BRETT'S KNEES FELT like they were going to cave in.

"Brett, who shot you?" Maddox caught him just before he collapsed. "Mama Mary, Rose, hurry, I need help!"

Sam was still clinging to Brett, looking scared to death.

"It's okay, son," Brett murmured in a soothing voice as he lowered him to the floor. "I'll be fine. Maddox is my brother." He gestured toward the badge on Maddox's shirt. "He's a good guy, the sheriff. He'll help us find your mommy and get rid of those bad men."

Mama Mary and Rose rushed in, both startled by the blood on his shirt.

"Oh, my word!" Mama Mary cried. "What's going on?"

"This is Willow's son, Sam," Brett said. *And my son, too.*

"Brett, this is Rose," Maddox said.

Brett muttered that he was glad to meet her. "Take care of Sam, Mama Mary. Two men took Willow and I need Maddox's help."

Rose gasped. "They took Willow?"

"You know her?" Brett asked.

Rose nodded. "I sell her quilts at my antiques shop."

Mama Mary dropped to her knees, her big bulk swaying as she rubbed Sam's arms. "Come on, little one. I bet you're hungry and tired aren't you?"

Sam hung on to Brett's leg. "I want my mommy," Sam said in a haunted voice.

Tears glistened on Mama Mary's eyelashes, but she didn't hesitate to comfort Sam, just the way she'd comforted him when he was little and his mother died.

"I know you do, sugar," Mama Mary said. "And don't you worry. Mr. Brett and Mr. Maddox are the two finest men in Wyoming. They'll have your mama back in no time." She dried his eyes with her apron. "Now your mama would want you to eat."

Sam leaned in to the big woman's loving arms. "Come on, little one. Mama Mary will whip you up some mac and cheese. I bet you like mac and cheese, don't you? It was Mr. Brett's favorite when he was your age."

Sam nodded against her, and Brett ruffled Sam's hair. "It's okay, bud. I'll be right here. My brother's going to patch me up."

Sam seemed to accept what he'd said, and Mama Mary carted him to the kitchen where Brett knew he was in good hands.

Maddox helped him into the den and onto the couch. "Rose, get some towels so we can stop this bleeding. Then call Dr. Cumberland. We have to remove this bullet."

"There's no time," Brett argued.

"Listen to me, Brett," Maddox said in a deep voice. "You won't be any good if you die on me."

Rose dashed from the room, and Maddox poured two whiskeys. He returned and handed Brett a glass, then took a swig of his own, his eyes dark with rage and worry.

"Now, what the *hell* is going on?"

Brett rubbed his hand over his eyes, then swallowed his drink. "You aren't going to like it."

"I know that." Maddox walked over and sat down beside him. "But I'm your brother, man. And if you need my help, I'm here. But I need to know everything."

Brett nearly choked on his emotions. He'd just found out he had a son. And now his brother was ready to help him.

Of course Maddox didn't know what all he'd done.

But it was time for him to come clean. He'd take whatever punishment came his way. As long as Maddox helped him save Willow.

"The night of the funeral," he began, "Willow called me, hysterical."

Maddox leaned his elbows on his knees. "This has to do with her husband, Leo, doesn't it? Did she know he was a crook?"

Brett shook his head, a bead of perspiration trickling down his brow. "They were separated, but he was supposed to come by her house and drop off divorce papers. On the way he picked up Sam. When Willow arrived home, she found Leo dead. And the men who'd killed him had abducted Sam."

Maddox muttered a curse, and let a heartbeat of silence pass. "Go on."

"They told Willow that if she called the law, they'd kill Sam."

"That's the reason you were snooping around on my computer?"

"Yes. The kidnappers said that Leo had a half million dollars. They wanted the money in exchange for her son." *His* son.

"What's the connection with the prisoner?"

"I think the kidnappers worked with Leo, they were his partners and he betrayed them so they killed him."

"His partners? You're talking about the cattle-rustling ring?"

"Yeah. When the police became suspicious about it, the leaders threatened Garcia's family, so he took the fall for all the charges."

Rose ran in with some towels, and Maddox cut Brett's

shirt off to examine the wound. They pressed towels to the bloody area, then applied pressure.

"So where's Leo's body?" Maddox asked.

Brett gritted his teeth at the pain. "I buried him, Maddox. Just until we could find Sam."

Maddox exploded and stormed across the room. Rose offered Brett a sympathetic look, folded another towel and pressed it to his bloody shoulder.

Brett cleared his throat. "I'm sorry, Maddox, but I didn't know what else to do. I did try to preserve evidence."

"How could you preserve evidence when you buried him?" Maddox crossed his arms as he stopped pacing. "Brett, do you realize what kind of position you've put me in?"

Brett let the silence fall. He could never live up to Maddox.

"Yes, and I'm sorry," he said honestly. "But Willow was terrified, afraid they'd kill Sam because we think he witnessed Leo's murder."

Maddox pinched the bridge of his nose.

Brett's lungs squeezed for air. "There's something else."

Maddox shoved his hands through his hair. "What?"

Brett swallowed hard. He couldn't believe it himself. But it was true. "Sam is my son."

WILLOW CLENCHED THE PIECE of rope that she'd found on the floor in her hand as if that piece of cord tied her to Sam.

She picked up the stuffed animal and pressed it to her nose. Sam's sweet little-boy smell permeated the toy just as his infectious laugh and insatiable curiosity filled her with love.

Footsteps echoed outside, then the door squeaked open. Remembering they'd set a deadline before they killed her, she barely suppressed tears.

They had removed their bandannas this time, revealing harsh faces, rough with beard stubble and scars. Faces that were now imprinted in her brain.

Which meant they were definitely going to kill her.

The bigger man with beefy hands strode over to her with a gun in his hand. The taller one stepped into the room with his phone.

The bigger guy grabbed her by her hair and jammed the weapon to her head. Willow cried out at the force, but froze when she felt the cold barrel at her temple.

Were they going to kill her now?

BRETT GRITTED HIS TEETH as the doctor removed the bullet, then cleaned the wound and stitched his shoulder.

"I didn't know doctors made house calls anymore." Although he knew this man had taken care of his father and had been friends with Joe McCullen.

Dr. Cumberland chuckled, but his eyes looked serious beneath his square glasses. "I usually *don't*, but this is a small town, and your brother is the sheriff."

"Yeah."

"He's a good man," the doctor said. "He takes care of this town and the people in it."

Guilt nagged at Brett. Unfortunately, Brett had put him in a terrible position.

From the doorway he heard Maddox discussing the situation with Rose. "I know he had reason," Maddox said, "but this is a mess. I have to retrieve Howard's body and have the crime scene processed."

"What about Willow?"

Maddox made a low sound in his throat. "We'll figure out a way to find her."

Dr. Cumberland handed Brett two prescription bottles. "Take these for pain when you need them. The other is an antibiotic to prevent infection."

Brett waved Maddox over. "I've already called my business manager. He should have a hundred thousand ready for me by morning."

Maddox scowled down at him where he lay on the couch. "Okay, but even if you give them the money, they may still kill Willow."

Brett clenched the pill bottles in one hand. "I won't let that happen."

Maddox studied him for a long moment while Rose watched, her expression concerned. "I want these guys," Maddox said. "Leo Howard was a crook. He was the leader of a cattle-rustling operation across the state. Our town isn't the first one he hit."

"Willow didn't know anything about it," Brett said earnestly.

"I don't doubt that. But he even stole from Horseshoe Creek, Brett. So this is personal."

More personal to Brett because the man had threatened Willow and Sam.

"Do you know who Leo was working with?" Maddox asked.

Brett thought hard. "There was a man named Wally Norman who was questioned about the cattle rustling."

Maddox nodded. "Yeah. Norman went to prison later on other charges. I think his partner was a man named Jasper Day. Day disappeared after Norman was locked up. I suspect he was lying low until the heat died down and he could get his hands on his share."

"I think Boyle Gates might have been involved, too," Brett said. "Willow and I talked to him, but he threw us out."

"Gates?" Maddox pulled his hand down his chin. "I wondered how that SOB grew his spread so quickly. Probably filled it with stolen cattle."

"He's smart, though," Brett said. "If he's involved, he helped set Gus Garcia up to take the fall." He tried to sit up, but he swayed slightly. Maddox steadied him, and Brett set the pills on the table. He didn't intend to take anything to impair his judgment. He needed a clear head to save Willow.

"I'll send a team to process Willow's house," Maddox said. "If we can match prints to whoever was there, maybe we can use it to track down the men who have Willow. Knowing their identities may lead us to a location where they're holding her."

Maddox reached for his phone. "I'll also get my deputy looking into Day's and Norman's whereabouts."

Brett started to thank Maddox, but his phone buzzed. His shoulder throbbed as he shifted and dug it from his jacket pocket. A text.

Fear ripped through him at the sight of the photo of Willow with the gun to her temple. Below the picture, the kidnapper had typed a message.

Twenty-four hours or she's dead.

Chapter Eighteen

Brett wanted to punch something. If those jerks hurt Willow, he'd *kill* them.

Maddox yanked on his jacket. "I'm meeting my head CSI guy, Hoberman, at Willow's. If the kidnappers left prints, we'll find them and get an ID."

Brett gripped the edge of the sofa to stand. "I'll go with you."

Maddox laid a hand on Brett's shoulder. "No, Brett. Let me do my job. You aren't going to be any good to anyone, if you don't get some rest."

Maddox leaned over and planted a kiss on Rose's lips. "I'll be back later."

"Be careful," Rose said softly.

Maddox's eyes darkened as he kissed her again, and Brett looked away.

He'd always seen his brother as the strong one, the one who didn't need anyone, but watching him with Rose gave him a glimpse of another side.

Maddox was just as vulnerable as he and Ray had been. Only Maddox had been the oldest, and his father had relied on him to be strong for his little brothers.

No wonder Maddox had resented the two of them when they let him down.

Mama Mary appeared at the door with Sam by her side. The gleam in the older woman's eyes told Brett all he needed to know. She'd fallen in love with the little boy at first sight.

Mama Mary was fierce and loving, had steered him back on track a few times when he'd strayed, but she always did it with a loving hand.

His heart twisted as his gaze rested on his son. His chin, those eyes, the dimple, even that cowlick reminded him of himself. And Sam looked just as lost as he had when his mother died.

But he was not going to let Sam lose Willow. Not as long as he had a breath in his body.

"Mr. Brett, he wolfed down that mac and cheese, but I believe this boy needs some sleep. I'm gonna take him upstairs. Which room do you want him in?"

Brett smiled at Mama Mary and pushed himself to stand. "My room. I'll take him."

Mama Mary's eyes twinkled with understanding. "There's a box of some of your old clothes in the storage room. I bet I could find some pajamas in there that would fit Sam."

"That would be great." Brett's shoulder throbbed as he made his way over to Sam, but he ignored the pain. "Come on, buddy. I'll show you my room."

Sam gave Brett a brave nod and slipped his small hand into Brett's.

Emotions flooded Brett.

A pity that now he'd come home, Brett's father was gone. And that Sam would never know his grandfather.

Sam tightened his fingers inside Brett's palm, and he squeezed his son's hand, amazed at the protective instincts that surged to life.

He would not let his kid down.

Together they climbed the steps, Brett walking slower to accommodate Sam's shorter stride. When they reached the landing, he took Sam to the last room on the right, his old bedroom.

Sam's eyes widened when he entered. Brett felt a sense of pride at the fact that his father had left all his rodeo posters on the walls. Men who'd been heroes to Brett and inspired his drive to join the circuit.

"Did you go to all those rodeos?" Sam asked.

Brett grinned. "Every last one. My daddy took me when I was little. And I'll take you."

Sam looked up at him in awe. "I wanna go, but Mommy always said no."

Brett stooped down to Sam's eye level and rubbed his arm. "Well, maybe together we can change her mind." Although hurt and anger with Willow gnawed at him— she'd deprived him of the first four years of Sam's life.

He pushed aside his own feelings, though. Sam would have to come first.

"You really think she'll let me come to one of your rodeos?"

To *one* of his? "I promise we'll work something out. Maybe I can teach you some tricks one day. Would you like that?"

Sam bobbed his head up and down, fighting a yawn.

Mama Mary appeared with a pair of flannel pajamas with superheroes on them. "I think these will fit."

Brett took them from her and thanked her. "Will these do, little man?"

Sam nodded and began to peel off his jeans. Brett squatted down to help him change, worried as he looked for bruises on the boy. "Sam, I know you were scared of those bad men. Did they hurt you?"

Sam pulled on the pajamas. "They locked me in that dark room and wouldn't let me out."

The quiver in his voice tore at Brett. He helped Sam slide on the pajama shirt, then folded down the quilt, and Sam crawled into bed. Then he sat down beside him and tucked the covers up over Sam.

"Do you know where you were? Was it a house or a barn? Was it in town or on a farm somewhere?"

Sam sniffed. "It was a house, but the windows was nailed shut."

Anger made Brett clench his jaw. "When you looked out the window, what did you see? Another building? Cows or horses?"

Sam twisted the sheet with his fingers. "Woods. There was trees and trees everywhere."

Brett sighed. "How about noises? Did you hear anything nearby? Maybe a train or cars? Or a creek?"

Sam scrunched his nose in thought. "I can't remember. I just heard that big man's mean voice. He tolded me to eat this gross sandwich, but I didn't want it, I wanted Mommy. And he got mad…"

Sam's voice broke and tears filled his eyes.

Brett held his breath. "What did he do when he got mad?"

"He yelled and throwed the food, and then he shut the door and locked me back up."

Brett hated the bastard more than he'd hated anyone in his life, but he softened his tone. "It's over now, little man. You'll never have to see those men again."

Sam collapsed into his arms again, and Brett rocked him back and forth, soothing him until the little boy's breathing steadied. He eased him back down on the bed and tucked him in again.

Sam's sleepy eyes drifted to the shelf, and Brett saw the stuffed pony he'd slept with as a boy. He took it down and handed it to Sam.

"This was my best friend when I was your age. His name is Lucky. He gets lonely up here. Can he sleep with you?"

Sam nodded, then took the pony, rolled to his side and tucked it under his arm. Brett planted a kiss on his head, his heart filled with overwhelming love.

"Night, little man."

Tomorrow he had to bring Willow home to his son.

But Willow hadn't told him about Sam, because she obviously thought he wouldn't make a good father.

How would she feel about letting him be part of Sam's life now?

WILLOW STRUGGLED AND FOUGHT to untie her hands and feet. Her fingers and wrists were raw, her nails jagged from trying to tear the rope in two. Finally, she fell into an exhausted sleep just before dawn.

But she dreamed Leo was standing over her with blood spewing from his chest while he held a gun against Sam's head. She motioned for Sam to stay still and begged Leo to let him go, but he waved the gun at her and ordered her to get on her knees and crawl outside.

Terrified for Sam, she did as he said. He shoved and kicked her until she reached the grave he'd dug for her. A sliver of moonlight illuminated the deep hole where snakes hissed and crawled along the edges, their tongues flicking out as if waiting to take a bite out of her.

Then Leo kicked her hard and she fell, tumbling down,

fighting and clawing as she tasted dirt and the snakes slithered over her body and bit her, poison shooting through her blood as she screamed.

A man's loud voice boomeranged through the room as he burst through the door. Willow jerked upright, disoriented.

Reality quickly interceded as he rammed his face into hers. "Shut up or I'll shut you up."

Willow bit her tongue. She'd obviously been screaming in her sleep.

She sucked in a breath and stared at him, determined not to show fear.

Tense seconds passed as he glared at her, daring her to make a sound.

More footsteps, then the thinner man appeared. "We need to set up the meet."

"I'll handle it."

Willow shivered as they slammed the door and left her tied up and alone again. Terrified they'd kill her even if Brett found the money, she started to work on the knots again.

If she could just free herself, when one of them came in again, maybe she could get past him and run.

BRETT DOZED FOR a couple of hours, but couldn't sleep for worrying about Willow. Every hour that passed intensified his fear that he wouldn't be able to save her.

He called first thing about the money, and his manager said all he had to do was pick it up at the bank in Pistol Whip. Brett took a quick shower and checked on Sam, but he was still sleeping, so he grabbed a cup of coffee and breakfast.

Maddox came in, looking tired and stressed to the hilt.

"My manager called. I'm meeting him at the bank to pick up the cash he liquidated for me," Brett told him.

Maddox accepted a cup of coffee from Mama Mary, then joined Brett at the table. "We found prints at Willow's. Jasper Day's and Wally Norman's. Norman escaped prison last week. He shanked a guard and killed him, then took his uniform to escape. We believe he contacted Day and they came hunting Howard."

"And when Leo refused to give them their share of the profit from the stolen cattle, they killed him."

"Exactly."

"And Willow and Sam got caught up in it because she married the jerk." Brett grimaced. She wouldn't have if he'd stayed around.

But you didn't. You left her alone and pregnant.

That realization made him feel like a heel. While Willow had been raising their little boy, he'd been sleeping around and smiling at cameras.

It was a wonder she didn't hate him.

"Hoberman will let me know if they turn up anything else useful. But finding those prints is enough to obtain a warrant for the men. I need Howard's body, though."

Brett stood and pushed his chair back. "All right, I'll show you where he is." He poked his head in the kitchen and called Mama Mary's name. "I have to go with Maddox. Will you take care of Sam this morning?"

"Of course. Rose is here, too. She loves kids and Sam knows her from when Willow stopped in at her store."

"Tell her I said thanks. We'll be back in a bit."

He grabbed his jacket and followed Maddox to his SUV.

"I wish you'd come to me before," Maddox said.

Brett winced as his stitches pulled. "I'm sorry, Maddox. I didn't want to put you on the spot."

"Didn't want to put me on the spot?" Maddox said gruffly. "You don't think burying a body and covering up a crime put me on the spot?"

"I know it did," Brett said. "But I couldn't let anything happen to Sam."

Maddox cut his look toward him. "Did you know he was yours?"

Pain rocked through Brett. "Not until we rescued him, and I saw him for myself."

Maddox mumbled something low beneath his breath. "He is definitely yours," he finally said with a small smile.

Pride ballooned in Brett's chest. "He is, isn't he?"

A silent understanding passed between them. Sam would be raised a McCullen from now on.

"Where is the grave?" Maddox asked.

Brett pointed to the east and gave him exact directions. Maddox had the ME and Hoberman waiting to meet them, and a few minutes later, Brett walked the ground and showed him the grave.

The CSI team began to dig, turning the damp earth, and Brett checked his watch.

He had less than twenty-four hours now to save Willow.

WILLOW'S SHOULDERS AND FINGERS ached from twisting and turning, and fresh tears of frustration threatened. She couldn't work the damn knot free.

The door opened again, and the thinner of the men appeared with a plate of scrambled eggs on it. He set a bottle of water beside it.

"I have to go to the bathroom," Willow said. Maybe there would be something in the bathroom she could use as a weapon.

He cursed, but gave a little nod, then jerked her up from the bed. "I can't walk," Willow said. "Please untie me so I can use the bathroom and eat."

His beady eyes met hers. "If you try to run, we'll kill you."

Fear nearly choked her, but she whispered that she understood. "I won't run. Brett will get you the money. I know he will."

"He'd better. We're out of patience."

He removed a knife from his pocket and cut the ropes. She shook her hands free, then wiggled her toes as he untied her feet. He gestured toward the hall, and she ducked in and used the facility, then did a quick desperate search for a razor or pair of scissors. Anything to defend herself.

But the cabinet was empty, the bathroom dingy and old, as if the house had been vacant for a long time.

That would make it harder for Brett to find her. She'd already looked out the window and realized they were off the grid and surrounded by woods.

The man pounded on the door and she opened it, trying to play meek as she glanced to the living area and kitchen. She didn't see the bigger man, so decided that he might be gone.

Getting away from one man would be easier than two.

He grabbed her arm, but she lifted her knee and kicked him in the groin. He doubled over and yelped in pain, and she ran toward the kitchen. She spotted a kitchen knife and grabbed it, then flung open the front door.

Cold wind assaulted her, then a man's fist came toward her face. She tried to scream as the man behind her yanked her hair, but her jaw screamed with pain from the blow the bigger guy had landed.

Another blow to her shoulder blade and she dropped the knife and crumpled, writhing in pain. The bigger guy hauled her up over his shoulder, and the world tilted and spun as he carried her outside.

A second later, he opened the trunk and threw her in. Her head hit something hard, a tire iron maybe, and she saw stars.

"I warned you what would happen if you tried to run," the thinner man snarled.

The trunk door slammed shut, pitching her into darkness. She tried to stay conscious, but nausea flooded her.

The last thing she thought before the car engine started and the car jerked away was that they were going to kill her and bury her just as she'd done Leo.

Except they'd do it out here in the middle of nowhere where no one would ever find her.

Chapter Nineteen

Brett's life flashed behind his eyes as he watched the men digging up Leo Howard's body.

A month ago, *hell*, two weeks ago, he'd been grinning for the cameras, at the height of his career, with his future bright in front of him. His agent had even suggested him for a part in a Western movie.

Now he'd not only discovered he had a son but he'd become an accessory to a murder and might be facing charges of tampering with evidence and covering up a crime.

Instead of riding for a living or starring in a movie, he might soon be sitting in a cell.

The plastic he'd wrapped around Leo came into view as the diggers dumped wet soil beside the grave. One of them paused when his shovel hit something. "He's here."

Brett breathed out in relief. For a fraction of a second, he'd actually been afraid that someone might have discovered Howard's body and moved him.

Maddox angled his head toward him. "You wrapped him in plastic?"

"And a rug." Brett grimaced. "I tried to preserve him as best I could."

Maddox motioned for the men to continue while he stepped aside. "Tell me exactly how you found him."

Brett inhaled sharply. "I can do better. I took a picture," Brett said. "I was planning to tell you everything once Sam was safe."

Maddox muttered a low sound. "All right. Let's see."

Brett pulled his phone from his pocket and accessed the picture. "Willow said Howard picked Sam up from a neighbor's then brought him home. We think the men must have been following him or watching the house, and confronted him about the money. When he refused to give it up, they shot him in the chest and took Sam."

Maddox studied the picture. "I'll have forensics process his body and compare evidence from the house to corroborate her story." His brows furrowed. "Did Howard have visitation with Sam?"

"I don't think so. Willow said he didn't want to be a father." Maybe because he'd known Sam wasn't his. Had Howard resented that fact? Had he taken his temper out on Sam?

"Then why did Leo pick Sam up and take him back to the house?"

Brett stewed over that. "Maybe he knew his partners were after him, and he intended to use Sam as leverage."

The breeze picked up dead leaves and dirt, scattering them at his feet. Brett rubbed his hands together against the chilly wind.

"What did Sam tell you about that night?" Maddox asked.

Brett swallowed hard. "Nothing. I...didn't ask him about it. I figured he'd been through enough."

The diggers had uncovered the length of Howard's body along with the bag of bedding. Two of the men climbed in the grave to hoist him from the hole where they'd laid him in the ground.

"I understand why you don't want to upset Sam, but he might have seen where Howard stashed that cash."

Brett's pulse pounded. He hated to make Sam relive that horrible day.

But if he'd seen where Leo hid the cash, he had to talk to him.

Willow's life depended on it.

Claustrophobia threatened to completely panic Willow. She was suffocating in the trunk of this car.

The constant rumbling and bumping over rocky roads intensified her headache and made her nauseous.

She reminded herself to breathe in and out and remain calm. Brett would bring the money and rescue her. And if he didn't…he'd take care of Sam.

The car finally jerked to a stop, brakes squealing. The sudden change in movement propelled her across the car trunk, and she rolled into the side. Doors slammed.

The men were getting out.

Terrified they'd carried her someplace in the wilderness to kill her and leave her body, she frantically ran her bound hands across the interior of the trunk. It was so dark, she couldn't see, but there had to be a release lever inside.

Although with her hands and feet tied, how in the world would she escape?

A noise sounded, then voices. "What are we going to do with her?"

"Get rid of her."

The female again. And she sounded so coldhearted.

"We need the money first."

"All right. Then do it. And kill that cowboy, too."

Willow's stomach knotted. Who was that woman?

Doris, Leo's former girlfriend? Or Eleanor, his grandmother's nurse? Maybe she'd lied and she had been involved with Leo.

"What should we do with the bodies?" one of the men asked.

"There's an old mine near here," the woman said. "Dump their bodies in there, then close up the opening so no one will ever find them."

Tears blurred Willow's eyes. If they killed her and Brett, what would happen to Sam?

BRETT WATCHED AS the medical examiner, a young woman named Dr. Lail, knelt beside Howard's body. One of the crime workers photographed the way he was wrapped in plastic and the rug, then folded those back so she could examine the body.

Brett ignored the pinch of guilt he felt over burying the man in the cold ground. Howard hadn't deserved any better.

"I'll do an autopsy," Dr. Lail said. "But judging from the gunshots, he probably bled out."

Maddox thanked her and supervised while they carried Howard's body to the ME's van to be transported to the morgue.

"We have to notify next of kin. Did he have relatives?" Maddox asked Brett.

"Father and grandmother." Brett gave him their names and addresses.

"I'll ask Deputy Whitefeather to make the notification."

"I need to go to the bank," Brett said. "Then I'll have

a talk with Sam." A talk he dreaded, but one that needed to happen.

Maddox gave a clipped nod. "Call me when you hear from the kidnappers. You aren't meeting them alone."

Worry nagged at Brett. "Maddox, if you come with me, they'll kill her."

Maddox stepped closer to him. "You can't afford not to have my help." Maddox lowered his voice. "Trust me for once, little brother. They won't know I'm there. But you could be walking into a trap. What would happen to Sam if you and Willow both got killed?"

A sick knot thickened Brett's throat. But his answer was immediate. "I'd want you and Rose to raise Sam."

Maddox's gaze met his, a sea of emotions in his eyes. "Of course I would raise him, he's a McCullen, but we aren't going to let anything happen, Brett. Not if we work together."

It had been a long time since they'd worked together on anything. But Sam and Willow were more important than any petty problem they'd had between them.

So he followed Maddox to the SUV, and they drove into town. Brett went in the bank while Maddox walked across the street to the jail to talk to his deputy about making the death notification.

Brett spotted his business manager, Frank Cotton, waiting in a chair outside the bank president's office. Cotton stood and greeted him with a worried expression, one hand clutching a leather bag.

"Are you going to tell me what this is about now?" Cotton asked worriedly.

Brett motioned for him to keep quiet and they moved against the wall. "I'm sorry, but I can't."

Cotton tugged at his tie. "Listen, if you're in trouble

with one of those rodeo groupies, just tell me and I'll make it go away."

Brett jerked his head back. "What are you suggesting?"

"I'm here to do whatever you need, Brett. If you want a girl run off, I'm your man. If you need a lawyer to, say… draw up a confidentiality agreement or adoption papers for a kid, or pay for an abortion, I'll handle it. We won't let anything stand in the way of your career."

Brett stared at him, disturbed by the offer. At one time, his career had been all that mattered. But now he didn't give a damn about it.

All that mattered was Willow and Sam.

And he'd just reconnected with Maddox. Granted they still had things to work out—whether or not Maddox would arrest him—but he wanted to be part of Maddox's life.

And part of Horseshoe Creek.

"Thanks," he told Cotton. "But I'm not paying off a girl. If I need a lawyer, I'll let you know."

He took the leather bag, then glimpsed inside. Cash, just as he'd requested. "Just keep this between us, Cotton."

"Of course."

Brett turned to leave. "Your agent's been calling," Cotton said. "She wants to talk about your schedule this spring."

"I'll get in touch with her," Brett said.

He stepped outside the bank and started to cross the street, but a truck whizzed by and he jumped back as a bullet flew toward him.

Chapter Twenty

Brett ducked behind a pole, just as another bullet whizzed by his head. Who was shooting at him?

He tried to get a look at the driver, but the truck roared down the road in a cloud of exhaust. Then someone slammed something hard against the back of his head, and he stumbled and went down. He tried to hold on to the bag of cash, but someone snatched it from his hands and raced away.

"Everyone get down!" Maddox yelled as he jogged from across the street, his gun drawn, his gaze sweeping the area for the shooter.

A few locals on the street screamed and darted in different directions. Brett pushed to his hands and stood, cursing as he hunted for the person who'd just stolen the cash. But he'd come out of nowhere and disappeared just as quickly.

Maddox was breathing hard, his gaze still surveying the street as he approached Brett. "Are you hit?"

"No. The shooter drove off, but another guy punched me and stole the money."

Maddox pivoted again. "The shooter was a decoy meant to distract you so the other man could sneak up behind."

"Yeah, and he succeeded."

"Did you get a look at either one of them?"

"No, not really. The license plate on the truck was missing. The one who took the money was big and wore a hoodie."

Brett's manager stepped from the bank, looking terrified. "Brett, man, are you all right?"

"Yeah, but he stole the money." Brett scraped his hand through his hair, frustrated. "I can't believe this is happening."

Maddox narrowed his eyes at the manager. "Did you see anything?"

The tall man fiddled with his bolo tie. "No, I heard the gunshot, and like everyone in the bank, we dropped to the floor and hid. We thought someone was coming in to rob the bank."

"It had to be the bastards who have Willow," Brett said. "They must have followed me here, and decided to take the cash and run."

His heart stuttered. Which meant that they might have given up on the other money and killed Willow.

AN HOUR LATER, Brett entered the farmhouse. Anxiety churned in his gut. Maddox had canvassed everyone in the bank, the street and business owners, but no one had seen anything.

Once the first shot had rent the air, panic had set in. It was a small town. The locals weren't used to high crime or random attacks…or murder.

But they would know soon enough that a kidnapping had occurred and that a man had been shot to death right here in their safe little town.

Rose greeted Maddox with a big hug and kiss. If Brett hadn't been so fraught with fear for Willow, he would have laughed at the mushy look on his big brother's face as he locked lips with her.

Sam raced in from the kitchen. "Did you get Mommy back?"

Brett's lungs squeezed for air. He'd never look at life the same way now that he had a little boy.

Maddox, Rose and Mama Mary gave him sympathetic looks.

"We were making cookies to surprise her when she comes home," Mama Mary said, wiping flour from Sam's cheek with a gentle hand.

"And Sam made her a card," Rose added with a smile.

Brett stooped down to Sam's level. "She's not with me now, but we're going to find her, little man. And she's going to love the cookies and card."

Sam's face fell into a pout. "We're making peanut butter. That's Mommy's favorite."

Emotions nearly choked Brett. He remembered that about Willow. One time she'd eaten half a dozen of Mama Mary's famous peanut butter cookies. He clasped Sam's hand in his. "Come in here with me a minute, bud. I need to talk to you."

Sam clamped his teeth over his lip, but followed him to the den. Brett wanted to wrap his arms around his son and swear to him that everything would be all right.

But he had to find Sam's mother first or he would be making empty promises.

"Sam, I'm trying to figure out where those bad men are keeping your mommy. Do you remember anything else about the place?"

"No. Just that it was dark, and it smelled bad." The little boy dropped his head and picked at the button on Brett's shirt.

"How about your daddy? What can you tell me about him?"

Sam turned his face up toward Brett. "He was mean to Mommy and he didn't want me."

The breath left Brett's lungs in a rush. He lifted Sam's chin with his thumb. He wanted to assure him that he wanted him, but that would take an explanation he didn't have time for right now. But it would happen. "You know, that's not your fault. You are a wonderful kid."

Sam simply stared at him with big frightened eyes. "Daddy didn't think so. He said I was a baby, and I was in the way."

Brett wrapped his arm around his son. He wished Leo was alive so he could kill him. "That's not true, Sam. You're very special and your mommy loves you with all her heart." *And so do I.* "I care about you, too."

Sam looked up at him. "I see why my mommy liked you when she was in school. You're nicer than Daddy. He yelled at Mommy all the time."

"That's because he was a bad man."

Sam looked down again. "But if he was bad and the other men killed him, why did they take me and Mommy?"

"Because your daddy stole money from them, and they're greedy and want it back."

"There was lots of it?" Sam said.

"Yes." Brett rubbed Sam's back. "Did you see your daddy with any money?"

He shook his head.

Brett hesitated, trying to word his questions carefully. "Daddy picked you up at your mommy's friend's house that day?"

"Yeah. I didn't wanna go with him, but Miss Gina said I should."

Brett chewed the inside of his cheek. "What happened when you and Leo got back to your house?"

Sam kept tugging at Brett's button, his little body trembling slightly. Brett rubbed Sam's back. "I know it's hard to think about, but buddy, it might help."

A long moment lapsed between them, then Sam's breath wheezed out. "We went inside, and he tolded me to hide in my room."

"What? Why?"

"He said some men followed him."

So Leo had tried to protect Sam. That was something.

"Did he have anything with him?"

Sam scrunched his nose. "Like what?"

"Maybe a briefcase or suitcase."

Sam's eyes lit up. "He gots a big gym bag and brought it in the house. Then he pushed me in the closet and shut the door and told me not to come out."

"You stayed in the closet?"

Sam nodded. "I was scared. I just wanted Daddy to go away. But he said he had to get some stuff he left with Mommy."

"Did she say what stuff?"

"No, and Mommy said she throwed the stuff he left away. But he said he hid it there. I was scared he'd get mad about that, so I didn't tell him."

Smart boy.

"After you got in the closet, what did your father do?"

Sam's finger twisted the button harder. "He took my toys out of my toy box and throwed them on the floor."

Brett imagined the scene, questions ticking in his head. He and Willow had searched the house, but what if Leo had stowed the money in that toy chest?

"Then someone busted in. I heard the door cracking,

then those awful men shouting and Daddy gots up and tried to talk to them."

Brett cradled Sam in his arms, holding him tight.

"They yelled and said ugly words, then Daddy jumped on one of them and…the gun went off."

His heart ached for his little boy. To witness a murder at such a young age was bound to affect him, maybe give him nightmares. Possibly for years to come.

He needed his mother to help him through the trauma.

He also needed a father.

"I'm sorry you had to see that, Sam, but you're very brave to tell me about it." Sam shivered, and Brett hugged him with all the love in his heart.

Then he cupped Sam's face in his hands. "I need you to be strong just a little while longer, okay?"

Sam nodded, the trust in his son's look nearly bringing Brett to his knees.

WILLOW'S BODY ACHED from being tied up and bound in the trunk of the car. She was suffocating.

But they didn't seem to be in a hurry to let her out. In fact, it had gotten quiet for a while and she thought they might have left her.

The sound of another engine roaring rent the air. Tires screeched. Then more doors slammed.

"Where have you two been?" the woman asked.

"We got that money McCullen promised."

"He found Leo's stash?" the woman asked.

"No, the money McCullen withdrew from his own funds. With that and Leo's money, we'll all be set for a long time."

"You idiot," the woman said. "He's liable to call the cops."

"And tell them what?" the man barked. "That someone stole ransom money? That he buried Leo's body? I doubt that rodeo star wants that in the papers."

"It's time for us to make the meet," the other man said. "If McCullen doesn't bring the cash Leo stole this time, let's get rid of the woman and get out of town before things heat up.

The trunk opened, and Willow clenched her teeth as the bigger guy hauled her to the ground. She stumbled, then gasped when she saw the woman.

Gina, her neighbor. The woman she'd thought was her friend.

Dear God... "Why?"

Gina gave her a nasty grin. "Because Leo was supposed to be mine. And so was this money. And with you out of the way, now it will be."

The big guy, Norman she'd heard him called, punched a number on his cell phone. It must be Wally Norman. A minute later, she heard Brett's voice.

"Hello. This is Brett McCullen."

"I'm texting you an address. If you want to see the woman again, bring the cash and come alone."

"Let me speak to Willow first," Brett said.

Willow shuddered as the big guy pressed a gun to her temple. "Say hello, honey."

"Brett, I'm okay, just take care of Sam!"

The man jerked the phone away, then whacked her on the back of the head again and shoved her back in the trunk.

Tears caught in her throat. The drop-off was a trap.

Chapter Twenty-One

Brett left Sam to finish the cookies and card with Mama Mary and motioned for Maddox to join him in the hall. "Maddox, I received a text about the drop."

"Where?"

Brett angled the phone for Maddox to see the address. "Do you know where that is?"

Maddox shrugged. "Yeah. It's not too far from here."

"I also may know where the stolen money is."

"Where?"

"Sam said that when Leo picked him up, he had a bag with him, and that he was digging around in Sam's toy chest."

"Did you look there before?"

"I saw the chest but all that was visible was toys. Maybe he hid it under them."

"Let's go." Maddox grabbed his keys, but Brett put a hand to his brother's shoulder.

"Not in your SUV, Maddox. If they see you, they'll kill Willow."

Maddox exhaled. "You're right. We'll drive your truck."

Seconds later, they raced to Willow's house. Crime-scene tape marked the house and fingerprint dust coated everything inside.

Worse, the house smelled of death and emptiness, not like a home, but like a place where a terrible wrong had been done. Would Willow want to return here?

"The toy chest?" Maddox asked, jarring him back to the moment.

Brett pushed all thoughts aside and hurried into Sam's room. Knowing Sam was his son made the toys and posters on the wall seem more personal and they tugged at his heart.

Toys had been dumped and scattered across the floor from the toy chest. A football, toy trucks, plastic horses, a plastic bat and ball.

"You see it?" Maddox asked behind him.

"No." He quickly emptied the remaining toys, then felt along the bottom and discovered a piece of plywood. Had that board come with the toy chest?

A nail felt loose, and he pulled at it until the board loosened, then he yanked it free. "I found it!" Cash was neatly stacked and spread evenly across the bottom.

Maddox handed him the duffel bag, and Brett quickly filled it with the money.

Nerves tightened his neck and Brett watched for another ambush as he carried it out to his truck. Seconds later, Brett sped from the house.

"Listen, Brett, when we get there, I'll stay down until we see what we're dealing with."

Maddox checked his gun, and Brett grimaced. His rifle lay on the seat between them. If he needed it, he'd use it in a heartbeat.

Dark clouds rolled overhead, the wind picking up as he turned down the road into the woods. Trees shook and limbs swayed as he neared the cabin, and he searched for signs that Willow was there.

"What do you see?"

Brett squinted through the dark. "An old cabin, looks like it's been deserted for a while. I don't see anyone. One light on in the house from a back room."

"How about a vehicle?"

"A dark sedan. Tinted windows. I can't see if anyone is inside."

"Park and sit there for a minute. Wait and see if anyone comes outside."

Brett did as he said, his senses alert as he scanned the exterior of the cabin. An old weathered building sat to the right. It appeared empty, but someone could be hiding inside.

A sound to the left made him jerk his head to see what it was. A deer scampered through the woods.

He hissed a breath, then reached for the door handle. "It's time. I have to see if she's here."

Maddox caught his arm and looked up at him from the floorboard of the truck. "Be careful, Brett. This could be a setup."

He knew that.

But he had to take that chance.

He eased open the door and slid one foot from the truck. Clutching the duffel bag with the other hand, he lowered himself to the ground. He visually surveyed the area again, his stitches tugging as he slowly walked toward the cabin.

"I've got your money," he shouted.

The front door to the cabin opened, and he braced himself for gunfire. If they killed him, at least Maddox was armed and could save Willow and take her home to Sam.

WILLOW FELT DIZZY from being locked in the trunk of the car and inhaling the exhaust as they'd driven.

The car jerked to a stop, and she forced tears at bay. Crying would do no good. These people didn't care about her.

All they wanted was money.

The trunk opened, and she squinted, blinded by the sudden light. Then a cold hard hand clamped around her wrist and dragged her from the car again. She stumbled, dizzy and disoriented.

"Day should be meeting with McCullen now," the man named Norman said.

Gina gestured to the right. Willow looked around, sick when she realized that they were in the middle of nowhere.

And that Gina was pointing to an old mine. Rusted mining equipment sat discarded, piles of dirt scattered around along with metal garbage cans and tools.

"How can you do this, Gina? Sam is just an innocent little boy. He needs me."

"He'll survive," Gina said.

"Did you kill Leo?" Willow asked.

"He deserved it. He tried to betray me, just like he did Norman and Day."

"Why did Leo take Sam to my house?" Willow asked. "Why didn't he just get the money and leave?"

Gina hissed. "He knew Norman broke out of jail, and he and Day were onto him."

Hate swelled inside Willow. Leo had taken Sam with him as insurance.

"And you followed him to my house and killed him," Willow said, piecing together the most logical scenario.

"No, that was Norman," Gina said. "He said Leo attacked him."

"So when he died that day, you kidnapped Sam?"

"We earned that money the hard way." Gina waved a hand toward the mine. "And when Jasper gets back with it, we'll flee the country and live the good life."

Panic clawed at Willow. Norman reached for her and she tried to run, but with her ankles bound together, it was futile. She stumbled, then he threw her over his shoulder like a sack of potatoes and carted her toward the mine.

BRETT PAUSED AT the foot of the steps. A thin man with a goatee and tattoos on his neck appeared, a .38 pointed at Brett. Jasper Day.

"Toss the money on the porch," Day ordered. "And you'd better not try to cheat us this time."

"You're the crook and the murderer, not me."

Day's laugh boomeranged through the silence as he waved the gun. "Throw it now."

Brett clenched the bag tighter. "First, I want to see Willow."

Day shook his head. "Not going to happen. I'm calling the shots here."

Brett had a bad feeling this was going south. That Willow wasn't here. If she was dead...

"Either you bring her out here, or I walk back to the truck."

Day cursed. "You're a fool. I've got a gun pointed at your head, and you think you can bluff your way out of this."

"I don't care about the money," Brett shouted, "but I'll give my life for Willow. Now show me that she's alive."

Day's hand shook as he took a menacing step toward Brett. "Put the bag down now, McCullen. This isn't one of your rodeo games."

Brett held his ground and yelled for Willow. "Is she in there?" He gestured toward the cabin, and Day glanced sideways with a cocky grin.

Brett took advantage of that small sideways look, swung the bag and threw it with all his might. The bag slammed into Day with such force that it threw him backward. But he managed to get off a shot before he fell.

Brett dodged the bullet, then Maddox jumped from the truck and fired at Day. One bullet into Day's chest, and he crumpled to the ground with a bellow. His gun skittered to the ground beside him as the man's arm fell limp.

Brett and Maddox ran toward him, then Maddox kicked the gun away, knelt beside the bastard and handcuffed him to the porch rail. Brett started toward the house, but Maddox called his name. He was right behind him, holding Day's gun. "Take this."

Brett snatched Day's revolver and inched up to the house. Maddox motioned for him to let him enter first, and Maddox eased through the door. He glanced in all directions, then gestured for Brett to go right and he'd go left.

Brett gripped the weapon with sweaty hands and inched across the wood floor. A bedroom to the right made his heart stop. A single metal bed sat by the wall, ropes discarded on the floor, a food tray, a ratty stuffed animal...

This was where they'd held his son. And they'd probably brought Willow to the same room.

But no one was inside now. He looked for blood but didn't see any. That had to be a good sign, didn't it?

He stepped into the hall and found Maddox frowning. "There's no one here, Brett."

Fear knotted his insides. "Where is she, Maddox?"

"Let's ask Day. He'll know." Brett followed him back outside but Day was barely conscious.

Brett dropped down beside him and snatched the man by the collar. "Where did your partner take Willow?"

The man looked up at him with glazed eyes. "Doctor…" he rasped.

Brett held up his phone. "I'll call for help when you tell me where they took her."

Day spit at him. "Go to hell."

Brett lifted Day's own gun to the criminal's head. "No, that's where you're going if you don't talk."

Chapter Twenty-Two

"You won't do it," Day rasped.

"You're sure about that?" Brett said darkly. "Because that little boy you kidnapped is my son. And his mother means everything to me."

The man's eyes bulged, and he coughed up blood.

Maddox aimed his gun at the other side of Day's head. "Where is she, Day?"

"The old mine off Snakepit Road."

Brett shoved away from the man, sick to his stomach. That mine had been shut down for years. And the road was dubbed Snakepit Road because miners had complained about the hotbed of snakes in the area.

"I have to go," Brett told Maddox.

Maddox looked down at Day. They both knew he wouldn't make it, but could they just leave him?

"Go ahead. I'll call for an ambulance and be right behind you." Maddox caught his arm. "Be careful, little brother. Don't do anything stupid. Wait for me to move in."

Brett muttered that he would, although if he had to go in on his own to save Willow, they both knew he'd do it.

Without Willow and Sam, his life meant nothing.

WILLOW SHIVERED WITH cold and fear as Norman tossed her to the ground inside the mine. She'd grown accustomed to the dark trunk, but this dark cavern wreaked of decayed animals and other foul odors she didn't even want to identify.

Norman cast his flashlight around the hole where he'd put her, and she cringed at the sight of the dirt walls. He must have dragged her a half mile inside. Wooden posts that supported beams inside the mine had been built when the mine was being worked, and Norman dragged her over to one and tied her to the post. Rocks and dirt scraped her arms and jeans, the jagged edges of loose stones cutting into her side.

"I wouldn't fight it too much," he said with an ugly sneer. "These beams are old and rotting. If one comes down, the whole mine may cave in."

"Why are you warning me?" Willow demanded. "You're going to leave me here to die anyway."

His thick brows drew together in a unibrow as he looked down at her. Then he turned and left her without another word. A snake hissed somewhere in the dark, and she pressed herself against the mine wall and pulled her knees up to her chest, trying to make herself as small as possible.

Not that the snake wouldn't find her anyway.

The light faded as Norman disappeared through the mine shaft, and she dropped her head forward, fighting despair.

Brett would have no idea how to find her. She was going to die here in this hellhole, and he would never know how sorry she was that she'd kept Sam from him.

Or that she'd never stopped loving him.

BRETT SCANNED THE DIRT road and deserted mine ahead as he sped down Snakepit Road.

There were no cars, no trucks, nothing to indicate anyone was here.

Fear seized him. Had Day lied to them? Had they taken Willow somewhere else?

His tires screeched as he barreled past the sign that marked the mine and threw the truck in Park. He jumped out, shouting Willow's name as he ran toward the opening of the mine, but just as he neared it, he noticed dynamite attached to the door and some kind of trigger, as if it was set with a timer.

Terror clawed at him, and he rushed to tear the dynamite away, but he was too late. The explosion sent him flying backward against some rocks, the sound of the mine collapsing roaring in his ears.

For a moment, he was so disoriented he couldn't breathe. Dust blurred his vision. His ears rang.

But fear and reality seeped through the haze. Was Willow inside that mine? Was he too late to save her?

He shoved himself up from the ground, raking dirt and twigs from his hair and clothes as he raced back toward the opening. "Willow! Willow, are you in there?!"

He dropped to his knees and started to yank boards away, but when he did, all he found was dirt. Mounds and mounds of it…

She might be buried alive in there…

Tears clogged his eyes and throat, and he bellowed in despair. But he lurched to his feet, ran to his truck, grabbed his cell phone and punched Maddox's number.

"I'm on my way, Brett."

"Get help!" Brett shouted. "They're gone, but there

was dynamite outside the opening of the mine and it just exploded. I think Willow's inside."

A tense moment passed, then Maddox's breath rattled over the line. "I'll call a rescue crew and an ambulance," Maddox said. "Just hang in there, man."

Brett jammed the phone in his pocket and ran back toward the mine, yelling Willow's name over and over and praying she could hear.

It seemed like hours later that Maddox arrived. His brother Ray shocked him by showing up on his heels. "Just tell me what to do," Ray said, his dark eyes fierce.

"We have to get her out," Brett said. "She has to be alive."

"A crew is on its way with equipment," Maddox said. "We need an engineer, someone who knows the mine, Brett, or we could make things worse."

How in the hell could they get worse? Willow was trapped, probably fighting for her life.

Ray cleared his throat. "Let me take a look. Maybe there's another entrance. Another way inside."

Ray's calm voice offered Brett a glimmer of hope, and he followed his younger brother, hoping he was right. They walked the edge of the mine shaft following it for half a mile, searching brush and rock structures for a second entrance.

"There had to be an extra exit for safety," Ray said.

He walked ahead, climbing a hill, then disappeared down an embankment. Brett was just about to give up when Ray shouted his name. "Over here. I found it!"

He looked up and saw Ray waving him forward. The sound of trucks barreling down the graveled road rent the air, and he looked back to Maddox who was waving the rescue crew toward the site.

"I'll tell Maddox I'm going in this end and check it out," Ray said.

Brett nodded and waited until Ray went down the hill, then he dropped to his stomach and crawled inside.

He couldn't wait. Every second that passed meant Willow was losing oxygen and might die.

The mine shaft was so low at the exit that he had to slide in on his belly. He used his pocket flashlight to light the way and slithered on his stomach, dragging himself through the narrow tunnel until he reached a taller section that had been carved under rock. It was a room with supports built, giving him enough room to stand up.

"Willow! Can you hear me?"

He waved the light around the tunnel, searching for other crawl spaces, and spotted one to the left. He dropped down again, ignoring the dust and pebbles raining down on him, well aware the whole damn thing could collapse in seconds.

"Willow!" He continued to yell her name and search until finally he heard a sound.

"Willow, can you hear me? If you can, make some noise!"

Please let her be alive.

He crawled a few more feet, then reached another clearing where more supports indicated another room, although it appeared the roof had collapsed in the center. Willow must be on the other side. "Willow!"

"Brett!"

He breathed out in relief. "Hang in there, honey, I'm coming."

He started to dig with his hands, but realized tools would make the process faster, so he crawled back the way he came. It seemed to take him forever to reach the exit. He sucked in fresh air as he crawled out and raced down the hill to where the other men were starting to get set up.

"I told you to wait," Ray said.

Brett blew off his concern. "I found her. But I need a shovel or pick to dig her out."

"We've got this, Mr. McCullen," one of the rescue workers said. "It's too dangerous for you."

Why? Because he was a damn celebrity. "I don't care. I have to save her."

"They're the experts." Ray stepped up beside him. "One wrong move in there, Brett, and you could bring the whole mine down."

Maddox placed a hand on his back. "Brett, let them do their jobs. Besides, it won't help Sam if you get yourself killed."

"Who's Sam?" Ray asked.

Brett rubbed a hand down his face and began to explain to his younger brother that he had a son.

WILLOW FADED IN and out of consciousness. She couldn't breathe, couldn't find the air.

What had happened? One minute she'd been tied down here, praying Brett would find her. Then…something had exploded.

The roof had come tumbling down, rocks and dirt pummeling her. She'd tried to cover her face and head, but it had happened so quickly, and now dirt and rocks covered her. She tried to move her legs but they wouldn't budge.

Either she was paralyzed or the weight of the dirt was too heavy…

Her head lolled to the side, and she forced herself to

inhale shallow breaths to conserve air. She thought she'd heard Brett calling her name.

Or had she been hallucinating because she was so close to death?

She closed her eyes and tried to envision someone rescuing her. Pictured Brett carrying her to safety and fresh air. Saw the two of them walking with Sam in the pasture, sharing a picnic, then telling Sam that Brett was his father.

Next, Brett was proposing, promising her they'd be the family they should have been all along.

The earth rumbled, some loud noise sounded and the mine began to tremble and shake again. She closed her eyes and mouth against another onslaught of debris, but when she opened them, her head was almost completely covered, and she choked on the dirt.

WITH EVERY SECOND that ticked by, Brett thought he was going to die himself. Maddox let the rescue crew take charge of finding Willow, while he issued an APB for Wally Norman. Authorities were alerted at airports, train and bus stations, and the police in states bordering Wyoming. He even notified border patrol in Mexico and Canada, although they didn't intend to let Norman get that far. Tire marks indicated that he'd been driving a sedan, although he could ditch that anywhere. *Hell*, he could have changed vehicles already and picked up a disguise.

"We're almost through!" one of the men shouted. They'd set up a man on the outside with receivers to communicate, as the two other rescue workers crawled inside.

Brett paced by the exit, grateful when an ambulance arrived.

"I can't believe you have a kid," Ray said.

"Me either." And he'd almost lost him and Willow.

But he was grateful Maddox and Ray were here. They hadn't exactly spent any time together since he'd returned. The three of them had retreated to their separate corners, just as they had as kids.

Except now Maddox had put his job on the line for him. And Ray...well, he'd come to his aid, no questions asked.

"They've got her!" one of the men shouted.

Brett rushed to the outside of the exit, desperate to see Willow. Ray stood behind him, silent but strong, as if he'd be there to catch him if he fell apart. It was an odd feeling, one he hadn't had in a long time.

Everyone in his business and the rodeo wanted something from him, wanted to build off his fame, wanted his money, wanted a part of him. But his brothers were here, just to support him.

Their father would have been proud.

Another agonizing few minutes stretched by, but finally one of the men slowly emerged, dragging a board through the opening.

A board with Willow strapped to it.

She was so filthy and covered in dirt and bruises that he could hardly see her face.

He held his breath as he dropped to her side and raked her hair back from her cheek. Her eyes were closed, and she lay terrifyingly still. "Willow?"

He looked up at the rescue worker, desperate for good news.

The man looked worried, his expression bleak as his partner emerged from the mine.

Brett cradled Willow's hand in his as the men lifted the board to carry her to the ambulance.

"Get the paramedics!" one of the rescue workers yelled.

More shouts and two medics ran toward them.

Brett whispered Willow's name again. "Willow, please wake up, baby. Sam and I need you." Suddenly he felt a tiny something in his hand. Willow's fingers twitching, grasping for him.

Brett choked on tears as she finally opened her eyes and looked at him.

THE NEXT TWO HOURS were chaos. Brett rode with the ambulance to the hospital, whispering promises to Willow that he wouldn't leave her side. She was weak and had suffered bruises and contusions and possibly a concussion. She also needed oxygen and rest.

"Gina," she whispered. "My friend."

"What? You want me to call her?"

"No. She was in on it," Willow rasped. "She was helping Leo. She told Norman to kill me."

"I'll tell Maddox to issue an APB for her, too."

She broke into a coughing spell, and he helped her sip some water. "Sam."

"He's home with Mama Mary," Brett said. "I called and told them you're all right. I'll bring Sam to visit tomorrow."

Willow clung to his hand. "No, I'll go home and be with him." A tear slid down her cheek. "Only I don't know where home is. I can't go back to that house where Leo was killed."

"Shh." Brett stroked her cheek. "Don't worry about anything tonight, Willow."

She breathed heavily, then looked up at him again. "About Sam, Brett…"

"I told you not to worry about anything," he whispered. "We'll find a way to work it out."

Although, as she faded into sleep again, Brett laid his head against the edge of the bed and clung to her hand. She had kept Sam from him once and bitterness still gnawed at him for what he'd missed.

Still…he loved Willow and wanted to be a father to his son.

But would Willow want him now after he'd let her down all those years ago?

Chapter Twenty-Three

Willow lapsed in and out of consciousness all night. She dreamt she was dying and that Brett saved her. She dreamt that he left her and walked away and was marrying someone else.

Every time she looked up, though, Brett was there. He stayed by her bed holding her hand and reassuring her she was all right. He fell asleep in the chair. He gave her water when she was thirsty and wiped her forehead with a cool cloth and held her when she woke screaming that she was drowning in dirt.

But sometime in the early morning, she stirred and heard him on the phone.

"Yes, Ginger, I know the movie offer is a big deal." Pause. "I realize it's a cowboy part, that it would take me to a new level."

Willow closed her eyes, her heart aching. Brett was already planning to leave her just as he had before. Except this time when he left, he would know he had a son.

She steeled herself to accept his decision. She would no more trap him now than she had five years ago.

And she'd never let him see how much he'd hurt her.

BRETT HAD NEVER prayed so much in his damn life.

Even when they'd finally moved Willow from the ER into a room, he'd been terrified she'd stop breathing.

Her screams of terror had wrenched his heart.

The nurse checked her vitals, the doctor appeared to examine her and Brett stepped out to call home. Maddox answered on the first ring.

"How is she?"

"All right. How's Sam?"

"Asking about her, but Mama Mary and Rose are feeding him funny-face pancakes and he's gobbling them up."

Brett had always loved Mama Mary's funny-face pancakes. Especially the chocolate-chip eyes.

"There's more. We caught Norman and Gina. They're being transported back here to face charges."

"Thank God." He swallowed hard. "What about me and Willow?"

"I explained everything to the local judge. And this morning I arrested Boyle Gates. Seems Day spilled Gates's involvement and the way they framed Garcia. Gus is going to be released. I offered him a job here on the ranch, so he and his wife and daughter can have a fresh start."

"You've been busy."

"I just like to see justice done. And Garcia needs a second chance."

Maddox was a stand-up guy. "Dad would be proud of you."

"He'd be proud of you, too, little brother."

"I don't know about that. Willow would never have gotten in this mess if I'd stuck around."

A second passed. "Maybe not. But that was then. What are you going to do *now*?"

Brett glanced back at the hospital room. "I'm going to fix things, if I can."

He ended the call and went in to see Willow. She was sitting up in bed, but her expression was guarded, her eyes flat.

"How are you feeling?"

"I need to go home and be with Sam."

"I'll tell Mama Mary to bring you some clothes and if the doctor releases you, I'll drive you back to the cabin."

Willow shook her head. "I can't go back there, Brett. Not with you." She hesitated and averted her eyes. "Our time has passed."

Brett's lungs squeezed for air. She wasn't even going to give him a chance?

He couldn't accept that. "Willow, you've been through a terrible ordeal. We all have. I was terrified that I'd lost you. Maybe you blame me for that, for everything."

She slipped from bed, hugging the hospital gown around her. "Don't, Brett. I'd appreciate it if you'd ask Mama Mary or Rose to bring me some clothes so I can shower and get Sam. Then we'll find a place to stay on our own."

Brett watched with a hollow feeling in his gut as she stepped into the bathroom and shut the door.

He phoned Mama Mary, and she agreed to bring Sam and some clothes. Willow must have gotten soap and shampoo from the nurse. By the time she was finished showering in the bathroom and in a clean hospital gown, Mama Mary was there.

She knocked and peeked in the door with a smile. When Willow saw Sam, her face lit up. She opened her arms and he fell into them.

The two of them hugged like they hadn't seen each other for years.

Suddenly Brett felt like the outsider. Like an intruder who didn't belong.

He stepped outside to gather his composure, his emotions in a tailspin. He'd thought he and Willow had gotten close again, that she had feelings for him. But had he hurt her too much for her to forgive him? Didn't she want him to be part of Sam's life?

Mama Mary patted his shoulder. "I'm sorry, son. But Willow asked me to drive her to a hotel. I don't understand what's going on between you two, but she probably just needs some time."

Or maybe he'd lost his chance years ago and Willow would never love him again.

THREE DAYS LATER, Willow was still miserable. She and Sam were temporarily staying in a small apartment above the fabric store in town. The lady who commissioned several of her quilts had been generous, and Willow had jumped at the chance to be close to town. Somehow she felt safer knowing the sheriff's office was down the street.

But she missed Brett, and so did Sam.

She pushed the boxes of pictures that she'd brought with her into the closet. *Out of sight, out of mind.*

Except she couldn't get Brett out of her mind. Which made her furious at herself.

Brett was probably packing to leave for his big movie role. Planning a hot, sexy, wild night with that woman, Ginger.

She would be only a whisper of a memory to him once he got to Hollywood and the sophisticated women who were probably dying to have a cowboy in their bed swarmed after him.

Sam lined his toy ponies on the floor, then pretended to gallop them around the pasture. How could she not look at her son and see Brett?

Worse, she didn't know what to say to Sam. How to explain why they weren't staying at the ranch anymore.

They still hadn't told Sam that Brett was his father. Brett hadn't pushed either.

Maybe he wanted it that way. If that was the case, it was best that Sam stay in the dark.

Determined to distract herself, she sorted through the mail. A white envelope written in calligraphy caught her eye. She opened the envelope, surprised to find a wedding invitation to Maddox and Rose's wedding.

It was to be a simple affair, just family and a few friends, and would take place at Horseshoe Creek.

She tucked the invitation back in the envelope, her heart aching. She wasn't family, but Sam was. Only he had no idea that he belonged to the McCullens.

Could she deprive him of that?

BRETT HAD TRIED to take Mama Mary's advice and give Willow time. But every day without her and Sam in his life was so painful he could barely breathe.

But today was his brother's wedding, and of course it made him think of Willow and the wedding they'd never had. The one they should have had.

The one he wanted.

But after all Maddox had done for him, he had to put his brother first today.

Chaos filled the house as Mama Mary ushered everyone around. The caterers, florist, the vendor with the tables and tent they'd ordered for the lawn.

And of course, him and Ray.

She'd insisted they wear long duster jackets and bolo ties, since they were standing up for Maddox.

Brett was his best man.

He felt humbled and honored and so damn glad to be home at Horseshoe Creek that he never wanted to leave.

The realization hit him, and he stepped into his old room and called his agent to tell her he was going to refuse the movie deal. He was done putting on shows.

He would stick around here and help Maddox run the ranch. And one day he would win Willow back.

Determination renewed, he left a message for Ginger, then strode down the steps. Maddox looked nervous but happier than any man had a right to be. He'd invited the ranch hands, Gus Garcia and his family, and Deputy Whitefeather, who seemed standoffish to him and Ray, though he didn't have time to contemplate the reason.

The weather had warmed today, a breeze stirring the trees, but the sun was shining, the flowers Rose had chosen dotting the landscape with color.

"Come on, brothers. It's time," Maddox said.

Brett and Ray followed Maddox and found the guests already seated in white chairs by the creek. Mama Mary and Rose had created an altar of flowers between two trees where Rose stood, looking like an angel.

The smile she gave Maddox sparkled with love.

Maddox was a damn lucky man.

Ray fidgeted with his tie, as if it was choking him, but Brett pasted on his camera-ready smile. As he and Ray took their places, he glanced at the guests and saw Willow and Sam sitting by Mama Mary.

His heart nearly stopped. She looked so beautiful in that pale green dress with her long hair billowing around her shoulders. Gone were the bruises and dirt from the mine, although her eyes still held remnants of the horror.

Was she still having those bad dreams? Who was holding her at night and soothing her when she did?

How about Sam? He looked handsome in that Western shirt and bolo tie. It was almost like Brett's. But did he have nightmares at night, too?

He was so enamored with watching the two of them that for a moment the ceremony faded to a blur and he imagined that he and Willow were the ones declaring their love.

Ray poked him. "The ring, brother."

He jolted back to the present and handed Maddox the simple gold band he'd bought for Rose.

Maddox and Rose exchanged vows, then kissed and cheers erupted. He and Ray turned to congratulate them, yet all Brett could do was wish he and Willow were the ones getting married today.

Champagne, whiskey, beer and wine flowed at the reception on the lawn by the creek that the ranch had been named for, and he took a shot of whiskey for courage, then went to talk to Willow before she could run.

He wanted her and Sam, and he didn't intend to back down without a fight.

He found her standing with Sam by the creek. She was trying to teach him how to skip rocks, but she had it all wrong.

He picked up a smooth stone, squeezed Sam's shoulder and then showed him the McCullen way. Willow's gaze met his, sadness and regret flickering in the depths.

But for a brief second, he saw desire spark. Enough

desire to warm his heart and give him a second jolt of courage.

Sam squealed when the water rippled at his next attempt, and Brett patted his back. "Good job."

Sam stooped to collect more stones, and Brett brushed Willow's arm. "You look beautiful tonight."

A sweet blush stained her cheeks. "I thought you'd be gone by now," she finally said.

Brett shrugged. "Maybe I don't want to go."

She gestured toward Maddox and Rose who were dancing in the moonlight while the wedding guests watched. "I'm sure Maddox is glad you stayed for the ceremony."

"That's not the reason I stayed."

Sam picked up another stone, raised his hand and sailed it across the creek.

"Good job, Sam."

Sam grinned. "You still gonna let me ride your horses like you promised?"

Willow laid a hand on Sam's shoulder. "Sam, honey, we'll get you lessons somewhere. Brett is a busy man. He has to leave soon. He's going back to the rodeo, and he's going to star in a movie."

Brett's smile faltered. "Where did you get that idea?"

Willow leaned down to speak to Sam for a minute. "If you want a cookie, you can go get one now."

Sam bounced up and down with a grin and ran toward the table with the cookie tray.

"I heard you on the phone with that woman, Ginger. I'm sure she's waiting for you with open arms."

Brett chuckled. Was that a note of jealousy in Willow's voice? "Ginger is my publicist and agent, Willow. Nothing more."

She averted her gaze. "Well, I'm sure there will be lots of women in Hollywood."

"What if I don't want Hollywood?"

"I know you, Brett, you always had big dreams. You belong in the limelight, not here."

Brett squared his shoulders. "You don't want me to be around Sam?"

"That's not what I said."

He cleared his throat, changing the subject. He had to get this out in the open. Had to know the truth. "Why didn't you tell me about him, Willow?"

She closed her eyes for a brief second, her breath unsteady. When she opened them, he saw regret and some other emotion that he couldn't define.

"Why, Willow? Because you didn't think I'd be a good father?"

"*What?* No." Her eyes flared. "You wanted to leave."

"You didn't give me a chance to choose the right thing."

"*The right thing?* What was that, Brett? What was I supposed to do, tell you I was pregnant and trap you into staying?" She waved her hand around the air. "You would have resented me for asking you to give up your dreams and it would have killed any love you had for me."

He hated to admit it, but she had a point. He had been young and restless. And he might have felt trapped.

But he'd changed. Grown up. Seen what was out there and figured out what was important in his life. "I'm sorry I wasn't the man you wanted, that you needed back then."

Sadness tinged her eyes. "I'm sorry that I didn't tell you about Sam, but I honestly didn't want to hold you back. Then you would have hated me, Brett, and I couldn't have stood that."

"I could never hate you, Willow." He lifted her hand into his. Hers was trembling. Or maybe it was his.

"I'm sorry for so many things, for not being here for you, for leaving so that you let Leo into your life, and into Sam's."

"That's not your fault," Willow said. "That was my mistake."

Brett kissed the palm of her hand. "We both made mistakes, but Sam is not one of them. And I'm not going back to the rodeo or starring in a movie."

Willow's eyes widened in surprise. "You're not?"

"No." Brett's heart swelled with love for her and his brothers and the land he'd once called home. He'd had to leave it to know how much it meant to him.

"I already told my agent, I'm done with rodeo, and that I don't want the movie deal."

"But Brett, it is a good opportunity for you."

"Maybe. But… I've wasted enough time. I want to be here."

"In Pistol Whip?"

He nodded. "I'm going to help Maddox run Horseshoe Creek." He grinned just thinking about his plans. "Being here will give me more time for you and Sam." He glanced at Sam, his heart nearly overflowing. "I promised him I'd teach him to ride."

Tears glittered on Willow's eyelashes. "He'll like that. That is, if that's what you want."

Brett took her other hand in his and drew her closer, then looked into her eyes. "What I want is *you*, Willow." He kissed her fingers one by one. "I love you and always have."

"But you're a wanderer, Brett. A dreamer."

"We can wander together," he said. "And I have lots

of dreams." He pulled her to him and kissed her. "I've been dreaming all week about marrying you and the three of us living on the ranch. That cabin is pretty small and Maddox and Rose are in the big house, but I have enough money to build us a house of our own."

"But you gave up your money to get Sam back."

Brett shrugged. "That was just a small part of my savings. Besides, when Maddox made the arrests, he retrieved the stolen money. A portion of it will go to Eleanor, who has agreed to continue caring for Leo's grandmother."

"What about her husband?"

"I told Maddox not to bother pressing charges. The man wasn't bad, just desperate."

"That's generous of you, Brett."

He shrugged. "I guess I understand what desperation can do to a man. The rest of the cash will be divided among the ranchers the men stole from. He also recovered my hundred K."

Willow licked her lips. "I...don't know what to say, Brett."

"Say you love me, Willow," he said huskily. "That you'll be my wife."

Willow's mouth spread into the smile that he remembered as a young man; the adoring, loving one she'd reserved only for his eyes.

She looped her arms around his neck. "I love you, Brett. I never stopped." She stood on tiptoes and kissed him tenderly. "But you're giving me so much. What can I give you?"

"You've already given me the greatest gift of all. A son."

Willow toyed with the ends of his hair. "He is pretty

special. I think he looks like his dad. He acts like him, too, sometimes."

Brett chuckled. "Then we're in for trouble."

Her look grew serious. "Are you sure, Brett? You won't get tired of being here? Of me?"

"I could never get tired of you, Willow. You're the only woman I've ever loved." He nuzzled her neck. "And there is one more thing you can give me."

Willow laughed softly. "What?"

He laughed and kissed her again. "A little girl."

Willow smiled and kissed him again, passion sparking between them just as tender and erotic as it always was when he touched her.

"Mommy, Brett, I gots cookies!" Sam raced toward him with cookie crumbs all over his mouth and they both laughed, then took his hand and walked along the creek.

Tonight they would tell Sam that Brett was his father, and that they were finally going to be a family.

And Sam would grow up a McCullen on Horseshoe Creek.

Brett could almost see his father smiling down at him from Heaven.

He would teach Sam to be a man just as his father had taught him.

Epilogue

Ray watched his brothers congratulate each other. Maddox married Rose. Brett was back with the woman of his dreams and had a son.

He wanted to pound their backs and wish them good luck. Tell them he was happy for them.

Find that kind of love for himself.

But the bitterness he'd felt for years ate him up inside like a poison.

Maddox and Brett still thought their old man hung the moon.

If they knew the truth, would they feel the same way? Or would they understand the reason he and his father had fought?

Maddox raised a glass of whiskey to make a toast, and Ray slipped into the shadows where he'd tried to stay all his life. He'd protected his brothers by keeping his father's secrets and lies.

As soon as the reading of the will was over, he'd leave Horseshoe Creek again. If he stuck around any longer, he might be tempted to tell them the truth.

But the old saying about the truth setting you free was a lie.

* * * * *

THE LAST McCULLEN

This one is for all the fans of
The Heroes of Horseshoe Creek series
who wrote asking for the twins' stories!

Chapter One

Ryder Banks needed a shower, a cold beer and some serious shut-eye.

Three months of deep undercover work had paid off, though. He'd caught the son-of-a-bitch ringleader of a human trafficking group who'd been kidnapping and selling teenage girls as sex slaves.

Sick bastard.

He scrubbed a hand over his bleary eyes as he let himself inside his cabin. The musty odor and the dust motes floating in the stale air testified to the fact that he hadn't seen this place in months.

Tired but still wired from the arrest, he grabbed a beer from the fridge, kicked off his shoes and flipped on the news.

"This is Sheriff Maddox McCullen of Pistol Whip, Wyoming." The newscaster gestured toward a tall, broad-shouldered man with dark hair. "Sheriff McCullen has just arrested the person responsible for three-year-old Tyler Elmore's abduction and for the murder of the boy's mother, Sondra Elmore. Sheriff?"

"The man we arrested was Jim Jasper, a sheriff himself," Sheriff McCullen said. "He confessed to the homicide."

"What about the man who was originally charged with the murder?" The news anchor consulted his notes. "Cash Koker, wasn't that his name?"

McCullen nodded. "Sheriff Jasper also admitted that he framed Koker, so Koker has been cleared of all charges." Sheriff McCullen offered a smile. "On a more personal note, my brothers and I learned that Mr. Koker—Cash—is our brother. He and his twin were kidnapped at birth from our family."

"That explains the reason his last name isn't McCullen?"

"Yes, he was given the name of the foster parent who first took him in." McCullen paused. "We're delighted to reconnect with him. We're also searching for Cash's twin. We hope he'll come forward if he's watching."

A photo of Cash Koker flashed onto the screen.

Ryder swallowed hard. Dammit, the man not only resembled the other McCullen brothers with his dark hair, square jaw, big broad shoulders and rugged build, but he looked just like *him*.

The number for the sheriff's office flashed onto the screen and Ryder cursed, then hit the off button for the TV.

Maddox McCullen was a damn good actor. The emotions on his face seemed real.

He wanted the world to believe that his twin brothers had been stolen from his family.

But that was a lie.

Ryder knew the truth.

The McCullens had sold those babies.

All for the money to expand their ranch, Horseshoe Creek.

Sure, on the surface, the McCullens looked like model

citizens, like a loving family. But that family had dirty little secrets.

Although he'd always known he was adopted, and that his adopted parents, Myra and Troy Banks, loved him, four years ago after Troy died, he'd had a bug to find his birth parents. A little research had led him to the McCullens.

He'd confronted his mother, and she'd broken down and admitted that she'd gotten him through a private adoption. That his birth parents had needed money at the time. She and Troy had wanted a child so badly they'd paid to get custody of Ryder.

A hundred thousand dollars. That's what he'd been worth.

The Bankses had sacrificed their entire life savings to take him in while the McCullens used the cash to buy more cattle and horses.

But they hadn't told him about Cash. Did his parents know he had a twin?

If so, why hadn't they adopted both of them?

Because they couldn't afford it…

So where had Cash been all these years?

His phone buzzed, and he glanced at the number. His boss, Connor Statham, assistant director of the FBI's criminal investigative division.

He pressed Connect. "Ryder."

"Listen, Banks, I know you just came off a major case, but I need you on another one."

The shower beckoned. So did a bottle of bourbon to stave off the anger eating at him over that news report.

"It's a missing baby and possible homicide—mother insists someone kidnapped her infant. Soon-to-be ex-husband suggested the mother did something with the child. She thinks *he* did something to the baby."

Ryder's stomach knotted. "She thinks he killed his own child?"

A tense heartbeat passed. "Either that or he sold him."

Statham's statement echoed in Ryder's head as if someone had hit him in the skull with a sledgehammer. The situation hit too close to home. "You think she's telling the truth?"

"He said, she said. Local deputy who took her statement thinks she's unstable. He issued an Amber Alert, but so far nothing's come of it."

Anger slammed into Ryder. What kind of world was it that people sold their children?

"I want you to investigate, watch her," Statham said. "If she's lying and gave the baby to someone or hurt the child, she'll slip up."

Ryder downed another sip of his beer. "Text me her name and where she lives." A second later, the name Tia Jeffries appeared on his screen along with an address.

He hurried to the shower. The bourbon would have to wait. So would the sleep.

If this woman had hurt her baby, she wouldn't get away with it. And if the father was at fault, he'd throw him in jail and make sure he never saw the light of day again.

TIA JEFFRIES SLIPPED the Saturday night special from her purse as she parked her minivan outside her ex-husband's apartment. A low light burned in the bedroom, the outline of a man—Darren—appearing in front of the window.

A woman sidled up behind him, hands reaching

around Darren's naked midriff, her fingers trailing lower to stroke his erection.

Bile rose to Tia's throat. How many times had she fallen prey to the man's charms and jumped into bed with him?

Only she'd believed he was marriage material at the time. Father material for the child she'd always wanted.

A baby that would be the beginning of the big family she'd dreamed about having.

The one that would replace the family she'd lost years ago.

Her mother, father and brother were all wiped out in a plane crash when they were on the way to her college graduation.

Her fault.

She would never forgive herself.

If she hadn't insisted on them attending, they would still be alive.

But the loss of her baby boy, Jordan, was even worse.

Only Jordan wasn't dead. At least, she didn't believe he was.

Someone had stolen him from her bedroom while she'd been sleeping. The police had questioned her as if she'd done something with him.

Guilt made her throat clog with tears. She certainly hadn't hurt Jordan. But she was supposed to protect him. Keep him safe.

Instead she'd been sleeping while he disappeared.

She'd begged the police to find her baby. Had told them that she suspected Darren.

But they hadn't believed her. Darren was a good old boy. Tight with the mayor's wife, because he could charm the pants off anyone.

But Darren had lied.

And Tia was going to find out the reason.

Her hands shook as she gripped the handle of the .33. Sweat beaded on her neck and forehead.

The bedroom excitement heated up, Darren and the woman moving together in a frenzied, harried coupling. Sickened at the sight, she closed her eyes to shut out the images.

Anger and bitterness welled inside her. How dare he move on to another woman when he'd left her empty and hollow inside?

When their son was gone?

She forced even, deep breaths in and out to steady the racing of her heart. She hadn't slept since Jordan had gone missing two days ago.

Damn Darren for not caring about his own son.

Letting her fury drive her, she whipped open her car door, clenched the gun inside the pocket of her black hooded sweatshirt and scanned the area to make sure no one was watching. Except for Darren's truck and the shiny BMW that must belong to his long-legged lover girl, the parking lot was empty.

Well, hell, except there was a black SUV parked at the corner by some bushes. She studied it for a second, nerves clawing at her.

Thankfully it was empty.

She glanced back at the apartment and saw Darren padding naked to the bathroom. Uncaring that anyone could see them through the window, the woman dressed slowly, drawing out her movements as if she was performing.

If that was the kind of woman Darren wanted, why had he connected with her? Why had he gone to the trouble to act like he cared instead of just leaving their relationship at a one-night stand?

The answer hit her swift and hard. Because he'd wanted access to the money in her charity.

Tia inched up the sidewalk, taking cover in the overgrown bushes as the woman sashayed back through the apartment. Seconds later, Darren's lover opened the door, wobbling on heels that made Tia dizzy as she hurried to her fancy car and slipped inside.

Adrenaline shot through Tia as the car sped from the parking lot.

The bastard was alone.

She couldn't survive one more sleepless night without knowing what had happened to her son. At night, she heard his cries, saw his tiny little face looking at her with trust.

Trust she didn't deserve.

The wind picked up, rattling trees and sending leaves raining down. A cat darted out from behind a cottonwood, startling her, but she bit back a yelp.

She inched her way up the sidewalk to Darren's apartment door. His was the end unit, shrouded in bushes.

She scanned the parking lot and surrounding area again as she reached for the door. Satisfied no one was watching, she turned the doorknob.

Shocking that the sleazy girl had actually locked it.

She bit her lip, then pulled the lock-picking tool she'd bought at the pawnshop from her pocket and jimmied the door. It squeaked as she opened it, and she paused, listening for Darren's footsteps or his voice.

The sound of the shower running soothed her nerves slightly.

A quick glance at the living room confirmed that Darren still hadn't mastered the art of picking up or cleaning. Dirty dishes filled a sink and clothes littered the sofa. A red bra hung from the end of a chair. The woman who'd just left or another lover?

Not that she cared who he screwed.

She just wanted to know where her son was.

Gripping the gun with both hands, she crept toward the bedroom. The low light burning accentuated the unmade, rumpled bed.

Her legs were trembling, so she sank into the wing chair by the dresser facing the bathroom door, then laid the gun in her lap and wiped her sweaty palms on her jeans.

Seconds dragged into minutes. Tension coiled inside her. Anger made her stomach churn.

But a calmness swept over her as the water kicked off. Tonight she would get some answers.

The shower door slammed in the bathroom. Footsteps sounded. Darren was humming.

A nervous giggle bubbled in her throat.

Darren stepped from the bathroom, wrapping a towel around his waist. His chest and hair were damp, and he was smiling.

When he spotted her, his smile faded.

She lifted the gun and aimed it at his chest. He was going to tell her the truth or she'd kill him.

RYDER LIFTED HIS binoculars and focused on Darren Hoyt's apartment, his instincts on full alert as Tia Jeffries confronted the man.

When Ryder first arrived at Tia's house, she'd been running to her car like she was on a mission. Then she'd tucked that gun inside her purse and his instincts had kicked in.

Dread had knotted his stomach as he'd followed her to Hoyt's apartment. For a while, she'd sat perusing the parking lot, and he'd thought she might abandon whatever plan she had tonight.

No such luck.

She'd watched Darren screw some woman, waiting patiently as if the scene didn't disturb her.

Then she'd slid from the car and slunk up to the apartment.

A movement inside Hoyt's apartment snagged his eye.

The lights flickered in the bedroom. Movement as Darren, wearing nothing but a towel, stalked toward Tia.

Maybe they'd gotten rid of the baby together and this was rendezvous time.

A shadow moved. Tia standing now.

The silhouette of her body revealed an outstretched hand.

No, not outstretched. An arm extended, hand closed around a gun.

He jerked the door to his SUV open and ran toward the apartment.

Just as he reached the apartment, a gunshot rang out.

Chapter Two

Tia's hand trembled as she fired a shot at Darren's feet. "Tell me what you did with Jordan."

Darren jumped back, his eyes blazing with fear and shock. "What the hell are you doing, Tia?"

She lifted the gun and aimed it at his chest. "I want the truth, Darren. Where is my baby?"

"I told you I don't know." He took a step backward. "Now put down that damn gun. You don't want to hurt me."

Oh, but she did. "Maybe I do," she said, allowing her anger at his betrayal to harden her voice. "You cheated on me, emptied my bank account, then left me pregnant and alone." Thank God she'd had the good sense to protect her charity so he couldn't touch those funds.

The eyes that Tia had once thought were alluring darkened to a menacing scowl. "I wouldn't have cheated if you'd satisfied me, baby."

Oh, my God. He was a total jerk. "I don't care who you sleep with or how many women you have. All I want is my son."

His eyes narrowed. "You're the one who lost him," Darren said sharply. "So tell me what *you* did with him, Tia?"

Rage boiled inside Tia. "I was exhausted from labor and the night feedings. I went to sleep." Still, the guilt clawed at her. "That's when you snuck in and stole him, didn't you? You were mad that I wouldn't give you more money, so you decided to get revenge. Did you hurt him or leave him with someone?"

"You're crazy," Darren shouted. "I can't believe the cops haven't already locked you up."

She was terrified they would. Then she couldn't find her baby.

He reached for his cell phone on the bed. "I'm calling them now—"

Panicked, she fired the gun again. The bullet zinged by his hand. He pulled it back and cursed. She started toward him, but a low voice from behind her made her pause.

"Put down the weapon, Tia."

A chill swept through her at the gruff male voice. She clenched the gun with a white-knuckled grip and pivoted slightly to see who'd entered the room.

"Put it down, Tia," a big, broad-shouldered man with dark brown hair said. "No one needs to get hurt here."

"She's insane. She tried to kill me," Darren screeched.

Tia inhaled a deep breath at the sight of the man's Glock aimed at her.

"He stole my baby," Tia cried. "I just want him to tell me where Jordan is." She swung the gun back toward Darren. She'd come too far to stop now. If this man worked for Darren, she didn't intend to turn over her weapon. Then she'd never convince Darren to talk.

Suddenly the big man lunged toward her. She screamed as he knocked her arm upward, twisted the other one behind her back and growled in her ear, "I said drop it."

"Who are you?" Tia said on a moan. It felt as if he was tearing her arm out of the socket.

"Special Agent Ryder Banks. FBI."

Shock robbed her of breath. Or maybe it was his strong hold.

A second later, he whipped the Saturday night special from her hand. She cried out as he pushed her up against the wall, and yanked her other arm behind her.

The sound of metal clicking together sent despair through her as he handcuffed her and guided her to a chair.

"You saw her. She tried to kill me," Darren shouted.

Tears blurred Tia's eyes. If she went to jail, she'd never find her son.

RYDER NEVER LIKED being rough with a woman. But he had no choice. This one was about to shoot a man.

Whether the guy deserved it, he didn't know.

He wished to hell he'd had more time to do a background check on both of these two.

"Thanks, man." Darren released an exaggerated breath and gestured toward Tia. "She's a total nut job. She was going to kill me."

"I was not." Tia shot him a rage-filled look. "I just want to know what you did with our baby."

"You fired at me," Darren shouted.

Ryder jerked a thumb toward Darren. "Sit down and shut up."

Darren sputtered an oath. "I didn't do anything. She broke in and pulled a gun on me."

Unfortunately she had done that—Ryder had witnessed it himself.

Perspiration beaded on Darren's forehead. "Arrest her and take her to jail."

Tia started to argue, but Ryder threw up a warning hand, then addressed Darren. "Do you know where the baby is?"

A vein throbbed in the man's neck. "No." He tightened the towel around his waist.

"Put on some damn clothes," Ryder said, annoyed that the man hadn't asked to get dressed.

Darren sauntered to the closet, yanked out a shirt and jeans, then disappeared into the bathroom.

Tia cleared her throat. "I wasn't going to kill him," she said again. "I just wanted to scare him into talking."

Ryder's gaze met hers. His boss had failed to mention that Tia Jeffries was gorgeous. Petite in height, but curvy with big, bright blue eyes that made her look innocent and sexy at the same time.

An intoxicating combination.

"You should have let the police handle it," he said, forcing a hardness into his statement. He had to do his job, find the truth, ignore the fact that when he'd hand-cuffed her, he'd felt a shiver ripple through her. That she felt fragile—well, except for that gun.

Still, she wasn't experienced with it. Her hand had been shaking so badly he'd had to wrestle the gun from her before she hurt her ex or shot herself.

"I tried," she said, anger mingling with desperation in her voice. "But that sheriff treated me like I'd hurt my own baby. He believed Darren instead."

"That's because Tia is unstable," Darren said as he stepped into the bedroom. "She did something to Jordan and now she's trying to blame me."

"That's not true." Tia's voice broke. "I would never hurt my son. I…love him."

She said *love* in the present tense. A sign that she might be telling the truth. Sometimes when people were questioned about the suspicious disappearance of a loved one, they used past tense, which meant they already knew their loved one was dead.

"She has emotional problems," Darren said. "Just check her history. She had a breakdown a few years ago."

Ryder raised a brow. "Yet you married her?"

The man's eye twitched. "Hell, I didn't know it at the time. But then she started acting weird and depressed and erratic. I encouraged her to get help, but she refused."

Hurt flickered in Tia's eyes. "That's not true."

"Yes, it is. When we met, she was all over me. Later, I realized that was just because she wanted a baby." His voice grew bolder. "I guess she thought she could trap me into staying with her. And I fell for it. But she was obsessed with the pregnancy. She stockpiled baby clothes and toys and furniture for months."

Tia's eyes glistened with tears. "It's true I wanted a baby, but I wasn't obsessed."

Ryder folded his arms. Some women did that to trap a man. Then again, if Darren hadn't wanted a child, he had motive to do something to the infant.

"You must have been angry when you discovered you were going to be a father," he said, scrutinizing Darren for a reaction.

"He was," Tia said. "But I didn't get pregnant on purpose."

"Yes, she did." Darren's eyes flickered with anger. "And, yeah, sure, I was mad, but I took responsibility."

The bastard made it sound as if he'd done Tia a favor, not as if he actually cared about his own offspring.

Darren pasted on a smile that looked as phony as a three-dollar bill. "I stayed with her for a couple of months, but she's impossible to live with." Another exaggerated sigh, as if he was a victim of a crazy woman. "She pushed me away, told me she wanted me gone. That she'd just used me to get the child and she didn't need me anymore."

Pain streaked Tia's face as she shook her head in denial. "That's not the way it happened at all. He started cheating on me, dipping into my money."

Ryder studied Darren then Tia. No wonder the local sheriff had asked for help.

Both stories were plausible.

Although Darren's attitude rubbed him the wrong way. The man seemed too slick, as if lying came easy.

The anguish in Tia's eyes seemed real.

Although her anguish could stem from guilt.

He steeled himself against the tears in her deep blue eyes.

He would find out the truth.

No child should have to suffer at the hands of the very people who were supposed to love and protect him.

THE COLD METAL felt heavy on Tia's wrists.

She could go to prison for attempted murder.

God…where had this federal agent come from? Had he been following her?

And why? Because the local sheriff had passed her case to the feds and thought she was guilty of doing something to Jordan?

Pain made her stomach clench. How could anyone think that?

She gulped back a sob. What was going to happen now?

She had to convince Agent Banks that she was telling the truth.

Darren strode across the room as if he owned the world and grabbed his belt. "Are you going to take her in?"

"You intend to press charges?" the agent asked.

Darren paused, his mouth forming a scowl. "I should. She would have killed me if you hadn't shown up."

"Don't do this, Darren. You know I'm not crazy or violent." Her voice cracked. "I just want my little boy back."

The agent crossed his arms. Darren walked over and stared into Tia's eyes with a coldness that chilled Tia to the bone. "Then tell the cops what you did with him and maybe they'll find him. And stop trying to make me sound like the guilty one."

Tia jutted up her chin, battling a sob. Her arms were beginning to ache from being bound behind her. "He's your son, Darren. But you really don't care about him, do you? If you did, you'd be asking the police to search for him, too."

"How do I even know he's mine?" Darren asked sarcastically. "Maybe you lied so I'd hang around."

Hurt robbed her of speech. How could he be so cruel?

Giving her one last icy look, he turned to the agent. "Lock her up so I don't have to worry about her shooting me tonight in my sleep."

"Darren, please," Tia whispered, desperate. "If you know who took Jordan, tell me. I won't even press charges. I just want him back."

Instead of answering, his jaw hardened. "Agent Banks, I told you to get her out of here. I have things to do."

A hopeless feeling engulfed Tia as the agent helped her stand.

"You need to come to the sheriff's office to file an official police report," the agent told Darren.

Darren gave a quick nod and muttered that he would.

Tia searched the agent's face for some hope that he believed her story, that he would help her.

But hope faded as he guided her outside to his car.

Dark storm clouds rolled in, obliterating the few stars that had shined earlier.

He opened the back door and gestured for her to get in. Emotions overwhelmed her as she sank into the backseat and he drove toward the jail.

Chapter Three

Tia hunched in the backseat of the agent's car, her nerves raw.

She was going to jail. She'd never see her baby again. If Darren had given Jordan to someone else, little Jordan would grow up without ever knowing her.

He might never know she'd looked for him, that she loved him.

A hollow emptiness welled in her chest. Hands still cuffed behind her, she leaned forward. She couldn't breathe.

Tears trickled down her cheeks, but she was helpless to wipe them away.

She closed her eyes, willing herself to be strong. An image of her son's tiny body nestled in the baby blue blanket and cap she'd knitted taunted her.

Even if she never got him back, she had to know he was safe.

But how could she do that locked in a cell?

The car bounced over a rut in the road, and she lifted her head and looked out the window. Rugged farm and ranch land passed by. Trees swayed in the wind, leaves raining down. Dark shadows hovered along the deserted stretch of land, signaling that night had set in.

Another night away from her baby boy.

Minutes crawled by, turning into half an hour.

She gulped back a sob and cleared her throat. "Where are you taking me?"

Agent Banks met her gaze in the rearview mirror. "The sheriff's office in Sagebrush."

Despair threatened again. The sheriff, Dan Gaines, had been less than sympathetic when she'd asked for help. He'd practically accused her of killing her child so she could be single, footloose and fancy-free.

He had no idea that footloose and fancy-free was the last thing she wanted.

Or that she'd spent her adult life missing the family she'd lost. That all she wanted was someone to love to fill the hole in her aching heart.

That she spent her days working with kids and families in need, helping them find housing and counseling so they could patch their lives back together. That the money she'd received from her parents' life insurance had gone toward a charity she'd started called Crossroads.

Agent Banks drove through the small, quaint town of Sagebrush, then parked at the sheriff's office. Dread made her stomach roil.

She had to find someone who'd believe her. Sheriff Gaines certainly hadn't.

Maybe Agent Banks would.

Somehow she had to convince him she wasn't the lunatic Darren had painted her to be.

RYDER CLENCHED THE steering wheel with a white-knuckled grip. Tia Jeffries looked tiny and frightened, and so damn vulnerable that he felt like a jerk for handcuffing her.

She had a damn gun and shot at a man.

Whether she'd been provoked made no difference. The law was the law. He was a by-the-book man.

Except sometimes there were grays…

Where did this woman fall on the spectrum?

He parked at the sheriff's office, killed the engine, then walked to the back of the car and opened the door. Tia looked up at him with the saddest expression he'd ever seen.

Eyes that could suck a man in with that sparkling color and innocence.

Except the innocence was yet to be proven.

He had to keep his head clear, his emotions out of the picture.

Only her lower lip quivered as he took her arm and helped her from the vehicle, making his gut tighten.

"I don't care what you do to me," she said with a stubborn lift to her chin. "But please find my baby."

What could he say to that? She wasn't pleading for him to release her, but she was worried about her child.

Wasn't the sheriff looking for the baby?

His gaze met hers. "I'll find him," he said. And if she was lying, he'd make sure she stayed locked up.

But…if there was any truth to her story, he'd find that out, too.

She inhaled sharply as he led her to the door of the sheriff's office. When they entered, a husky man in a deputy's uniform sat at the desk. He looked up with a raised brow.

"Where's the sheriff?" Ryder asked.

"On a call." The man stood and extended his hand. "Deputy Hawthorne." He gave Tia a once-over. "What's going on?"

"Miss Jeffries needs to cool down awhile. Pulled a gun on her ex." He didn't add that she'd fired that weapon.

The deputy grabbed a set of keys, jiggling them in his hand. "I'll put her in a holding cell."

Ryder nodded, although the terrified look on Tia's face twisted his insides. Dammit, he didn't have a choice.

"Can I have my phone call?" Tia asked.

"In time," Deputy Hawthorne said.

"Let her make the call," Ryder said. For some reason, he didn't trust how quickly the deputy planned to follow through.

Deputy Hawthorne shrugged and gestured toward the phone. "Is it local?"

Tia nodded, and he handed her the handset. The handcuffs jangled as she punched in a number.

Ryder gestured for the deputy to step to the side. "Miss Jeffries claims her baby was kidnapped from her home. Has the sheriff been investigating?"

The man shrugged. "He thinks she got rid of the kid. No proof yet, though."

"Anything on the Amber Alert?"

"So far nothing."

"He talked to the baby's father, Darren Hoyt?"

Deputy Hawthorne nodded. "Man had an alibi."

Ryder wondered how solid it was. "Did the sheriff tape his interview with Miss Jeffries?"

The deputy narrowed his eyes. "Not when he got the call and went to her house. But she came in and he recorded that conversation."

"I'd like to watch the tape."

Hawthorne worked his mouth side to side. "Maybe you should wait on the sheriff to return."

"I can look at it here or get a warrant and take the tape with me, so why not make it easy on both of us?"

The deputy seemed to think it over, then muttered agreement. Tia hung up the phone, her hands trembling as she placed them back on her lap. Hawthorne wasted no time. He escorted her through the back to a holding cell. Ryder scanned the space as he followed. Two cells. The other was empty.

At least she wasn't being thrown in with some dangerous derelict. He removed the handcuffs before he motioned her inside.

The cell door closed with a clang. Tia looked small and helpless behind those bars, yet he'd seen the fight in her when she'd confronted her ex.

"Please find Jordie," she whispered in a pained voice. "He's just a few weeks old. He…needs me."

Yes, he did.

But Ryder had seen the worst of society on that last case. The head of the damn ring had seemed like an upstanding citizen. But evil had lurked beneath the surface.

Did Tia deserve to have her son back?

For the life of him, he wanted to believe her. Maybe because no kid should grow up thinking his mother had gotten rid of him like Ryder had.

"I will find the baby." And he'd put away whoever had taken the child.

He gestured to the deputy. "The video?"

The man frowned but led him to a small office across the hall from the cells. Another room was designated for interrogations.

Ryder took a seat. Seconds later, Hawthorne started the video feed of his initial interview at his office with Tia after her son disappeared.

Ryder knotted his hands in his lap as he watched the recording.

Tia paced the interrogation room. "Sheriff, you have to find my baby. I think my ex did something to him." She looked haggard in a worn T-shirt and jeans, her hair yanked back in a ponytail and her eyes swollen from crying.

Sheriff Gaines, a robust man with a scar above his left eye, pointed to a chair. "Sit down. Then tell me what happened again."

"I don't want to sit down," Tia cried. "I want you to find Jordan."

Sheriff Gaines jerked a thumb toward the chair, his voice brusque. "I said sit down."

Tia heaved a breath and sank into the chair in front of the rickety wooden table. She fidgeted with a tissue, wiping her eyes then shredding it into pieces. "I think Darren is responsible."

Sheriff Gaines folded his beefy arms on the table. "Start at the beginning and tell me what happened."

"For God's sake, we went through this when I first called you yesterday." Tia ran a hand through the front of her tangled hair. "Jordie is only six weeks old." She pressed a hand over her chest. "I fed him at midnight the night before, and he fell asleep in my arms." A smile curved her mouth as if she was remembering. "He's so little, and he eats every three hours, so I was exhausted from being up at night." She looked down at her hands. "I shouldn't have, but I laid him in the crib, then went to my room and crawled on my bed. I was only going to close my eyes for a minute, but I must have fallen into a deep sleep."

Instead of reassuring her that it was okay to rest while her baby slept, the sheriff grunted. "Go on."

Guilt streaked her face. "Anyway, a little while later, a noise woke me up."

"A noise?" the sheriff asked. "The baby crying?"

"No." Tia closed her eyes and rubbed her temple as if she was trying to remember. When she opened her eyes again, she exhaled a shaky breath. "It sounded like a gunshot, but then I realized it was a car. Backfiring. I looked out the window and saw taillights racing away." She rubbed her arms now as she paced. "Then I went to check on Jordan, but…his crib was empty."

A heartbeat passed, the silence thick with tension. "You believe that someone broke into your house and stole your baby while you were asleep?"

Tia nodded miserably. "I told you that already. I usually put him in the cradle by my bed, but I'd been rocking him in the nursery so I left him alone in there. I… thought I'd hear him if he woke up."

The fact that she'd varied her routine must have struck the sheriff as suspicious, because a scowl darkened his face. "So the one night you put him in the other room, he disappears?"

Tia nodded. "It's all my fault. I should have put him in the cradle, but I'd barely slept since he was born and I wasn't thinking."

"I see. You were exhausted and tired of dealing with a fussy baby, so you left the baby where you couldn't hear him," Sheriff Gaines said.

"No." Tia stopped pacing long enough to throw up her hands. "That's not what I meant! But I thought he'd be safe in his nursery and I was only going to take a nap, and we were alone." Her voice cracked and she dropped into the chair again. "But someone came in and stole him."

The sheriff leaned forward, arms still folded. "Don't you mean that you were sick of taking care of a crying infant so you wanted to get rid of him? Maybe you lost it and smothered him, then you panicked and buried him in the yard or put him in the trash."

"No, God, no!" Horror turned Tia's skin a pale color. "That's not what happened. I love my baby—"

"It happens, Miss Jeffries. Mothers are exhausted, suffering from postpartum depression. They can't take it anymore and they snap. They shake the baby to get it to be quiet or they put it in the bed a little too hard or—"

"No!" Tia shouted. "I love my son. I came here for your help, not for you to accuse me of hurting my son." She launched herself at the man and grabbed his shirt. "You have to do something. Look for him!"

The sheriff gripped her hands and pried them from his shirt. "Listen, Miss Jeffries, it'll be easier on you if you cooperate. Tell me what you did with your baby. Maybe he's still alive and we can save him."

Tia sucked in a sharp breath. "I didn't do anything with him except feed him and put him to bed. I think my ex took him."

"Why would he do that?" Gaines asked.

"Because he didn't want a baby in the first place."

"But you got pregnant anyway," the sheriff said in a voice laced with accusations. "You thought if you got pregnant he wouldn't leave you, didn't you?" Sheriff Gaines growled. "Then you had the baby and he left anyway, so you did something to the kid and are trying to get revenge by blaming him."

Tia shook her head vehemently. "No," she cried. "Please believe me."

The sheriff set her away from him. "I will investigate, Miss Jeffries. In fact, my deputy and I are going to search your place again now."

Ryder chewed the inside of his cheek. Gaines was playing tough cop, pushing Tia, just as he might have done.

But had he ignored the possibility that Tia might be telling the truth?

Had he even checked into Tia's ex or canvassed the neighbors to see if anyone had heard that car backfire or seen someone snooping around Tia's place?

Ryder's phone buzzed. He checked the number.

McCullen.

Dammit. He hadn't planned on ever talking to the family.

But one of them had obviously found him.

What the hell was he going to do about it?

Chapter Four

Ryder checked the video where the sheriff interviewed Darren.

Hoyt seemed cocky, self-assured. He insisted he hadn't been in Tia's house and that he hadn't taken the baby. He also accused Tia of trying to trap him into marriage, just as he'd told Ryder.

Had the bastard practiced his story?

For some reason, the sheriff didn't push Hoyt. Didn't pursue his past or the financial angle.

Because he'd decided that Tia was the guilty party.

"Hell, Tia was jealous that I was moving on with my life," Darren said. "She probably faked the kidnapping to get my attention, hoping I'd come back to her."

Damn. The federal agent in him agreed that Darren's story was plausible.

But Tia didn't appear to be in love with Darren—she was only concerned about the baby.

Although it was true that the parents were always suspects in a child's kidnapping, disappearance or death. He couldn't clear her just yet.

But what if she was telling the truth?

Just because his parents had sold him didn't mean this

woman had done the same thing. But if she had, he'd make sure she paid.

He didn't give a damn if her hair looked like sunshine and her blue eyes poured tears as big as a waterfall.

Or if she looked terrified and pale. That could be explained from guilt. Criminals or people who committed crimes in a fit of passion often experienced guilt.

Sometimes they imploded on themselves.

Unless they were pathological liars or sociopaths.

But she didn't fit that profile.

He had to run background checks on both of them, look at their computers, phone records, talk to neighbors and friends.

He scrubbed a hand over his bleary eyes, a good night's sleep beckoning. But the image of Tia in that cell made him decide to put bed on hold for a while, at least until he did some work.

He shut off the tapes, phoned his boss and requested warrants, then stepped back into the front office. The deputy was leaning back in his desk chair, feet propped on the desk, a grin on his face.

"Yeah, Martha, I should be there in about an hour."

Ryder folded his arms and stared at the man, sending him the silent message to get off the phone.

The deputy scowled, tilted his head sideways so Ryder couldn't hear his conversation, then ended the call.

The idea of Tia sitting alone in a dark cell all night rubbed Ryder the wrong way. "You're leaving the woman alone in here tonight?"

Hawthorne frowned. "The night shift deputy is coming in. Why? That woman probably killed her kid. She deserves to rot in prison."

Anger shot through Ryder. "Have you ever heard the phrase *innocent until proven guilty*?"

Hawthorne barked a laugh. "Yeah, but don't let those blue eyes fool you."

"What makes you so sure she's the culprit? Why not the baby's father? He didn't want a child in the first place."

Hawthorne cut his gaze to the side. "I know women, that's why."

Ryder leaned forward, hands on the desk, body coiled with tension. "Just make sure she's safe in there," he said in a low growl.

A muscle ticked in the deputy's jaw. "I know how to do my job."

Ryder gritted his teeth. Small-town sheriffs and deputies disliked the feds encroaching on their territory.

"Did you need something else?" Hawthorne asked.

Ryder met his gaze with a stony look. "Darren Hoyt is supposed to come in and file an official report. Let me know if he shows up."

Hawthorne gave a clipped nod.

"Do you have Miss Jeffries and Hoyt's computers?"

"The sheriff already looked at them but didn't find anything."

"Phone records?"

Hawthorne shrugged. "Have to ask Sheriff Gaines."

"I will." But he'd prefer to look at them himself anyway, especially since the deputy and sheriff had already made their decision about Tia's guilt.

Ryder tossed his business card on the desk. "Let me know if you hear anything." He didn't wait for a response.

Even if the sheriff had investigated thoroughly, which

it didn't appear he had, Ryder would conduct his own inquiry.

If Jordan had been kidnapped for money, Tia would have received a ransom call.

Which meant whoever took him had a different motive.

Worse—every day this baby was missing meant the chance of finding him diminished.

TIA SHIVERED AS she hunched on the only piece of furniture in the cell—a tiny cot. The low lights in the small hallway barely lit the inside of the tiny barred room. A threadbare blanket lay on top of a single mattress that was so thin you could feel the metal springs beneath it.

Tia curled her arms around her waist, clenching her fingers into her palms so tightly she felt the pain of her fingernails stabbing her skin.

She deserved the pain. She was a terrible mother. If she hadn't fallen asleep, her baby wouldn't have been taken.

How could she have been so deep in sleep that she hadn't heard someone break into the house?

The sheriff said there were no signs of a break-in.

But there had to be.

Unless she'd been so exhausted she'd forgotten to lock the door.

No…she always locked the door. She was compulsive about it and checked it at least three times a night.

A squeaking noise alerted her to the fact that someone had opened the door between the cells and the front office. Footsteps echoed on the concrete floor.

Her stomach knotted. Had Sheriff Gaines returned to make more accusations? To taunt her?

A big, hulking shadow moved across the dimly lit hall. More footsteps. A breath rattled in the quiet.

She tightened her hands again in an attempt to hold herself together and braced herself for whatever Gaines or his deputy dished out.

"Tia?"

She jerked her head up. Not Gaines's snide voice. Special Agent Ryder Banks.

God, had he come back to rescue her from this nightmare?

He stopped in front of the cell, his big body taking up so much air that she could barely breathe. Then he shoved a notepad and pen through the bars. "I need you to write down all your contacts. The people you work with, your friends, neighbors, anyone you can think of who might vouch for you or who had access to your house."

Hope warred with despair. What if it was too late?

"Tia?" This time his voice was gruff. Commanding. "If you want my help, take the pad and start writing."

She pulled herself from her stupor, stood on shaking legs and crossed the small space. Her hand trembled as she grabbed the pad and pen. "You're going to help me?"

Silence stretched for a full minute while he stared at her. She felt his scrutiny as if he was dissecting her.

"I'll find your son. Then I'll make whoever kidnapped him pay."

The coldness in his tone suggested he hadn't decided on her innocence yet.

But at least he was going to investigate. That was a lot more than Gaines had done.

She sighed, then walked back to the cot, sank onto the mattress and began the list.

Her coworkers and the volunteers at the shelter came first. Two of her neighbors next.

"Don't leave anyone out," he said.

She ignored the distrust in his tone. As long as he looked for her son, she could put up with anything. "I won't. Are you going to have Darren do this, too?"

"Absolutely." He paused, then cleared his throat. "You said you run a charity for families in need. Is this for abused women and children?"

Tia shrugged. "Yes. But it's also open to anyone who needs help. Sometimes mothers come to us when their husbands or children's fathers abandon them. They need help finding housing and food and jobs. We've also had families in crisis—it could be drug or alcohol related, one of them has lost his job, even a long-term illness where the parent has to go into a hospital for treatment. We work through social services, but we also find temporary foster homes through local churches and provide counseling to help them get back on their feet. Our goal is to keep the family intact or to reunite them if there's a separation period."

"Admirable." His dark eyes narrowed. "Can you think of anyone you've angered? Maybe a father or mother who lost their kids to the system, someone who'd want revenge against you."

Tia's pulse jumped. There were a couple of names.

"Write them down," he said as if he'd read her mind.

Tia nodded, then scribbled every name she could think of, including the hospital staff and attendants as well as Amy, a young delivery nurse, who'd befriended her.

Finally she handed the agent the list. Her fingers brushed his big hands, and a tingle of something dangerously like attraction shot through her.

She yanked her hand back quickly. She'd never be foolish enough to fall for another man.

When she got Jordan back, he would be the only one in her life.

RYDER LEFT TIA, shaken by the spark of electricity he'd felt when she'd touched his hand. Then she'd looked up at him with those damn sea-like blue eyes and he'd thought he would drown in them.

She had some kind of pull on him.

A pull he had to ignore.

He was a loner. Always had been. Always would be. There was no place for a woman or family in his line of work.

It was still odd, since he wasn't usually drawn to gun-carrying women who shot at their husbands or to suspects in his cases.

His reaction had to be due to lack of sleep. He wasn't thinking clearly.

He needed that beer and a bed. Although an image of Tia sprawled naked on the sheets with her hair fanned out taunted him.

He shook the image away.

The list of names in his hand meant he had work to do. Sleep would have to wait.

He just prayed Tia would be safe in that cell. At least she couldn't get herself in any more trouble by killing her ex.

He bypassed Hawthorne, who was on the telephone again, strode outside to his SUV and headed toward Crossroads. Although it was getting late in the evening, hopefully someone would still be awake.

The old Victorian house was nestled on an acre of

land literally at the crossroads of the town limits and the countryside. The porch light and lights inside were on, indicating someone was there.

Ryder swung down the drive, surprised at the wild-flowers growing in patches along the drive. A cheery-looking sign in blue and white boasted its name, and underneath, etchings of children and parents linking hands in a circle as if united had been carved into the wood.

He passed a barn and spotted two horses galloping on a hill to the east.

Rocking chairs and porch swings filled the wrap-around porch, making the place look homey and inviting.

He climbed the porch, wiped his feet on the welcome mat, and banged the door knocker, which was shaped like the sun. Through the window, he noted a kitchen with a large round oak table and a woman at the sink washing dishes.

A second later, a twentysomething blonde with pale green eyes opened the door. She couldn't be more than five feet tall and couldn't weigh a hundred pounds. Her eyes widened as her gaze traveled from his face down to his size-thirteen boots and back to his face.

He flashed his identification. "Special Agent Ryder Banks, FBI. I need to ask you some questions about Tia Jeffries."

She blinked, a wariness in her expression. "Yes, Tia told me you'd probably be coming. I'm Elle Grist, Tia's assistant."

"When did she tell you I was coming?"

"When she called after you arrested her," the woman said, disapproval lacing her tone.

So she'd used her one phone call to call the charity. Why? To request they cover for her?

"Before you even ask, no, Tia would never do anything to hurt her baby or anyone else. She's the most loving, caring person on this planet."

"You're loyal to her. I get that."

"Yes, I am, but with good reason," Elle said. "Tia lost her family—every one of them—on the day of her college graduation. They were flying to the ceremony when the plane went down." Her voice cracked with emotion. "She still blames herself. More than anything in the world, she values family. That's why she started this place. She's helped so many people over the past five years that she deserves a medal."

Elle dabbed at her eyes. "Tia also took me in when I lost my mother two years ago. She let me live with her until I could get a job. She saved me from…"

Ryder arched a brow. "From what?"

Elle rubbed a finger over a scar on her wrist. "I wouldn't be alive if it weren't for her." Footsteps sounded, and the heavyset woman he'd seen through the window washing dishes appeared, drying her hands on a checked cloth.

"Miss Elle speaks the gospel. Everyone loves Miss Tia." She planted her beefy hands on her hips. "You gonna find the evil one that took her baby?"

Ryder swallowed, choosing his words carefully. From Tia's list, he guessed this woman must be Ina, the cook and housekeeper. "I'm certainly going to try. But I need your help."

"We'll do anything for Tia," Ina said.

He gestured to the notepad. "Then let me come in. I

want you to look over this list Tia made and tell me about the people on it."

The women exchanged questioning looks, then a silent agreement passed between them, and they motioned for him to enter.

"Just be quiet now," Ina said. "We have two families here with little ones. Took their mamas forever to get them to sleep tonight."

Ryder glanced at the stairs and nodded. It certainly appeared that Tia was some kind of saint to these people. If that was the case, who had stolen her son?

And what had they done with the little boy?

Chapter Five

Ryder studied the photos on the wall of Tia's office. She and the staff had taken pictures of several families who'd come through Crossroads and displayed them on the wall to showcase that their efforts were working.

Personalized thank-you notes and cards were interspersed, creating a collage that triggered Ryder's admiration.

"Darren Hoyt claims Tia is unstable, that she suffered from depression," Ryder said.

Elle's mouth grew pinched. "She is not unstable and she certainly doesn't suffer from depression."

"That girl had it rough a while back," Ina interjected. "Losing her mama and daddy and brother all at once. Anyone would have been grief stricken. On top of that, she blamed herself 'cause they were on their way to see her."

That would have been tough.

"She was only twenty-one at the time," Elle said. "She was suddenly alone and didn't know what to do. But one of her friends convinced her to go to an in-house therapy program. So she did. No shame in that."

No, he supposed not.

"I admire her," Elle continued. "She took her own

personal tragedy and used it to make her stronger and to help others by building this place."

That was admirable. Ryder addressed Ina. "What did you think about Darren Hoyt?"

Ina folded her arms. "He was a con man. He knew Tia had money from her folks and married her to get hold of it. But that girl was smart and set up the charity so no one could touch it."

A wise move. "She didn't trust Darren from the beginning?" Ryder asked.

Elle shrugged. "It wasn't that. She just wanted to protect her family's money and for their deaths to stand for something."

"She barely paid herself a salary," Ina said. "But she gave openly to others."

"When Darren realized he would never get her inheritance, he left her," Elle said. "That man was a manipulative SOB—he never loved her."

"She loved him?" Ryder asked, wondering why that thought bothered him.

Elle blew out a breath. "At first I think she did."

"She was young, vulnerable, lonely and naive," Ina said. "Darren Hoyt took advantage of that."

Ryder gritted his teeth. "Do you think she was jealous that he moved on? She wouldn't have done something to get Darren's attention and win him back?"

"Heavens, no," Ina murmured.

Elle shook her head. "Tia had never seemed happier than during that pregnancy."

Ina smiled softly. "She wanted that baby more than anything."

Ryder rubbed his chin. "Can you think of anyone

who'd want to hurt her? Maybe someone whose family came through Crossroads?"

Both women shook their heads no.

He consulted the notepad. "Tell me about Bennett Jones."

"He was furious when his wife left him and took their son," Ina said.

"Do you think he kidnapped Tia's little boy for revenge?" Elle asked.

Ryder shifted on the balls of his feet. "I don't know—do *you* think he did?"

Elle chewed her bottom lip. "It's hard to say how far he'd go. Tia suggested he attend anger-management classes."

"He did have a mean streak," Ina agreed, her cheeks puffing out.

Ryder checked the list again. "What about Wanda Hanson?"

Ina fanned herself. "Lord help, that woman had her issues."

"What do you mean?" Ryder asked.

"She had back problems and became addicted to pain meds, then escalated to harder stuff," Elle said. "Husband found her passed out while their baby was left unattended. They lived on a lake, and their toddler was outside alone."

Ina tsked and shook her head. "It's a wonder the little fellow didn't drown."

Ryder arched a brow. "What happened?"

"Father tried everything to convince her to get help. He finally divorced her and moved with the boy to Texas to be close to his folks."

Ryder thanked Elle and Ina, then extended his business card. "Please call me if you think of anything else that could be helpful."

Ina caught his arm. "Agent Banks, you gonna help our Tia?"

Ryder cleared his throat. These women had sung Tia's praises. If everything they said was true, she was a victim. "I'm going to find Jordan," he said.

Both women nodded, and he headed out the door.

If Bennett and Wanda had lost custody of their children, they might blame Tia.

It was a place to start.

TIA COUNTED THE scratches on the wall of the cell beside the cot. Foul language mingled with crude sketches and another area where someone had drawn lines counting the days.

She wondered if she should start her own calendar.

A cold chill washed over her at the thought. Knowing Sheriff Gaines, he'd keep her locked up until he finished making his case against her for hurting her baby and she went to trial. Now, he'd probably add attempted murder for threatening Darren.

The blasted man. If he'd done his job and found her son, she wouldn't have been forced to take matters into her own hands.

She stretched her fingers, shocked at herself for firing that gun. She'd never believed she had it in her to hurt another human.

Not until she'd held her baby. The very second she'd looked into his little face, she'd known she'd do anything to protect him.

Yet she'd failed.

Tears blurred her vision. She blinked in an attempt to

hold them back, but it was futile. The enormity of her loss struck her again and she walked over to the bars of the cell and curled her fingers around them.

She had no idea what time it was, but the windowless cell and the dim light made it feel like it was the middle of the night.

She wrapped her arms around her waist, and rocked herself back and forth. She felt empty inside and ached to hold her little boy again.

Where was he now? Was he safe?

He ate every few hours. Was he hungry?

Just the thought of feeding him made her breasts throb. They'd shared a tender bond when she'd nursed him.

The tears broke through as she realized she might never get to hold him again. No one would ever love him as much as she did.

She just prayed that whoever had kidnapped him takes care of him and keeps him safe until she finds him.

And she *would* find him, no matter how long it took or what she had to do.

RYDER'S STOMACH GROWLED. He hadn't eaten all day. And he'd never gotten any sleep.

He would take care of the food, though, while he did a little research on Darren Hoyt.

He parked at the Sagebrush Diner, a place that reminded him of an old Western saloon. The log cabin sported rails outside to tie up horses. Considering the closest stable was twenty miles away, he doubted it was used much, but it was a nice touch.

Several cars filled the parking lot, and a group of teens had parked in the back corner and were sitting on the hoods of their cars hanging out. The flicker of a lighter lit the air, and smoke curled upward. Cigarettes or weed—he didn't know which.

Not that he cared at the moment. He had more important things to do—like finding Jordie Jeffries.

Country music blared from an old-fashioned jukebox in one corner, chatter and laughter buzzed through the room, and burgers sizzled on a griddle in the kitchen area. He claimed a seat at a booth just as a twentysomething waitress approached.

She gave him a once-over, then a big smile. "Hey, tall, dark and handsome, what can I get you?"

He bit back a chuckle at her attempt to flirt. He wasn't interested and didn't take the bait. "Burger, chili and a beer." He set his laptop on the table. "You have Wi-Fi?"

She nodded. "Finally. Password is Sagebrush."

The name of the diner—original.

He thanked her, then booted up his machine, ending the conversation. He quickly connected to the internet, then the FBI's database and plugged in Darren Hoyt's name.

A preliminary background check revealed the man had been born in Houston to a preacher and his wife, who'd died when Darren was in college. Had he used that fact to bond with Tia?

His work history showed that he'd dabbled in real estate and had touted himself as an entrepreneur. He'd lived in Montana and Colorado and had been single until he'd married Tia.

A couple of speeding tickets, but no charges filed against him. No rap sheet.

The waitress returned with his beer and food and he muttered thanks. Hoyt was no saint. If Elle and Ina were correct and he was a con man, there had to be something in his history that was suspicious.

He sipped his beer, then dug into the food. By the time he'd finished, he'd found a photo of Darren online from a charity fund-raiser Tia had organized the year before and plugged it into facial recognition software.

Seconds later, he had a hit. Only the man in the photograph wasn't Darren Hoyt. His name was Bill Koontz.

Bill Koontz was born in a small town in Texas. His mother was Renee Koontz, who had a record for solicitation and had served prison time for drug dealing when her son was fifteen. He'd been in and out of foster homes for a few months, then lived on the streets. At eighteen, he'd disappeared for a while.

Around twenty-five, he resurfaced in Montana, where he'd worked odd jobs, then had become a groomer at a country club stable.

Several women at the club had reported that he'd swindled them out of their savings. Eventually the guy had served three years in prison. When he was released, he moved to Wyoming, where he eased his way back into another country club and resorted to his old tricks.

At first, life must have been good. But then reports of him trying to con members out of their savings cropped up, and he was fired.

Two years later, Darren Hoyt had been born. The name was new, but Ryder would bet his life that the con game had continued.

Tia had simply been a mark.

The waitress appeared, the flirtatious smile joined by a gleaming in her eyes. "Another beer, sugar?"

"Just the check." Another beer and she might take it as a sign that he was interested.

Her smile dipped into a frown and she handed him the bill. He tossed some cash the table to cover it, then dug around another minute for more information on Hoyt. Nothing again on that name.

Curious, he ran a search on country clubs in the area and found one about five miles from Crossroads.

His pulse jumped. Maybe Tia had approached members to donate to her charity.

He found the number and left a message identifying himself and asking for a return call from the director.

Exhaustion knotted his muscles, and he finally stood and left the diner. The waitress waved to him as he left, but he ignored her. He didn't have time for women.

Not when a baby needed him.

A HALF HOUR LATER, Ryder pulled down the drive to his cabin. An image of Tia alone in that prison cell sleeping on that cot taunted him.

From what he'd learned, she didn't deserve to be in jail. While she was locked up, her son's kidnapper was getting farther and farther away.

He had to do something.

Tomorrow he'd confront Darren about his past. Then maybe he'd persuade the man to talk.

Woods backed up to his cabin, trees swaying in the wind. He'd chosen the place because it was virtually deserted, a retreat after working undercover or dealing with criminals.

He tucked his laptop beneath his arm, then climbed from the SUV, scanning the area for trouble as he always did. Once a detective, always a detective.

Satisfied the area was clear, he let himself into the cabin. He flipped on the light switch, then headed straight toward the shower. Before he could undress, a knock sounded at the door.

Startled, he gripped his gun and eased into the living room. He'd made too many enemies on the job to trust anyone.

He inched to the side window in front, eased the curtain aside and checked the yard. A beat-up pickup truck sat in the drive.

Hmm.

Holding his gun to his side, he stepped over to the front door and opened it.

Shock stole his breath at the sight of the man standing on his porch.

A man who looked like him.

It had to be his twin brother, Cash Koker.

Chapter Six

Ryder blinked to clear his vision. It was almost eerie, seeing himself yet knowing the man in front of him wasn't him. Same dark brown eyes, wide jaw, broad shoulders.

Except Cash looked freshly shaven where Ryder was scruffy, with three-day-old beard stubble on his jaw and hair that needed a wash and a trim.

Cash shoved his hands in the pockets of his denim jacket. "Damn," Cash muttered. "They told me I had a twin, but I couldn't believe it."

Words tangled on Ryder's tongue. He swallowed to make his voice work. "You knew about me?"

Cash shook his head. "Not until recently." His gaze traveled up and down Ryder as if he too couldn't believe what he was seeing. "You knew about me?"

Ryder shook his head. "Not until I saw that news report where Sheriff McCullen was interviewed."

"That's Maddox." Cash glanced inside the cabin. "Uh, can I come in?"

Ryder squared his shoulders. Was he ready for this conversation? Hell, no.

But he had questions and couldn't turn this man away, not when he looked so much like him it was shocking. They *were* brothers, twins.

And none of this was Cash's fault. Judging from Maddox's statement, Cash had only recently learned about the McCullens, too.

"Sure." He stepped aside and gestured for Cash to enter, then led him to the small den. "Sorry this place is a wreck. I haven't been here for a while."

Cash studied him, arms folded. "You're with the FBI, aren't you?"

"Yes." Ryder clenched his jaw. "How did you know that? And how did you find me?"

Cash shrugged. "My—our—brothers have been looking for you awhile. Ray's a private investigator and Maddox used his connections in the sheriff's department to expedite the search."

Ryder gritted his teeth. What did you say to a brother you didn't know you had? "Do you want a beer or something?"

A small grin tugged at Cash's mouth. "Yeah. Thanks."

Ryder grabbed two cold ones from the refrigerator just to have something to do. He knew how to handle hardened criminals, but he had no idea how to handle this situation.

When he turned back, Cash was watching him. "Sorry for just showing up here." He popped the top of the beer and took a sip. "But once Ray found you, I…had to see for myself."

Ryder gave a nod of understanding, then gestured toward the back deck. It offered a great view of the woods and was his favorite spot to think and unwind after a case.

He and Cash stepped outside, a breeze stirring the warm air. Ryder claimed the rocker and Cash settled on the porch swing. It creaked back and forth as he pushed it with his feet, the silence between them thick with questions and the revelation that they were identical twins but also strangers who knew nothing about each other.

He sipped his beer, stalling.

"So how did you grow up?" Cash finally asked.

Ryder heaved a wary breath. "I was adopted by a couple named Troy and Myra Banks. They told me I was adopted when I was little, but not about my birth family."

Cash's jaw tightened.

"You weren't adopted?"

Cash shook his head. "Nope, I was sickly. Bounced from foster home to foster home."

Guilt gnawed at Ryder. "That must have been rough."

"I survived," Cash said, although the gruffness of his voice hinted that it had been tough.

No wonder Cash had welcomed the McCullen brothers.

"So how did you find out about the McCullens?" Ryder asked.

A sardonic chuckle escaped Cash and he swallowed another sip of beer. "A few months ago I got arrested. Maddox and Brett and Ray showed up at my bail hearing. Took me home with them and paid for my defense."

Ryder narrowed his eyes. "Just like that? No strings attached?"

Cash frowned. "Well, Maddox made it clear that if I was guilty he wouldn't cover for me. But they investigated and helped me clear my name."

Ryder stared at the sliver of moon trying to peek through the trees.

"Your turn," Cash said. "How did you find out about the McCullens?"

Ryder silently cursed. "After my dad died, I became curious and did some digging. Finally I asked my mom."

"You mean your adopted mother?"

"Same thing," Ryder said, his loyalty to the woman who'd raised him kicking in. "She told me what happened."

Cash narrowed his eyes. "She told you that you were kidnapped, that your real mother died trying to find you?"

Ryder locked his jaw and debated what to say. But he refused to lie. "Not exactly."

"Then what did she tell you?"

Ryder leaned forward, arms braced on his thighs as he studied Cash. "That the McCullens needed money to expand their ranch, so they made a deal with a lawyer and sold me."

A startled look passed across Cash's face. "What? Damn, that's not the way it happened."

"How do you know?" Ryder asked. "We were both babies at the time."

Cash scraped a hand over his face, drawing Ryder's gaze to the long scar on his forehead. Ryder's gut pinched. How had he gotten that?

Cash settled his Stetson on his lap. "That's right, but once the McCullens found me, they explained everything. It's a long story. The doctor who delivered us made a mistake with another delivery, a mistake that cost another couple their child. That baby's father stole us from the hospital to replace the child he lost, and the doctor covered out of guilt. He told our parents that we were stillborn."

Shock rolled through Ryder. "That's the story the McCullens told you?" Ryder said, well aware his comment sounded like an accusation. "How do you know it's true?"

Cash sucked in a sharp breath. "Because Maddox investigated. That doctor remained friends with the Mc-Cullens, especially Joe, our father. He finally admitted what happened—that Mom was murdered because she didn't believe we'd died and because she was searching for us. Dunn, the man who'd taken us, killed her to cover up the truth."

Ryder's mind raced. "If that's true, why didn't the man who kidnapped us raise us?"

Cash grunted. "Apparently his wife figured out what he'd done and insisted he take us back to the McCullens. The man was afraid of being arrested, so he dropped us off at a church instead."

Ryder swallowed hard. But Myra and Troy Banks claimed they'd gotten him from an attorney and led him to believe the McCullens orchestrated the deal. They hadn't mentioned anything about a church.

Ryder stood and walked to the edge of the deck. A wild animal growled from the woods. He could almost see its predator eyes glowing in the dark.

"Last year, our father, Joe, realized what had happened. He started looking for us, too. Then he was murdered."

Ryder drained his beer. "Listen, Cash, it sounds like you had a rough childhood. I'm sure it feels good to think the McCullens want you." He balled his hand into a fist and pressed it over his chest. "But I have a family—a mother, at least. And I don't want or need the McCullens in my life."

Emotions wrestled in Cash's eyes. He'd obviously thought Ryder would be thrilled to learn about his roots.

Ryder might—if he didn't already know the real story. Of course the McCullen brothers wouldn't admit that their parents had been greedy enough to trade two of their children for money.

Cash removed a manila envelope from the inside of his jacket. He laid it on the coffee table. "Inside are letters and cards our mother wrote to you. I have an envelope just like it."

Ryder raised a brow in question.

"She—our mother, Grace—wrote to us after we went missing. She bought cards for Christmases and birthdays. Read them and you'll see I'm telling the truth."

Without another word, Cash set his empty beer bottle on the table with a thud, then strode back through the house and outside. Ryder stared at the envelope, his heart pounding, until he heard Cash's truck spring to life and chug away.

Anger and resentment mingled with doubt. He squashed the doubt. His mother loved him. She wouldn't have lied to him.

He didn't need any letters or cards or for his life to be disrupted by the McCullens.

He was fine on his own. He always had been. He always would be.

THE HOURS DRAGGED BY. Tia had felt alone when her family had died, but she'd never felt more alone than she did now, without her baby in her arms.

Her eyes felt gritty from staring at the ceiling of the jail cell, and her body ached from fatigue. But that discomfort was nothing compared to the emptiness inside her.

She might never see Jordie again.

She'd read stories about children who went missing and were never recovered. There were other accounts where the child was located years later but had bonded with whoever had raised them.

Jordie was only an infant. Babies changed every day. What if it took months or years to find him and she didn't even recognize him?

She paced the cell for the millionth time, mentally retracing the events of the past couple of days.

Darren had moved out months ago. But he'd contacted her two weeks before she was due, offering to set up a fund for the baby—with her money. He wanted to invest in a surefire project that would double the money in a week's time.

She had refused. At that point, she didn't trust him. He'd already cleaned out her savings account and most of her checking account.

He could have kidnapped Jordan for revenge. Maybe he was even working with someone else.

Although if he'd taken Jordan because of the money, why hadn't he asked for a ransom?

Everything was normal. He was eating and gaining weight. Although the doctor insisted he was too young to smile, he had smiled at her as she'd hugged him on the way back to the car.

Of course he'd had a fit when she put him in the car seat. Apparently he didn't like to be confined.

The bars on the cell mocked her. Neither did she.

She closed her eyes and saw his little face again. So trusting. So sweet and innocent. He'd smelled like baby wash. He had her blue eyes and a full head of light-colored hair.

At the doctor's office, two other mothers had commented on how beautiful he was. The nurse who'd delivered him, Amy Yost, had phoned to see how the checkup went. Tia had invited the young woman over for coffee the next day. They'd chatted and become friends. Amy suggested she and her three-year-old daughter, Linnie, get together more often.

After Amy left, Tia's neighbor Judy Kinley had dropped by with brownies and a basket of goodies for Jordie—diaper wipes, baby washcloths, onesies and a blanket she'd crocheted herself.

Tia had enjoyed the visit but finally admitted that she needed a nap, that she'd been up half the night and maybe they could visit another day.

But none of those memories were helpful. She hadn't seen anyone lurking around the house watching her. No strangers had come to the door. She hadn't seen any cars following her. And she hadn't received any odd phone calls.

She closed her eyes and flopped back on the cot, her head spinning. Just as she was about to drift to sleep, the sound of a baby crying echoed in her ears.

She jerked upright in search of Jordie and realized she was still in jail. Emotions racked her body.

She was no closer to finding her son than she had been the day before.

JUST AFTER DAWN, Ryder crawled from bed, irritated that he'd let thoughts of his conversation with Cash keep him awake. When he'd finally gotten the McCullens off his mind, Tia's big blue eyes had haunted him.

He showered and shaved, then dressed and strapped on his holster. He called Darren Hoyt on his way out the door.

"Meet me at the Sagebrush jail in half an hour. If you

aren't there to file a report, I'll assume you're dropping the charges and I'll release Miss Jeffries."

He'd also fill Sheriff Gaines in on what he'd learned about Hoyt.

Then he wanted to search Tia's house himself. Maybe the sheriff had missed a clue.

Storm clouds hovered in the sky, painting the woods a bleak gray and making the deserted land between his cabin and town look desolate. As he drove into town, he noted that the diner was already filling up with the breakfast crowd and several young mothers strolled their babies on the sidewalk and at the park while their toddlers and preschoolers ran and squealed on the playground.

He parked at the jail and went inside, his stomach clenching at the sight of another deputy at the desk. The old-timer had gray hair and a gut, and was slumped back in the chair, snoring like a bear.

Had he even checked on Tia?

Ryder rapped on the wooden desk. The man jumped, sending the chair backward with a thud as the edge hit the wall.

"Wha-what's going on?" The man fumbled with his wire-rimmed glasses.

Ryder identified himself. "I need to talk to Sheriff Gaines."

The man's face grew pinched as he adjusted his glasses. "This about the prisoner?"

"Yes," Ryder said between clenched teeth. "That and her missing child."

The man yawned. "Sheriff'll be in here soon. You can wait."

Ryder opened his mouth to ask him what he knew about the missing baby case, but the door swung open and Darren Hoyt barreled in. His clothes were disheveled, his eyes bloodshot and he reeked of whiskey.

"I'm here," Hoyt snapped. "Now let me sign those damn papers. I've got stuff to do."

Ryder grabbed the man by the collar and led him to the corner.

"Listen to me, you jerk. I did some digging on you last night and I know about your past."

"What are you talking about?" Hoyt growled. "I don't have a record."

"Not as Darren Hoyt, but you do under your real name."

Panic flared on Hoyt's face.

"Now, I suggest you tell me where Jordie Jeffries is."

"I told you last night, I don't know." He flung his hand toward the door leading to the cells. "Go ask my ex. She's the one that took the runt to her house."

Ryder jammed his face into the man's and gave him a warning look. "Because I don't believe she did anything but love that baby. You, on the other hand are a dirtbag of a father, a con man and a criminal."

Hoyt shook his head in denial. "That's not true—"

"Yes, it is," Ryder said coldly. "But if you confess and tell me where to find the baby, I'll go to bat for you with the judge."

"I don't know where he is," Darren screeched. "I swear I don't."

Ryder studied him for a long, frustrating minute. He wanted to beat the bastard until he confessed, but he couldn't do that here, not with that deputy watching.

"If that's true, prove it and drop the charges against Tia. The best way to find your son is for me to work with her."

Hoyt's breath rasped out. "You gonna watch her, see if she leads you to the baby?"

Ryder's gut tightened, but the lie came easy. "Exactly. You do want your son found unharmed, don't you?"

Hoyt's eyes darted toward the deputy, then the door opened and Sheriff Gaines strode in.

"What's going on?" the sheriff asked.

Ryder reluctantly released Hoyt. "Hoyt and I were just making a deal. He wants us to find his baby real bad."

The sheriff's eyebrows climbed his forehead as he jerked his head toward Hoyt. "That so?"

Hoyt nodded. Ryder patted his arm. "And you're dropping the charges against Miss Jeffries, right?"

Hoyt hissed a curse word, then gave another nod. "Just tell that crazy bitch not to come near me again."

Ryder barely resisted slugging the jerk. But he would keep Tia away from Hoyt for her own protection.

He gestured toward the deputy. "Please bring Miss Jeffries to the front."

The older man ambled through the door, and Ryder turned to Gaines. "I need everything you have on this missing child case."

"Wait just a damn minute," Gaines said. "This is my jurisdiction."

"Kidnapping is a federal offense. I'm officially taking over the case now."

If he didn't, Gaines would probably railroad Tia to prison and they'd never find her son.

Chapter Seven

Ryder watched as Hoyt stormed out the door. If the bastard cared about his baby, he'd be pushing him and the sheriff to find him.

Instead, Hoyt was more concerned with himself.

"Sheriff Gaines, did you search Tia's house after she reported her child missing?"

Gaines shifted, his chin set stubbornly. "Of course."

"What did you find?"

"Like I put in my report, the window was unlocked. No prints. No sign of foul play or that anyone had been in the house except Miss Jeffries."

"Can I see that report?"

Gaines shoved a file folder from his desk toward Ryder. Ryder quickly skimmed the notes on Tia's interview and photos of the empty crib and nursery.

"Did you take pictures when you searched the outer premises?"

Sheriff Gaines shook his head. "Wasn't nothing to photograph."

Ryder frowned. If an intruder had broken in, he would have expected to find something. Maybe footprints, brush disturbed.

He wanted to conduct his own search. "You can release her now."

The sheriff glared at him. "You sure that's a good idea?"

Ryder nodded. "Keep an open mind, Gaines. If Tia is innocent, whoever abducted her baby could be getting away."

FOOTSTEPS ON THE concrete floor startled Tia. What was going to happen now? Was the sheriff or that agent taking her to court for a bail hearing?

Had one of them found Jordie?

An older deputy appeared, his scowl menacing. Keys jangled as he unlocked the cell.

She rubbed her wrists. Even though the agent had removed the handcuffs, she could still feel the weight of the cold metal. Was he going to handcuff her again?

"Let's go," the deputy barked.

Tia inhaled a deep breath, stood and crossed the floor to the cell door. The deputy gestured for her to follow him, but he surprised her by not cuffing her. Exhaustion pulled at her, but she held her head high.

Darren had depleted her checking and savings. If she needed bail money, she could ask her assistant at Crossroads to dip into their funds to bail her out.

But that was a last resort.

Except for paying herself a small salary, she *never* used the charity's money for personal reasons.

But if her parents had been alive, they'd agree that she should do anything to find her baby.

When the deputy opened the door to the front office,

she blinked at how bright it seemed, a reminder that life in prison meant missing fresh air and sunshine.

A shadow caught her eye, then the figure came into focus. Agent Banks.

Her lungs squeezed for air. If he hadn't arrested her, she might find him attractive.

He *was* attractive. Tall, dark and handsome.

But he'd locked her up the night before and left her alone in jail when she should have been out looking for her baby.

RYDER SCRUTINIZED TIA to make certain she was okay. Leaving a woman alone in a jail with a male-only staff, especially with men he didn't know, always worried him.

She looked exhausted and frightened, but there were no visible signs that she'd been abused or manhandled.

"What's going on?" she asked.

"Hoyt decided to drop the charges," Ryder said.

She glanced at the sheriff for confirmation.

"Guess it's your lucky day," the sheriff said in a voice harsh with displeasure. "But I suggest you stay away from your ex or you'll be right back here."

Tia gave a nod. "Do you have new information on my son?"

Gaines cut his eyes toward Ryder. "You'll have to ask him. It's his case now."

Another surprised look flitted across Tia's face, then relief. She obviously didn't trust Gaines to do his job.

Ryder gestured toward the door leading outside. "I'll drive you home."

Tia rubbed her hands up and down her arms as if she was trying to hold herself together as they crossed the room to the door.

"Don't leave town, Miss Jeffries," Gaines muttered.

She paused, animosity streaking her face. "I'm going to find my little boy," she said sharply.

Gaines started to say something else, but Ryder coaxed Tia out the door before they shared another exchange.

He placed his hand to Tia's back as they stepped onto the sidewalk and felt a shiver run through her.

"Are you all right?" he asked gruffly.

She shook her head. "I won't be all right until I'm holding Jordie again."

He understood that. "Let's talk at your house. I'm sure you want a shower and some food."

She didn't comment. She simply slid into the passenger seat of his SUV.

"I don't know how you convinced Darren to drop the charges, but I appreciate that."

He started the engine. "I don't like him," he said bluntly.

A small smile tugged at her mouth, making him wish he could permanently wipe the anguish from her face. "You mean you saw through his act. Sheriff Gaines certainly seems to believe whatever Darren says."

"I know. I don't understand that." He gripped the steering wheel tighter, then veered onto the road leading to Tia's house.

She angled her head, her eyes narrowed. "How do you know where I live?"

He winced. "It's my job, Tia."

She heaved a breath. "You were watching me, weren't you? That's the reason you were at Darren's when I confronted him."

Confronted was putting it mildly. "Yes," he said, deciding to be straightforward. "Kidnapping and a missing baby warrant the feds' attention."

He pulled into the drive of the small bungalow. Flowers danced in the window boxes, the house was painted a soothing gray blue and a screened porch made it look homey—and totally at odds with Tia's current situation.

"Do you own or rent?" Ryder asked.

"I own it," Tia said. "I was living in an apartment before, but I wanted Jordie to have a real home with a yard to play in." Her voice broke. "I thought when he got older, we'd get a dog."

Ryder swallowed hard. There was no way this woman had hurt her child.

"I know Sheriff Gaines searched the house and property, but I intend to conduct my own search."

Ryder grabbed his kit from the trunk then followed Tia up to the front porch. She opened the door, and he followed her in.

Just as he'd expected, signs of a new baby were everywhere—a basket of baby clothes from the laundry. An infant bouncy seat. Toys scattered on a dinosaur blanket on the floor.

"The nursery is this way." Tia picked up a stuffed bear from the couch and hugged it to her as if she needed something in her arms to fill the void of her missing baby.

She led him across the den into a small hallway. A bathroom was situated between two bedrooms.

"Jordie's room is in here."

The moment he stepped inside the nursery, the love Tia had put into decorating the room engulfed him.

"Has anyone been inside the house since Jordie was born?" Ryder asked.

Tia rubbed her temple. "Elle and Ina dropped by and brought dinner and a basket of baby things."

"I spoke with them. They sang your praises." He paused, mentally eliminating them from his suspect list. He needed to look into the two people they'd suggested might hold a grudge against Tia.

"They're both wonderful and are godsends with the women and families who come through. I wish I could afford to pay them more, but they don't seem to mind."

"Who else?"

"A neighbor dropped by to bring me some treats and a gift for Jordie."

"Which neighbor?"

"Judy Kinley, the lady who lives behind me."

Ryder made a mental note to check her out. "Anyone else?"

She scrunched her mouth in thought. "Darren stopped by to drop off the finalized divorce decree."

He bit back a curse. "What a guy."

"I know. I was an idiot to ever believe he cared."

Ryder didn't comment. Men like Darren Hoyt were predators. He saw it all the time.

"I'm going to look around the room and check outside," he said instead.

Hopefully he'd find a clue that the sheriff had missed.

Tia desperately wanted a shower, but she felt uncomfortable with the federal agent in the house, so she watched as he combed through the nursery.

"What are you looking for?" she asked.

"Fingerprints. Forensics that would prove someone broke in."

He dusted the crib and the windowsill for prints.

"Did you find anything?"

He shook his head. "Not yet. But the kidnapper could have worn gloves."

Because he'd planned this. But who would do such a thing? Darren was the only one who knew about her inheritance. And he hadn't asked for money. He'd denied knowing anything about the kidnapping, when in private he could have blackmailed her into paying.

Ryder examined the window lock, then knelt to check the floor below, then the wall. He removed a camera from his kit and took a picture.

"What do you see?" she asked.

"Scuff marks. It's not enough to cast, but it might be important."

He examined the lock again. "This definitely wasn't jimmied. Did someone else come in the house that day? Someone who might have unlocked the window without you being aware?"

Tia pressed two fingers to her temple as she mentally retraced her movements that day. "Judy came by and a friend I made at the hospital, my delivery nurse, Amy, stopped in with her little girl. We had coffee. Elle and Ina came later. They dropped off a casserole and saw Jordie for a minute. But none of them would have unlocked the window."

"I asked Elle and Ina about two people on your list, Wanda Hanson and a man, Bennett Jones. They mentioned they might hold a grudge against you."

"They were both angry," Tia said. "But I can't imagine either one of them kidnapping Jordie to get back at me."

"I want to talk to them anyway," Ryder said. "Sometimes people crack and do unexpected things."

She followed him outside to the back of the house, to the nursery window.

"Stay put," he said bluntly. "If there is something here, you don't want to contaminate it."

Tia wrung her hands together and hoped that he found something that would lead them to her baby.

RYDER CIRCLED THE house outside, searching the patches of grass and weeds. An area near the window looked as if the foliage had been mashed—as in footprints.

It could have happened when Gaines conducted his search, although the man obviously hadn't been very thorough. If he had, he would have photographed the window and surrounding area.

He snapped photos of his own, capturing the disturbed bushes and dirt. A partial shoe print was embedded in the ground, which at least suggested someone—a man?— had been outside the room.

That lent credence to Tia's story.

Of course, Gaines could argue that Tia had paid someone to take the baby.

He texted the tech team at the Bureau, instructing them to check Tia's financials for anything suspicious, and also to look into Wanda Hanson and Bennett Jones.

He peered closer and discovered smudges on the wood beneath the window frame. Another partial boot print where the intruder had climbed onto the ledge and slipped through the window. He snapped pictures of the ledge, noting broken splinters around the edge and smudges on the windowpane.

He studied it for a print, but the kidnapper must have worn gloves, as there was no clear print.

Something caught his eye below, wedged into the weeds, and he stooped and combed through the area.

A pack of matches, with a logo for the Big Mug.

He hadn't seen ashtrays or any evidence that Tia was a smoker in her house.

His pulse kicked up. The matches could have belonged to the person who'd taken her son.

Chapter Eight

Still grungy from the jail cell, Tia stepped onto the porch for air. When she'd first bought the house, she'd imagined rocking Jordan out here on cool spring and fall nights, doing artwork with him as he grew older and adding a swing set to the backyard.

She blinked back more tears, then spotted Judy, the neighbor whose house backed up to Tia's, standing on her deck. She was peering at Tia's house through binoculars.

Ryder stepped onto the porch, his phone in hand. "Who's the woman with the binoculars?"

"That's Judy Kinley."

"Tell me about her."

Tia bit her lower lip. "She seems friendly, although she's a little nosy. She works at home doing accounting for a couple of small businesses."

"Married? Kids?"

"No." Tia shook her head. "At first I thought it was comforting to have a neighbor close by, in case of an emergency, one who'd watch out for my property, but she tends to just drop by. I guess she's lonely."

Agent Banks arched a brow. "She comes by a lot?"

Tia shrugged. "A few times. Once she brought cookies and another time a pie. Apparently she likes to bake."

"Did she know your ex?"

"No," Tia said. "I wanted a fresh start, so I moved here after he and I split up."

He nodded. "Is she always peering at the neighbors?"

Tia tucked a strand of hair behind her ear. "She started a community watch program."

"Was she home the night Jordie disappeared?"

"Yes," Tia said. "When I found his crib empty, I called the sheriff. A few minutes after he arrived, Judy rushed over to see what was wrong and what she could do to help."

An odd expression flickered in Ryder's eyes. "I'm going to talk to her. I also want to speak to some of your other neighbors. Maybe one of them saw something."

Although if so, why hadn't he or she come forward?

RYAN CROSSED TIA'S BACKYARD, then strode toward the neighbor's back deck. He waved his identification. "Ma'am, my name is Special Agent Ryder Banks. I'd like to ask you some questions."

She lowered the binoculars and stepped back as if startled. Ryder paused at the bottom of the steps, studying her. She was probably in her early forties, with a face already weathered from too much sun. A few strands of gray hair mingled with the muddy brown, and she wore a drab T-shirt and jeans that hung on her thin frame.

"Tia said your name is Judy. Is that right?"

"Yes. I assume you're investigating the disappearance of her baby."

Ryder nodded. "Yes, ma'am. May I come up and talk to you for a few minutes?"

She clenched the binoculars by her side. "I don't know how I can help, but sure, come on up."

Ryder wasn't buying the innocent act. Anyone who watched their neighbors through binoculars knew what was going on in the neighborhood.

His footsteps pounded the wooden steps as he climbed them.

"Can I get you some lemonade or tea?" Judy asked.

"No, thanks." He gestured toward Tia's house and saw her watching. "How well do you know Tia Jeffries?"

Judy shrugged and leaned against the deck railing. "We've chatted a few times."

"You were living here when she moved in?"

"No, I moved in after her. My husband passed away and I wanted to downsize."

"Tell me what you know about Tia."

Judy fluttered her fingers through her short hair. "Tia seems like a nice young woman. She was alone, too, so I introduced myself."

"Did you meet her ex-husband?"

Judy pursed her lips. "No, I can't say I wanted to, either. Any man who'd abandon his pregnant wife is pretty low in my book."

He agreed. "Tia said you started a neighborhood watch program. You were also home the night her baby disappeared. Did you notice any strangers lurking around? A car that was out of place?"

She shook her head no. "Although Darren stopped by, Tia said he brought the divorce papers."

"Was she upset about that?"

"No, she seemed relieved it would be final."

Ryder shifted. Darren could have slipped into the nursery and unlocked the window without Tia's knowledge.

"Tell me about the night the baby went missing."

"What do you mean?"

"Tia said she'd fallen asleep and when she woke up and checked on the baby, he was gone. She called 911, then you came over when you saw the police."

"That's right."

"How was she?" Ryder asked.

"How do you think she was?" Judy said with a bite to her tone. "Someone kidnapped her child. She was hysterical."

"What exactly did she say?"

"She was crying so hard she could barely talk." Judy sighed wearily. "But she said someone had kidnapped Jordan from his bed. I tried to calm Tia while the sheriff searched the house and outside."

"Did Tia say anything else?"

Judy rubbed her forehead. "She just kept begging the sheriff to find her son. He asked about her marriage. She told him about the divorce, then she said she was afraid Darren abducted the infant."

"According to Tia, he left her because she refused to give him money from her charity."

"True." Judy made a low sound in her throat. "But if he took the little boy for money, why hasn't he demanded a ransom?"

Good question. And one Ryder wanted the answer to.

UNABLE TO BEAR the scent of her clothes any longer, Tia stripped and stepped into the shower. The hot water felt wonderful, but as she closed her eyes, images of her little boy taunted her.

"I promise I'll find you," she whispered. "I will bring you home and I'll never let you out of my sight again."

She scrubbed her body three times to cleanse the ugliness of the jail cell, then soaped and rinsed her hair.

When she climbed out, she brushed her teeth, pulled on a clean T-shirt and pair of jeans, and dried her hair.

The agent still hadn't returned.

The hole in her heart continued to ache, and she stepped back into the nursery and ran her fingers over the baby quilt she'd hand sewn. Each square featured an appliqué, a hodgepodge of different breeds of puppies. She'd imagined naming the dogs on the quilt with Jordie. And when he was older, they'd visit the animal shelter and choose a dog to adopt.

She'd painted the room a bright blue and his dresser a barnyard red. She opened up one of the drawers and touched the sleepers she'd neatly folded, the tiny bootees and socks, then hugged the little knit cap he'd worn home from the hospital to her chest. She blinked back more tears as she inhaled Jordie's newborn scent.

She had to do something to find her son.

Maybe a personal plea on the news.

She'd talk to that agent when he returned.

If he didn't agree, she'd find a way to do it herself.

RYDER CANVASSED THE NEIGHBORHOOD, but no one had seen or heard anything suspicious the night before or the night of Jordie's disappearance. Several of them hadn't even met Tia, as she'd only moved in a few weeks before.

Two older women claimed they'd seen Tia strolling the baby in the mornings. She'd looked tired but doted on her child.

He walked back to Tia's, frustrated that he hadn't discovered anything helpful.

On a positive note, he hadn't heard anything derogatory about Tia, nothing to make him doubt her story.

He banged the horse door knocker, and Tia opened

the door. She'd showered, and her hair looked damp as it hung around her shoulders.

His gut tightened. She was damn gorgeous.

Not something he should be noticing or thinking about.

"Did you learn anything?" Tia asked.

He shook his head. "Afraid not. None of your neighbors seemed suspicious, but I'm going to run background checks on each of them just to be on the safe side. I want to talk to the hospital staff next."

Tia frowned. "Why? Jordie was taken from my house."

"I know. But we have to consider every possibility. Perhaps a stranger or another patient was in the hospital looking at the babies, someone who didn't belong."

Tia's eyes widened. "You mean someone could have been watching Jordie, looking for a chance to take him?"

Ryder shrugged. "Either him or another child. We could be dealing with a desperate, possibly unstable parent. Perhaps someone who lost a child or couldn't have a baby was depressed, desperate. He or she could have scouted out the nursery. It's happened before."

Tia shivered.

Ryder couldn't resist. He gently took her arms in his hands and forced her to face him. "If someone took him because they wanted a family, that means Jordie will be well taken care of, that he or she will keep him safe."

Tia released a pent-up breath, then gave a little nod. "I want to appear on television and make a plea for whoever took Jordie to return him to me."

Ryder hesitated. "That could work, but it could backfire, Tia. Sometimes going to the media draws out the crazies and we waste time on false leads."

Her eyes glittered with emotions. "Maybe. But if the

person who abducted Jordie wants a family like you suggested, seeing how much I love and miss my baby might make them rethink what they've done and bring him back."

He couldn't argue with that.

"Please, Agent Banks," she whispered. "I have to do everything I can to find him."

Ryder inhaled. "All right, I'll set it up."

"For today," Tia said. "I want to do it right away."

"All right, but call me Ryder." After all, they were going to be spending a lot of time together—as much as it took until they recovered her son.

"All right, Ryder," she said, her soft voice filled with conviction. "I want to speak to the press as soon as possible."

Ryder nodded then stepped aside to make the call.

TIA'S HEART RACED as Ryder returned, his phone in hand. "Did you set it up?"

"Yes. At six. They'll air it on the evening news."

"Good. That will give us time to go to the hospital."

Ryder agreed and they hurried to his SUV. Ten minutes later, she led the way to the hospital maternity floor. The nurses at the nurses' station looked surprised to see Tia, their nervous whispers making her wonder what they thought.

Hilda, the head charge nurse, hurried around the desk edge and swept her into a hug. "Oh, my God, Tia. I'm so sorry about the kidnapping. Did the police find Jordie?"

Tia shook her head no and introduced Ryder. "Agent Banks is looking for him."

"I need to talk to each of the staff members who were on duty the night Tia delivered."

Hilda looked eager to help. "All right, I'll get a list and text them."

"Also, I need to know if anyone suspicious has been lurking around the nursery area and this ward."

"Not that I know of," Hilda said. "But I'll ask around."

"Do you have security cameras on this floor?"

"Absolutely," Hilda said. "We take our patients' and their children's safety very seriously."

"Good. I want to review all the tapes the week prior to Jordie's disappearance as well as the week he was born."

Hilda nodded, then stepped to the desk to set things up.

Tia held her breath. If Ryder was right, maybe the person who'd taken her son was on one of those tapes.

Chapter Nine

Tia hurried toward the nurse who'd coached her during labor. Amy spoke to her, then Tia introduced Ryder.

"This is Special Agent Ryder Banks," Tia said. "He's helping me search for my son."

Ryder flashed his credentials. "I'm talking to all the staff," he said. "You were here the night Tia delivered her son?"

Amy nodded. "I worked night shift that week."

Tia offered her a smile of gratitude. "Amy was my labor coach. I couldn't have done it without her."

Amy shrugged. "You did the hard work, Tia." Her voice cracked. "I'm just sorry for what's happened."

Tia swallowed the fear eating at her. "I'm going on television to make a plea to get Jordie back."

Amy squeezed her hand. "I hope that helps."

Ryder cleared his throat. "Amy, have you noticed anyone lurking around the maternity floor? Maybe someone near the nursery?"

Amy fidgeted with the pocket of her uniform. "Not really."

"How about a patient who lost a child?" Cash's story about the McCullens echoed in his head. "A grieving mother might be desperate enough to take someone else's child to fill the void of her own loss."

Amy squeezed Tia's hand again. "That's true. But I can't discuss other patients' medical charts or history."

"You don't have to. Just tell me if there's someone who fits that description."

Amy worried her bottom lip with her teeth. "There was one woman who suffered from complications and delivered prematurely, only twenty weeks."

Tia's heart ached for her. "That must have been devastating."

Amy nodded. "She and her husband were in the middle of a divorce, so she blamed him. She thought the stress triggered her premature labor."

Hilda returned and motioned for them to join her at the desk. "The security guard is waiting whenever you want to take a look at those tapes."

"Thanks." Ryder turned back to Amy. "Why don't you watch the tapes with us? If you see anyone you think is suspicious, you can point them out."

Amy and Hilda exchanged concerned looks, then Amy followed them to the security office. They passed a nurse named Richard who grunted hello.

Amy exchanged a smile with him and introduced Ryder. "I'm canvassing the staff to see if anyone saw or heard anything strange when Miss Jeffries was here."

"I didn't see anyone suspicious." Richard gave Tia a sympathetic look. "I'm sorry about your baby, Miss Jeffries."

Tia murmured thanks, then Richard had to go to the ER.

Hilda led them into the security room, and she, Ryder and Amy gathered to view the tapes.

When the guard zeroed in on the camera feed showing her at admissions, Tia's heart gave a painful tug. That night she'd been so excited. After nine months of carrying her baby inside her, of feeling his little feet and fists push at her belly, of listening to his heartbeat during the ultrasounds and imagining what he might look like, her son was going to be born.

She was going to have a family of her own.

He had cried the moment he'd come out, a beautiful sound that had brought tears to her eyes. He had a cap of light blond hair, blue eyes and tiny pink fingers that had grasped her finger when she'd caressed him to her breast.

But now he was gone.

RYDER PARKED HIMSELF in front of the security feed, anxious to find a lead. Amy certainly seemed to care about Tia and wanted to be helpful.

Tia's breath rattled out with nerves as she sank into the chair beside him. One camera shot captured her entering the ER—apparently she'd driven herself. She held her bulging belly with one hand, breathing deeply, as she handled the paperwork.

Although her hair was pulled back in a ponytail and she was obviously in pain, she looked…happy. Glowing with the kind of joy an expectant mother should be feeling.

All his life, he'd thought his birth mother had sold him. But if Cash was telling the truth, she hadn't done any such thing.

She died trying to find us.

Cash had insisted that was the truth.

Had his biological mother felt that anticipation over

giving birth to him and Cash, only to be grief stricken when she was told her twins were stillborn?

His lungs squeezed for air. How she must have suffered.

Tia was wheeled into a triage room, then a delivery room, where they lost sight of her.

"Let's look at the hallways near the nursery the week before—"

"Go back to the day he was born," Amy suggested quietly.

That must have been around the time when the other woman lost her baby.

The next half hour they studied each section of the tape, zeroing in on parents and grandparents and friends who'd visited—most of whom looked elated as they oohed and aahed over the infants in the nursery.

Couples came and went, huddling together, smiling, laughing and crying as they watched the newborns.

Emotions churned in Ryder's belly. He'd never imagined having a family of his own—a wife, kids. Not in the picture. Not with the job he did.

A long empty space of tape, then another crew of family members appeared, gushing and waving through the glass window.

Just as they left, a young woman emerged from the shadows, her thin face haggard and lined with fatigue. She was hunched inside an oversize raincoat, her hair pulled back beneath a scarf, her face a picture of agony as she studied the infants. The nurse, Richard Blotter, paused as he passed, his gaze narrowed.

"There's Jordie," Tia said in a raw whisper.

The woman hesitated as she walked along the window,

eyeing the pink and blue bundles. She paused in front of Jordie's bassinet.

Tia straightened, her body tensing as she leaned forward to home in on the woman's face.

"She's looking at Jordie," she said in a low voice.

Yes, she was.

Richard passed the nursery, but the woman hurried away.

Ryder swung his gaze toward Amy, but she quickly glanced toward the floor, avoiding eye contact as she bit her lower lip.

"Do you know who this woman is?" Ryder asked.

"I don't remember her name," Amy said, "but she's the woman I mentioned who lost her baby."

"I need a copy of this tape," he told the security guard.

The tech team could work wonders with facial recognition software. He'd also get a warrant for medical records and find out her name.

She might be the person who'd stolen Tia's child.

TIA CONSTANTLY CHECKED the clock as Ryder questioned other staff members. Hilda discreetly ran a check for any patients who'd required mental health services.

As they left the hospital, Ryder drove to the county crime lab and dropped off the partial print and matches he'd found outside the nursery along with the tapes for analysis. He wanted the ID of the woman who'd been watching those babies.

He received a text from the FBI analyst as they walked back to his SUV. "One of our analysts located Bennett Jones."

"Where is he?"

"Jones remarried and moved to Texas. Been there four

months. His first wife claims he's made no move to see their baby since he met the other woman."

Tia gritted her teeth. "That's not uncommon. He was angry when she left, had a bruised ego, but he quickly replaced his family with another one."

Ryder grunted a sound of disapproval. "I also have an address for the woman, Wanda Hanson. She entered a rehab program after her husband gained custody of their infant."

"Where is she now?"

"A few miles outside Pistol Whip." He started the engine and pulled onto the highway. Tia contemplated the woman in the security tape as he drove. Sympathy for her situation and her loss filled Tia. If she'd taken Jordie, hopefully he was in good hands.

But Jordie belonged to her. *With* her.

And she would do whatever necessary to bring him home.

The sun dipped behind a sea of dark clouds, painting the sky a dismal gray. The farmland looked desolate, with dry scrub brush dotting the landscape, the ground thirsty for water.

Ryder drove down a narrow two-lane road past a cluster of small, older homes that needed serious upkeep. A few toys and bicycles were scattered around, the yards overgrown and full of weeds.

He checked his phone for the address, then turned in the drive of a redbrick ranch. Anxious to see if Wanda had her son, Tia slipped from the vehicle and started up the drive. Ryder caught her before she made it to the front door.

"Let me handle this," Ryder said in a gruff voice.

"She hates me, Ryder. If she took Jordie, the minute she sees me, she'll know the reason I'm here."

And Tia would know by the look on Wanda's face if she was guilty.

RYDER PUNCHED THE DOORBELL, his gaze scanning the property for any sign Wanda was home, but there was no car in the drive. It was impossible to see in the tiny window-less garage.

Tia stepped slightly to the right and peered through the front window. From his vantage point, the house looked dark.

"Do you see anything? Any movement?" he asked.

"No one in the kitchen or den."

He rang the bell again, then banged on the door. Seconds passed with no response. He jiggled the doorknob, but it was locked.

"I'm going to check around the side and back."

He veered to the left and Tia followed.

"You're sure this is her place?" Tia asked.

"Yes, our analyst, Gwen, is good at her job. Apparently Wanda had no money for rent or to buy a house. This place belonged to her mother, who passed away last year. She's been living here since the custody hearing."

He passed the side window. No lights inside. The curtains hung askew, clothes scattered around the room. Dry leaves crunched as they inched to the back door. He jiggled the door but it was locked.

Dammit, he wanted to search the interior. He removed a tiny tool from his pocket just as Tia did the same.

"I've got it," he said, remembering the way they'd met. "Don't touch anything, Tia. If we find evidence, I don't want it thrown out because you were present."

"Don't you need a warrant?" Her brows furrowed at the unpleasant reminder, and she jammed the tool back in her pocket.

Hell, he was breaking the rules. "Technically, yes. But it's acceptable if I have probable cause. I can always say we heard a noise and thought the baby was inside."

Ryder yanked on latex gloves, opened the door, flipped on the overhead light and called out, "FBI Special Agent Banks. Is anyone here?"

Silence echoed back. Then Ryder stepped into the tiny kitchen. Outdated appliances, linoleum and a rickety table made the room look fifty years old. A dirty coffee cup sat in the sink along with a plate of dried, molded food. The garbage reeked as if it hadn't been taken out in days.

Ryder opened the refrigerator, and Tia spotted a carton of milk, eggs, condiments and a jar of applesauce.

On the second shelf sat two baby bottles, half full of formula.

Her pulse jumped. Why would Wanda have baby formula and bottles when there were no kids in the house?

Her child was a toddler, too, not a baby, so why the bottle?

Ryder crossed the room into the den and flipped on a lamp. The soft light illuminated the room just enough for her to see that Wanda wasn't a housekeeper.

Magazines, dirty laundry and mail were spread across the couch and table. A worn teddy bear had been stuffed in the corner along with an infant's receiving blanket.

Tia followed Ryder into the hall. The first bedroom had been turned into a nursery. Tia scanned the room, her heart racing at the sight of a tiny bassinet.

Wanda's baby had long ago outgrown it, but a receiving blanket lay inside, along with an elephant-shaped blue rattle.

A baby had been here recently. Was it Jordie?

Ryder paused to look at it, then walked over to the changing table and lifted the lid on the diaper pail.

"Was Wanda allowed visitation rights?" Tia asked.

He shrugged, then made a quick phone call and identified himself. "Mr. Hanson, was your wife allowed visitation rights to your child?"

Tia held her breath while she waited for the answer.

"No. Hmm," Ryder mumbled. Another pause. "When did you last see her or speak with her?"

Silence stretched for a full minute. Ryder thanked the man then his gaze darkened.

"He hasn't heard from her. Said she hasn't seen the kid, but he's safe with him. The last time he talked to her, she'd fallen off the wagon and screamed at him that she hadn't deserved to lose her little boy."

Tia trembled. Wanda blamed her, not her drug addiction.

Ryder opened the dresser drawer—several baby outfits, all for newborn three-month-old boys. He hurried to the next bedroom while she stood stunned at the sight of the clothes.

Ryder's gruff voice made her stomach clench. "It looks as if her suitcase is gone and her clothes have been cleaned out, like she left in a hurry."

Tia gripped the edge of the baby bed. Had Wanda abducted Jordie and gone on the run?

Chapter Ten

Fear paralyzed Tia. "Look at these clothes and baby things," she said to Ryder. "If Wanda has Jordie, with the border less than a day's drive away, she might have taken him out of the country."

Ryder snatched his phone from the belt at his waist. "I'm going to issue a BOLO for her. Do you know what kind of car she drives?"

Tia searched her memory banks. "She used to drive a black Honda, but that's been over a year or so."

"I'll have Gwen check her out. Look through that basket on the kitchen counter. See if you find a pay stub or anything else that might indicate where she's going."

He riffled through the desk in the corner as he phoned the Bureau.

She focused on the basket. Piles of overdue bills, a lottery ticket, a speeding ticket that hadn't been paid, a letter from the rehab center asking her to call her counselor.

A manila envelope lay beside the basket. Tia opened it as Ryder stepped back into the room. She sighed at the legal document granting custody of Wanda's child to her husband.

She dug deeper and discovered a pack of matches.

Her heart thumped wildly. The logo on the outside read the Big Mug.

The same logo was on the matches Ryder had found in the bushes outside her baby's nursery. "Look at these."

"We need to stop by that bar," Ryder said. "I sent those other matches to the lab for prints. I'll do the same with these and see if they have the same prints."

Hope flared in Tia's chest. "If the prints match, that means Wanda took Jordie."

"Don't jump the gun," Ryder said. "Let's canvass the neighbors and see if anyone noticed Wanda acting strangely or if they saw her with an infant."

He gestured to the laundry basket. "Look through those clothes and the laundry and see if any of the baby things are familiar. What was Jordie wearing the night he was abducted?"

The memory of that baby sleeper haunted her. "A light blue sleeper with an appliqué of a wagon and horse." She rushed toward the laundry piled on the couch.

An assortment of receiving blankets, caps, outfits, bootees and…a sleeper. She quickly examined it. No appliqué of a wagon and horse—a teddy bear instead. She frantically searched the rest of the laundry, but the sleeper wasn't there.

Relief mingled with worry. She didn't want to think that Wanda had taken Jordie because she was angry. If the woman was drinking or taking pills again, she might have an accident or hurt him.

No. She had to remain optimistic. She closed her eyes and said a silent prayer that Jordie was safe.

Ryder touched her elbow. "Gwen is alerting airports, train stations and bus stations to watch for Wanda. She's sent photos of Jordie and Wanda nationwide. If they try to get out of the country, we'll stop them."

"I hope so," Tia said.

Ryder took another look through the house while she checked the chest in the nursery.

Ten minutes later, they walked to the neighbor's house next door. A tiny gray-haired woman opened the door, leaning on a cane.

Ryder identified himself, flashed his credentials, then explained the reason for their visit.

"I'm Myrtle." The little woman gave Tia a sympathetic smile. "I'm sorry about your baby, miss. People coming in your house and stealing your children—I don't know what the world is coming to. It's just plain awful."

Ryder cleared his throat. "When did you last see your neighbor Wanda?"

"About three days ago," Myrtle said.

"You mean Wednesday?" Ryder asked.

Myrtle nodded. "Early that morning, I saw her carrying some kind of bundle out to the car. Then she sped away."

Tia's lungs squeezed for air. Tuesday night was when Jordie disappeared.

RYDER AND TIA spent the next half hour questioning other neighbors. They met a young woman strolling twin toddlers into the driveway across the street. Tia gushed over the children, a boy and girl, who looked to be about a year and a half old.

Ryder made the introductions.

"I'm Dannika," the young woman said. "I'm not sure how I can help."

"Tell us about your neighbor Wanda," Ryder began.

Dannika claimed Wanda liked to entertain late at night, and that she'd seen several men come and go over the last month but had never been introduced to any of them. One drove a black Range Rover and another a dented white pickup. She made sure her children stayed in the fenced backyard instead of wondering to the front because she was worried about Wanda's driving.

Tia's face blanched at that statement.

Ryder didn't like the picture this neighbor was painting. "She was driving while intoxicated?"

"It appeared that way," the young woman said. "She was reckless, weaving all over the road. One night she smashed her own mailbox."

Tia wiped perspiration from her forehead. "Did she have family around?"

"Not that I know of."

"Did you see her with a baby?" Ryder asked.

The woman took a sip of her bottled water. "No, although sometime Wednesday afternoon, she was carrying a bundle to the car. It could have been a baby wrapped up in a blanket."

Ryder's jaw hardened, but he worked to maintain a neutral expression. So if she'd left early that morning, she might have returned for some reason. "Was anyone with her that day?"

"No. But an SUV was parked in the drive that morning."

"What kind?"

She rubbed her forehead. "Black. I think it was a 4Runner."

"Did you see the driver?"

She shook her head. "I'm afraid not. I didn't think much of it at the time."

Ryder handed her a business card. "If you think of anything else that might help, please give me a call."

She accepted the card with a nod then knelt to console the little girl who'd woken from her nap and started to fuss.

Tia looked longingly at the toddlers as they said goodbye and walked to the next house.

A teenage boy answered the door wearing a rock band T-shirt, his arms covered in tattoos, a cigarette dangling from the corner of his mouth. His eyes looked bloodshot. "Yeah?"

"Are your parents home?" Ryder asked.

The kid's fingers curled around the door edge as if he might slam it in their face—or run. "No."

"Where are they?"

"Daddy lit out when I was three. Mama's working at the dry cleaner's down the street." He shoved his hand in his back pocket and shifted nervously. "Why?"

"I need to talk to them."

Panic streaked the teen's eyes when Ryder flashed his badge. "Look, man, I ain't done nothing."

Ryder chuckled sarcastically. "I don't care if you're smoking weed or have drugs here at the moment, buddy. We're looking for a kidnapped baby."

The teen cursed. "I didn't steal any kid."

"It was my baby," Tia said quickly. "And we don't think you took him. But the woman next door, Wanda, might have."

"Have you seen her around?" Ryder asked.

The boy tugged at the ripped end of his T-shirt. "Not today."

"Did you see her with a baby?" Tia asked.

"Naw." He shot a quick glance down the street.

"What's going on down there?" Ryder asked.

The boy looked down at his shoes. "That's where she gets her stash."

"Her dealer lives on the street?" Ryder asked.

The boy shrugged.

"Is he your supplier?" Ryder asked.

"No, hell, no." Fear darkened his face. "And don't tell him I said anything. I don't want him coming after me."

Ryder grimaced. "Don't worry, I won't mention you. I'll tell him we're talking to all the neighbors, which is true."

Relief softened the wariness in the teen's eyes.

Ryder pushed his card into the boy's hand. "Call me if you see Wanda come back, or if you think of anything that could help."

The boy nodded, his eyes darting down the street again.

Ryder turned to leave, his gaze scanning the area in case someone was watching.

PURE PANIC SEIZED TIA. "Oh, my God," Tia said as the young man closed the door in their faces. "What if Wanda is high and driving around with Jordie? She might have an accident or lose her temper—"

"Shh, don't go there," he said softly. Ryder gripped Tia's arms and forced her to look at him. "We don't know that she took Jordie."

"But what if she did?" Tia cried. "I've heard of desperate addicts actually selling their children or trading them for their fix."

"I know it's difficult not to imagine the worst," Ryder said, "but we need to focus. We still have a lot of possibilities to explore. The woman in the security footage at the hospital, for one."

Tia inhaled a deep breath. "All right. What do we do next?"

"I'm going to talk to the drug dealer," Ryder said. "You need to wait in the car."

"But I want to hear what he has to say."

Ryder's jaw tightened. "It's too dangerous. We have no idea if he's armed or if there are thugs working with him."

He walked her back to his SUV.

"Be careful," Tia said as he started down the sidewalk toward the drug dealer's house.

She accessed the pictures on her phone and studied each one she'd taken of Jordie while she waited. Although she didn't need to look at them—she'd already memorized each detail.

RYDER SCRUTINIZED THE yard and house as he approached. The windows were covered with black-out curtains, the window in the garage covered as well.

Could be a sign that the man who lived inside had something to hide.

He raised his fist to knock, his instincts on alert. The yard was unkempt, and a black sedan with tinted windows sat in the drive. He banged his fist on the door, one hand sliding inside his jacket, ready to draw his weapon if needed.

Inside, a voice shouted something, then footsteps pounded.

Ryder knocked again, and the voice he'd heard called out, "Coming."

Ryder glanced to the side of house, looking for signs of a meth lab—or a runner.

The door squeaked open, and gray eyes peered back, a twentysomething male with a head of shaggy hair glaring at him. "Yeah?"

Ryder flashed his credentials and was rewarded by a panicked look from the guy. "I'm canvassing the neighbors to see if anyone has seen Wanda Hanson, who lives in that house." He pointed to the run-down ranch they'd come from.

"Listen, man, I don't know many of the neighbors," the guy said. "We don't exactly have cul-de-sac parties around here."

No, but maybe crack parties. "But you may have seen the news about a missing infant, a six-week-old boy named Jordie Jeffries?"

"Do I look like I've got a kid in here?" the guy said, belligerence edging his tone.

Suddenly a movement to the right caught Ryder's eye, then the door slammed shut in his face.

A second guy exited a side door and darted to a truck parked at the curb.

Ryder pulled his gun from his holster and shouted for him to stop. But the man he'd been talking to at the door ran out the side after the truck.

Suddenly Tia bolted from the SUV and dashed toward the truck.

He yelled for her to go back, but a shot rang out, the bullet zinging toward Tia.

Chapter Eleven

Ryder grabbed Tia and wrapped his arms around her, then threw her to the ground, using his body as a shield to protect her as they dodged another bullet.

Tia screamed and clutched his back as he rolled them toward the bushes.

"Stay down," he growled in her ear.

She nodded against his chest, and he lifted his head and peered up at the truck. Another bullet flew toward them.

He motioned for Tia to keep cover in the bushes as he drew his gun and fired at the driver. He missed and the man jumped in the truck.

Ryder pushed to his knees and inched forward, gun at the ready. The engine fired up. Tires squealed as the driver accelerated and pulled from the curb. Ryder jogged forward and shot at the tires, memorizing the tag as the truck sped down the road.

He turned and saw Tia running toward him. Dammit. "I told you to stay down."

"They're getting away," Tia cried.

Ryder stowed his gun in his holster and coaxed Tia back to his SUV. She sank into the passenger seat, and he phoned his superior and explained the situation, then gave him the license plate and the address of the house.

"Get an APB out on this truck. I also need a warrant to search his place."

"You got it. I'll contact the local sheriff and have him bring the warrant."

Ryder bit the inside of his cheek. He didn't particularly want Sheriff Gaines in the middle of this, but excluding him would cause more trouble. Pissing off the man in his own jurisdiction could work against him.

Connor transferred him to the tech analyst Gwen.

Ryder gave her the home address. "Tell me what you find on the man who lives here."

Tia tucked a strand of hair behind her ear, her hand trembling. He tilted her chin up with his thumb. "You okay?"

She nodded, expression earnest as they waited.

Seconds later, Gwen came back on the phone. "House is owned by a couple in Texas. They've been renting it for the last year to a twenty-five-year-old student named Neil Blount. But…" She hesitated and Ryder thumped his boot on the ground.

"Arrest record?"

"A couple of misdemeanors for possession. Looks like he dropped out of college."

"Job history?"

"Nothing substantial. He worked at a couple of hamburger joints. Last job was at a bar called the Big Mug."

Ryder hissed. The matches outside Tia's place had come from that bar. "Find out everything you can on that bar, its owner and history. They could be running drugs out of there."

TIA WATCHED AS Ryder and the sheriff entered Neil Blount's house. If Jordie had been with those men at any time, what had they done with him?

Her phone buzzed, the caller display box reading Crossroads.

It was Elle. "Hey, Tia, I just called to see how things are going."

Tia relayed what had happened. "At this point, I don't know if Wanda or this man had anything to do with Jordie's disappearance, but Ryder is looking into them. What's happening at Crossroads? Do you need me to come in?" Tia asked.

"No, everything is going smoothly," Elle assured her. "The new family has settled in. I already set up a job interview for the mother. She seems anxious to accept our help so she can get back on her feet."

"Good. That's half the battle," Tia murmured. Sometimes families resisted accepting help or, in some instances, emotional issues and addictions kept them from following through on good intentions.

"I'm saying a prayer for you," Elle said. "I know you're going to find him, Tia. I just know it."

Tia wished she felt as optimistic.

"Call me if you hear something."

Tia thanked her and disconnected just as Ryder exited the house. She rushed toward him. "Any sign of Jordie?"

He shook his head. "No. We did find drugs, enough to indicate Blount is into dealing big-time. Sheriff Gaines agreed to get his deputy to work with one of the DEA's special agents to see just how big his operation is."

"Where is my baby, Ryder?" Tia said in a hoarse whisper.

Ryder wanted to console her, but he couldn't lie to her. "I found a laptop and am sending it to the lab for analysis. If there's any mention of a kidnapping or possible child-stealing ring, they'll find it."

Tia nodded, although anxiety knotted her shoulders. A child-stealing ring? God…that could mean that whoever had taken Jordie might have sold him to a stranger.

That stranger could be halfway across the world with her son by now.

RYDER HATED CHASING false leads, and Blount and Wanda both might be dead ends. Although at this point, he had no other clues. "We have time before the interview," Ryder said as he and Tia got in his SUV. "I want to go by the Big Mug on the way."

Tia twined her hands in her lap, twisting them in a nervous gesture. "What if they're long gone? Maybe in Mexico or Europe or Brazil?"

Ryder covered her hand with his to calm her. Her fingers felt cold, stiff, her anxiety palpable. "That would mean passports, flight plans. We didn't find anything in Wanda's house to indicate she'd made arrangements to leave the country. And with the Amber Alert and airport, train and bus stations on guard, someone would have seen them."

"Not necessarily," Tia argued. "A woman cuddling a baby wouldn't arouse suspicion."

"No, but authorities will be watching for anyone behaving suspiciously. Also, to travel with an infant, you have to provide a birth certificate."

Ryder started the engine and pulled onto the road, heading toward the Big Mug.

"Can't people fake birth certificates?" Tia asked.

Ryder veered around a curve, staying right when the road forked. It definitely had happened, especially with criminals who stole children as a business. But he didn't want to panic Tia any more than she already was.

"It's difficult, but it can be done," Ryder said. "Knowing there's an Amber Alert for an infant, security personnel and authorities will scrutinize documents carefully." At least he hoped they would.

A slacker could miss crucial signs on faked documents, though. Worse, if the kidnapper was smart, he or she might have altered the baby's name, birth date and even his sex. People were looking for a baby boy. They might not take a second look at an infant swaddled in pink.

Tia lapsed into a strained silence while they drove, the deserted land stretching before them a reminder that a kidnapper could have vanished somewhere in the Wyoming wilderness and stay hidden until the hype surrounding the baby's disappearance died down.

Then he or she would try to make a hasty escape.

They had to find Jordie before that happened.

The gray clouds overhead darkened, casting a dismal feel as they ventured into the outskirts of town. The Big Mug sat off the country road next to a rustic-looking barbecue place called the Tasty Pig, a place Ryder had heard had the best barbecue this side of Cheyenne. His mouth watered at the thought, but one peek at Tia told him that food wasn't on her mind.

All she wanted was to find her baby. He didn't have time to feed his stomach when she was hurting and Jordie's kidnapper might be getting farther and farther away.

He parked in the graveled lot. Pickup trucks, SUVs and a few sedans filled the lot. Country music blared from the bar, smoke curling outside as they walked up to the door. A few patrons huddled by the fire pit on the rustic planked porch to the side, a gathering spot for smokers and people wanting to escape the loud music inside.

"I know Wanda had addiction problems, but I can't see her hanging out here," Tia said beneath the beat of the music as they walked to the entrance.

"But it would be a good spot for drug exchanges," Ryder pointed out. "She slips in, orders a drink and leaves with a small package in her purse."

Tia nodded. "I feel for her little boy. I kept hoping she'd get her act together, for his sake."

"Addiction changes people," Ryder said in a gruff voice. "They lose perspective."

"That's true," Tia said softly. Sadness clouded her eyes. "After my folks died, I was prescribed antidepressants, but I didn't like taking them and quickly stopped. I always thought that if I had a child and took care of him, my child would grow up healthy and happy. But… I failed him in the worst way."

Ryder's gut clenched. "This was not your fault, Tia."

He pulled her up against him. Her labored breathing puffed against his neck as he rubbed one hand up and down her back to soothe her.

"Let's just focus on finding your baby," Ryder said in a low voice. "Hang in there, okay?"

She didn't move for a second, but he felt her relax slightly against him.

He was not going to disappoint her or her baby. Jordie deserved to know his real mother, that she loved him.

The sentiment resurrected the memory of his twin brother's visit. Cash had insisted their mother loved them.

He pinched the bridge of his nose. He didn't want to think or believe that his mother, Myra, had willingly accepted a stolen child.

If she had, she'd lied to him. And if that was true, he didn't know if he could ever forgive that.

TIA BRACED HERSELF for the bar scene. She had to be tough. Not fall apart in Ryder's arms.

It would feel so good if she could lean on him, though.

But leaning on a man wasn't an option.

Especially this man—he had handcuffed her and hauled her to jail.

"You can go back to the car," Ryder said. "I'll handle this."

Tia wasn't a cop or federal agent, but the bar patrons hanging around outside in the parking lot didn't incite a safe feeling. She was surprised there were so many here, too. Judging from the motorcycles, there must be a biker rally nearby.

"This is a seedy-looking crowd," Tia pointed out. "I'd feel better going in with you."

A tense heartbeat passed. For a moment, he looked around, sizing up the situation. When he settled his dark gaze on her, admiration for her mingled with concern in his eyes. "You're right, but keep a low profile. Don't forget that we were shot at earlier."

Tia shivered. "How could I forget?"

Guilt flashed on his face. He didn't have to remind her about their close call. She knew their search was dangerous.

That whoever had taken Jordie didn't want to be found. That he or she would kill to get away.

But she didn't care.

Being close to Ryder Banks was dangerous in another way.

Tia steeled herself against letting her guard down around him, though. He was a tough federal agent. He seemed intent on doing his job.

And he was sexy and strong—just the kind of man a woman wanted to lean on.

She'd seen enough women fall into that trap and come through Crossroads, broken and desperate and in need of help.

She would never forget the lessons she'd learned.

"Just stay beside me," he growled as they went inside.

Tia put on a brave face.

She'd keep her eyes open and her senses alert. Maybe someone in the bar knew who had her son.

Chapter Twelve

Ryder tucked Tia close by his side and visually scoped out the bar as he entered. Protective instincts kicked in, and he looked for male predators, drunks on the watch for a one-night pickup who might target Tia, possible drug dealers or patrons who were high or looking to cut a deal.

Then Wanda.

He didn't know the woman, but this establishment definitely boasted a rough crowd. Booze, conversation, flirting, boot-scooting music and hookups driven by beer and drugs created a chaotic atmosphere. No women with children inside and no couples with an infant.

He kept one hand on Tia's lower back and guided her toward the bar. Two stools on the end opened up as a couple took to the dance floor, and he led her to it, then sank onto one of the stools.

The bartender, a cowboy with an eye for the ladies, slid two napkins in front of them. "What'll you have?"

They weren't here to drink, but he wanted to fit in. "Whatever you have on draft." He slanted his gaze toward Tia with an eyebrow raise.

"The same." She plucked a matchbook from the basket on the counter and rotated it between her fingers.

A robust guy wearing a bolo tie approached to her

right, his short-cropped hair making his cheeks look puffy. He raked a gaze over Tia, then frowned and walked on past.

"Do you know that guy?" Ryder asked.

Tia studied him as she accepted her beer. "No. Why?"

"Just wondering." Something about the way the man had looked at Tia raised questions in Ryder's mind. Had he been simply assessing her to determine if she was single or if she was with him?

Or did he know who she was?

He took a sip of his beer, removed his phone and accessed a picture of Wanda, then laid the phone on the counter. He motioned for the bartender. "Do you know this woman?"

The bartender pulled at his chin as he glanced at it. "Seen her in a couple of times, but I don't really know her."

"Was she with anyone?" Ryder asked.

The bartender wiped the counter with a rag. "Not really."

Ryder had to push. "Was she here to score some drugs?"

The bartender leaned closer, lowering his voice. "Listen, man, I don't know what you've heard, but this is a legitimate place."

"I'm not concerned about the drugs." Ryder eased his credentials from his pocket and discreetly showed them to the man. Then he flicked a finger toward Tia. "This woman's baby is missing. I'm looking for a lead on the kidnapper."

Unease darkened the guy's face. "I don't know anything about a kidnapping."

Tia touched the man's hand, her eyes imploring.

"Please think. Wanda may have taken my son. He's only a few weeks old and he needs me."

The man gestured for them to wait, took two young women's orders, gave them their drinks, then returned with the bill.

He slid the check in front of Ryder as if dismissing them. But he'd scribbled a name at the bottom of the bill—Bubba.

"He holes up in an old shack behind the bar," the bartender murmured.

"He took my baby?" Tia asked.

The guy shook his head. "No, but if anything was going on with Wanda, he'd know."

Ryder tossed some cash on the bill to pay for their drinks, then shoved back. The big guy who'd been watching Tia stood by the door as they left, his scowl so intense that Ryder hesitated.

But the moment he returned the man's lethal stare, he jammed his beefy hands in the pockets of his jacket and lumbered out the door.

Ryder stepped outside with Tia, his senses alert as he scanned the parking lot. The tip of a cigarette glowed against the dark night. The big guy folded himself inside a jacked-up black pickup, then sped off.

"Who was he?" Tia asked.

"No idea," Ryder replied. "He was watching you inside, though."

Tia shivered. "If Wanda wanted her son back, coming to this bar wasn't the way to do it."

"She made her choices," Ryder said. He just wondered if taking Jordie was one of them. Ryder took Tia's arm again. "The bartender said Bubba lives back here. Let's find that shack."

She fell into step beside him as they wove down the dark alley. The scents of garbage, smoke and urine filled the air, and Ryder led her past a homeless man sleeping in a cardboard box, which he'd propped behind a metal staircase.

Tia paused, her look sympathetic as if she wanted to offer the man assistance, but Ryder ushered her on. Ryder spotted the shack the bartender had referenced, a weathered structure with mud-and-dirt-coated windows.

Not knowing what to expect, he coaxed Tia behind him, removed his gun and held it by his side as he knocked.

A second later, a sound jarred him. Another popping sound, then an explosion.

He grabbed Tia and dragged her away from the building as the glass windows shattered and fire burst through the rotting wooden door.

TIA SCREAMED, DUCKING to avoid flying debris and glass as Ryder pushed her beneath the awning of a neighboring building. He covered her head with his arms and held her, his warmth and strength suffusing her as wood splintered and popped and glass pellets pinged around them.

She heaved for a breath, trembling as they waited for the worst to die down. Finally the force of the explosion settled, but fire blazed behind them, heat searing her.

Ryder breathed against her neck. "You okay?"

She nodded and turned in his arms to face him. He was mere inches away, his gruff expression riddled with anger and worry.

He felt so solid and strong against her, the weight of his body like a wall protecting her. His gaze raked over her face, then dropped to her eyes. A flicker of something masculine darkened his expression, causing a flutter in her belly that had nothing to do with the fact that they could have died in that explosion.

And everything to do with the fact that Ryder was the sexiest man she'd ever laid eyes on. "What happened?" she asked, her voice cracking with emotion.

His chest rose and fell against hers as he inhaled a deep breath. "Someone warned Bubba we were coming." Ryder rubbed her arms and lifted his body away from her. "My guess is that he was destroying evidence."

"It was a meth lab?" Tia guessed.

"That's what I'm thinking." He pulled away, retrieved his phone, called for backup and a crime team.

Seconds later, a siren rent the air.

"What if Jordie was in there?" Tia said, panic flaring in her eyes.

"There's no reason to think that." Ryder squeezed her arm. "We'll search the house, but meth dealers generally stick to the drug business."

Still, fear paralyzed Tia as she looked back at the burning building.

THE NEXT TWO hours passed in a blur of law enforcement officers, rescue workers, firemen and DEA agents. The area was cleared due to fumes from the meth lab, forcing Ryder to get Tia away from the scene.

Thankfully the search indicated that no child or baby had been inside. In fact, no one, adult or otherwise, was inside when the building blew. The theory was that Bubba lit up the place to destroy evidence and any links to himself. Ryder was turning the case over to the DEA.

He had more important work to do.

His phone buzzed as he and Tia drove away from the chaotic scene. "Agent Banks."

"Ryder, we have info on Wanda Hanson," Gwen said. "A cashier at a convenience store called in that she stopped for gas, and confirmed she had a baby with her. No word if it's a boy or girl or the age. But when she left the store, she drove across the street to a motel and checked in for the night."

Ryder's pulse jumped. "Text me the address. I'm on my way."

"What was that about?" Tia asked as he ended the call.

"Wanda Hanson's car was spotted. We're heading there now."

"Did she have Jordie?"

He bit his tongue to keep from offering her false hope. "I don't know. We'll find out."

He pulled to the side of the road, entered the address into the GPS, then swung the SUV around and headed west, toward the highway where the motel was located.

Tia's hands went into motion again, fidgeting and twitching. He laid his hand over hers. Her skin felt cold, clammy. "Try to relax. It's about sixty miles from here."

"What if she's gone by the time we get there?" Fear made her voice warble.

"She checked into a room for the night."

"Hopefully she's feeding Jordie," Tia said.

Ryder wanted to assure her that that was exactly what the woman was doing. But if she was high, drinking or coming down from a high, there was no telling what her mood would be.

Or if she'd even be coherent.

"Did Wanda have a gun?" he asked.

Tia's brows pinched together as if she was thinking.

"Not that I recall. Why? Did someone report seeing her with one?"

He shook his head and squeezed her hand again. "No, I was just asking. It's better to be prepared." She could have picked up a gun from a gun shop or borrowed one from a friend.

"When we get there, I need you to remain in the SUV," Ryder said. "I'll go to Wanda's room and see if she's home."

"I'm going, too," Tia whispered. "Jordie needs me."

Ryder shifted back into agent mode. "Let me assess the situation, Tia. We can't go in guns blazing or someone could get hurt." Her. The baby.

"You're right." She released a shaky breath. "If Wanda is doing drugs or drunk, she might panic."

"Right." Half a dozen scenarios of how the situation could go bad flashed through his mind. He wasn't green at this. Drug addicts and criminals weren't predictable. And when they were backed into a corner, they did things they might never do under normal circumstances.

Tia lapsed into silence. Dark clouds rolled in as the truck ate the miles, the occasional howl of a wild animal breaking the quiet. Traffic thinned, deserted farmland and broken-down shanties a reminder that this highway led out of town and into the vast wilderness.

A good place to hide or get lost. Or disappear with a stolen child.

Ryder sped up and passed a slow moving car, then checked the clock. The minutes rolled into half an hour.

Wanda Hanson was not going to get away tonight, though. Not if she had Jordie Jeffries with her.

TIA GRIPPED THE edge of the seat as Ryder pressed the accelerator and took the curve on two wheels. His calm demeanor was meant to soothe her, but his big body was tense, hands clenching the steering wheel in a white-knuckled grip.

In spite of what he said, he was anxious to get to the motel in case Wanda didn't stay the night.

She fought panic as the time passed.

"Ryder, what if Wanda is meeting someone at the motel? She could be giving Jordie to that person."

Ryder's thick brow rose. "Just try to keep up the faith."

She ran her fingers through her hair, fighting thoughts of the worst-case scenario—that Wanda had disposed of Jordie.

As they neared the motel she noticed a truck pulling an oversize load was parked on the side of the road, a tiny house behind it.

Cheap neon lights glowed ahead, illuminating a graveled parking lot. Ryder veered into the lot and parked between an SUV and a pickup. Two minivans and a sedan were parked at the opposite end, and another vehicle stood in front of the corner unit.

"That's Wanda's van," he said as he killed the engine.

"Do you know which room she's in?" Tia asked.

"Gwen talked to the motel manager. Room twelve, at the end."

Tia zeroed in on the corner unit. A low light burned inside, shrouded by the motel's thin curtains.

Ryder eased his weapon from his holster and reached for the door handle. "Stay here."

Tia nodded, but as Ryder left the SUV and walked toward the minivan, adrenaline and fear made her open her door and follow. Her footsteps crunched on gravel as she hurried up behind Ryder.

He cut her a sharp look. "I told you to wait in the SUV."

Tia peered through the front window of the minivan, but the windows were tinted, making it difficult to see.

Ryder pulled a small flashlight from his belt and shined it inside, waving it across the front seat. No one there.

He moved to the side window and shined the light across the backseats. Tia's breath caught.

A car seat.

"Look," she whispered. "She has an infant carrier, and there are baby toys."

Ryder gripped her arm. "We have to be careful, Tia. We don't want to spook her. If she has a weapon, this could go south."

Panic seized Tia. If that happened, Wanda might hurt Jordie.

"Trust me," he said on a deep breath.

Ryder's gaze met hers, his dark eyes steady. Determined.

Odd that she did *want* trust him, especially after he'd arrested her. But she did. "You're in charge."

Tension vibrated between them for a long second. The air stirred around them, bringing the scent of damp earth and garbage. An engine rumbled, doors opened and slammed, and a child's voice echoed in the wind as a family climbed out, gathering toys and suitcases as they walked to their room.

They passed several rooms, then a housekeeping cart. Tia lifted a set of towels from the cart along with a pillow. Ryder nodded in silent agreement and they passed two more rooms, then paused at the last unit.

His right hand covered his weapon, which he held by his side as he knocked with his left.

Tia swallowed hard then called through the door, "Housekeeping. I have extra towels and pillows."

Ryder eased Tia behind him. A voice sounded inside, then footsteps and the door creaked open.

Tia's heart pounded as Wanda appeared. Her eyes were glazed, hair stringy and unwashed, and she reeked of cigarette smoke. As soon as she spotted Tia, she spit out a litany of curse words, then tried to shut the door in their faces.

Ryder shoved the door open, drew his gun and shouted, "Stop and put your hands up!"

Wanda came at him fighting and hissing like a crazy woman, but he yanked both arms down beside her and pushed her against the wall.

Tia spotted a blue bundle lying on the bed between two pillows. Jordie.

She raced toward it.

Chapter Thirteen

Tia ignored Wanda's shrill scream as she approached the bundle on the bed. Ryder wrestled the woman's arms behind her and handcuffed her. She kicked and shouted obscenities as he shoved her into a chair.

Hope speared Tia as she slowly sank onto the bed. She didn't want to startle the baby, so she gently pressed one hand to his back.

Cold fear washed over her. He wasn't moving.

"You can't take my baby!" Wanda shouted.

"Shut up," Ryder growled.

Tia's gaze met his, terror making her heart pound. If Jordie was hurt or sick, she had to help him.

She leaned over and scooped up the bundle, but as she turned him in her arms, shock robbed her breath.

There was no baby.

She was holding a doll in her arms. A life-size doll that felt and looked like a real infant.

But it wasn't Jordie.

"Let me go!" Wanda fought against the restraints so hard that the chair rocked back and forth.

Tia whirled on her. "What did you do with my son?"

Ryder's brows puckered into a frown and he strode

over to her to examine the baby. "Good God," he muttered when he realized the truth.

Tia carried the doll over to Wanda. "Where's my baby?"

Wanda shook the chair again as she rocked the chair backward against the wall. "You took my boy away from me. You can't have this one!"

Tia shoved the doll into Ryder's arms, grabbed Wanda's shoulders and shook her. "What did you do with my son, Wanda?"

"I don't know what you're talking about," Wanda muttered. "You're the one who took my son from me."

Ryder rubbed Tia's back. "Let her go, Tia. She's so strung out she doesn't know what she's doing or saying."

But Tia couldn't let go. She'd been so sure Wanda had her son. So sure he was here, that she'd take him home tonight and feed him and rock him to sleep and wake up in the morning with her family at home.

That this nightmare was over.

"Tell me, Wanda," Tia said in a raw whisper. "Where's Jordie? What did you do with him?"

Wanda went still, her lips curling into a sick smile, yet her eyes weren't focused. They were glazed over with the haze of drugs.

Tia choked on a sob and stepped back, her heart shattering at the realization that Wanda might not have taken Jordie at all.

RYDER GRITTED HIS teeth at the agony on Tia's face. Wanda started another litany of foul words, and he barely resisted smacking her in the mouth.

"Shut up," he barked.

Tia ran a finger over the doll's cheek. The damn thing looked so real he expected it to start crying any minute.

Forcing himself into agent mode, he planted himself in front of Wanda, dropped to a squat and tilted her face to look at him. "Wanda, listen to me. Kidnapping is a felony offense. You need to tell me if you abducted Tia Jeffries's baby."

Her lip quivered as she flattened her mouth into a frown. "Go to hell."

"That's where you're going if you hurt that baby," Ryder said, his tone lethal. "But if you cooperate, I'll see that you get a fair shake, that you receive counseling and treatment for your addiction."

A bitter laugh rumbled from Wanda's throat. "You don't scare me," Wanda said. Her head lolled from side to side as if she was suddenly dizzy or about to crash. "I didn't take that bitch's baby, although it would serve her right if I did, since she ruined my family."

Tia folded her arms and faced Wanda, her body vibrating as if she was grasping to maintain control. "You lost your child because you chose drugs over him."

Ryder pressed a hand to Tia's arm to encourage her to let him handle the situation. "But we can change that," he said, giving Tia a warning look. "Tell me, Wanda. You were hurting because you missed your son. You were angry at Tia. You found out she had a child, and you wanted to get back at her so you—"

"I hope you never get your kid back," Wanda yelled.

Ryder put his arm out to keep Tia from pouncing. Tears flowed from her eyes, ripping at his emotions.

Ryder spoke though gritted teeth. "I told you I'd help you, Wanda, but you have to talk first. Now, you slipped into Tia's house and you took her newborn—"

"I didn't take the kid." Wanda slid sideways in the chair, her eyes rolling back in her head.

Ryder caught her just before she passed out.

A strangled sob erupted from Tia, her pain and frustration palpable as he phoned 911.

DESPAIR SUCKED AT Tia as the medics rushed in and took Wanda's vitals.

One of the medics gestured toward the doll as they loaded Wanda onto the stretcher. "Is there a child here?" he asked.

Tia shook her head. "She has emotional issues." Whether Wanda's drug addiction or her instability had come first, Tia didn't know.

"She under arrest?" the medic asked.

Ryder cleared his throat. "For now."

"For what?" Tia asked. Being cruel? Traveling with a doll?

"Attacking an officer," Ryder said. "At least that gives us a reason to hold her until she's coherent."

So he hadn't completely ruled out Wanda as the kidnapper. Although if Wanda had taken Jordie, Tia would have expected her to brag about it, to rub it in her face.

Ryder retrieved Wanda's purse from the desk chair and dumped the contents on the bed as the medics carried Wanda to the ambulance. A baby bottle, wipes, keys, tissues, a pack of gum, a small bag of powder that Tia assumed was cocaine, a tube of dark red lipstick, a pack of matches from the Big Mug, a ratty wallet and a cell phone.

He scrolled through her contacts. "Husband's name is still in here. A few others, but not many. I'll have the lab check them out."

Tia looked over his shoulder. "What about her recent calls?"

A couple of unknowns. The motel number. The name Horace Laker. A woman named Elvira Mead. The bus station.

Did one of these people know where Jordie was?

RYDER WENT DOWN the list, calling each number. The two unknowns did not respond. Horace Laker was the owner of Laker Car Rentals. Wanda had rented the van from him.

"Did Ms. Hanson have any children with her when you saw her?" Ryder asked.

"Didn't see any. Said she was in a hurry, though. Had to meet up with someone."

Someone who'd taken Jordie, or her dealer?

"Was she high when she talked to you?"

The man coughed. "Didn't think so. But she did seem antsy. But everyone's in a hurry all the time these days so I didn't think much of it."

Ryder thanked him, disconnected, then called the last number. Elvira Mead answered. Ryder introduced himself and explained the situation. "How do you know Wanda?"

"I'm her neighbor," Elvira said. "She called and asked me to feed her cat for a few days. Said she was going out of town."

"Did you see her with a child? An infant, maybe?"

"No, she lost her boy a while back. Thought that might straighten her up, but it sent her into a downward spiral."

"Did she mention a woman named Tia Jeffries?"

"She hated that woman," Elvira said. "Blamed her for her husband leaving her, but we both knew it was Wanda's addiction. He had to take that boy away from Wanda."

Ryder's gut pinched. Hopefully the woman hadn't gotten her hands on Tia's son. "Did she mention getting revenge against Tia?"

A hesitant pause. "She mouthed off some, but if you think she kidnapped that baby, you're wrong. I saw the story on the news. The night the baby went missing, Wanda was passed out at home."

"You're sure about that?"

Elvira gave a sarcastic laugh. "Damn right I am. She barreled in driving like a maniac. Left her car running, crawled out and practically collapsed in the driveway. I went out to check on things, turned off the engine and helped her inside."

"That was nice of you."

A pause. "I've been in AA for twenty years. Kept trying to talk Wanda into joining. I promised her I'd be her sponsor, but she refused to go."

Ryder thanked Elvira for her help and disconnected.

Tia was watching him. "Anything?"

He hated to dash her hopes, but he refused to lie to her. "That was Wanda's neighbor. Wanda was home the night Jordie disappeared—she said she passed out and was there all night."

Ryder checked his watch. It was almost time for the early evening news. "We'll drop her phone off at the crime lab. Gwen can check out her contacts while we go to the TV station."

He hated to put Tia through a public appearance. And it could bring false leads.

But sometimes a parent's grief and fear in a personal plea touched viewers and strangers enough to make them take more interest in helping to find a missing child.

They needed all the help they could get.

Tia freshened up in the bathroom at the TV station, well aware she looked pale and gaunt. Desperate.

God, she *was* desperate.

The past three days had taken its toll on her body and her mind.

But she had to pull herself together to talk to the press.

On the drive to the station, she'd rehearsed in her mind what she wanted to say. In each scenario, she wound up screaming for the kidnapper to return her baby.

You are not going to fall apart. You're going to be calm, reasonable, tell the truth and...beg.

She tucked her brush in her purse, wiped her face with a wet paper towel, then dried her hands.

Several deep breaths, and she summoned her courage and left the restroom. Ryder was waiting, his gaze deep with concern.

"They're working on Wanda at the hospital," he said. "Gwen just phoned. She didn't find anything suspicious in Wanda's bank records. In fact, Wanda is broke. Probably depleted her money feeding her habit."

"Then she might have been desperate enough to take Jordie and try to sell him," Tia said, her voice laced with horror.

He shrugged in concession. "I'm not ruling out that possibility, although her phone records haven't turned up a lead. And she has an alibi the night of the abduction."

Tia clung to the theory because they had no other clues. "Then she had a partner or help."

Ryder kept his expression neutral. "So far, nothing we've found supports that theory, Tia. According to a neighbor Gwen talked to, Wanda didn't have any friends visiting. She'd alienated all her family. Another neighbor saw a shady-looking character confront her at her car once. She owed him for drugs."

An attractive blonde woman in a dark green dress approached. "I'm Jesse Simpleton. I'll be handling the interview with you, Miss Jeffries."

Tia shook her hand. "Thank you. I appreciate you taking the time to do this."

"Of course." The young woman's voice softened with compassion. "I'm so sorry about your baby. We'll do whatever we can to help."

"I've set up a tip line." Ryder pushed a piece of paper into the woman's hands. "Here's the number."

"We'll make sure it appears on-screen and rebroadcast it with each news segment." Jesse showed them where to sit by the anchor's chair, and the director instructed them regarding the cameras.

Jesse squeezed Tia's hand. "Just talk from the heart."

Tia didn't know what else to do. Before they started, she removed the photo of Jordie she'd taken the night she'd brought him home from her purse and rubbed her finger over her baby's sweet cherub face.

The director signaled it was time to start. Jesse introduced her. Tia angled the photograph toward the camera.

"My name is Tia Jeffries. Six weeks ago was the happiest day of my life. I gave birth to my son, Jordan Timothy Jeffries. He weighed seven pounds, eight ounces and was nineteen inches long." The memory of holding him for the first time made tears well in her eyes. "I carried him home the next morning, ecstatic. He was a good eater and was growing and healthy and happy. But three nights ago, someone slipped in my home while I was sleeping and stole him from his crib." She swallowed, battling a sob.

"I know he's out there somewhere. I can hear him cry at night. I can feel him wanting to come back to me, to be with his mama where he belongs." She pressed a kiss to the photograph. "I don't care who you are or why you took my baby. I don't want revenge or even to see you in jail. All I want is my little boy back." She swallowed hard. "If you have him, please drop him at a church or hospital. No questions asked."

Jesse announced the information about the tip line, but Tia had to say one more thing.

"I'm offering a reward of a hundred thousand dollars to whoever brings him back to me or provides a lead as to where my baby is."

She felt Ryder's look of disapproval, but kept her eyes on the camera as the reward was posted on-screen.

If she had to, she'd use every penny she had to get her son back.

Chapter Fourteen

Tia prayed the TV plea brought in answers, that someone had seen her baby or knew who'd taken him and decided to do the right thing.

Ryder stopped at the diner and insisted she eat dinner, although she could barely taste the food for the fear clogging her throat.

An hour and a half later, he pulled into her driveway, the silence between them thick with tension and the reality that night had come again, another night where she would go into an empty house, with an empty nursery and an empty bed.

"I'll come in and check the house." Ryder slid from the SUV and walked her to the door. Tia swallowed back emotions as she unlocked the door.

Ryder flipped on a light and strode through the house, checking each room. "The house is clear," he announced as he returned to the kitchen.

She nodded. She hadn't expected the kidnapper to have returned.

Ryder hesitated, his dark gaze penetrating hers as he brushed his fingertips along her arm. She sucked in a breath.

"You did good during the interview, but—"

"If you're going to tell me I shouldn't have offered a reward, don't bother. If the kidnapper took Jordie for money, this should prompt a call. And if not, maybe someone who knows where Jordie is or who took him might step up."

"I just want you to be prepared in case we receive prank calls or false leads."

"I know." Despite the fact that she told herself not to lean into him, she did it anyway. "But we—I—have to do something."

Understanding flickered in his eyes. "You are doing everything you can," he said. "Trust me. We won't stop until we find your baby."

Tears pricked at her eyes. She needed to hear that, to know that she wasn't alone and that he wouldn't give up. She'd read about cases where leads went cold, other cases landed on their desks and police essentially stopped looking. Children were lost for decades.

Fear nearly choked her. Ryder must have sensed she was close to breaking. He wrapped his arms around her and held her tight.

"Hang in there, Tia."

She battled tears, blinking hard to stem them as she nodded against his chest. His chest felt hard, thick, solid. His arms felt warm and comforting—safe.

His steady breathing and the gentle way he stroked her back soothed her.

But that was temporary. Nothing had changed.

Except that at least she wasn't alone.

She lifted her head to look into his eyes. "Thank you, Ryder. I'm…glad you're here." She hesitated. "Working the case, I mean."

"I'll let you know if I hear anything." He eased away

from her, making her instantly feel bereft and alone again. "Try to get some rest."

She nodded and bit her tongue to keep from begging him to stay.

He walked to the door, shoulders squared, his big body taut with control. "Lock the door behind me," he said as he stepped outside onto the front porch.

She rushed to do as he said, then watched through the window as he climbed in his SUV.

RYDER PINCHED THE bridge of his nose as he drove away from Tia.

He didn't want to leave her, dammit.

But he had no place in her life. Except as an agent working her case.

He checked his phone, but no messages or calls yet. He hoped to hell the TV plea and tip line worked. Or maybe Gwen would locate the woman on that tape at the hospital.

Dark clouds rolled above, thunder rumbling. Most people had tucked their children into bed by now so they'd be safe and sound for the night.

Like Tia had thought her baby was.

Predators were everywhere, though. Watching and stalking innocents. Waiting to strike when the victim let down his or her guard.

By the time he reached his cabin, his thoughts had turned to possibilities other than Tia's ex or Wanda. What if the kidnapping wasn't personal? What if it had nothing to do with revenge against Tia, but simply that she'd crossed paths with a desperate person who wanted a baby, and she'd become the target because she was a single mother?

Images of the agonized look on Tia's face haunted him as he went inside. The rustic place was empty, a chill in the den. He shrugged off his jacket and holster but carried his gun with him, then planted it on the coffee table. The envelope of letters Cash had left was sitting in the center of the table where he'd left them.

He stared at it, struck by the pink rosebuds on the wooden keepsake. His birth mother's doing.

Myra Banks was his mother. She'd rocked him to sleep when he was a baby and nursed his fevers and bandaged his skinned knees and…loved him as much as any mother could.

But this woman… What about her?

Cash insisted he read them, that he understand how much Grace McCullen had wanted the two of them.

He lifted the envelope. Just as Cash said, it was filled with dozens of letters and cards.

He thumbed through them. He didn't know where to start.

Pulse pounding, he walked to the bar in the corner, poured himself a whiskey, then returned. He tossed the first drink back, then poured another and set it on the table.

The picture sitting on the table of him and Myra at Christmas last year mocked him. It had been four years since his father had died. They'd both missed him, although the last few years his father had let his own drinking get out of hand. He'd blamed financial problems, a backstabbing partner who'd cheated him out of half his building supply company.

Even if Ryder and his father hadn't always gotten along and he'd been a bastard to his mother when he was drinking, Myra and Troy had been there for him.

Cash's face, identical to his own, flashed behind his eyes. Cash, his twin, who'd been tossed around in foster care all his life.

Cash, who was now friends—and brothers—with Maddox, Brett and Ray McCullen.

Ryder heaved a sigh. He didn't need a brother. Or to be part of that family.

Still…he had to know the truth.

He dug through the pile, checking the dates, until he found the earliest dated envelope. He opened it and drew out a photograph inside a folded sheet of paper.

He lifted the picture and studied the dark-haired pregnant woman. She was holding a basket of wildflowers. She had her hand on her pregnant belly, and she was smiling up at the sun.

This was the woman who'd given birth to him. She was beautiful.

Emotions flooded him, and he opened the sheet of paper and started to read. Her handwriting was feminine, soft, delicate—her words music to his soul.

Dear son,

This morning, I had an ultrasound and learned I was having twin boys. This is the most exciting day of my life!

I'm not only blessed with one more baby, but two.

As much as the McCullen men need more women around Horseshoe Creek, I honestly believe that God meant for me to have a ranch of boys. The world needs more good men and husbands, and I know you and your brothers will fill that role.

I've already experienced the joy and chaos little

boys bring, and also the love and camaraderie they share. I can't wait to add you and your brother to the McCullen clan.

Your father, Joe, is a tough cowboy, but a loving man and father, and you will be blessed by having a role model and leader to guide you through life.

I wish my own mama, your grandmother, could have lived to see this day.

I love you so much my heart is bursting and exploding with emotions. Just a few more weeks, and I'll get to hold you in my arms.

Until then, I'll sing you a lullaby each night while you nestle alongside your twin inside me.
Love always,
Mama

"MAMA LOVES YOU, JORDIE," Tia whispered as she stepped into the nursery. The soothing blues and greens of the room reminded her of the day she'd painted the room in anticipation of her son's arrival.

Ina had knitted baby bootees, and Elle had brought a basket of baby toys. She picked up the blue teddy bear Amy had given her, turned on the musical mobile of toy animals dancing above Jordie's crib and hugged the bear to her as she sank into the chair.

The toy train, football, blocks, arts and crafts corner, puzzles, rocking horse and farm set were all waiting. She rocked the chair back and forth and began to sing "Twinkle, Twinkle Little Star" along with the musical mobile, pushing the chair back and forth with her feet as she cradled the bear to her like she had her son.

For a while, she allowed herself to imagine her little boy playing in the room. She saw him riding the little pony, drawing pictures to hang on the wall, learning to walk, running outside in the backyard and splashing in a rain puddle, then waving to her from the jungle gym at the park.

Of course he'd learn to ride and they'd have picnics and feed the horses and ducks.

A smile tugged at her mouth as she envisioned birthdays and Christmases and marking his growth on the wall chart that she'd hung by the door.

The Hickory Dickory Dock clock on the wall ticked another hour away. Another hour that her son was missing.

ONCE RYDER STARTED with the mail, he couldn't stop himself until he'd read every letter and card. His mother poured out her heart, telling him how much she missed him every day, how she envisioned him and his twin and what they would have looked like, how she put flowers and toys and gifts on their tiny graves, how she quietly celebrated their birthdays.

Then there were disturbing letters where she chronicled her search for the twins. On pink flowered stationery with ink blurred from her tears, she'd written heart-wrenching descriptions of the nightmares that had plagued her. Sleepless nights when she'd wake up sobbing into the pillow because she could hear her babies' cries.

Ryder rubbed a hand over his eyes. God.

Cash was right.

The words on those pages were not from a woman who'd sold her children to fund her and her husband's ranch.

She told about the distance her grief had created between her and Joe, about his affair with Barbara, about how she'd forgiven him because they'd both sought comfort in different ways.

In each progressive letter, she'd promised not to give up looking for them, that she would find them and bring them back to Horseshoe Creek.

The last letter made his heart pound. She'd sensed someone following her. Had felt like she was being watched.

She'd been afraid…

Grief for the woman who'd given birth to him mushroomed in his chest. He traced his finger over her picture, and sorrow brought tears to his eyes.

Next came the face of the woman who'd raised him—Myra Banks.

Dammit. Had she lied about how she'd gotten him, or had the person who'd kidnapped him and Cash lied to her?

He stood and paced. He had to talk to her.

He checked his watch. Ten o'clock.

Dammit, she'd be in bed now.

He'd pay her a visit first thing in the morning. And he'd get to the truth.

TIA DRAGGED HERSELF to the bedroom, forced herself into pajamas and crawled into bed, hugging the teddy bear to her. She sniffed the plush fur, her son's baby scent lingering.

She closed her eyes, but the dark only accentuated the quiet emptiness in the room and in her house.

Her chest ached so badly she could hardly breathe.

Fatigue clawed at her. Just as she was about to drift asleep, her phone trilled.

Tia's pulse jumped.

She swung her legs to the side of the bed and snatched her cell phone. Her hand was trembling so badly she dropped the phone on the floor. Heart racing, she flipped it over.

The caller ID display box showed *Unknown*.

Panic snapped at her nerve endings, but she jerked up the phone and stabbed Connect.

"Hello."

"I saw you on the news."

Tia's breath stalled in her chest. "What? Who is this?"

"Your baby is safe. But he won't be if you keep looking for him."

Terror crawled through Tia. Before she could ask more, the phone went silent.

Chapter Fifteen

Tia trembled as she stared at her phone. The voice had belonged to a woman.

Who the hell was she? Did she really have Jordie?

And what had she meant—he was safe for now? If she kept looking...what would she do to him?

Terror and rage slammed into her. She punched Call Back but it didn't go through.

Tia lurched from bed, strode to the window and peeked out through the blinds. No cars outside. No one in the backyard.

She rushed to the front and looked through the window—no one there, either.

Heart pounding, she pressed Ryder's number. She paced the living room while she waited on him to respond. Three times across the room and he picked up.

"Ryder, I just got a call from a woman who said she has Jordie, that he's safe."

"What?" Ryder said. "Is she bringing him back?"

"No." Tia wiped her forehead with the back of her hand. "She said if I wanted him to stay safe that I should stop looking for him."

Ryder murmured something below his breath. "Dammit, I'm sorry, Tia. I warned you that your interview might draw the crazies and pranks."

"What if it isn't a prank?" Tia cried. "What if she's telling the truth, and we keep looking and she hurts him?" She choked back hysteria. "I'd never forgive myself if something bad happened to him because of me."

RYDER SILENTLY CURSED and walked outside onto the back porch. No way in hell he'd sleep now.

"Listen, Tia, I'll be right over. Meanwhile, I'll call the tech team and see if they can trace that call. Did a name show up?"

"No, it was an unknown."

Of course it was. "Probably a burner. I'll see if anything has come in over the tip line. Stay put and don't panic."

"I'm trying not to," Tia said, her voice cracking with tension. "But I'm scared, Ryder."

"I know." His own gut was churning. If that woman had abducted Jordie, she might be panicking. And if she didn't have him and was just playing some sick, cruel game, she was heartless and deserved to be locked up.

"Hang in there, Tia, I'll be there soon."

Ryder threw a change of clothes and toothbrush in a duffel bag. Then he strapped on his holster and gun, slipped on a jacket, snatched his keys, and headed outside. Out of the corner of his eye, he noticed the mail from his birth mother. He hurried over, stacked everything back inside the envelope and closed it.

The night air hit him, filled with the smell of impending rain.

He jumped in his SUV and sped toward Tia's, calling Gwen as he drove onto the main road.

He explained about the call Tia had received. "I need you to find out where that call came from."

"I'm on it, but if it was as quick a call as it sounds, I doubt we can trace it."

Frustration knotted his shoulders. "I know it, but do your best." They couldn't ignore any call or lead. "Anything from the tip line?"

"Not yet. There have been a few calls, and I have people checking them out."

"What about the woman in the video feed from the hospital nursery? Any ID on her?"

"Afraid not. We're running her through facial recognition and waiting to get the medical records from legal, but so far nothing. I'll keep you posted."

"Thanks." Ryder ended the call, his experience as an agent warring with his worry for Tia and her baby.

You are not supposed to get involved.

But after reading his birth mother's heartfelt words and realizing the pain she'd suffered had only grown deeper with every passing day and hour he and Cash were missing, he realized that Tia was experiencing the same emotions now.

Grace had sensed someone was watching her because she was asking questions about him and Cash.

Tia had just received a threatening call.

Still, he couldn't talk Tia out of giving up her search. Her love—a mother's love—was too strong, just as his birth mother's was.

Only his birth mother's search had gotten her killed.

TIA PACED THE living room, too terrified to sit or lie down. By the time Ryder arrived, she'd worked herself into a sweat.

She yanked open the door and met him on the porch. "Could you trace the call?"

Ryder's boots pounded the wooden porch floor as he strode toward her. "Gwen's trying. But most likely it came from a burner phone, Tia. If she calls again and you keep her on the phone long enough, maybe we can get something."

Tia's chest tightened. "But what if she doesn't call again?"

Ryder gripped her arms to stop her constant motion. "We'll find her another way."

"But how?" Tia whispered.

Ryder pulled her into his arms and held her. "This is what I do," he murmured.

She pressed her hand against his chest. His heart beat steadily beneath her palm, soothing her slightly. Ryder was strong and caring and he knew what he was doing.

She had to trust him.

Hard to do when the last man she'd trusted had been Darren, and he'd tried to con her out of her inheritance, then abandoned her when she was pregnant.

He pulled away slightly, then took her hands in his. "When she called, did you hear anything in the background that might indicate where she was?"

Tia strained to remember. "I don't know, I was so terrified…"

"Think. Was there any street noise? Cars? A train? Water?"

"I think I heard a siren."

"Like the police?" Ryder asked.

She shook her head. "No, maybe an ambulance?"

"So she might have been near a hospital," Ryder said.

Tia pressed her fingers to her temple. "Maybe. I don't know, Ryder. It could have been a fire engine."

He squeezed her hands. "Okay, just think about it. Something might come to you later."

Although later might not be soon enough.

RYDER STRUGGLED NOT to show his own anxiety. Tia needed comfort, encouragement and hope.

Lying to her wouldn't be fair.

He insisted that she lie down, but from the couch where he'd stretched out he could hear her tossing and turning.

Just as dawn streaked the sky, she finally settled and fell asleep. She needed rest, so he changed clothes and made coffee, then decided to pay his mother that visit.

By eight o'clock, he'd swung by his place, picked up a couple of Grace's letters and was knocking on Myra's door. She always enjoyed her coffee in the sunroom in the mornings and greeted him with a cup in hand.

"Ryder, what a nice surprise." She wrapped him in a hug. Ryder stiffened slightly. She might not be so happy when he told her the reason for his visit.

Myra pulled back, a small frown creasing her eyes. "Is something wrong, honey?"

Ryder gave himself a second to grasp his emotions before he cleared his throat. "We need to talk. Can I join you in the sunroom for some coffee?"

"Of course." She swept her hand through her wavy chin-length hair and gestured toward the coffeepot. "Do you want some breakfast, too?"

Ryder shook his head. He couldn't eat until this conversation was over.

He chose a mug from her collection, filled it with coffee and they walked to the sunroom together.

She sank into her wicker chair while he took the glider. His father had owned a fifty-acre farm outside town, but when he died, his mother sold it and bought this little bungalow a mile from town. It was a small neighborhood, but catered to retirees who didn't want to deal with yard upkeep.

"What's going on, Ryder?" she asked, tone worried.

"I've been working a case," he said, stalling. "A baby kidnapping."

"Oh, the Jeffries woman. I saw her on the news last night."

He sipped his coffee and gave a nod. "We're hoping the tip line turns up a lead."

"I'm so sorry for her," his mother said. "It must be horrible to have your baby stolen from your home like that."

He studied her but saw no sign of an underlying meaning that she could relate because of him. "She's devastated. She wanted a family more than anything in the world."

Myra traced a finger around the rim of her mug. "Well, I hope you find the baby."

"I will." An awkwardness stretched between them in the silence that ensued. Ryder took another long sip of his coffee. He didn't know where to begin, so he removed a couple of Grace's letters from inside his jacket and laid them on the wrought-iron coffee table.

His mother looked down at them with a frown, then lifted her gaze to meet his. "Talk to me, son. What's going on?"

"It's about my adoption," Ryder said. "I need to know who handled it. How you and Dad got me."

Myra's hand trembled as she lowered her coffee mug to the table. "We've already been through this, Ryder. We wanted a baby and couldn't have one. Your father met this lawyer who said he'd found a little boy for us."

"What was the lawyer's name?"

A seed of panic flared in her eyes before she masked it. "Frost. William Frost."

Ryder made a mental note of the name. "You said he told you that my birth parents needed money, so they sold me in exchange for relinquishing custody."

Frown lines creased her forehead. "Yes."

Ryder had to tread carefully here. This woman loved him and had raised him. He couldn't treat her like a suspect in an interrogation.

But…he had to know the truth. If she'd lied to him or if someone had lied to her…

He gestured toward the envelopes on the table. "That's not true, Mom," he said gruffly. "I know who my birth parents are now. The McCullens."

His mother gasped. "You talked to them?"

He shook his head. "No, unfortunately they're both dead."

She rubbed her forehead with two fingers. "I don't understand, Ryder."

"They didn't sell me," he said bluntly. "I was kidnapped, stolen from them at birth, along with my twin brother."

Shock and some other emotion resembling guilt streaked her face.

"You knew I had a twin," Ryder said, his throat thickening. "Didn't you?"

Pain and guilt darkened her eyes, then she turned away

and wrapped her arms around herself as if she needed to physically hold herself together.

His anger mounted at her silence. "You did, didn't you? You knew about Cash?"

She stiffened her spine. "We were told there were twins, but that one of them was sickly. And...your father didn't think we could handle a sick child."

"So it wasn't about the money?" Ryder asked. "Not to the McCullens. And you and Dad lied about paying for me, so you could have taken Cash in, too."

She shook her head, eyes wild with a myriad of emotions. "No, we did pay," she said sharply. "That lawyer wanted a fee, and we used every ounce of our savings to adopt you. We couldn't afford hospital bills for a sick baby and...we thought he'd find a place for your brother."

Rage at the situation fueled Ryder's temper. "But he didn't, Mother." Ryder stood, the glider screeching as it shifted back and forth. He walked to the door and looked out at the woods, needing air.

When he turned back to her, he slammed a curtain down over his face to mask his emotions. "Cash was tossed around from foster home to foster home. He never had a break."

"You met him?" she asked, her voice cracking.

"Yes, he came to see me." The turmoil in Cash's eyes taunted Ryder. "He never had a family, Mother, because you and Dad separated him from me." He pounded his chest with his fist. "And before that, someone kidnapped me and Cash from our birth parents."

Tears blurred her eyes. "I...don't know what to say, son, except that I only knew what the lawyer told us. I raised you. I love you."

Ryder jerked the envelopes from the table and pulled

out the photograph of pregnant Grace McCullen, looking up at the sun.

"She was my mother, Cash's mother, and she wanted us. She didn't choose to give us up for adoption."

"That can't be true."

"It is true, Mother. She kept cards and letters she wrote to us. She poured out her heart because she missed us and loved us."

She shook her head in denial. "I'm sorry, Ryder, I had no idea..."

"Maybe not," Ryder said. "But she—her name was Grace—Grace and Joe McCullen not only looked for us, Mother—they died trying to find us."

Chapter Sixteen

Ryder sat in silence as his mother read the first letter. She wiped at tears as she picked up two of the cards and skimmed them.

"My God," she said in a haunted whisper. "I...can't believe this. I...really didn't know, son."

Ryder stood, gripping his coffee mug with clammy fingers. "Maybe not, but you should have told me I had a twin." He faced her, his heart in his throat. "I had other brothers, too, Mother. And parents who grieved that I was taken from them." Just as Tia was grieving.

She jammed the card she was reading back into the envelope. "I'm sorry, Ryder. I don't know what else to say."

He didn't know what else to say, either.

Except the disappointment, sadness and regret for the McCullens—along with his own, for missing out on knowing his brothers—was eating him up inside.

Memories of arguments his mother and father had had when he was a child echoed in his head. His father had been harsh at times, demanding, had always pushed to get his way.

"I know Dad was a tyrant at times, Mother, and that you gave in to him. Do you think he knew the truth?"

She pressed her lips into a thin line. "How dare you

disparage your father when he's not here to defend himself, Ryder. He and I both loved you and we did the best we could." She snatched the letters and cards and pushed them into his hands. "There's nothing good to gain by harping on what happened years ago. I've told you the truth, and I'm done talking about this."

Ryder crossed his arms. His mother could be stubborn. She'd always defended his father, even when she knew he was wrong. Now that he was dead, though, he hoped she'd think for herself.

"Fine, then you're right. We're done talking." Furious and confused, he strode back through the house.

Even if his father had known about Cash and the kidnapping, Ryder couldn't confront him. His father was dead.

But...the lawyer might have answers.

His phone buzzed as he sped from the driveway. Gwen.

Hopefully she had news for Tia. He'd also see what Gwen could find out about William Frost.

TIA WOKE TO find Ryder gone. Disappointment mingled with hope that he might be chasing a lead.

Groggy from too little sleep, she showered, scrubbing her hair vigorously to calm her nerves.

Her TV appearance had aired the night before.

Then that call...

But how had the caller gotten her personal cell phone number? They hadn't released the number on TV.

Surely other reliable calls would come in. Someone who'd seen her baby. Someone who wanted that reward money badly enough to turn the kidnapper in, even if that person was a friend or someone he or she loved.

She checked her phone for missed calls or messages before drying her hair, but there were none.

Outside, she heard a noise. An engine? Car slowing?

She peeked through her bedroom window and scanned the yard. A slight movement. A shadow.

It disappeared as fast as it had come.

Her pulse quickened. Had someone been outside? Was someone watching her or her house?

Or was she simply paranoid?

She blew her hair dry, gathered the strands into a ponytail and brushed her cheeks with powder to camouflage the bags beneath her eyes. Lip gloss helped with her parched dry lips.

She hurried to get coffee and forced herself to eat a piece of toast. The rumbling sound of a car engine startled her, and she rushed to the front window and checked outside.

Ryder.

She swung the door open before he stepped onto the porch. "Gwen just called. It might be nothing or we might have a lead."

She snatched her purse and phone on the way out the door, then ran back and plucked the baby quilt from the crib just in case they found her son. Pressing it to her chest, she jogged down the steps and crossed to his SUV. "What kind of lead?" she asked as she dived into the passenger seat.

"Someone reported seeing a woman with a baby at the bus station outside Sagebrush acting suspiciously."

Tia's breath caught. "Was it a little boy?"

Ryder covered her hand with his. "I don't know, Tia. It might not be Jordie or the person who kidnapped him.

For all we know, the woman is just a nervous traveler, or she could be in trouble for another reason."

"Like an abusive spouse," Tia said, his logic ringing true. Still, she clung to hope as he sped toward Sagebrush.

RYDER TRIED TO banish the image of his mother's pain-filled face from his mind. He had to focus on Tia now.

But…when he had the time, he'd talk to Maddox. As the sheriff of Pistol Whip, Maddox might have information on that lawyer.

Tia twisted her hands together. "Who called about the woman?"

"A ticket salesperson at the bus station."

"Did she get a look at Jordie?"

"She didn't say." He didn't want to squash the light in Tia's tone, but he also didn't want to feed false hope.

Tia chewed on her bottom lip, then lifted the baby blanket and pressed it against her cheek. Early morning sunlight slanted off her face, making her skin look golden and her face young.

He thought of his birth mother, Grace, in the picture where she was her pregnant. She'd looked radiant and happy, just as he imagined Tia had during her pregnancy.

He wished he could have seen Tia like that, before the horror and agony of this kidnapping had taken its toll.

She remained quiet as he maneuvered through town.

Just as they pulled up, a bus was loading, a line of passengers boarding. Tia leaned forward to search the group as he swung into a parking space. Before he killed the engine, she threw the door open and started toward the bus.

But the bus door quickly closed, the engine fired up and the bus pulled away.

Tia cried out in frustration.

Dammit. Ryder motioned to the entrance of the station and darted inside. He strode straight to the ticket counter, flashed his ID and explained he needed to speak to the person who'd phoned the tip line.

A white-haired woman in a green shirt emerged from the back. "I'm Bernice, the lady who called."

Tia rushed up behind him, her breathing choppy. "This is my son, Jordie." She shoved the photograph toward Bernice. "Did the woman you saw have this baby with her?"

Ryder placed a hand to her back as they waited on a response.

TIA'S HEART WAS pounding so hard she thought it would explode in her chest.

Bernice leaned over the counter and scrutinized the photograph. "Hmm, I can't be sure. She had him wrapped up tight in a baby blanket and kept him to her chest, so I couldn't see the baby's face."

Tia gripped the counter. "Did you see the baby's hair? Was it blond or dark?"

Bernice settled her reading glasses on the end of her nose. "I… I'm sorry, I can't say."

Ryder gave Tia's waist a squeeze, a silent message to hang in there.

"Why did you think she was acting suspiciously?" Ryder asked.

Bernice worried her glasses with her fingers, settling and resetting them again. "Well…she was awkward, you know, like she didn't know how to take care of the baby. It was fussing and crying and she jostled it to try to quiet the poor thing and kept looking around as if she was afraid."

Because she had Jordie?

Or had Ryder been right—was she running from someone else? God knew, Tia had worked with enough women coming through Crossroads that that was a distinct possibility.

"Did she call the baby by name?" Ryder asked.

Bernice glanced at the other ticket attendant, but the heavyset woman simply shrugged. "I was on my break, didn't see or hear nothing."

"A name?" Ryder asked again.

Bernice shook her head no. "She just kept saying, 'Hush, little darlin'.' That's all."

"What was the passenger's name?" Ryder asked.

Bernice checked the computer. "Vicki Smith."

"Did you check her ID?" Ryder asked.

The woman nodded. "All she had with her was a discount store card, one of those big warehouse deals where you have to have a membership."

"No driver's license?" Tia asked.

She shook her head no. "Said her wallet was stolen. Sounded down on her luck."

"What's her destination?" Ryder asked.

Bernice glanced at the computer again. "Cheyenne."

"Can you give me a description of her?"

"She was wearing a scarf, so I don't know how long her hair was, but it was a dirty brown."

"Height and weight?"

Bernice shrugged. "About your height, ma'am. But she was plumper, although hard to tell how plump with the baby pressed to her like that. Could have been baby weight, too."

"Did she have any distinguishing marks on her body? A tattoo or birthmark?"

"Not that I saw," Bernice replied.

"Did she mention meeting anyone?"

"No."

"Did she make any calls? Maybe on a cell phone?"

Bernice hesitated again then shook her head. "I didn't see a phone. Like I said, though, she was acting strange, like she didn't want to talk to people. So I didn't push it."

Ryder thanked her, then pressed a card on the counter. "If you think of anything else she said or did, call me."

Tia clutched the baby blanket to her as she followed Ryder back to the SUV. "What are we going to do?"

Ryder started the engine, a muscle ticking in his jaw. "We're going to follow that bus."

He gunned the engine and sped onto the highway. Tia buckled up for the ride.

RYDER HONKED HIS horn as a sedan nearly cut him off when he pulled out of the bus station. The black car ignored the horn, sideswiped him then raced on.

Ryder swerved, hit the curb and bounced back onto the road. He wanted to go after the son of a bitch, but following that bus and the woman on board took priority.

Tia's breathing filled the strained silence. She gripped the dashboard and said nothing, though.

Instead she kept her gaze trained ahead, eyes darting back and forth in search of the bus.

Ryder spotted it ahead, flew around an ancient pickup and roared up beside it.

"Look!" Tia pointed to a side window near the back, where a young woman wearing a dark scarf turned to watch them.

Dammit, she had a baby on her shoulder, swaddled in a blanket, and her eyes were wide with fear.

"That has to be her," Tia said in a raw whisper.

Chapter Seventeen

Ryder considered pulling the bus over, but decided to wait until the next bus station. It was only twenty minutes away.

Meanwhile, he phoned Gwen and asked her to dig up what she could find on Vicki Smith.

"I'm following the bus she's on now," Ryder said. "She used a discount store's ID, no driver's license, so it may be a fake name."

"Smith is an extremely common name," Gwen said. "Let me see how many Vickis there are."

A traffic light turned yellow, but the bus coasted on through just as it turned red. Tia looked panicked. Ryder quickly checked the intersection for cars, then sped through.

No way were they going to lose this bus.

"Ryder, I found dozens of women named Vicki Smith, but none match the description you gave, either. But if this woman is the unsub, she could have changed her appearance."

"I know. Cross-check with those medical records we got warrants for and see if any of those women recently delivered a baby or lost a child."

"On it."

The bus slowed at another light. The woman turned around again, fear flashing on her face when she realized they were still behind her.

"Okay, a woman named Vicki Smith gave birth to a baby girl a month ago in Sagebrush."

"Find out where she is now and the status of the baby."

"Okay, I'll keep you posted."

She disconnected just as the bus moved forward. It swung a wide left at the intersection and Ryder followed it into the parking lot of the bus station.

TIA DARTED AROUND the front of the bus just as the door opened and passengers began to unload.

Ryder rushed up behind her. "Stay calm and let me handle the situation," he said in a low voice next to her ear.

Tia felt anything but calm. She rose on tiptoes to see over the passengers, desperate to find the woman and baby. The bus was full, though, and the woman had been sitting near the back, so she couldn't do anything but wait.

"What did you learn about her?" Tia asked as an Asian woman and small child walked past her, followed by two teenagers, earbuds in, immersed in their music.

"Nothing, really. A woman named Vicki Smith gave birth to a baby girl a month ago. Gwen's looking into her."

Several more passengers left the bus, then the bus driver peered to the back of the bus, seemed to decide that was everyone getting off at this stop and closed the door.

"No!" Tia hit the door with her palm.

Ryder stepped in front of her and rapped his fist on the door, then flashed his badge at the window. "FBI, open up."

The bus driver flicked a hand up, indicating he was going to comply, then opened the door. Tia started to board, but Ryder gently urged her to stay still.

"Let me handle it, Tia." He flashed his badge as he climbed the steps. Tia followed on his heels.

Whispers and murmurs passed through the remaining passengers still seated.

"FBI Special Agent Ryder Banks," Ryder announced.

Tia scanned the people on board and spotted the woman in the back huddling down in the seat, her head buried against the baby. A scarf covered her hair, shadowing her face.

Ryder held up his hand. "Please stay seated, folks. I need to talk to the young woman in the back, the one with the baby."

The woman remained crouched in the seat, face averted as she soothed the crying child.

Tia's heart ached. Was that Jordie crying for her?

Ryder motioned for the woman to come with him. She stood slowly, hugging the baby to her as she followed Ryder.

"This should just take a moment," he said to the woman and the bus driver.

Tia shaded her eyes from the sun as she exited the bus into the parking lot. Ryder guided the woman to the sidewalk.

The woman pivoted, covering the baby with her hand to hide its face.

"Miss," Ryder said, "what is your name?"

She cast a terrified look at Tia then patted the bundle in her arms. "Vicki Smith."

"And your baby's name?"

"Mark," the woman said. "Why? What do you want with us?"

Tia cleared her throat. "Do you know who I am?"

Vicki adjusted her scarf, drawing it tighter. "No. Should I?"

Tia barely restrained herself from yanking the child from the woman's arms. "I was on the news last night. My baby was kidnapped I've been looking for him ever since."

The woman backed away. "I don't have your baby. This is my child. I'm going to visit my mother in Cheyenne."

Ryder gently touched the baby's cap. "Then we can clear this up really quickly. Just let us see the baby."

She shook her head vigorously, clutching the child as if to protect it from them. "You can't take my baby. I won't let you."

Tia inhaled sharply. The fear in the woman's voice was real. Whether it was because she was a kidnapper or for another reason, she couldn't tell.

Ryder gently touched the baby again. "I'm not going to take the child. But I need to verify that this is not Miss Jeffries's son."

"It's not," the woman cried. "Now let me go. If I miss that bus, I can't get to my mother's."

"Just show me that it's not my son," Tia said, softening her tone. "Then we'll let you be on your way."

The woman trembled, her eyes wary as she studied them. But she slowly tilted the infant back into her arms and eased the blanket from its face.

Ryder gently pushed the cap back to reveal a thick head of wavy black hair.

It wasn't Jordie.

TIA'S LEGS BUCKLED. Ryder steadied her, sensing her disappointment.

"I'm sorry, you're right," Tia said. "I just thought…"

"Someone phoned the tip line and said you were acting suspiciously," Ryder said, still unwilling to release her before he heard the real story.

She *was* acting suspiciously and hiding something.

Alarm speared the woman's eyes. "I…don't know what you mean." She hurriedly rewrapped the infant and started back toward the bus.

Ryder caught her arm. "Wait, I need to ask you some questions."

Vicki's eyes darted around the parking lot. "Please, you can see I don't have that woman's child. Now let me and my baby go."

"Something's wrong," Ryder said. "Is that child really yours?"

"Of course it is," she gasped.

"Then why the fake ID? Because I know Vicki Smith is a fake name."

"No, I'm Vicki. I'm from Pistol Whip—"

"There is a Vicki Smith from Pistol Whip, but she gave birth to a baby girl a month ago."

The woman sagged against his hold. "Please don't do this. If he finds us, he'll kill me and take Mark. He's already hurt him once. I won't let him do it again."

Tia had eased up beside him. "I'm sorry for scaring you, Vicki."

"Are you talking about your husband or boyfriend?" Ryder asked.

Embarrassment heated the woman's cheeks. "Yes."

"He's Mark's father?"

"Yes—"

"How did he hurt him?" Ryder asked.

The woman rocked the baby. "He can't stand it when he cries. He shakes him so bad. And the other night he threw him against the wall."

Pure rage shot through Ryder. If she was telling the truth, the bastard should be locked away.

"The real Vicki and I are friends," she continued. "She loaned me her discount card so I could use it as an ID to get on that bus."

"Is your mother really waiting?" Tia asked.

The woman shifted, then shook her head, fear and defeat streaking her face. "No,.. I have no place to go, but I had to get away from him." She dropped a kiss on the baby's head. "I put up with him hurting me, but I refuse to let him beat up our son."

"Good for you," Tia said with a mountain of compassion in her voice.

"I'm sorry about your situation," Ryder said injecting sympathy into his voice. "But if what you're saying is true, you should go through the proper channels."

"I filed a police report once, and they came and talked to him." Her voice grew hot with anger. "Then do you know what he did?"

"He was enraged and took it out on you," Tia said.

"Yes," the woman whispered brokenly. "He beat me so bad I couldn't walk for days. Where were the police then?"

Ryder silently cursed. He'd heard this story before, too.

"I can help you," Tia said. "I run a program called Crossroads. It's for families in crisis. There are other women like you, women who will help you."

"But he'll find me," Vicki cried. "He always finds me."

"No," Tia said emphatically. "I promise you he won't."

"She's right," Ryder said. "If everything you're telling me is true, I'll make certain you and your child have protection."

The woman began to sob, and Tia drew her and Mark into a hug, comforting them while Ryder motioned to the driver that he could leave.

TIA'S HEART ACHED for the woman. Unfortunately her story was a common one. The cycle of abuse would repeat itself if she didn't break it. That took strength and courage and help from strangers.

She could offer that. And if Ryder was willing to help...

The woman's body trembled next to Tia as she helped her into the SUV. She wished they had a car seat for the infant. They would take care of that ASAP.

Ryder phoned a friend with a private security company, and he agreed to guard the center for the evening. She phoned Elle to give her a heads-up about the situation. Vicki admitted her real name was Kelly Ripples.

Tia hugged Kelly again as they arrived at the center. "Everything will be okay now, I promise."

Elle and Ina met them at the door. "We fixed a room for you and the baby," Ina said. "I hope you don't mind sharing a room. Susan and her little girl are really nice. They just got here a couple of days ago. I think you'll like them. The little girl loves babies."

Kelly looked skeptical, but thanked Ina and followed her to one of the bedrooms, where a portable crib was set up in the corner. "I need to feed him," Kelly said.

"Of course," Tia said. "We'll let you have some privacy."

Ina gestured toward the rocking chair. "When he's

settled, please join us in the dining room. I cooked a pot of homemade vegetable soup and some corn bread."

"That sounds wonderful," Kelly said in a low voice.

Tia joined Ryder in the hallway. "Thank you for arranging for the security guard."

He nodded. "I called Gwen. She's checking Kelly's story."

"I believe her," Tia said.

Ryder crossed his arms. "Time will tell. Until then, she'll be safe here. And if her story is confirmed, I'll see that her husband never gets hold of that child again."

Tia had never trusted a man the way she did Ryder. His fierce protectiveness and drive for justice was admirable.

She wanted to tell him that, but her growing feelings for him terrified her.

THE COMPASSION TIA showed for the woman astounded Ryder. She had gone from suspecting Kelly of kidnapping to an offer to help her in minutes.

Ryder's cell phone buzzed. He motioned to Tia that he needed to take it, so he stepped into the other room. "Gwen, that was fast."

"It's not about Kelly," she said quickly. "We have a hit on the woman in the security footage at the hospital nursery, and I cross-checked it with the hospital records. Her name is Bonnie Cone. She lives outside Sagebrush. She lost a baby recently and suffered serious depression. Her husband claimed she was obsessed with having another baby right away, but the doctor advised against it. The husband said they separated last month. He hasn't been able to reach her for a couple of weeks and he's worried."

A desperate, grieving woman. "Where is she?"

"I'm texting you her address now."

Ryder considered pursuing the lead on his own, but if they found Bonnie Cone, Tia could tell them really quickly if she had Jordie.

Chapter Eighteen

Tia assured Kelly that she and Mark would be safe at Crossroads. The private security agent seemed to take his job seriously.

His eyes also lit up with a spark when he met Elle.

Tia would love to see her friend with a nice man. She'd had her own troubles before joining Crossroads and deserved happiness. But she definitely had built walls to protect herself.

Just as Tia had done.

Maybe that was the reason they were such good friends.

Ryder explained the phone call, and they rushed toward Sagebrush. She fidgeted, determined not to get her hopes up.

"The woman we're going to see was the one on the security camera at the hospital. Her name is Bonnie Cone. She lost a baby over a month ago. According to Bonnie's husband, she was despondent and obsessed with having another child."

Tia's heart went out to her.

But...her sympathy would only stretch so far.

The afternoon sunlight beamed in the car and slanted off farmland as they passed. Beautiful green grass, cows grazing, horses galloping on a hill in the horizon—a reminder of Wyoming's natural beauty. Normally those things soothed her, but today nothing could erase the grave feeling in her chest.

Bonnie's house was an older ranch, set off the road in a neighborhood about five miles from town. Although the house had probably been built fifty years ago, it looked reasonably well kept, except for the yard.

A gray minivan was parked in the drive. As they passed it, she peeked in and spotted a car seat.

They walked to the front door in silence. A welcome home wreath on the door and a wooden bench on the front stoop indicated that Bonnie had tried to make the house more homey and inviting.

Ryder punched the doorbell, his gaze scanning the property. He was always on alert. A product of his job, she supposed.

How did he live this kind of life, facing danger and criminals every day, and not become jaded? Did he ever relax?

He punched the bell a second time and Tia peeked through the front window. Living room with a brown sectional sofa, magazines dotting the coffee table, along with a baby bottle and an assortment of infant toys. A colorful blanket was spread on the floor, a toy rabbit and squeaky toy on top.

Seconds later, footsteps sounded and she quickly moved away from the window. If the woman saw her, she might bolt.

RYDER FLASHED HIS ID as Bonnie opened the door. "Miss Cone, my name is Special Agent Ryder Banks, and this is Tia Jeffries."

Bonnie's gaze darted to Tia, her eyes widening in recognition. "You're the woman on TV last night."

"Yes, that was me," Tia said softly. "Can we come in?"

Bonnie glanced back and forth between Tia and Ryder. "I don't understand."

Bonnie looked pale and thin, her eyes were dark with circles, her medium brown hair curly and tousled as if she hadn't slept in days. She was also still wearing a bathrobe.

Ryder shouldered his way through the door. "We need to talk. It'll just take a moment."

Bonnie tugged the belt of her robe tighter around her waist and gestured toward the sofa. Baby clothes and crib sheets overflowed a laundry basket, spilling onto the sofa.

Tia exhaled and slid the basket to the floor so she could seat herself beside Bonnie. Ryder claimed the club chair opposite her.

Bonnie plucked a receiving blanket from the basket and wadded it in her hands. "What is this about?"

"We're investigating the disappearance of Miss Jeffries's baby," Ryder said.

"I'm sorry about your son." The woman gave Tia a sympathetic smile. "But what does that have to do with me?"

"You delivered your baby at the same hospital where I gave birth," Tia said.

Pain darkened Bonnie's eyes. "Yes."

"I know you lost a child," Tia said gently. "That must have been awful."

Bonnie's lower lip quivered. "It was."

"I'm so sorry," Tia said. "I understand the heartache."

"No one understands," Bonnie said with a trace of bitterness. "I carried him for nine long months inside me. I had dreams for him."

Tia placed her hand over Bonnie's. "I do know. I carried my baby just like you did, I dreamed about holding him and watching him grow up. I started a college fund for him before he was even born."

Ryder swallowed hard at the emotions her words stirred.

"We were watching the video feed from the hospital," Ryder cut in. "You were on it."

Bonnie narrowed her eyes. "What?"

"After your baby was gone, you came back to the hospital and you were looking at the newborns."

Bonnie made a strangled sound in her throat and placed her hand over her stomach. "Yes, I wanted a baby so badly. I missed my son."

"That's understandable," Ryder said. "You missed him so much that you were out of your mind with grief."

Bonnie nodded, tears welling in her eyes. She swiped at them, unknotted the blanket and began to fold it methodically, as if the task was calming.

Tia picked up a burp cloth from the basket and ran her fingers over it. "We know you were grief stricken and in a bad place, Bonnie. I understand that, I do."

"Maybe you were so distraught you did something you never would have done otherwise," Ryder said. "You wanted to replace your baby, so you found another one."

Bonnie's startled gaze shot to Ryder's. "Yes, I did. My husband didn't understand, but I had to have a baby." Her voice was raw, agonized. "What's wrong with that?"

"Nothing," Tia said. "Not unless you took my son to replace yours."

Bonnie stood abruptly, knocking the basket of laundry over. Clothes spilled out, but she didn't seem to notice. "My God, that's the reason you're here. You think I kidnapped your baby?"

Ryder stood, sensing the woman might turn volatile. "We have to ask."

Bonnie fisted her hand by her side. "That's completely insane," Bonnie stuttered. "I would never do such a thing."

A mixture of emotions welled in Tia's eyes. Ryder wanted to comfort her, but she needed answers instead.

"But you got another baby," Ryder asked.

Fear deepened the panic in Bonnie's expression. "Yes, but that baby is mine now." She whirled toward Tia. "He's not yours, do you hear me? He's mine and you can't take him away."

Tia pressed a hand to her mouth.

"Then where did the baby come from?" Ryder asked.

"I didn't steal anyone's baby," Bonnie shouted. "I adopted a little boy."

Tia's sharp breath rent the air. "Then you won't mind showing him to me."

Anger slashed Bonnie's expression. "If it'll get you to go away and leave me alone, then yes. I'll get him."

She stalked toward the bedroom, and Tia and Ryder followed. For all he knew, she was going to grab the baby, go out a back door and run.

TIA RUSHED TO stay close to Bonnie in case she snatched the baby and tried to get away.

Bonnie stumbled, then grabbed the bedpost to steady herself as she crossed to the bassinet.

"He's sleeping," she said in a voice both tender and filled with fear. "I hate to disturb him."

Tia and Ryder remained in place, though, so she gently lifted the infant, swaddled in a blue blanket with turtles on it, his tiny fingers poking out.

Tia's pulse pounded as Bonnie gently pulled the blanket back to reveal the baby's face.

He had a fuzzy blanket of brown hair, his chin was slightly pointed, his face square. He was beautiful.

But he wasn't Jordie.

Disappointment nearly brought her to her knees.

Tia grabbed the bedpost this time, choking back a cry.

"Tia?" Ryder's low, gruff voice echoed behind her.

She shook her head, then turned to face him, her heart in her eyes.

Ryder crossed the room and took her arm, then glanced at the baby.

"How old is he?" Ryder asked.

"Four weeks today." Bonnie dropped a kiss on the baby's head, making Tia's heart yearn for Jordie even more. "Isn't he beautiful?" Bonnie said in a voice reserved for doting mothers.

"Yes," Ryder said. "You said you adopted him?"

"I did. After I lost…my child, I was devastated. Then my doctor advised against another pregnancy and I thought I couldn't go on." She paused and swiped at tears. "One of the counselors suggested adoption. I thought it would take a while, but someone else in the hospital gave me the name of a lawyer who handled private adoptions, and I contacted him." She rocked the infant back and forth in her arms. "It was a miracle. He said he knew of a teenager who had decided to go the adoption route. I couldn't believe it." She hugged the infant tighter. "As soon as she gave birth, he called me. I rushed to the hospital and there he was in the nursery, all wrapped up, just needing some love."

Her eyes brightened. "Love I could give him. I knew he was meant to be mine. I needed him and he needed me."

"He's lucky to have you," Tia said.

Bonnie nodded. "I named him after my father, David. He was a good man."

"It's a lovely name," Tia said. "I'm sure your father would be happy."

"What was the lawyer's name?" Ryder asked.

"He's a reputable attorney," Bonnie said defensively.

Ryder arched a brow. "His name?"

"Why do you want to know?" She clutched the baby tighter. "Did you talk to my husband? If you did, he probably told you I was crazy, that I was obsessed with having another child. And I was, but that doesn't mean I won't be a good mother to this little guy."

"I'm not questioning that," Ryder said. "But I'd like to talk to the lawyer just in case whoever abducted Tia's baby might have done so to sell him."

"Sell him?" Bonnie gasped. "My God. It's not like I bought him off a black market. What kind of person do you think I am?"

"It's no reflection on you, Bonnie," Ryder said. "But in a missing child case, I have to consider every possible theory."

Tia wanted to reassure her everything would be all right. But if, by chance, she had adopted a child obtained illegally, that adoption would be illegal and the courts would intervene.

That scary realization must have occurred to Bonnie.

"You can't take him," Bonnie said. "I can't lose him, too."

Tia stepped closer to calm her. "We're not going to do that, Bonnie. We just need the name of that lawyer."

Her expression wilted, and she closed her eyes for a second as if in a silent debate. When she opened them, she clenched her jaw. "His name is Frank Frost. His office is in Cheyenne."

"Frost," Tia said. "Thank you, Bonnie. We'll let you go and rest." She stroked the back of the baby's head. "You sleep tight, sweetie. Bonnie loves you and will take good care of you."

Ryder glanced at Tia. "Let's go."

Anxiety tightened her shoulders as she followed him outside. "Ryder, what's wrong?"

"I don't know," Ryder said as he climbed in the front seat.

A muscle ticked in his jaw as they pulled away.

"Are you keeping something from me?" Tia asked.

Emotions glittered in Ryder's eyes, but he quickly masked them. "No."

"Yes, you are," Tia said earnestly. "You promised not to lie to me, Ryder. If you heard something about Jordie—"

"I didn't," he said, his wide jaw hard with anger. "But I recognize that name Frost."

Tia pulled the baby quilt into her lap and twisted her hands in the soft fabric. "What about him?"

Ryder heaved a weary breath. "I was adopted myself. I've always known it, but recently I learned who my birth family was—is. I have a twin brother, Tia. We were kidnapped as babies and our parents were told we were dead."

A cold chill swept over Tia. "You were kidnapped?"

He nodded. "My twin brother has reconnected with our birth family. He came to see me the other day."

"Oh, my God." Tia laid a hand on his shoulder, aching to comfort him for a change. "That must have been a shock."

"It was." He hesitated, then cleared his throat. "The lawyer who handled my adoption was named Frost."

Tia froze. "You think it was the same man?"

"No, his name was William. But they could be related."

"Are you suggesting the lawyer knew that you and your brother were stolen?"

Ryder shrugged, but his look indicated he did.

Chapter Nineteen

Another thought occurred to Ryder as he drove toward Cheyenne.

If Frost had intentionally been an accomplice in the kidnapping and selling of babies—him and Cash—was that the first instance?

How many more had there been since?

He'd have to talk to the McCullens—see if they'd looked into the lawyer. But the thought of meeting his brothers made his gut clench.

He wasn't ready for that. Not with the memory of those letters fresh in his mind.

Worse, now he'd divulged his secrets to Tia. She'd grown silent, obviously contemplating the implications of his statement.

He spotted a barbecue restaurant and pulled into it. "Let's get a quick lunch. I need to call Gwen."

Tia nodded, worry radiating from her features as they made their way inside. They grabbed a booth and ordered, then he stepped outside to phone Gwen.

"I checked into Kelly Ripples's story," Gwen said. "She's telling the truth. She's been in the hospital three times over the past year with injuries consistent with spousal abuse. A neighbor reported a domestic at her place six weeks ago. Found a pregnant Kelly on the floor bloody and bruised."

"Son of a bitch."

"Yeah, he's a bad one. Good for her for getting away from him."

"We just have to keep him away," Ryder said. It was a damn shame women needed help to escape the men who supposedly loved them. But better for the child to not have a father than have one who hit him.

"I have someone else I want you to run a background check on. A lawyer named Frank Frost. He has a practice in Cheyenne. Also look for info on William Frost."

"What are you looking for?"

Ryder explained his personal situation, including the history behind his own adoption, brushing over Gwen's murmur of sympathy. "The woman in the video, Bonnie Cone, used Frank Frost for legal services in a recent adoption. I need to know if that was legitimate, if adoptions are his specialty, if there have been any complaints against him—"

"I got it. I'll get back to you ASAP."

He thanked her, then hung up and started inside. A breeze blew in, stirring dust. A ranch in the distance reminded him of the McCullens and Horseshoe Creek.

He had to put aside his feelings and talk to the McCullens. See if they had insight on either of the Frost men. If Maddox had investigated him, it could save Ryder time.

Stomach knotted, he punched Cash's number.

"Ryder?"

"Yeah," Ryder said. "I read the letters."

A tense moment stretched between them. "They wanted us."

"I know that now."

"You want to come by Horseshoe Creek and talk?"

Did he? "Sometime. But I'm mired in this kidnapping case right now. Actually, that's the reason I called."

"What do you need?"

An odd feeling tightened his chest. He'd always worked alone. Been a loner all his life.

Now he had brothers.

Cash had offered to help, no questions asked.

"I need to know if you or any of the McCullens know anything about a lawyer named William Frost."

A heartbeat passed. "Frost?"

"Yeah. He's the lawyer who handled my adoption. I wondered if he was in on our kidnapping."

Cash's breathing echoed over the line. "I'll talk to Maddox and Ray and call you back."

Ryder thanked him and disconnected. He had to get back to Tia. She was anxious for news.

He wished to hell he had some.

TIA TRIED TO eat her pulled pork sandwich, but she could barely swallow the food. Her stomach was churning.

Ryder had been kidnapped as a baby. Her son had also.

And now that Ryder knew the truth, it was too late for him and his birth parents to reconcile.

What if that happened to her and Jordie? Was she doomed to a life where she searched the crowd everywhere she went, hoping to see a child that was her son? As the years went on and he changed, would she even recognize him?

She sipped her tea to wash down the sandwich. "I've been thinking." She set her tea glass on the table. "If this lawyer is involved in something illegal, he's not going to just come out and tell us."

Ryder's jaw tightened. "No. I'll need a warrant for his records."

"That's not easy," Tia said. "Not with adoption or medical records."

"Gwen's seeing what she can dig up, and I called Cash to see if the McCullens know anything about Frost. They're both going to get back to me."

He dug into his sandwich, and Tia toyed with an idea in her head. "You're planning to talk to Frank Frost?"

Ryder nodded as he chewed. "I'm hoping to find out something to use as leverage to persuade him to talk."

"I have an idea." Tia tapped her nails on the table. "Why don't we pose as a couple wanting to adopt a baby?"

Ryder scrubbed a hand through his hair. "That's not a bad idea, Tia, but you were on TV. He'll recognize you."

Tia's pulse jumped. She hadn't thought of that. "Wait a minute," she said, her mind spinning. "I'll wear a disguise."

He took another bite of his sandwich and wiped his mouth with the gingham napkin. "I don't know. He might see through it."

Tia's mouth twitched. "Trust me, Ryder. I've done this before." At his perplexed look, she continued, "I mean, for other women."

Ryder studied her as he finished his meal. "I don't need to know details," he said.

Because he sensed what she'd done might have crossed the lines with the law. It had a few times. But sometimes the law failed.

"All right. But I think it could work."

Ryder ordered a cup of coffee and pie. "It's worth a

shot, although if he recognizes you and realizes what we're doing, it could be dangerous."

"I don't care," Tia said. "I don't want Jordie to be lost to me forever like you were to your parents."

Her comment hit home and brought pain to his eyes.

"I'm sorry. I—"

"You're just speaking the truth," Ryder said. "I admire that, Tia. I've been lied to enough in my life."

Tia laid her hand over his and stroked it. "What do you mean?"

He glanced at their hands, and she expected him to pull away. But he didn't. He turned his hand over beneath hers and curled his big fingers around hers.

"My father is dead, but I talked to my mom. She claims she didn't know I was kidnapped, but she and Dad knew I was a twin. They didn't take my brother because he was sickly." His tone turned gravelly with anguish. "Cash was never adopted. He bounced from one foster home to another and had a rough life."

Tia had heard similar stories.

"That's sad," Tia said. "Is he all right now?"

Ryder nodded, his frown softening. "He's connected with the McCullens and is married. He even adopted two kids."

Tia rubbed his palm. "That's a great ending to the story. He used what happened to make him stronger and to give back to needy children."

"But he could have grown up with me, had a decent upbringing—"

"You feel guilty that you got the better deal," Tia said, sensing guilt beneath the surface of his words.

His troubled gaze lifted to hers, and he gave a quick nod.

"It's not your fault," Tia rushed to assure him. "You were an innocent kid, a baby when you were taken. You didn't know about him."

"Not until this week." Resentment deepened his tone.

Tia's heart ached for him. "You're angry at your mother because she didn't tell you about him."

He nodded again. "How could she keep that from me?"

A tense silence stretched between them.

"I don't know, Ryder," Tia said honestly. "It was obviously a complicated situation. Maybe she was trying to protect you."

"Protect me from what?" Ryder barked. "From knowing I had a sibling?" He shook his head. "No. She was protecting herself and Dad," Ryder said. "She said they didn't have enough money to raise both of us."

"Was that true?"

He shrugged. "Maybe. But they claimed they paid to get me. That the McCullens sold me. That's what I thought until Cash showed up and told me the truth."

"I don't completely understand, Ryder," Tia said softly. "But they must have loved you, so give it some time."

He didn't look convinced, but the waitress appeared and he left cash to pay the bill. His phone buzzed just as she walked away.

Ryder glanced at the number then back at Tia. "It's Cash. I need to take this."

Tia decided to stop in the ladies' room while he answered the call. Her emotions were all jumbled. Hearing Ryder's story reminded her that Jordie was in someone else's arms now.

And that she had to get him back. She couldn't spend a lifetime wondering where he was and if he was safe.

RYDER INHALED THE fresh air as he stepped outside. He shouldn't have confided his story to Tia. But when she'd taken his hand and looked at him with those tender, compassionate eyes, he hadn't been able to stop himself.

His phone buzzed again. He pressed Connect. He had to get his head back in the case. "Cash?"

"Yeah. I spoke with Maddox. When he and Ray were trying to find us, they learned we were left at a church. The name Frost did come up. He was a lawyer in Sagebrush, but he died ten years ago."

"Did he have a son?"

"Yeah, his son is about our age. He took over his father's practice." Cash paused. "Maddox questioned him about us, but he said he had no clue. Adoption records were private and sealed."

"I'll work on obtaining warrants," Ryder said. "Tia and I are going to question Frank Frost this afternoon."

"Keep us posted," Cash said.

"I will." When this case was settled, he'd meet his other brothers, too.

He ended the call, then phoned Gwen. "I need you to work on obtaining warrants for a lawyer named Frank Frost and for his files. Also, see if you can get one for his deceased father's case files."

"That'll take time."

"I think Frank Frost may be involved in the Jeffries baby kidnapping."

"Any evidence to support it?"

"That's why I need the warrants." A double-edged sword. Judges were hesitant to force situations without probable cause.

"Bonnie Cone said Frost handled her baby's adoption.

Since the name Frost surfaced regarding my adoption, I think there's a connection."

"I'll get on it ASAP."

He explained about his plan with Tia, and Gwen agreed to rush to set up a profile for the couple, complete with a background, bank information and accounts, and job history along with a cell phone he could use in dealing with the lawyer, one that couldn't be traced back to him if Frost looked. "I had Elle contact Frost's office for an appointment," Tia told him. "They emailed paperwork for us to fill out, so I'll do that before we go. I'm going to say that we've tried in vitro fertilization and it's failed several times."

"Good idea," Ryder said.

"Let's stop by Crossroads," Tia said. "I have clothes there to create a disguise."

He agreed and they drove to the center. When they arrived, Tia and Elle filled out the paperwork from Frost's office and faxed it to them, then she disappeared into a back room while Ryder checked in with the security officer he'd asked to watch the place, an ex-military guy named Blake Bowman.

"Any problems?" Ryder asked.

Bowman shook his head. "No." He lowered his voice. "The people here are something else. They're doing good work."

All thanks to Tia and her generosity.

Elle joined them, her body language exuding anxiety. "Any word about Jordie?"

"We may be on to something," he said. "How is Kelly?"

"She's settled in and seems willing to accept our help."

"Good."

Elle tucked a strand of hair behind her ear. "You are going to find Jordie, aren't you, Agent Banks?" She glanced toward the door. "Tia doesn't deserve this."

"I'm doing everything possible."

The door opened, and a woman with curly blond hair, bright green eyes and wearing a Western skirt appeared. She was almost as tall as Ryder, with big bosoms, and wore a wrist brace on one arm.

"What do you think?"

Ryder's eyes widened at the sound of Tia's voice.

He hadn't recognized her at all.

Hopefully Frost wouldn't, either.

"I didn't know it was you," he said gruffly.

She smiled. "I told you I could pull it off." She offered him a long Duster coat, hat and glasses to disguise himself, then they hurried to his SUV.

"Let me take the lead when we see Frost," he said.

She slipped something from her pocket and opened her palm to him.

Two simple gold wedding bands lay in her palm. "If we're going to inquire about adoption, we have to pose as a married couple."

Ryder considered balking, but she was right.

Still, for a single man who liked being alone, it felt odd as hell when he slid that wedding band on his third finger.

Chapter Twenty

Tia and Ryder practiced their story on the way to the lawyer's office.

Thankfully Gwen was on top of things, and Frost's personal assistant had already emailed that they had been approved and everything was in order.

Tia adjusted her wig as they parked in front of Frost's office.

"Are you sure you're up to this?" Ryder asked as they made their way up to the man's office.

Tia nodded. "I'll do whatever it takes."

Ryder gave her an encouraging smile. "You're a brave woman, Tia."

She shook her head. "Not brave. I'm a mother. It's just what mothers do—protect their children at any cost."

"Unfortunately not all mothers are that way," Ryder said darkly. "Believe me, I've seen some shocking examples over my career."

Tia sighed. "I'm sure you have. And all your life you thought your own mother had sold you." She pressed a hand to his cheek. "Now, you know that's not true. She loved you and Cash."

She was right. Emotions clouded his expression, and

he reached for the door to the lawyer's office. "Let's do this."

Tia offered him a brave smile and entered first. Playing the loving husband, Ryder kept his hand at the small of her back.

"Jared and Emma Manning," Ryder said. "I called earlier to see Mr. Frost."

The perky redhead announced their arrival to her boss. "Follow me."

Tia held on to Ryder's arm as they entered. The receptionist made introductions and offered them coffee, but she and Ryder declined.

Frank Frost was midthirties, with neatly groomed hair, a designer suit and caps that had probably cost a fortune. Framed documents on the wall chronicled his education and legal degree, along with photographs of him and an older man who resembled him, most likely his father. Another picture captured him with a leggy blonde in an evening gown posing in front of a black Mercedes. A Rolex glittered from his left arm.

Tia gritted her teeth. Had he made his money by selling babies?

Frost ran a manicured hand over his tie. "Have a seat, Mr. and Mrs. Manning, and tell me how I can help you."

Ryder started to speak, but Tia caught his arm. "Let me tell him, honey."

Ryder's gaze met hers. "Of course, sweetheart."

His look was so strained that Tia bit back a chuckle. But she focused on Frost and her act. "We've wanted a baby forever," she said earnestly. "But it hasn't been in the cards, what with my endometriosis and all. We've been through all the tests and spent a small fortune on in vitro, but it didn't work."

"I'm sorry to hear that," Frost said, injecting sympathy in his voice. "It always saddens me when folks such as yourself, who would obviously make good parents, aren't blessed in that way when others who aren't parent material spit kids out left and right."

"Thank you for understanding," Tia continued. "I was just about ready to give up, but I met this woman at the hospital when I was leaving the other day. She had the saddest story ever and told me that she'd lost her own child, but that she was adopting a baby." Tia dabbed at her eyes. "So it hit me then, that that's what we had to do."

"There are a lot of unwanted children in the world," Frost said.

"I really want an infant," Tia said. "I...just love babies and want to get a little one so he or she will bond with us from the beginning."

Frost shifted, pulling at his tie. "Infants are harder to come by and in higher demand."

"I tried to tell my wife that," Ryder said. "But she wants a baby so badly." He removed a checkbook and set it on his lap. "I'm willing to pay the adoption fees and any extra costs if we can expedite finding us a child." He tapped the checkbook. "Money is not a problem. I..., have done well for myself."

Tia pressed a kiss to Ryder's cheek. "Isn't he wonderful? He's going to be an amazing father."

Frost looked back and forth between them as if searching for a lie. But Tia swiped at tears and leaned into Ryder, playing the desperate woman and adoring wife.

"Please help us," Tia whispered. "I don't think I can go on if I don't have a baby in my arms." That much was true.

Ryder curved an arm around her, pulled her to him and dropped a kiss on her head. "I promised Emma that we'd have a family," he said, his voice cracking with emotions. "You understand how difficult it is for a man to not be able to give the woman he loves everything she wants."

Frost nodded slowly. "I'm sure it's difficult."

"Not just difficult," Ryder said. "It's painful and frustrating." He opened his checkbook and reached for a pen. "Just tell me what you need to make it happen so my sweet wife here will finally get to have the child she deserves and wants."

A thick silence fell for a moment, then Frost gave a conciliatory nod. "I will see what I can do. Although it might take a few days."

Tia gripped Ryder's hand and kissed it, then shot Frost a smile of gratitude. "You have no idea how much this means to me, to us."

"I'm happy to be able to assist you." Frost shook Ryder's hand. "I'll let you know when I have a baby that suits your needs and then we'll make the arrangements."

Tia's heart pounded. She didn't want to leave without something concrete to go on. But Ryder gently pulled her to stand, keeping her close to him and playing the loving husband.

"Come on, sweetheart, it's going to be all right now." He arched a brow at Frost. "You won't let us down, will you, Mr. Frost?"

A sly grin tilted the man's face. "Just have your finances in order when I call."

"No problem." Ryder coaxed Tia to the door.

She chewed the inside of her cheek to keep from screaming at Frost and demanding that he tell her if he had her son.

Ryder pulled her out the door then back to his SUV. As soon as they climbed inside, she collapsed into the seat and closed her eyes.

RYDER'S PHONE BUZZED as they drove away. Gwen again. Hoping she had good news, he quickly connected it.

"Ryder, we just received a call through that tip line. A woman. She wouldn't talk to me, but said she needed to speak to the woman on the news."

"Maybe she'll talk to me."

"I suggested that, but she said no. It has to be Tia."

Dammit.

"Where did the call come in from?"

"I don't know, she was only on the phone for a minute. Said she wanted Tia's number."

"Did you give it to her?"

"No, I told her I'd have to speak to Tia first. But she insisted that she had information that could be helpful."

Ryder cursed. Then why the hell hadn't she just given Gwen the details? "All right. When she calls back, give her Tia's number. But keep a trace on her phone so we can track down this woman. If this is some kind of prank or if she's the one who threatened Tia earlier, I'll find her." Although the earlier caller had Tia's cell number.

Ryder ended the call then relayed the information to Tia. They were halfway back to Tia's when her phone trilled. She startled, then glanced at it and showed Ryder the display.

Unknown.

He bit back a curse, then motioned for her to answer it and place the call on speaker.

She laid the phone on the console and connected. "Hello."

Heavy breathing echoed over the line. Ryder clenched the steering wheel tighter, braced for a threat.

"Is this Tia Jeffries?"

Tia inhaled sharply. "Yes, who is this?"

"I don't want to give my name," the woman said in a low voice.

Tia twisted her mouth to the side in agitation. "Then what do you want?"

Another tense moment passed. "I don't know if this will help, but I delivered my baby at the same hospital where you did. It was six months ago, so I don't know if it's connected."

"If what's connected?" Tia asked.

"I'm a single mother," the woman continued. "I was down on my luck, moneywise, and lost my job a few weeks before the baby was due."

Ryder and Tia exchanged a questioning glance. Where was she going with her story?

"Anyway, when I was in the hospital in labor, this nurse came in to be my coach. At first he was nice and supportive, but he said he heard me telling the nurse at check-in that I had no insurance and that I was going to raise the baby alone."

Tia took a deep breath. "Go on."

"That's when things got odd."

"What do you mean odd?"

"He asked me if I'd considered giving my baby up for adoption."

Tia paled. "Had you?"

"No...well, maybe it occurred to me, but that was only because I was so broke and was afraid I couldn't take care of my child on my own. But I didn't think I could do it." The woman hesitated, her breathing agitated again.

"What happened?" Tia asked.

"I told him I'd think about it." She cleared her throat. "But once I held little Catherine in my arms, I knew I couldn't let her go. Then the nurse came in to visit me in the hospital room and pressured me. Said he knew someone who wanted a baby really badly, that we could go through a private adoption and I'd be compensated well enough to take care of my hospital bills and set me up for the future."

Ryder's blood ran cold.

"Then what?" Tia asked, her voice shaky with emotions.

"I told him no, again. And again. Then the day I brought my little girl home, he showed up at my house. It freaked me out, and I threatened to call the police if he contacted me again."

"What did he do then?" Tia asked.

"He got angry. But I held firm. When I picked up the phone to call 911, he left."

"Have you heard from him since?"

"No. But when I saw your story, it reminded me of how much that experience disturbed me. I mean, he knew where I lived. That I was alone. He even made me feel bad, that I was being selfish for raising a child on my own."

Tia rubbed her forehead. "You said *he*. It was a male nurse."

"Yes, his name was Richard." Her voice wavered. "Maybe I was just paranoid, but I...just thought it might be important."

"Thank you," Tia said. "Actually, Richard was one of my nurses when I went into the hospital, too."

Ryder swung the SUV off the side of the road and

parked. Tia thanked the woman and asked her to call if she thought of anything else.

As soon as they disconnected, he phoned Gwen. "I need an address and everything you can find on a nurse named Richard Blotter."

TIA RACKED HER brain to remember if Richard had mentioned adoption to her.

She'd been half-delirious with excitement and pain that night when she had arrived at the ER.

He had helped her into the wheelchair and gotten her settled into a labor room. When she'd told him she had no labor coach, he assured her he'd help her through the process, but then Amy had stepped in.

"Tia?" Ryder's gruff voice broke into her thoughts. "What do you know about Richard Blotter?"

She massaged her temple, where a headache was starting to pulse. "Not much. He was nice to me, and seemed caring. But that night was chaotic."

"He knew you were a single mother?"

Tia nodded. "Yes, he was actually ending his shift, but he must have stayed, because he came by to see me after Jordie was born."

"So he knew you lived alone?"

"Yes." Bits and pieces of their conversation trickled through her mind. "He said he wasn't married, but he wanted to have a family someday. That he chose nursing because he liked to help people. He especially liked labor and delivery because he enjoyed being part of such a happy day for people."

"Did he seem suspicious to you? Like anything was off?"

Tia struggled to recall specifics. "Not really. He said

he was raised by a single mother, and that it had been hard on her and him. That he always wanted a father." She hesitated. "I told him I wanted my baby to have a father, too, but the father wasn't interested."

Horror struck her.

She had been scared and in pain and nervous over the delivery and had spilled her guts about those fears.

Had Richard befriended her so he could gain access to her baby?

Chapter Twenty-One

Ryder gritted his teeth as the pieces clicked together in his mind.

Richard Blotter grew up in a single-parent home, missed having a father and resented it—perhaps he had projected his own bitterness on Tia and other women who chose to raise babies on their own.

The profile fit.

He also had access to patient files, worked in the labor and delivery unit and had personal contact with Tia. Bonnie had delivered at the same hospital, lost her baby and wanted another child.

But if Blotter was trying to place kids in two-parent homes, why would he have helped Bonnie adopt a baby when her husband had left her?

Unless he didn't know about the separation...

"Did Blotter ever call you at home or drop by to see you?"

Tia shook her head no. "But he could have found out where I lived."

"I know." Ryder punched the number for the hospital. "This is Agent Ryder Banks with the FBI. Is Richard Blotter on duty today?"

"Just a moment, please. I'll check," the receptionist said.

Tia bounced her leg up and down in a nervous gesture. Ryder rubbed her arm to soothe her.

"Agent Banks, actually, he was scheduled to work today, but he didn't show."

"Did he call in?"

"No, and that's odd. He's usually very dependable. Maybe there was a mix-up and he didn't realize he was on the schedule."

Or maybe he suspected his days were numbered, that the police were on to him.

"All right, if he shows up, please give me a call."

"May I ask what this is about? Do you think something happened to Richard?"

"I can't say at this point," Ryder said. "Just please let me know if he shows up at the hospital."

He checked his text messages. Gwen had sent him Blotter's home address. "He's not at the hospital today," he told Tia as he turned the SUV around and began to follow his GPS. "We're going to his house."

"I can't believe that Richard would do this," Tia said. "He seemed so nice and caring. I…trusted him."

"He was a nurse at the hospital," Ryder said. "You had no reason not to trust him."

"But I should have picked up on something."

Ryder blew a breath through his teeth. "People can fool us, Tia. Believe me, I've dealt with sociopaths who can lie without blinking an eye. Besides, you met him when you were vulnerable."

"I should have been smarter," Tia said, anger lacing her tone. "I let him get close and he kidnapped my child."

"We don't know that yet," Ryder said, although his gut instinct told him they were on the right track.

Tia shifted and turned to look out the window as they

drove. "I don't know whether to wish that he was involved or to hope that he wasn't."

"You're strong, Tia. If he is, at least we're getting closer to finding your baby."

He pressed the accelerator and sped toward Blotter's.

GUILT NAGGED AT Tia as Ryder drove. If her conversation with Richard was the reason he'd abducted Jordie, she'd never forgive herself.

She mentally replayed the night she'd given birth over and over in her head. Jordie had been a normal delivery— alert, his Apgar score high. She'd nursed him right away and kept him in the room with her all night.

She hadn't wanted him out of her sight.

Amy had assured her that her reaction was normal, that a lot of first-time mothers were paranoid about their newborn being away from them for even a moment.

She'd been right to be paranoid.

She'd just thought she and Jordie were safe in her own house.

They should have been, dammit.

Ryder veered into an apartment complex a mile from the hospital.

He checked the address, then wove through the parking lot in search of Blotter's building. "There it is." Ryder gestured to an end unit. The parking spots in front of it were empty, a sign Blotter wasn't home.

"I'm going to check it out. You can wait here if you want." He opened the car door and Tia jumped out, close on his heels.

Anger surged through Tia, pumping her adrenaline, and she removed her wig and dropped it on the seat. She wanted to confront Richard herself.

"Let me do the talking," Ryder said when they reached the door.

Tia nodded, although if Richard admitted he'd abducted her baby, she couldn't promise that she wouldn't tear his eyes out.

Ryder rang the doorbell, his gaze scanning the parking lot while they waited. Afternoon was turning to evening, and the lot was nearly empty.

Ryder punched the bell again, then pushed at the door. To her surprise, the door squeaked open.

Ryder motioned for her to stay behind him, then he removed his weapon from his holster. "Mr. Blotter, FBI Special Agent Ryder Banks."

Tia peeked past him. The foyer was empty. Ryder inched inside. "Mr. Blotter?"

Silence echoed back.

Holding his gun at the ready, Ryder moved forward. Tia stayed behind him, her gaze scanning the living room, which held a faded couch and chair. A small wooden table occupied the breakfast nook, paper cups and fast-food wrappers littering it.

No sign of a baby anywhere.

Ryder checked the bathroom and bedroom. "Clear. He's not here."

Tia stepped into the small bedroom. A faded spread, dingy curtains—no sign of Blotter. Ryder opened the closet door, and disappointment filled Tia.

No clothes inside.

She checked the dresser drawers. Empty.

Richard Blotter was gone.

"Dammit," Ryder said. "It looks like he left quickly."

"You think he knew we were coming?" Tia asked.

Ryder shrugged. "I don't know how he could. Not unless the nurse at the hospital gave him a heads-up we were asking about him." He phoned Gwen. "Get a BOLO out on Richard Blotter. He's cleaned out his apartment."

"On it," Gwen said. "I'm looking at his bank account now, Ryder. He cleaned it out, too."

"Were there any suspicious transactions before today?"

Tapping on computer keys echoed in the background. "He made a couple of big deposits over the last four years but quickly moved the money into an offshore account."

Could those have been payoffs for kidnapping babies or convincing single mothers to choose the adoption route?

"What about another house or property that he owns?"

"I don't see anything." She hummed beneath her breath. "Wait a minute, he has a sister."

That could be helpful. "What's her name?"

"Judy Kinley," Gwen said.

"Judy?" He glanced at Tia and saw her skin turn ashen. "Yes, she lives—"

"Across the street from Tia Jeffries." Ryder's pulse jumped. "Find out everything you can on her and Blotter. If there's a second address or other family members, let me know. And examine both their phone records."

If Blotter and his sister were working with Frost or with another party, they might find a clue in their contacts.

Tia was staring at him with a sick expression when he ended the call.

"Judy is Richard's sister?"

Ryder nodded.

"She never mentioned that her brother worked at the hospital," Tia said. "She came into my house and pretended to be my friend. She brought me food and a gift when Jordie was born." She gasped. "Oh, my gosh, she even brought me a dessert that day. I had some that night. Do you think she put something in it to make me sleep?"

Ryder silently cursed. "It might explain why you didn't wake up when Blotter came in. And why there were no signs of a break-in on the window," Ryder said.

Tia dropped her face into her hands. "Because she was in the nursery. She must have unlocked the window that day she visited me and Jordie." Tia pressed a hand to her chest on a pained sigh. "It's all my fault. I welcomed her in. I let her hold my baby."

Ryder rushed to console her. "This was not your fault," he said firmly. "These people are predators."

Anger replaced the hurt on her face. "We need to go to Judy's."

Ryder's gaze swept the room. He doubted she was home. If Blotter had skipped, she'd probably left with him.

"Help me look around here before we go. Maybe he left a clue to tell us where he went."

"I'll check the kitchen," she said.

Tia raced to the other room while he dug through the drawers and closet. But Blotter had cleaned them out as well, leaving no sign as to his plan.

TIA HOPED TO find something in the kitchen, an address or contact they could trace to her son, but the drawers and cabinets were empty.

Pain and hurt cut through her.

They had to find Richard and Judy. They were the key to her son.

Ryder appeared a second later. "Nothing in there. Gwen's searching their contacts, bank records, history."

Tia rushed to the door. "Let's go. Maybe Richard hasn't gotten to Judy yet."

They hurried outside, and Ryder raced toward Tia's neighborhood. She mentally beat herself up all the way.

How could she have been so stupid? She'd trusted Darren, and he'd deceived her. She'd trusted the hospital, the staff and nurses, but one of them had conspired to take her son. Then she'd trusted her neighbor who seemed friendly and helpful.

That was one of the worst deceptions. How could a woman do that to another woman?

Judy had taken betrayal to a new level—she'd consoled Tia the very night Jordie had disappeared.

No wonder Judy had been so quick to rush over. She'd known what was coming. She'd been watching the house, had probably alerted her brother when the house was quiet. When Tia had turned out the light.

Maybe she'd even stalled when she'd come to Tia's rescue to give her brother more time to make his escape with her son.

Ryder took the turn into the neighborhood on two wheels. He screeched into Judy's driveway, and they both hit the ground running.

Ryder gestured for her to wait behind him, then he drew his gun and held it at his side as he pounded on the door. "Judy? It's Agent Banks. We need to talk."

Tia checked the garage, but Judy's car was not inside. Her heart sank. "Her car's gone, Ryder."

His jaw tightened. He knocked again then jiggled the door. Just like Blotter's, the door swung open. Ryder stormed in, Tia behind him, calling Judy's name.

The empty bookshelves looked stark now, a reminder that Judy hadn't added any personal touches to the place. No family photos or mementos.

Now Tia understood the reason.

Ryder raced through the house searching while Tia checked the kitchen drawers and desk. She fumbled through a few unpaid bills, then found a small note pad with several pages ripped out.

An envelope caught her eye, and she pulled it out and gasped. Several pictures of her when she was pregnant were tucked inside.

She checked the drawer again, hoping for an address or phone number of someone Judy or Richard might be working with.

Her fingers brushed something wedged inside the top desk drawer, the end caught. She stooped down and gently pulled at it until it came loose.

Rage shot through her. It was a photo of Jordie the day she'd brought him home from the hospital.

Ryder's boots pounded on the staircase as he rushed down. "Nothing upstairs."

Tia's hand trembled as she tossed the picture on top of the desk. "I was so stupid. She was watching me all along."

Ryder cursed and reached for the photo, but suddenly the sound of something crashing through the window jarred them both. A popping sound followed.

Then smoke began to fill the room.

Chapter Twenty-Two

Ryder dragged Tia outside into the fresh air as smoke billowed into the room. He pulled her beneath a cottonwood, and they leaned against it, panting for breath.

Tires screeched. Instantly alert, he scanned the yard and street and spotted a dark car racing down the road.

Did it belong to the person who'd thrown that smoke bomb in the house?

"What was that?" Tia said on a cough.

"Someone who doesn't want us finding the truth," Ryder said, jaw clenched.

Tia pushed her hair from her face. "Judy Kinley and Richard Blotter are definitely involved."

"I agree."

Ryder removed his phone to call 911, but a siren wailed and a fire truck careened around the corner. Someone on the street must have seen the explosion and called.

The fire engine wheeled into the driveway and firefighters jumped into action. "Are you okay?" Ryder asked Tia.

"Yes, go talk to them."

One of the firemen met him on the lawn. "What happened?"

Ryder explained.

"Anyone hurt or inside?"

"No. I'm going to call a crime unit to process the inside of the house, though. I believe the woman who was living here was involved in a baby kidnapping."

The fireman lifted his helmet slightly, expression dark, then gave a nod and went to join the others. Ryder phoned for the crime unit, then made his way back to Tia as they waited.

She paced the yard, looking shell-shocked. "I can't believe Judy would do this to me. Why?"

Ryder shrugged. "Maybe she was protecting her brother or needed money."

"But who did they give my baby to?"

He wished to hell he knew. "We'll find him, Tia. We're getting closer."

"If Richard was involved, do you think someone else at the hospital knew?"

Good question. "Let's go back to the hospital and see." Maybe by then Gwen would have something on Richard and his sister, like an address where they might be hiding out. She was supposed to be checking their prints against the matchbook he'd found outside the baby's nursery.

The crime team arrived ten minutes later, and Ryder explained the situation to the chief investigator while Tia walked across the street to her house to change from her disguise.

"I want the place fingerprinted," he said. "Then let's compare the prints to the matchbook we found outside the nursery." He had a feeling Blotter and Judy were accomplices.

Frost still ranked high on his list as the leader.

One of them might be able to point them to the person who actually had Jordie.

TIA BATTLED NERVES as she and Ryder entered the hospital. Each time she walked through the door, the memory of giving birth to her son returned. She had been so proud when she'd carried him home that day, so elated and full of plans for the future.

That future looked dismal without Jordie in it.

Ryder went straight to the nurses' station. Hilda, the charge nurse, waved to her. "Tia, I saw the news story," Hilda said. "Is there any word?"

"Not yet." Tia motioned for Hilda to step aside and they slipped into the break room while Ryder canvassed the other staff for information on Richard.

"Hilda, I have reason to think that Richard Blotter might have been involved. Did you ever see or hear him do anything suspicious?"

Hilda's eyes widened. "No, he was always so helpful, especially with the single mothers." Alarm flashed across her face as if she realized the implications. "Are you suggesting he was friendly because he was up to something?"

Tia nodded. "I don't think he was working alone, though. His sister lived across from me. I think she was watching me and unlocked the window in the nursery so he could come in and take Jordie."

"But why would they do such a thing?" Hilda asked.

That was the big question. "I don't know yet," Tia said. "But some people are willing to pay a lot to adopt a baby."

Hilda gasped.

Tia's stomach knotted. "Was Richard close to anyone here at the hospital? Did he have a girlfriend?"

Hilda scowled and peered down the hall. "Not that I know of."

Tia bit her tongue in frustration. "Is Amy here today?"

"She just left, sweetie." Hilda's phone buzzed, and she checked the number. "I have to get this. I'm praying for you, Tia."

Tia thanked her and followed her back to the nurses' station. She punched Amy's number then left a message asking Amy to call her.

Amy had worked more closely with Richard than Hilda. Maybe she knew something about him that could help.

RYDER'S NEWLY ISSUED phone vibrated as he ended his conversation with an orderly who stated that he'd always thought Blotter showed a peculiar interest in the single mothers. He'd thought Blotter was interested in striking up a romance, but it was an odd place to look for female companionship.

Ryder agreed with that.

The phone vibrated again. Frost's number showed up on the screen. Surprised to hear something so quickly, he hesitated. Frost might be on to them.

"Jared Manning speaking."

"Yes, Mr. Manning, I reviewed your information and everything seems to be in order."

"Great. When do you think you'll have a baby for us?"

"Actually, that's the reason I'm calling. Typically it takes months to find an infant, but it just so happens that we were placing a baby today, but the couple we were working with backed out. So, it may seem sudden, but if you and your wife are interested, we could arrange for you to take this child."

Sweat beaded on Ryder's neck. He wasn't buying the man's story. Maybe Frost had checked out the phony bank account and decided the Mannings had more money than the other couple so his profit would be larger.

Whatever, he couldn't turn down this opportunity. "Of course we're interested. Is it a boy or a girl?"

A pregnant pause. "I believe it's a little girl. I didn't think you were particular about the sex."

"We're not," Ryder said, careful to keep his tone neutral. "I just wanted to tell my wife. She's going to be so excited. I'm sure she'll want to pick up some clothes and girly things."

"Good. I'm glad. Now we have some details to work out."

"Just tell me what you need," Ryder said.

"My secretary will send you an account number for a wire transfer and the amount. Once that's taken care of, we'll schedule a time and place for you to pick up the baby."

"How soon will this happen?"

"Since we already had this adoption arranged, the placement can happen tonight. That is, unless that's too soon."

"No, tonight is great. I can't wait to tell my wife."

"Good. You'll receive the details shortly. I hope you and your wife and the little girl will be very happy."

Ryder assured him they would be, then stared at the phone in silence when the man hung up.

He hurried toward Tia. "Frost just called. He has a baby for us."

Hope lit Tia's eyes. "A little boy?"

He shook his head. He'd probably already placed Jordie. "A baby girl. But if we catch him in the act, we can force him to talk."

Renewed determination mingled with disgust on Tia's face. "When do we get her?"

Ryder's phone dinged with a text. He quickly skimmed for details.

"Tonight. Eight o'clock. I'll have Gwen wire money into his account now."

His mind churned. If they were about to crack a baby stealing/selling ring, he wanted to take Frost and whoever else was involved down. His first thought was to call Maddox, the sheriff of Pistol Whip.

But he'd never even met the man.

This was not how he wanted to meet, either.

So he phoned his boss. Statham would send backup with no questions asked.

AN HOUR LATER, Tia dressed again in her disguise. Tonight she was no longer Tia Jeffries—she was Emma Manning.

Looking to adopt a child.

Granted, she'd hoped the baby that the lawyer would bring was her own son, but at least they were one step closer to finding him.

If Frost was selling babies to the highest bidder, they would catch him and put him away.

She certainly didn't want any other mother to suffer the pain she'd felt the past few days.

Ryder donned his disguise as well. They didn't want anyone to immediately recognize him and run. Anxiety filled Tia as they drove to Frost's office to finalize the paperwork.

He wasn't in the office, but his receptionist handed him the documents and they signed them, anxious to complete the exchange.

When the lawyer's personal assistant left the room,

Ryder photographed the documents and sent a copy to the lab for analysis.

Then they went to the outdoor café next door to pick up the baby. She and Ryder had both agreed that was an odd place for an adoption exchange, that it indicated something fishy, but they had to follow through, pretend to be the desperate couple who asked no questions but paid to get what they wanted.

Ryder visually scanned the parking lot as he parked. "Are you ready?"

Tia nodded. He'd insisted they bring a rental van in case they were being watched. Richard and Judy might recognize Tia's. She had insisted Ryder install the car seat. Whoever this baby belonged to, she intended to protect the child at all costs.

Ryder squeezed her hand. "Remember, play it cool. We'll wait until the child is handed over and then move in to ask questions or make an arrest."

"Do you think Frost or Richard Blotter will show?"

"I have no idea what to expect, but we have to be prepared for anything."

Tia braced herself and adjusted her wig. She'd never felt so alone.

Except for Ryder. He was here.

She'd hang on to him as long as possible. And when she got Jordie back, she'd once again learn to manage on her own.

"How are we supposed to know who we're meeting?" she asked.

Ryder gestured toward the entrance and then asked for a table. "Frost's assistant sent our photograph to whoever is bringing the baby."

Tia fidgeted with her purse, trying to act normal, but

her pulse was racing. Ryder threw his arm around her, nuzzling her neck, perpetuating the image of a young couple in love as they made their way to the hostess's station.

Ryder pointed out a corner table toward the back of the outdoor seating area. "We want that table."

Tia realized he'd chosen it to give them a good view of the entrance so he could look for the person they were supposed to meet.

She draped herself around him as they walked to the table, half faking the kisses yet needing his strength to help her through the nerve-racking ordeal. When they sat, the waitress immediately deposited water on the table and took coffee orders.

Ryder positioned his chair to watch the entrance and pulled her close to him again, twining his fingers with hers. She stared at their laced fingers—her hand so small in his, his so large and callused yet so tender, and a wealth of emotions swelled in her throat.

Suddenly he stiffened, and she jerked her gaze to the door. Her heart stalled in her chest.

Amy, the young labor nurse who'd befriended her, appeared, holding an infant.

"My God, not Amy," Tia whispered.

Amy scanned the seating area, shifting back and forth, her movements jittery. A second later, she looked at Ryder and must have recognized him.

Panic streaked her expression, then she turned and ran.

Chapter Twenty-Three

"Amy?" Tia rose to go after the young woman, but Amy had disappeared.

Ryder shot up. "I'm going after her!"

He jumped the gate to the patio and Tia jogged to the gate entrance, pushed it open and followed. Amy was running across the street toward a white SUV, clutching the baby to her.

Ryder caught up to her and cornered her by the vehicle. Tia's breath rasped out as she wove between cars.

Shock mingled with hurt and disbelief. Tia removed her wig and Amy gasped.

"You took my son?" Tia cried.

Amy shook her head in denial. The baby started to cry and she jiggled the infant in her arms, trying to shush it. "No, I didn't do it, Tia. I swear."

Ryder folded his arms, his big body blocking her from escaping and pressing her against the side of the SUV.

"Who does this child belong to?" Ryder asked, his tone hard.

Tears blurred Amy's eyes. "A teenager. She gave her up for adoption."

"Just like I supposedly did," Tia snapped.

Amy's face contorted in pain.

"Where's my son?" Tia shouted.

"You have to believe me, Tia," Amy said. "I...didn't take Jordie. I swear."

"Then what's going on?" Ryder demanded.

Amy trembled, the baby crying louder. She patted its back, but Tia reached out and took the infant. Her arms had felt empty for so long. This little girl wasn't Jordie, but she could comfort her until they brought her home to her mother.

"Explain," Ryder said sharply.

Amy wiped at her eyes. "I... I swear I didn't know about Jordie or anything about babies being kidnapped."

"Yet here you are," Ryder said with no sympathy.

"I got a call, was told to drop this baby off with its adopted parents."

"Who called you?" Ryder asked.

"Richard Blotter," Amy said. "He...threatened me, threatened my little girl." More tears trickled down her cheeks. "You know my daughter is handicapped. She needs surgery. I didn't have the money..."

"He paid you to steal babies from the nursery," Ryder cut in.

"No." She sucked in a sharp breath. "A while back, I caught Richard Blotter hacking into patient files. He said he worked with a lawyer who handled adoptions. I threatened to tell the hospital that he was violating patient confidentiality, but he assured me he was only helping mothers and families by connecting them with the lawyer. I thought it was legitimate."

Amy looked miserable. "I had to do something to help Linnie. She needs braces to straighten her legs so one day she can walk. I...just wanted to give her a normal life, as normal as she could have."

The baby had quieted in Tia's arms as she swayed back and forth.

"But you eventually figured out what was happening?" Ryder asked.

Amy gulped. "I heard Richard on the phone a couple of days ago. He sounded upset, nervous. He said they had to lie low, that the police were asking questions." She twisted her purse strap between her fingers. "That's when I realized what had happened."

"Then why didn't you come forward and tell me?" Tia cried.

"I confronted Richard, but he said if I told I'd be arrested for my part, that I'd go to jail for aiding in a kidnapping." She gave Tia an imploring look. "I couldn't go to jail, not when my little girl needs me."

Compassion for the woman's situation filled Tia, but hurt over Amy's betrayal overpowered it. "So you just kept quiet and let them take my baby. Where is he, Amy? Where is Jordie?"

Amy's face wilted again and she shook her head. "I don't know, Tia. I...honestly don't know."

"I'm sorry, Miss Yost," Ryder said. "But you're going to have to come with me until we sort this out."

Amy shot Tia a panicked look. "But I'm supposed to go home to Linnie."

"Who's with her now?" Tia asked.

"My mother." Amy's voice cracked. "She'll be devastated if I go to jail. And if I lose my job, I can't support us."

"Let's take it one step at a time." Ryder guided Amy to the rental van. Tia carried the baby, soothing the infant with her soft voice.

She strapped the baby into the car seat in the back

beside Amy, who was staring into space, ashen-faced and terrified.

Ryder needed a safe place to leave her, but he didn't want to take her to Sheriff Gaines. He considered the McCullens, but this wasn't the way he wanted to meet his brothers. He still had to bring Frost in for questioning and find Blotter and Judy.

He drove to the FBI office instead then escorted Amy to an interrogation room. "Do you have information on the mother of that baby?" Ryder asked.

She shook her head no. "I was just told that she'd signed away her rights and that another couple wanted her."

He pushed her again for more on Frost, but she didn't seem to know anything else helpful.

A kind woman named Constance from the Department of Family Services arrived to take the baby until they sorted out the custody issue.

"I'm sorry, Tia, really," Amy said for the dozenth time.

"Just cooperate and tell the police whatever you know," Tia said. "I don't want what happened to me to happen to anyone else."

Ryder's chest clenched. Even though Tia was suffering, she still had compassion for Amy. She was an unusual woman.

"My little girl needs me," Amy said in a pained whisper.

"Tia's baby needs her, too," Ryder said. "Cooperate and we'll see what we can work out."

They left Amy in federal custody and the baby with Constance then drove back toward Frost's office.

"I'm sorry your friend was involved," Ryder said.

Tia muttered a sarcastic sound. "It seems like everyone I meet lies to me." She touched Ryder's arm. "Promise me you won't do that. If you find out something about Jordie, promise you'll tell me no matter what."

Ryder didn't want to be the bearer of bad news. He wasn't giving up now, either. "I promise."

She relaxed slightly, and he sped into the lawyer's office parking lot. Although he was gone earlier, Frost's Mercedes was in the parking lot now.

Ryder led the way, anxious to get this bastard and make him talk. Early evening shadows played across the parking lot, accentuating the fact that most everyone had gone home for the day.

He snatched the warrants he got at the FBI office from his pocket as he reached the office door, then gave a quick rap on the door and pushed it open. He paused in the entryway to listen for sounds that Frost was inside or had a client but heard no voices. Only the faint sound of a familiar machine.

A paper shredder.

Adrenaline pumping, he rushed through the reception area, following the noise. Frost was in the file room behind the shredder, feeding files into it.

"Stop, Mr. Frost. I'm Special Agent Ryder Banks." Ryder waved the envelope. "I have warrants for your files."

Frost shifted, then reached down. Ryder thought he was going for the files, but Frost lifted a pistol and fired at them.

Tia screamed and ducked behind the door. Ryder pulled his weapon and fired back, hitting Frost in the chest. Frost grunted in shock, dropped his gun and collapsed to the floor.

Ryder kept his gun aimed on the man as he rushed toward him. Frost was reaching for his pistol again when Ryder made it to him, but Ryder kicked it out of the way.

"It's over, Frost," Ryder barked.

Tia ran up behind him. "Where's my son, you bastard?"

Frost coughed, his eyes closing then opening again.

Ryder stooped down and grabbed the man around the neck. "Where's the baby?"

Frost gasped and tried to speak, choking for a breath. Blood gushed from his chest wound, soaking his white designer shirt. Then his eyes rolled back in his head and he faded into unconsciousness.

Ryder released the man abruptly. "Don't you dare die, you bastard."

Tia dropped to her knees and shook the man. "Wake up and tell me where my baby is!"

But Frost's only response was to gurgle up blood.

Ryder cursed, afraid it was too late, and called for an ambulance.

TIA FOUGHT DESPAIR as the paramedics loaded the lawyer's unconscious body onto the stretcher and into the ambulance. Ryder instantly went to work searching the files while the crime unit began processing the office space and sorting through the shredded documents.

Tia looked over Ryder's shoulder into the file cabinet. "Anything on Jordie?"

"Not yet." He offered her a smile of encouragement. "But don't give up. We still have mountains of papers to sort through, plus we need to search his computer."

Tia tried to hang on to hope. They couldn't have come this far and not find her baby.

Although if Frost had destroyed the documents pertaining to Jordie and he died, and they didn't find Richard Blotter, her son might be lost to her forever.

Chapter Twenty-Four

Ryder hoped the search of Frost's files would turn up an address for the person who had Tia's son, but no such luck. There was a list of other adoptions, which appeared to be legitimate, but he turned them over to the Bureau's unit that worked with the National Center for Missing and Exploited Children—NCMEC—to verify the adoptions and their legitimacy.

He and Tia sat in silence in the waiting room of the hospital, their nerves raw. A few minutes later, a doctor appeared with a grave expression on his face. "I'm sorry, but Mr. Frost didn't make it."

Tia sagged against him, devastated. Their only lead was gone.

"We're still looking at his computer, and if we find Blotter, he may have the information we need."

She nodded against him, although her despair bled into his own. He didn't want this case to end without answers.

He wrapped his arms around her. "I'm driving you home to get some rest."

"I want to do another press conference," Tia said. "Tonight."

Ryder debated on the wisdom of the idea, but what did they have to lose?

He phoned the station and spoke with Jesse, the anchorwoman who'd interviewed Tia before. She was anxious for more of the story and agreed to the late-night segment.

If Ryder had exposed a major baby-selling ring, the public had a right to know. They also needed eyes searching for Blotter and his sister, Judy.

They stopped for Tia to change out of her disguise. She looked exhausted and sad, but she held her head up and faced the camera with a brave face.

Ryder spoke first. "Tonight we have information regarding the missing Jeffries baby, although we do not have the baby back in custody." He explained about the lawyer's alleged adoption setup and his theory about Blotter and his sister serving as accomplices.

"If anyone has seen or had contact with Mr. Blotter or Ms. Kinley, please phone our tip line." The station displayed pictures of the man and his sister. "Or if you have information regarding Mr. Frost and his adoption practices, please come forward."

Tia clenched the microphone with a white-knuckled grip. "I'm Tia Jeffries and I'm pleading with you again. I believe these people abducted my son. It's possible that whoever adopted my baby isn't aware that he was stolen from his own bed, from his mother. If that is the case, there will be no repercussions. I just want my son back safely."

She wiped at a tear but managed to maintain control as the anchorwoman summarized the story and repeated the number for the tip line.

"Good luck, Miss Jeffries." Jesse gave her a hug.

Tia thanked her and Ryder drove her home. When they reached her house, Tia rushed inside.

She darted into the bathroom and shut the door, then he heard the shower water kick on and her sobs followed.

TIA FELT LIMP when she climbed from the shower. She dried off and combed through her wet hair on autopilot, numb from the day's events. She yanked on a tank top and pajama pants and left the bathroom in a daze.

Ryder was standing in the living room, a bottle of whiskey in front of him along with two glasses. He raised a brow and she nodded. Why not?

Maybe it would dull the pain for a while. Maybe when she woke up tomorrow, Jordie would be home in his crib and her life would be normal again.

Then Ryder would be gone.

She wanted her son back. But she realized she didn't necessarily want Ryder to leave.

Not a good sign.

He handed her the whiskey, and she swirled it around in the glass, lost in the deep amber color and the intoxicating smell.

Ryder tossed his drink down, then pressed his lips into a thin line. "We're not giving up, Tia. Don't think that."

His words soothed her battered soul. But she wanted more. His touch. His kiss. His mouth on hers, his lips driving away the pain with pleasure.

She sipped her drink. "I trust you, Ryder. I know you'll find him."

He slowly walked toward her. "You are the strongest woman I've ever known."

"I'm not strong," Tia said in a hoarse whisper.

"You are." He reached out and tucked a strand of damp hair behind her ear. His movement was so gentle and tender that her throat closed.

Yet her heart opened to him, and her body screamed with need. Unable to resist, she placed her hand against his cheek. His skin was tanned, rough with dark beard stubble, his eyes liquid pools of male hunger, desire and strength.

She needed that strength tonight.

She finished her drink, then pushed the glass into his hand.

"Another?"

She shook her head no. "I don't want a drink."

He swallowed hard, his jaw tightening as she traced a thumb over his lips.

"Tia?"

"Shh, don't talk." Her body hummed to life with the desire to be closer to him.

She gave in to it, stood on tiptoe and pressed her lips to his. The first touch was raw, his breath filled with hunger. Her skin tingled as he deepened the kiss.

She whispered his name on a breath as he plunged his tongue into her mouth, and she tilted her head back, offering him free rein on her neck and throat as passion drove her to pull him closer.

She fumbled with the buttons of his shirt, and he brushed her cheek with the back of his hand, then lower to trace over her shoulder and down to her hip.

He pressed her into the vee of his thighs, his thick sex building against her belly, a sign that he wanted her just as she wanted him.

That was all she needed.

She was tired of hurting all the time.

For this one minute in time, she wanted to feel pleasure. Pushing the guilt aside, she clutched his arms and pressed her breasts against his chest.

Her nipples throbbed, stiffening to peaks, the warm tingle of electricity in her womb a reminder that she hadn't felt this way about a man in a long time.

She didn't bother to question what was happening. Life made no sense. All she'd known was pain for days.

Tomorrow the pain would be back.

But tonight, Ryder could alleviate it.

EVERY OUNCE OF Ryder's ethical training ordered him to stop. To walk away.

But his body didn't seem to be listening to his brain.

Instead, the hunger inside him surged raw and primal, driving him to hold Tia closer, to stroke her back and shoulders, to brush her breast with one hand until he felt her chest rise and fall with her sharp intake of breath.

He deepened the kiss, savoring the heat between them as she met his tongue thrust for thrust. Her hands raked over his shoulders and back, her touch stirring his body's need.

He shifted, his erection throbbing against her belly and aching to be inside her warm heat.

She coaxed him to the bedroom until they stood by her bed. Soft moonlight spilled through the room, painting her in an ethereal glow. Yet that glow accentuated the paleness of her skin and the sadness in her eyes.

He took a deep breath and forced his hands to be still, to look into her face. "I won't take advantage of you," he said gruffly.

Her gaze met his, turmoil and pain and some other emotion he couldn't define flaring strong. "Then I'll take advantage of you."

With one quick shove she pushed him onto the bed.

His chest clenched. "Tia?"

"Shh." She pushed him to his back then crawled on top of him, straddling him and moving against him in a sensual move that sent white-hot heat through him.

He cupped her face with his hands and drew her to him for another kiss. Lips met and melded. Tongues mated and danced. His hands raced over her body as she tore at the buttons on his shirt.

She shoved the garment aside and the two of them frantically removed it, then she tossed it to the floor. Her hands made a quick foray over his chest, making his lungs explode with the need for air.

"You're beautiful, Tia," he murmured. God, she deserved better than this.

She kissed him again, then lowered her head and trailed kisses and tongue lashes along his neck. She teased and bit at his nipples, stroking his sex with one hand while she worked his belt and zipper with the other.

He wanted her naked before he exploded, dammit.

He slowed her hands, then settled her hips over his sex, moving her gently so he could cup her breasts in his hands. They were full, round and fit into his palms.

He kneaded them then lifted his head, pushed her tank top up and closed his lips over one ripe nipple. She moaned, threw her head back and clung to him.

He flipped her to her back then straddled her this time, loving both breasts with his hands and mouth, her moans of pleasure eliciting his own.

He trailed his tongue down her abdomen, then shoved her pajama bottoms off and spread her legs. She clawed at his back, but he wanted her, sweet and succulent in his mouth, hard and fast below him.

Pushing her legs farther apart, he drove his tongue to her sweet heat and suckled her. She groaned, writhing beneath him as he plunged his tongue deep inside her and tasted her release.

The sound of her crying his name as she came apart sent erotic sensations through him, and he rolled sideways long enough to discard his jeans and pull on a condom.

Then he rose above her, kneed her legs apart again and looked into her eyes.

The raw passion and pleasure on her face stole his breath.

He wanted to see her look like that again and again.

She closed her hand around his thick length and guided him inside her. He moaned her name and found his way home.

TIA CURLED INTO Ryder's arms, closed her eyes and savored the sensual aftermath of their lovemaking.

Although guilt niggled at her. How could she enjoy herself when her baby was still missing?

Still, her body quivered with erotic sensations, and she clung to him as if hiding in his arms could erase reality.

Finally she drifted into sleep. But sometime later, a ringing phone jarred her awake.

Ryder rolled from the bed, snatched his cell phone and answered. "Yeah? Okay. I'll be right there."

He reached for his shirt as he ended the call.

"Who was that?" Tia asked.

"Gwen. Someone spotted a man they think is Blotter at a motel near the airport. I'm going after him."

Tia pushed at the covers. "I'll go, too."

Ryder eased down on the bed beside her. "No, Tia, stay here and rest. He didn't have the baby with him. He might be dangerous."

Ryder's touch reminded her of their night of lovemaking, the frenzied, harried hunger, the gentle touches, the pleasure his touch evoked. She didn't want him to go.

But he had to do his job. And if he found Jordie...

She lifted one hand and placed it over his, grateful for his tenderness. "Please be careful, Ryder."

He nodded, eyes dark with the memories of their night together as well. "I will." He dropped a kiss on her lips, then gathered his jeans and yanked them on along with his socks and boots.

She watched him dress, silently willing him to come back to bed and make love to her again. But she bit back the words.

Finding her son was more important. She wanted him back in her arms so they could start their life together.

Her heart squeezed. Only Ryder wouldn't be part of that life.

RYDER PHONED LAW enforcement in Cheyenne, explained the situation and requested backup. A detective named Clay Shumaker met him near the airport.

Ryder checked with the motel clerk, who claimed a woman had signed herself in as Mrs. Jerome Powell.

Ryder showed him a picture of Judy Kinley and he identified her as the woman. Finally they were catching a break.

He and Shumaker approached the room with caution. Shumaker circled to the back to cover the bathroom window in case the couple tried to escape.

Ryder knocked on the door. "FBI. Open up, Blotter. Ms. Kinley. It's over."

The curtain slid aside and two eyes peered out. Judy Kinley.

"Give it up and no one will get hurt," Ryder shouted.

But the door opened and a gunshot rang out. Ryder cursed and jumped behind the rail to dodge the bullet. Blotter raced out, gun aimed and firing.

Ryder raised his weapon and fired back, catching Blotter in the shoulder. Blotter twisted and fired at Ryder.

Ryder's body bounced back as the bullet skimmed his arm.

Chapter Twenty-Five

His arm stung, but the bullet had only grazed him.

Another one skimmed by Ryder's head, missing him by a fraction of an inch. Ryder cursed and released another round, this time sending Blotter to his knees with a gunshot to the belly.

"He's down!" Ryder shouted to the detective.

Shumaker appeared, pushing Judy in front of him, her hands cuffed. She was crying. "Richard!"

Ryder kicked Blotter's gun aside and knelt to check his wounds. Blood oozed from his abdomen, and he'd lapsed into unconsciousness. Dammit.

He wanted Blotter alive and talking.

Ryder called for an ambulance then confronted Judy at the police car. Fear and panic flared in the woman's eyes. "Where is Tia's son?"

"I don't know," Judy said.

"Don't lie to me, Judy. You pretended to be Tia's friend, then you unlocked that window for your brother to come in and kidnap the baby. Why?"

Judy closed her eyes and released a pained sigh. "Money. Richard...he needed it. The people he owed threatened to kill him if he didn't pay up. I...told him I'd help this once, but that was it."

"So you and Richard conspired to kidnap Tia's baby, then sold the child for cash," Ryder said, not bothering to hide the derision in his voice.

"It wasn't like that. That lawyer convinced me that the baby would be better off with two loving parents."

"That wasn't his or your decision," Ryder said. "Tia loves her son and would be—will be—a wonderful mother."

Judy hung her head in shame.

"Who did he give the baby to?" Ryder pressed.

"I told you, I don't know," Judy said.

"Nothing? Didn't your brother tell you a name or where the couple was from?"

Judy shook her head. "He said it would be better if I didn't know."

Then she wouldn't be culpable. But that was a lie. She was an accomplice to a felony.

The siren wailed, lights flashing as the ambulance arrived. Ryder gestured to the detective. "Book her."

"Please don't let my brother die," Judy said as the detective guided her into the back of his car.

Ryder didn't respond. He told the medics he'd follow them to the hospital.

As soon as Blotter regained conscious, he was going to talk.

He followed the ambulance to the hospital then stayed with the man in the ER.

"He needs surgery," the doctor told him.

"Make sure he survives," Ryder said. "That man kidnapped a child. I want to talk to him."

The doctor scowled. "I understand."

Ryder went to the vending machine for coffee then

phoned Gwen for an update. "Please tell me you found something on Frost's computer or in his files."

"We've collected information on at least half a dozen adoptions that might be in question and are assigning a task force to investigate them individually."

"What about a couple who got Jordie Jeffries? An address where he might be?"

"I'm afraid not. We won't give up, though, Ryder."

He closed his eyes in frustration, then returned to the waiting room to pace while he waited on Blotter to get through surgery.

A SOFT KNOCK at the door woke Tia. She stirred and stretched, then realized that it might be Ryder returning.

Maybe with news.

She pulled on her robe and knotted it at the waist, then hurried into the living room. Morning sunlight spilled through the front sheers and warmed the floor against her bare feet.

She hesitated at the door. "Ryder?"

"Yeah, open up, Tia."

Tia jerked the door open, her heart in her throat. Ryder faced her but stepped aside. "There's someone here who wants to see you."

A slender twentysomething woman was stooped down beside a baby carrier. A baby carrier holding a small blue bundle.

Tia gasped and dropped to her knees in front of the baby. "Jordie?"

Ryder cleared his throat. "Yes, it's him, Tia. He's fine."

Tia's gaze met the young woman's and she scooped her son up into her arms, tears spilling over. "Oh, my Jordie, I thought I would never see you again." She kissed and hugged him, then held him away from her to soak in his features before she planted more frantic kisses all over his face and head. "Oh, baby, I've missed you so much."

His little chubby face looked up at her, a tiny smile pulling at his mouth. "I love you so much, Jordie." She glanced at Ryder. "How did you find him?"

"Blotter was shot but he regained consciousness long enough to tell me the name of the adopted party."

He gestured toward the woman. "This is Hilary Pickens."

Hilary sniffed and dabbed at her eyes. She was shaking and looked terrified and sad at the same time. "I'm sorry... I didn't know." The woman's voice cracked on a sob and she touched the baby's head lovingly. "I didn't know he was stolen. The lawyer told us that he was ours, that his mother didn't want him."

A myriad of emotions flooded Tia. Rage at the people who'd done this.

Compassion for this woman, whom she believed had been a victim just as she had.

"I took good care of him, I swear," the woman said. "I wanted a baby so badly, and when he came to us, I couldn't believe it finally happened."

"You went through Frank Frost?"

The woman nodded, tears streaming down her face. "But then I saw you on the news and...at first I ran. I thought I couldn't give him back." She gulped a sob. "But then I kept thinking about you and hearing your voice begging to have him home, and I looked into his eyes and knew I couldn't keep him. That it would be a lie, that he wasn't really mine." She glanced at Ryder. "I was packing his things to bring him here when Agent Banks showed up at my door."

Ryder nodded in confirmation.

Tia cuddled Jordie closer, then reached out and took the woman's hand and led her inside.

Then she and Hilary hugged and rocked Jordie together while both of them cried.

RYDER STOOD ASIDE as Tia and the young woman cooed over the baby. He had never met anyone like Tia.

She had suffered while her son was missing, yet she'd accepted the woman who had her child into her home and forgiven her within seconds.

The other woman was suffering, too, he realized. She had wanted a child, but she'd done the right thing when she discovered Jordie had been stolen from his mother without the mother's consent.

His own mother's face taunted him. The pain in Myra's eyes when he'd shown her his birth mother's letters.

He had been hard on her. Had walked away.

He had to see her.

Knowing Tia would be fine now she had her son, he slipped out the back door. She no longer needed him. She had her family.

It was time he reconciled with his own.

Anxiety knotted his gut as he drove to his mother's house. He knocked on the door, childhood memories bombarding him.

The times he was sick and his mother nursed him back to health with her homemade chicken soup and tenderness. The bedtime stories and holidays baking cookies together. His father teaching him to ride a bike and a horse.

The door opened, and his mother appeared, her face pale, eyes serious and worried. "Ryder?"

He offered her a smile. "Mom, I… I'm home."

A world of relief echoed in her breathy sigh, and she pulled him into her arms and hugged him.

Ryder hugged her in return. Nothing could change the way he'd come to be in this woman's life, or the fact that his birth mother had loved him and suffered when he was taken.

But Myra Banks was family, and he loved her.

Three days later

IT WAS TIME he met the rest of his family—the McCullens.

Nerves crawled up Ryder's back as he drove to Horseshoe Creek.

He had tied up the case. With Gwen's help and the task force in place, they had found three more cases in Frost's files of unlawful removal of a child from its birth parent, all three teenagers he had coerced into handing their babies over to him for placement. However, the young women had not been blessed with the hefty payment Frost received—he had kept that for himself.

The mother of the baby Bonnie Cone had adopted agreed to leave her with Bonnie, although Bonnie encouraged the teen to be part of the child's life. Tia's Crossroads program stepped in to facilitate the arrangement.

Tia did not press charges against Hilary, but Hilary joined Crossroads. Helping other families was filling the void left by her own loss, and she'd decided to become a foster parent.

Tia's kindness and Crossroads program were a blessing to so many.

He had been blessed to have met her.

Rich farmland, pastures and stables drew his eye as he wound down the drive to the main farmhouse on Horseshoe Creek. Cash had asked all the McCullens to join him at the house for the meeting.

God. Ryder was so accustomed to being alone, he wasn't sure how to handle this.

Although being alone had its downside. He missed Tia, dammit.

The beauty of the land reminded him that this property had belonged to his birth parents, that they had worked the land and animals and built a legacy for their sons.

And that he was one of them.

It was still difficult to wrap his head around that fact.

The sight of trucks and SUVs at the rambling farmhouse made his pulse clamor. They were all here waiting to meet him.

What if he didn't fit?

Dammit, Ryder, you're an FBI agent. You've faced notorious criminals. This is family.

Except he felt like a stranger—an outsider—as he parked and walked up to the door.

Before he could knock, Cash met him outside. "Hey, man, glad you came."

Ryder shook his twin's hand, an immediate connection forming. He was no longer alone.

Cash had been out there all along.

Cash looked slightly shaken as well. "The others are waiting."

Ryder nodded, his voice too thick to speak. He'd done his research, knew all the names and faces.

But he wasn't prepared for the warm welcome.

"I'm Maddox, the oldest," the man in the sheriff's uniform said. "Welcome to Horseshoe Creek." He gestured for him to follow. "Everyone is out back on the lawn. Mama Mary fixed a big dinner. We thought we'd do it picnic style."

Cash gave him a brotherly pat on the back, and Ryder shot him a thank-you look, then he walked through the house to the back porch and onto a lush lawn with picnic tables and food galore.

A chubby woman with a big smile and wearing an apron greeted him first. "I'm Mama Mary," she said with a booming laugh. "Nice to finally have all the family here together."

Cash had told him about the bighearted woman who had served as mother to the McCullen boys after Grace was murdered.

She swept him into a hug and he patted her back, emotions thrumming through him when she released him and his brothers lined up to meet him.

Tia hummed a lullaby to Jordie as she rocked him, the warmth of his little body next to hers so wonderful that she didn't want to put him in his bed. Each time she did, she feared she'd wake up and find him gone again.

Since his return, she'd had a security system installed, along with new locks. He had been sleeping in the cradle in her bedroom, but one day he would outgrow it and she'd need to move him to the crib.

Still, for now, she clung to him. Listening to his breathing at night gave her peace. His little movements and smiles filled her with such joy that she thought she would burst from happiness.

Except…she missed Ryder.

Her bed seemed big and lonely without him. His scent lingered on the pillow. Images of his naked body tormented her. And when she closed her eyes, she imagined

Ryder beside her, holding her, loving her, his big body there to protect her.

But…she hadn't heard a word from him. He'd brought her baby back to her as he'd promised, then disappeared.

Probably onto another case.

He didn't need her or a ready-made family.

She tucked Jordie into the cradle and stroked her thumb over his baby soft cheek. "I love you, little man. Mommy will always take care of you."

She had to be both a mother and father for her son. Somehow she'd find the strength to raise him alone.

And to forget Ryder.

Chapter Twenty-Six

One week later

Ryder parked his SUV on a lush stretch of Horseshoe Creek and studied the pastures, the horses galloping along the hill and the open spaces and imagined a log home built on the property. A swing set out back. A screened porch overlooking the pond.

Family dinners and picnics.

He had tried to stay away from Tia. She needed time to settle with her son. Time to recover from the trauma.

He had helped her on the case, but he wanted more. But he didn't want to play on the fact that she might feel indebted to him.

His feelings for her had nothing to do with debt.

He'd fallen in love with her, with her kindness and compassion, with her strength, with the way she loved her son and helped others.

But what did he have to offer?

He was a loner who worked a dangerous job. What kind of father would he be?

He wanted to be like Joe McCullen.

The past week he'd spent hours visiting and getting to know the family. They'd taken him in as if he'd always been part of them. He'd also gotten to know Deputy Roan Whitefeather, who turned out to be his half brother. The McCullens had even welcomed Myra into the fold.

He studied the piece of ranch land they'd given him to build on with emotion in his throat. He had a home here if he wanted it.

He did want it. But he didn't want it alone.

What are you going to do about it?

Damn. He swung the SUV around and headed toward Tia's, even though doubts filled him as he left the ranch. Tia had been burned by so many people. She'd admitted she didn't trust anyone. Darren had betrayed and hurt her.

What if she didn't want him?

TIA FINISHED HER morning coffee as she read Jordie a story. Granted, he was too young to really understand, but he seemed to like the sound of her voice.

The doorbell buzzed just as she laid him in the crib. She hurried to the door, brushing her hair into place as she went, then peeked through the window.

Ryder's SUV.

The fear she'd lived with when Jordie was missing returned, yet she reminded herself he was safe now. Richard Blotter and Judy were in jail. Frost had died.

Her son was home and no one would take him from her again.

She took a deep breath and opened the door. Ryder stood in front of her, looking big and tough and so handsome that her lungs literally squeezed for air again.

"Tia?"

His face looked so strained that fear returned. "Is something wrong?"

He shook his head. "No. Can I come in?"

She swept her arm in a wide arc. "Of course."

"How are you and Jordie doing?" he asked.

She glanced toward the nursery door. "Good. I…still get nervous sometimes when I put him in his room, but I have a security system now and baby monitors everywhere."

He nodded, his body rigid. Finally he released a breath. "Would you and Jordie like to take a ride with me?"

She rubbed at her temple. "A ride?"

"Yes, I have something to show you." His dark gaze softened. "Trust me."

She did, with every fiber of her being. "All right, I'll get him. But you'll have to put my car seat in your SUV. or we can take my minivan."

"I've got it covered."

He had a car seat?

She didn't ask questions, though. She went and scooped Jordie up, then wrapped him in his blanket. Ryder brushed his finger over Jordie's head, his expression tender.

"He's growing."

"I know," Tia said, proud that the ordeal hadn't stunted him.

They walked outside together and he opened the back door for her to settle her baby in the infant seat.

"Does he mind car rides?"

"He sleeps through everything," she said with a smile. She was the nervous one.

Ryder seemed stiff and uneasy, but he slowly relaxed as he drove. She studied the farmland as they left town, then was surprised when they reached a sign that read Horseshoe Creek.

"You met the McCullens?" she asked.

"Yes," Ryder said, his voice gruff. "I've spent a lot of time with the family this past week. They took me in like I was part of them."

"You are part of them," Tia said, sensing the pain that he'd felt and how difficult it was for him to accept the change in his life.

"They even welcomed Myra, my mother," Ryder continued.

"I'm happy for you, Ryder." She leaned her head on her hand. "Family is everything." She still missed her mother and father and brother and wished they were alive to see her son.

Emotions glittered in his dark eyes as he met her gaze. Then he turned down a drive and wound past several stables. Finally he parked at a stretch of land by a pond.

He cut the engine and angled himself to face her. "This is beautiful, Ryder."

A broad smile curved his serious face. "It's mine."

Tia gasped. "Yours?"

"Apparently Joe McCullen left the ranch to all his sons."

"I'm so happy for you. Do you plan to build a house and live here?"

He lifted her hand in his. "Yes. I thought a big farmhouse with a porch with rockers on it." He pointed toward the left side. "A play yard with a swing set could go right there."

Tia's heart began to race. "A swing set?"

He nodded. "And there's a lot of room to ride bikes and horses, and we could teach Jordie to fish one day."

Her breath caught. "Ryder?"

He squeezed her hand, then pressed a kiss to her palm.

"I don't just want a house, Tia. I want to build a home here, and I want you and Jordie to be part of it."

"You do?"

"Yes. I love you, Tia." He dug in his pocket and lifted the gold bands they'd worn during their disguise. "I like the feel of this on my hand. I thought we might make it real." He shrugged. "Of course we can get new ones. A diamond for you if you want."

She'd seen the discomfort on his face when she'd handed him the rings that day. But now...now he seemed relaxed. Happy.

Sincere.

"You aren't doing this just so Jordie will have a father?"

He shook his head. "I want to be his father, if you'll let me." He kissed her fingers one by one. "But I miss you and love you, Tia. I want us to build a life together. To be a family."

Tears welled in Tia's eyes. Happy tears this time.

She gently brushed her hand against his cheek and Ryder swept her in his arms and covered her mouth with his. The kiss was deep, passionate, sensual, filled with promises and yearning.

"Is that a yes?" he murmured.

She nodded and kissed him again. "Yes, Ryder, I love you, too."

She didn't need diamonds. She had her son back. And with Ryder and the McCullens, she would have the big family she'd always wanted.

Epilogue

Six months later

Tia's heart overflowed with love as the reverend announced she and Ryder were husband and wife.

Ryder kissed her thoroughly, the passion between them building. But that would have to wait.

Their family was watching now.

"Later," Ryder whispered against her neck.

She gently touched his cheek. She would never grow tired of touching him. Or hearing his voice. Or looking into his impossibly sexy eyes.

She certainly wouldn't get tired of loving him. "That's a promise."

He gathered her hand in his and they turned to face the guests. Mama Mary smiled from the front row. Just last month she'd married the foreman of the ranch. But she still held the family together with her big warm hugs and comforting food and motherly love.

Maddox, Brett, Ray, Roan and Cash had bonded with Ryder and helped build the house she and Ryder were moving into, while their wives had helped Tia organize the wedding on the lawn.

Cheers and clapping erupted, shouts of joy and happi-

ness and congratulations as she and Ryder stepped from
the gazebo to accept glasses of champagne.

She looked across the beautiful ranch and the wonderful McCullens, grateful for their boisterous chaos.

Rose jiggled her baby boy, Maddox's son, Joe, in the
stroller while Ryder's mother, Myra, nestled Jordie to her.
Willow and Brett's son, Sam, was chasing fireflies with
Cash and BJ's adopted boys, Tyler and Drew.

Maddox lifted a champagne flute. "Let's toast to the
last McCullen."

Ryder laughed and so did everyone else.

"Hell, he's not the last." Brett touched Willow's bulging belly. "We're just getting started."

"So are we," Ray said as he pulled a pregnant Scar-
let against him.

Megan, Roan's wife, smiled sheepishly. "So are we,"
Roan admitted with an affectionate hug to his wife.

Ryder and Tia exchanged a secretive look. They
planned to have more children as well and so did Cash
and BJ, but Ryder vowed not to push Tia. Jordie was only
a few months old.

Still, as she sipped her champagne and nuzzled his
neck, love and passion exploded inside him. Tia wanted
at least four, maybe six kids.

Tonight might not be too soon to start.

* * * * *

SPECIAL EXCERPT FROM

◆ HARLEQUIN
INTRIGUE

*After forensic investigator Lena Love is attacked and
left with a partial heart-shaped symbol carved into her
chest, her hunt to find a serial killer becomes personal.*

Read on for a sneak preview of
The Heart-Shaped Murders,
*the debut book in A West Coast Crime Story series,
from Denise N. Wheatley.*

Lena Love kicked a rock out from underneath her foot, the
bent down and tightened the twill shoelaces on her brow
leather hiking boots.

The crime scene investigator, who doubled as a forensi
science technician, stood back up and eyed Los Angeles'
Cucamonga Wilderness trail. Sharp-edged stones and ragge
shards of bark covered the rugged, winding terrain.

"Watch your step," she uttered to herself before continuin
along the path of her latest crime scene.

Lena squinted as she focused on the trail. Heavy foliag
loomed overhead, blocking out the sun's brilliant rays. Sh
pulled out her flashlight, hoping its bright beam would hel
uncover potential evidence.

An ominous wave of vulnerability swept through he
chest at the sight of the vast San Gabriel Mountains. She spu
around slowly, feeling small while eyeing the infinite view
of the forest, desert and snowy mountainous peaks.

The wild surroundings left her with a lingering sense c
defenselessness. Lena tightened the belt on her tan sued
blazer. She hoped it would give her some semblance c
security.

It didn't.

Lena wondered if the latest victim had felt that same vulnerability on the night she'd been brutally murdered.

"Come on, Grace Mitchell," Lena said aloud, as if the dead woman could hear her. "Talk to me. Tell me what happened to you. *Show* me what happened to you."

A gust of wind whipped Lena's bone-straight bob across her slender face. She tucked her hair behind her ears and stooped down, aiming the flashlight toward the majestic oak tree where Grace's body had been found.

Lena envisioned spotting droplets of blood, a cigarette butt, the tip of a latex glove…*anything* that would help identify the killer.

This was her second visit to the crime scene. The thought of showing up to the station without any viable evidence yet again caused an agonizing pang of dread to shoot up her spine.

Grace was the fifth victim of a criminal whom Lena had labeled an organized serial killer. He appeared to have a type. Young, slender brunette women. Their bodies had all been found in heavily wooded areas. Each victim's hands were meticulously tied behind their backs with a three-strand twisted rope. They'd been strangled to death. And the amount of evidence left at each scene was practically nonexistent.

But the killer's signature mark was always there. And it was a sinister one.

Look for
The Heart-Shaped Murders *by Denise N. Wheatley,*
available June 2022 wherever
Harlequin Intrigue books and ebooks are sold.

Harlequin.com

Love Harlequin romance?

DISCOVER.
Be the first to find out about promotions,
news and exclusive content!

 Facebook.com/HarlequinBooks

 Twitter.com/HarlequinBooks

Instagram.com/HarlequinBooks

Pinterest.com/HarlequinBooks

You Tube YouTube.com/HarlequinBooks

ReaderService.com

EXPLORE.
Sign up for the Harlequin e-newsletter and
download a free book from any series at
TryHarlequin.com

CONNECT.
Join our Harlequin community to
share your thoughts and connect
with other romance readers!
acebook.com/groups/HarlequinConnection

HSOCIAL2021

HARLEQUIN

Heartfelt or thrilling, passionate or uplifting—Harlequin is more than just happily-ever-after.

With twelve different series to choose from and new books available every month, you are sure to find stories that will move you, uplift you, inspire and delight you.